BRANDYWINE

JACK ROWE

BRANDYWINE

A GROLIER COMPANY

FRANKLIN WATTS
NEW YORK   TORONTO   1984

Also by Jack Rowe:
Inyo-Sierra Passage

Library of Congress Cataloging in Publication Data

Rowe, Jack.
Brandywine.

I. Title.
PS3568.0926B7   1984   813'.54   83-23409
ISBN 0-531-09828-1

BRANDYWINE

In loving memory of my parents,
Aloysius F. Rowe and Elizabeth Farren,
and the Powdermen of the Brandywine

PROLOGUE

1800

Tis a lovely place, Maggie! All green with meadows and trees, and the river flowin' between!"

"Ah, a muddy bog, likely. All I've seen since we stepped off that reelin' boat is mosquitoes and swamps."

"And hills all around, Maggie; soft and gentle humps above the stream, and thick with trees. Oh, the *trees*, Maggie. You've not seen the like in all Kildare."

"And snakes."

"Denis and me both has jobs at the cotton mill . . . and the others, too. Eighty cents for every day we work. That's nearly five dollars a week! And Maggie, the great news—I've bought a plot of land for us to build on!"

"Bought land . . ."

"From the mill owner himself. A piece of the new country, lass!"

"A piece of farmin' land, you mean?"

"Oh, not so big as all that, Maggie, love. But big enough fer a house and garden surely, and snuggled in the woods."

"In the woods! What can we grow in the woods? Merciful heavens, Patrick, have y'squandered our savings on a wild patch of sumac and thistles?"

"Ah, Maggie, don't be judgin' the place till y'see it. The woods goes on as far as kingdom come and full of game, and we can fish almost from where the house will stand."

"Didja spend all o'the money, then?"

"Do ye take me fer a complete fool, woman? I kept some back to do the buildin' with. The rest...Well, the rest I'm to pay him off outta me wages."

"Y' didn't sign yerself into indenture!"

"Now, Maggie, it's not like that at all....Just a note, it was, a note fer Mr. Broom to hold the land."

"Mother Mary, an Englishman!"

"Ah, now, there y' go....The man's American, same as we'll be, too. He's one of them Quaker folk, and well t'do, from the look of him."

"Aye, well t'do. Gettin' rich off the likes of us is what it is."

"It's me golden opportunity. Just wait till you see it, Maggie. It's grand. I can't wait to move you and the babies out of this foul place."

"When will that be?"

"Tomorra or the day after. No later."

"Are we to live in the bushes, then, until you throw up our shanty?"

"We'll double up with Feeney's gang. Just temporary."

"With Nora and Denis? When did they get a place?"

"From Jacob Broom. A small place near ours."

"Y'mean Denis Feeney *bought* a house?"

"Ah, no, Maggie. He's rentin' the place. You know Denis and how he feels about bein' tied down."

"I don't know, Patrick. Sure and it's a kind thing for them to take us under their roof, but rubbin' elbows with Nora for very long might wear our friendship thin."

"It won't be long, darlin'. A month or two. No more. And another thing, our place will be no shanty with earth underfoot, nor cottage neither, but a proper house of stone, with plank floors, and..."

"And?"

"A private room for us to bed at long last."

"Oh? Tell me, Patrick, is there aught you've been keepin' from meself fer lack of privacy?"

"Mebee."

"Well, now, I will be holdin' ye to *that*, Mr. Gallagher!"

"Ah, Maggie, 'tis a scandalous woman I've married, and that's a fact."

PART ONE

1801-
1811

CHAPTER 1

Eleuthère Irénée du Pont ran his hand over the gleaming silver inlays of his fowling piece. The sporting gun balanced nicely in the crook of his left arm, and he was eager to try its accuracy with a moving target. He watched with admiration as the well-trained hunting dogs of his host, Colonel Louis de Tousard, worked the frost-covered stubble of the barley field and threaded their way through scarlet and gold thickets along its borders. Tousard stood a little to his left as the two hunters waited for a sign that the dogs had spotted any game.

Suddenly the lead animal froze in point. Following on cue the two trailing dogs slid to a halt, and the two hunters moved into position for the shot. As he stepped forward, keeping abreast of the colonel, Irénée swung the Damascus steel barrel of his weapon to high port and checked his priming. Then he swept his eyes to the front, scanning the bracken several yards ahead of the point dog.

When the two men were almost abreast of the pointer, a clump of taller grasses erupted into a white and beige fountain of drumming wings. The covey immediately fanned out in protective scattering flight as each quail thrummed frantically along its shallow flight path.

Irénée thrilled with the beauty of the sight and drew a quick bead on one of the birds. They were close enough to allow time for a leisurely shot, and when he squeezed the trigger he knew he had an absolute kill. As the pan flashed, his reflexes tensed for the shock of the main load, which always came a second later, but this time it did not.

The crash of Tousard's shotgun made him flinch, but he kept his own barrel on target, tracking the small bird out of range until it settled into a clump of briers and disappeared. Then unexpectedly his piece fired with a sickly whoosh.

Irénée cursed softly as he examined the firing pan and touch hole. The new gun was so befouled with gummy residue from unburned powder that it was impossible for him to tell if the misfire had been caused by the explosive or the mechanism.

"It's not the gun, my friend," Tousard said as he strode forward to retrieve his bird. "You of all people should recognize inferior powder. Were you not the prize student of Lavoisier?"

Irénée twisted off the cap of his powder flask and spilled a small quantity of the substance into his palm. It was lumpy and lacked a uniform texture. He gave his host a questioning look.

Tousard laughed self-consciously and shrugged. "You are surprised that a military man should provide his guest with gunpowder of such poor quality, eh?"

"Is it quite old?"

"I'm afraid not, my friend. It came from a fresh shipment delivered to the storekeeper last month."

Irénée shook his head. "Then your search for economy has robbed you of any bargain."

The colonel shook his head. "Ah, du Pont, I am afraid you do not understand. The powder in your hand is the highest quality anyone can buy in America."

"But what of imported powder—French, even English?"

"Impossible to get." He gave Irénée a hard look. "Surely you are not unaware of the feelings in this country toward our homeland. As for England . . . well, I think she is of the opinion that any good explosives she sends here might be used against her in the future."

Irénée du Pont weighed the words of his companion with respect. At fifty-two, his host was twenty-two years older than Irénée, but more important was the fact that he had lived in his adopted country since serving under Lafayette in the American Continental Army during the Revolution. Irénée had been just four when that war had started, and now, in 1801, he found it hard to accept the discrimination against the foreign born that was evident everywhere in the United States. The fact that he had difficulty with English further chilled the reception he got from Americans. Well, blood was thicker than water, as the saying went, and these descendants of the original English colonists treated their erstwhile British enemies with more deference than they offered anyone else who came visiting America.

The two men worked at the hunting throughout the November morning, adding a few brace of birds and one large cottontail to their bag. But it was a frustrating diversion. One shot in three misfired, and Irénée was furious at one point when a weak charge bloodied a rabbit but did not bring it down. He knew when it had outrun the dogs that it would probably die slowly, holed up somewhere in the briers.

Later that evening as he and his wife, Sophie, dined with the Tousards at their elegant table, the subject of the poor gunpowder came up again—but indirectly.

Madame Tousard was delighted to have the young du Pont couple as her guests. She was a dozen years younger than her husband and felt a mild confinement in their farm community a few miles west of Wilmington, Delaware. Their neighbors were also French, a collection of colonial nobility lately from the West Indies, which they had fled to escape the rebellion of their own slaves. French custom and language persisted here, but social affairs were constrained by the fact that Wilmington was dominated by English Quaker mercantile families. Neither group had much interest in the other.

That Colonel Tousard's credentials as an American military officer with the illustrious Lafayette gave him status did not change the realities of their isolation. As the years slipped by after the Revolution, even that distinction began to erode, and Jeannette de Tousard found infrequent need to draw upon her extensive wardrobe of exquisite finery. Except for an occasional party at their own modest estate, Jeannette had lately dressed rather plainly. She accepted the respectable retirement of her colonel and contented herself with memories of the years in Philadelphia and Boston when she was an eye-catching beauty on the dashing artilleryman's arm.

Tonight she had put on her favorite gown. It had been sent from France for her to wear on the occasion of General Washington's

Inaugural, and although she had been only twenty-eight at the time, her rigorous attention to diet enabled her to slip into the dress with practically no alterations.

Jeannette was desperate to hear news of French society, but she chose to open the dinner conversation with Irénée less directly. She looked across at their guest and inquired as to the health of his family.

"It has been some time since we have seen your brother Victor, Monsieur du Pont. How are he and his wife and children?"

Irénée did not respond for a moment. He was working on a mouthful of quail and was having some difficulty. Although he was only thirty, he had lost many of his teeth. In a hurry to cover his embarrassment he bolted the food and wiped his mouth with a napkin before answering.

"They are fine, madame. I envy Victor's familiarity with this country, especially the language."

Jeannette smiled. "Yes, as I recall, your brother is quite a social lion. He would not be one to let a loss for words compromise convivial affairs."

"And de Nemours," Colonel Tousard interjected. "How is Pierre? I understand that he has been closeted with Jefferson regularly. I do not understand where the man gets his vitality—at his age!"

"My father is quite well. He has occasional attacks of gout, but they do not slow him down. This new enterprise has him bouncing all over the countryside. Every week he seems to come up with a new project."

"How *is* the venture progressing?" asked Jeannette. She addressed the question to du Pont's wife, trying to draw her into the conversation.

Sophie gave Irénée a dismayed look and spoke reluctantly. "It is not progressing at all, I'm afraid." When Jeannette rewarded her frank answer with an attentive silence, she went on, "Even his connection with Jefferson has not helped. Father Pierre has a dream of putting his physiocratic theories into practice. Unfortunately the cost of land is much greater than any of us imagined. It does not appear that Pontiania, as he likes to call it, will ever come to be."

"Pontiania?" Jeannette was becoming more interested in Madame du Pont, and began to revise her estimate of Irénée's wife as being rather dowdy and unimaginative. "I'm afraid I have not followed the career of de Nemours enough to know of his philosophy."

Irénée responded, "It is basically a belief that all true wealth—prosperity—comes from the land. Theoretically a shared agrarian community would be the ideal way to live and prosper."

"Share and share alike?" Tousard ventured.

"Put simply, yes." Irénée shook his head. "I'm afraid my father's ideas are somewhat impractical at times."

Sophie countered, "It is not the impracticality of his idea as much as it is the poor welcome this country extends to investors of foreign birth. I for one would dearly love to see the project undertaken. The countryside in America is lovely, primitive, waiting. Heaven knows how much I miss our farming estate at Bois des Fossés. Were it not for that madman Bonaparte, we would still be there!"

Irénée reached awkwardly across the wide table to comfort Sophie with a squeeze of the hand.

Colonel Tousard rose to refill the wine glasses, breaking the sad little silence in the room. "I must agree with your husband, Madame Sophie. To undertake a collective farming plan in this country would be a disaster. We Americans are too frank about our greed for that. I speak as one, like you, uprooted from my homeland, who would like to share the blessings of my adopted country with other Frenchmen. It is pleasant to sit here and converse easily in French and maintain the familiar niceties we have salvaged from our transplanted culture." He paused to let the words sink in. "But it cannot last. Even if we keep ourselves apart for a time, our children will let it go. As a matter of fact, Jeannette and I would be doing you a service if we spoke only English."

An awkward silence followed the colonel's words, and Jeannette gave her husband a sharp look. It seemed to her that Tousard's well-intentioned remark might be interpreted as a rebuff. She tried to smooth things over. "But, my dear, it would be silly to play such a game with our friends. Besides, I was about to press Sophie for the latest news of fashions abroad and for whatever tidbits of scandal she could remember. Such a discussion can be properly enjoyed only in French!"

Their shared laughter lightened the moment, and she caught a brief look of gratitude from Madame du Pont.

Irénée, however, chose to continue the point. "What you say is quite true, Colonel Tousard," he began earnestly, "but only if our stay here is permanent. Frankly, for me the struggle with this unwieldy and inconsistent tongue would not be worth the trouble unless I were assured of spending a considerable time here. At the moment, that prospect seems quite dim."

Sophie was quick to agree. "We shall probably return to France, once things quiet down a bit."

Tousard looked at her gravely and shook his head. "I hate to disagree with you, madame, but I fear the France you and I remember will never return. Oh, I think it only a matter of time until Napoleon's power wanes, but France is permanently changed." He reflected a moment, then added, "And as difficult as it might be for you to understand at the moment, I think it is a good thing."

"You speak with the conviction of a convert to American republicanism, sir. There are those who predict the collapse of the United States in due course," Irénée said mildly.

Tousard's fervor surprised even Jeannette. "I cannot guarantee this government, Irénée, but if it fails, another will be fashioned to support the American way of life. These people—*we* people—as diverse as our heritage may be, have had a taste of independence and opportunity undreamed of in the Old World. We will never relinquish it."

Jeannette felt somehow that her husband's speech called for applause, but she sensed an edge of antipathy between them and their guests. She rose abruptly and came around the table to stand by Sophie.

"Well, I've had enough of politics, gentlemen. I suggest that we ladies leave you to your wine while we catch up on Paris and London in the parlor."

After Sophie and Jeannette had left, Tousard looked Irénée hard in the eye. "You spoke of your father's failure to bring any of his projects to fruition. I have heard from Victor what some of these attempts have been, Irénée, and I must confess that I expected as much."

Irénée shifted uneasily in his chair, somewhat rankled, and shot back, "Colonel Tousard, you have the advantage of host, but I think you are pressing too hard, sir!"

"Hear me out, du Pont. It is not my wish to put you ill at ease.

I know both Victor and your father well enough to point out that neither man is gifted in the ways of business. Victor is a born diplomat, but he could not sell a blanket to a freezing man. De Nemours is a gifted scholar with marvelous skill in theoretical science and philosophy, but the fact that he barely escaped France with his life should indicate that as a practitioner he is a bad risk."

Irénée remained quiet and attentive, but anger spots rose to his sallow cheeks. Tousard was distracted momentarily by the sudden observation that this man of thirty appeared to be much older. The strain of the last few years must have affected him more than it did the others in his family, he thought sadly. He pressed on with his argument.

"Today while we were hunting, the solution to your problem was in the palm of your hand. Don't you see, Irénée? You are the one du Pont able to make a success of any business venture because you are the only one with enough practical sense and hard fiscal responsibility to make it work." Tousard grinned and slapped Irénée on the knee. "You are so practical that you were unable to see opportunity when it flew up before your very eyes. A pity you do not have a bit of the dreamer in you, for you would have snapped at it in a moment."

"You are speaking about the manufacture of black powder," Irénée said.

"Bravo, my dear du Pont," chuckled Tousard, watching as the idea took hold in Irénée's mind. "After all, have you not been the only productive member of the family since your father was stripped of his government stipends? Was it not you whom the great Antoine Lavoisier chose as his protégé? Have you not already designed powder mills a half-century advanced over the best that can be found in all of the colonies?"

Irénée nodded thoughtfully.

"Tomorrow," said the colonel, "we shall make the rounds of some of the better powder mills. You will need to know how weak your future competitors will be. Then I shall send you packing back to your father to get a share of the investors' cash . . . before he and Victor fritter it all away."

Irénée stood and gripped Tousard's hand. "Thank you, Colonel, you have given me the first glimpse of hope I have seen in the last year."

Tousard waved off the thanks, but he was smiling broadly. "One more thing, my friend," he said.

"And what is that?" asked Irénée.

"Beginning tomorrow, Paris fashion and scandal notwithstanding, you and Madame Sophie will speak only English in this house!"

Federal City, or Washington, as some were beginning to call it, was hot and muddy on the last day of May 1802. As his carriage brought him through the as yet unpaved thoroughfares of the new capital, Thomas Jefferson felt his impatience mounting. It was a bad way to start the week.

By the time he reached his offices this Monday morning, he would be hopelessly behind schedule. The traffic was a nightmare of wagons and carriages wrestled by their cursing drivers through a hub-deep yellow quagmire produced by a weekend of constant drizzle. Jefferson was beginning to agree with most of the government personnel recently shifted to the District that it would have been better to base the federal agencies in Philadelphia at least until the main streets were paved. As he looked out through the flapping side curtains of the carriage through the gray, misty rain, he was depressed by the stark view of partially completed buildings rising out of an unlandscaped plain of muck.

His first appointment was not going to be pleasant either. His old friend, Pierre du Pont de Nemours would be waiting, eager for reassuring news. The President leaned back against the clammy leather upholstery and sighed. The least he could have done was manage not to keep the old man waiting when all he had to tell him was bad news. The fact that in exchange for the bad news Jefferson planned to ask a favor of his friend was a further source of gall.

As soon as he reached his office he gave orders to send du Pont in. He was pleased to note from the appointment calendar on his desk that Pierre would be accompanied by his younger son, Irénée.

When he heard the door open, Jefferson rose from his chair and came around the desk to meet his visitors. He greeted them in fluent French, embracing them in an effort to extend a Continental welcome in spite of his usual reserved manner. Pierre du Pont de Nemours waved off the French.

"No, no, my friend," he boomed happily. "It is necessary that we use English. For the past many months, my son has insisted on the use of the common American tongue."

Jefferson smiled and turned to Irénée. "You are finding it difficult to deal with us in French, eh? I think you are wise to make the effort. Unfortunately there is suspicion of foreigners, and," he added sadly, "unfair advantage is taken in business matters."

"I have noticed," Irénée said flatly.

"Come, sit here by the window," Jefferson said, indicating a settee and chairs clustered near his desk. As he walked behind the limping French aristocrat, he commented gently, "The gout has come back to plague you again, eh, Pierre?"

De Nemours collapsed onto the settee with a grateful wheeze. "Agh, my old ailment. Well, it is nothing, really."

Jefferson came right to the point. "My good friend," he began, "I'm afraid I have nothing but bad news for you again." He paused to let the words sink in, hating to dash the Frenchman's hopes. "The cost of land is even higher than I had feared. To acquire a tract such as the one you envision would be far beyond your capitalization."

De Nemours managed a weak protest. "But Thomas, I myself have heard of land prices well within reach of our budget."

Jefferson ran a freckled hand through his thatch of graying red hair and regarded father and son in silence before he continued. "For many months now we have looked for a suitable place for Pontiania that would be within your means. We must not delude ourselves further. It is simply not to be. I think that you, too, my good friend, have come to realize that these rumors of cheap land are mere sorcery—the siren songs of land speculators. This office has been besieged with entreaties of honest folk who have lost small fortunes at the hands of such rascals. Do not be tempted to become one of those unfortunates. Take your pledged funds and invest in a project that has hope."

Irénée spoke for the first time. "As you can see, Mr. President, the hope of my father and those who have entrusted him with shares is for precisely what you insist they cannot get."

Jefferson nodded. "Indeed, Irénée, I am all too painfully aware of the distress your father must feel at this time."

There was another silence. Jefferson assessed the composure of the elder du Pont before he spoke. "Frankly, Pierre, I have never approved of your idea."

"But you have given your support..."

"Of course." Jefferson laughed. "My friend, you have no idea... Well, you must; you have certainly been in compromising situations of your own!" The three smiled at this oblique reference to the elder du Pont's near fatal confrontation with Napoleon.

The President's face became serious again, and he pressed his argument. "The idea of having a settlement that would be occupied exclusively by French-born people is what troubles me. What you are proposing in essence is the building of yet another colony. I think we have had enough of separate colonies. It is time now for all of us to think of ourselves as Americans—free from the crutch of Europe. Your plan would tend to delay the process."

"I see." There was a grimness in the comment from de Nemours.

"My opinions, however, are of little consequence in this matter, Pierre," Jefferson reminded his friend firmly. "Pontiania is ninety percent undercapitalized in any event."

"Mr. President," Irénée began with a quick glance in his father's direction, "what do you think of our starting a gunpowder business?"

Pierre du Pont sputtered with exasperation. "That factory idea of yours again! I should as likely return to my boyhood trade of watchmaking. Our stockholders would ridicule the idea of starting a competitive industry in America when France is the acknowledged leader in the manufacture of explosives. Forgive my son, Thomas. We have been over this ground before, but he persists in his dream of becoming a factory slave."

Jefferson laughed. "Oho, Pierre! That goes against all your physiocratic ideals, does it not?"

"To be serious, sir," said the younger du Pont, "I have visited your powder mills and sampled your powder, and I am convinced that there is a need for sporting powder of quality."

"He thinks that Lavoisier's laboratory training qualifies him as a builder of factories," injected de Nemours, indulgently dismissing the idea.

"Lavoisier?" murmured Jefferson. "Of course, Irénée. I had forgotten your boyhood enthusiasm. Well, that does sound like a worthy idea." He probed Irénée for more information, testing his commitment to the idea more than his grasp of the methods of manufacture. Lavoisier, eh? That was certainly a guarantee. Given the strained relations between England and France, and the back-handed treatment the United States was getting from both, the existence of a dependable source of high-quality musket and cannon powder would be in the national interest. Jefferson decided that Irénée's project should be encouraged.

He turned to the elder du Pont, who was as near to being in a sulk as he had ever seen him. "Good friend, de Nemours," he began, trying to mollify his disappointed visitor, "let this young man have part of your company's funds. I think he may have struck the wellspring of your financial success. Forget your station for the moment; it is no crime here for a gentleman to engage in manu-facture—especially if he gets rich at it."

Pierre's demeanor gave every indication of his displeasure, but his curt nod of assent was a guarantee of support, and that was all Irénée needed. He rose and thanked his father and Jefferson in turn by shaking their hands and then standing awkwardly ill at ease.

Jefferson relieved him of his discomfiture very quickly. "Irénée, I have a matter of government to discuss with your father, and it is diplomatically of some delicacy. Would you excuse us for a few moments?"

Irénée looked relieved and took his leave promptly.

After the door closed behind his son, Pierre turned to the Pres-ident, his eyes now gleaming with the prospect of involvement in diplomatic intrigue. Jefferson could not miss the sudden animation in his friend's face, and he mentally congratulated himself on a diplomatic move of his own.

"Pierre," he began gravely, "I would like you to deliver a letter to a friend of yours in Paris. Your trip to report to your shareholders comes at the most propitious time for the United States."

"Most certainly, I will be honored to deliver it, Mr. President," de Nemours replied, using Jefferson's title with feeling. "May I ask the nature of this letter?"

Jefferson smiled at the irony of his request.

"Certainly, de Nemours. I want to see if your Napoleon will sell *us* some real estate. It is a rather sizable parcel called Louisiana."

CHAPTER 2

1802

Maggie Gallagher padded sleep-
ily through the predawn gray of the cottage, her bare feet scuffing
softly on the planked floor. She was carrying something heavy, and
she grunted once or twice with the weight of it as she made her
way to the back door. She felt for the latch with the back of her
hand, and when the cold iron handle brushed against it, she hooked
it with one finger and tugged it open.

A frame of light widened as the heavy door swung inward, and
she bumped it fully open with her backside. She was holding an
earthen pot at arm's length.

Somewhere above her in the trees a crow squawked angrily at
being disturbed and flapped off to a quieter roost. Maggie muttered
something unpleasant and rolled her eyes in the direction of the
sound. The weight of the slop jar was giving her shoulder cramps
now, and she grimaced from the stink of it as she struggled along
the dirt path leading uphill to the privy at the edge of the woods.
Although the sun had not yet risen, the July day was already warm
with clammy humidity.

When she reached the outhouse, she placed the pot securely
between the gaping holes of the bench, tugging back her full apron
with one hand and tipping the pot with the other. She held her
breath as it spilled into the dark pit beneath the seat, and did not
breathe again until she was able to dash from the place.

"Holy Mother of God," she gasped. "'Tis a foul duty to start the day with!"

At the corner of the house she set the pot down and scooped water from a rain barrel to rinse it clean. Each pitcherful was alive with skippers dancing around in the cloudy stuff. She washed the pot several times, emptying it into a shallow trench that began near her washtub and ran downhill along the stone wall of the white-washed cottage.

Before going back into the house she peered critically into the murky barrel. Me wash will be gray with muck if I use any more of this, she thought. I'll have Sean and Joseph scrub it out and fill it from the Crick.

After setting the chamber pot where it would catch the drying sun, Maggie ducked into her kitchen to start breakfast for her Patrick and the three boys.

"The Crick," as Maggie called it, was the Brandywine, but that was a name seldom used by the Gallaghers or by any of their scattered neighbors in Chicken Alley. The mapmakers had labeled it Brandy-wine Creek for some reason nobody could remember, but it was no mere creek. More water rushed through its banks in a day than flowed down many a river. It was twisting, steep, and clogged with tumbling rapids in places, and while that made for pretty scenery in this wooded wilderness, it also made for poor transportation. A proper river would have its share of boats—small ones, at least. The Brandywine was hard going even for a canoe.

Upstream a few miles and a quarter-century earlier, General Washington had come to grief at Chadds Ford, and six miles lower as the stream goes, seagoing vessels could turn in from the great Delaware River for a few hundred rods and berth. In between it was just a wild and rushing pretty thing to fear in floods and worry over in drought.

It had been tamed in places. Every few miles a stone dam blocked the current to drive a grain or cotton mill. The Crick was good at that. Even at low water there was always enough water to back up into a millrace and spin the power wheels to run a mill.

So the Irish of Chicken Alley called it that—the Crick. And they talked about it often. Since it drove the cotton mill where they all worked, they often had reason to think about its health—and its moods.

At the moment, however, Maggie was thinking about what to make for breakfast besides the cold mush from the night before. Eggs would have been nice, but they had been boiled the day before against the need for dinner. Boiled eggs and a handful of potatoes with whatever greens she could find in the woods would make a passable noon meal. But breakfast? There was barely sugar enough to sweeten the tea. She couldn't squander even one lump on the cornmeal mush.

She went to the table and raised the cloth covering the cold slab of mush, sniffing at it to make sure it had not gone sour overnight. Under the cupboard, on a workboard that ran the width of the kitchen, Maggie began sorting out the contents of her larder. The food was skimpy enough to gather in one bowl and a small heap, and for a moment she felt a panic grip her that she had not felt since they got off the ship that brought them here years before. What in the world would they eat tomorrow?

The mill fire had put them all in a fix. One day the cotton mill had been running steady as ever, giving regular pay to two dozen families, and then they had smelled smoke in the night. That had been over a month ago now, that morning when they had all stood around the blackened foundations with Jacob Broom telling them that he would not be rebuilding and that all debts at the company store had to be paid up with no more credit.

Maggie wondered if Patrick would be able to find any steady work this year. Times were getting tight everywhere, and there wouldn't be a prayer of his starting out at one of the other mills farther downstream. They were all grain mills anyway, running in fits and starts with the harvests.

She began to sort out the boiled eggs, one for each of them. There was one extra, and she set it aside for Brendan. It would help fatten the poor dinner pail she was fixing. A slab of bread and mush was little enough to keep a strapping boy like him from starving.

It was lucky they had Brendan. The poor job he had at the tannery was keeping them alive. Child's wages was all he earned, but the two dollars he brought home on Saturday kept them in flour and potatoes, at least.

She made quick work of fixing the light dinner box, glanced ruefully at what was left, and went to the money jar to count it up again. Somehow they would have to get some meat on the table this week, even if it meant snitching it from the savings.

The counting didn't take long. Fourteen fat copper pennies lay in a row on her workboard. The flannel sack with the drawstring holding the separate savings was so light she could feel only the weight of the cloth. There was no point in opening it; she knew full well what was inside. Her fingers undid the knot anyway, spread the soft mouth open, and probed for the coins. The three wafer-thin ten-dollar gold pieces gleamed up at her. As always the sight of them gave her a shiver of pleasure. Two months' pay. Just having the feel of them was worth the year of scrimping. So out of place they seemed in her kitchen.

She picked out one coin and calculated how much food it would bring to their pantry. Even if she spent part of it and took a couple of two-dollar coins in change, there would be food enough for weeks. Ah, the thought was blasphemy. They would have to manage some other way. She popped the gold pieces back into the bag and drew the strings.

Stacking the greenish red pennies carefully against the splash-board, she decided to spend the lot at the store this morning. It would be hardly worth the walk, even if she found a bargain, but blowing the whole fourteen cents seemed important somehow. It would be her reward for resisting temptation again.

She chuckled at the game she was playing. It did not matter much if she did hoard those gold beauties. They were spent already as it was. In two months they would go to Jake Broom as the year's payment on their land. Thirty dollars this fall, another thirty the next and the house would finally be Patrick Gallagher's free and clear.

If they hadn't starved to death by then.

She shrugged off the thought and went back to rouse Patrick and the three boys.

By midmorning Maggie had finished hanging out her wash and had sent the twins off with a bucket to see if they could find a berry patch that had not been picked over. The five-year-olds grumbled halfheartedly at the new chore, but finally took up the bucket and started out.

"Mind ye stay away from the Crick," Maggie called after them, "and don't eat everything y' pick. Save a bit for the pail."

When she came back into the house she found her husband on his hands and knees under the kitchen table.

"Didja lose something, Mr. Gallagher?" she demanded, watching his backside wiggle as he gripped each leg of the table and gave it a shake. "Or is that some new kind of dance you're favorin' me with?"

"It's the table what's doin' a jig," a gruff voice rumbled. "A man can't eat a decent meal without it slidin' from under his nose."

The angry edge to his words was not lost on her, and she stepped aside as he backed out and started to rise. Not enough breakfast and no work, she thought, and he's taking it out on the table.

As Patrick Gallagher straightened up on his knees, his head caught the corner of the plank table with a sharp crack.

"Goddammit!" he roared, leaping to his feet and clamping a great hand just above his ear. He stepped away and stood scowling at the wobbling table.

He looks ten years older than his thirty two, she thought. She wondered how much older than thirty *she* looked these days. She tried to sound cheerful. "Well, I'm off to see what I can buy to fatten you up. I'll ask at the store if there's news of work." She jiggled the table with her hand. "Why don't you fix this while I'm gone?"

At the back of the house she slung a bucket yoke over her shoulder. As long as she was passing by, she would leave it at Halloran's spring and pick up fresh water on her return. That was one thing to be thankful for. At least the spring had not gone dry.

Maggie's trip to the store did not do much to lift her spirits. The handful of coppers bought her a peck of potatoes and a few pounds of meat. There was nothing left over for anything else, but she did talk the storekeeper out of some lard, which she claimed was going rancid in the heat.

With the potatoes, her basket was a lot lighter than she would have liked, even faced as she was with a half-hour walk home in the noon heat. Well, she wouldn't think of it. She tried to focus her mind on the springhouse. It was close to home, and she let her imagination exaggerate the pleasure of taking a rest in the shade of the mossy wall and drinking her fill of the icy water running crystal pure from the wooden pipe the Hallorans had driven into the hill.

By the time she got to the spring, she was so thirsty with the heat and the thinking of it that she nearly upset her basket in a rush to get at the tin hanging by the pipe. Oh, it was lovely sitting there with the cup at her lips letting the cold stuff clear away the sticky dryness of her throat. She closed her eyes and rested.

A sound startled her, and her eyes flew open. One of the Halloran boys stood shyly a few feet away. He was holding a chicken carcass in each hand. They were not plucked, and the white feathers were smeared with blood and filth.

"Good day t'ye, Jimmy," she said, sitting up.

The boy shifted awkwardly and looked down at the chickens, which were half-dragging on the ground.

"And what have you there, lad?"

"Ma...Ma said to give these to you...if you can use them."

Maggie got to her feet and looked closely at the fowl. They were sorry-looking chickens. The heads were gone on both, and one was partly gutted. A ragged hole gaped in the feathers where its tail had been.

"What happened, Jimmy?"

"A 'possum...or maybe two...got the whole flock, every single one! Even the cock! And all they ate was the heads.... Some they just killed." He held the birds up for her to take. "Ma says we got too much to eat before it spoils."

"I'm sorry to hear you lost all yer chickens, Jimmy. 'Tis an awful thing."

"No more eggs now," the child piped with adult inflection. Then, finding himself free of the chickens, he turned and began to run back toward the Halloran cottage.

"Tell yer mother thanks from us...and we're sorry."

She felt sorry for the lot of them. Mary Halloran had told her only the week before that they would have to begin to butcher their chickens, as Maggie and Patrick had. They couldn't afford the cracked corn to feed them. Better to buy meal, put it into their own mouths, and eat the chickens one at a time while they were still plump. But to lose a dozen or so in one night to a 'possum was a catastrophe for the Hallorans...and bounty for the Gallaghers.

"Feast before famine," Maggie said aloud, gathering up her basket and hanging it on the yoke to balance the weight of the full water bucket. As she started the last leg home, she hoped it was just a saying and not a prophesy.

CHAPTER 3

She was all in a sweat when she finally reached the house, and the thought of its thick walls and stone coolness propelled her into a rush to get there. She trotted the last few yards, bursting through the kitchen door eagerly.

As soon as she entered, waves of heat engulfed her, and a rotten stench filled her nose. A fire was roaring on the hearth! She stood glaring at her husband's back as he stooped over the flames, stirring some vile mess in her best pot.

"Jesus, Mary, Mr. Gallagher! What are ye about? Is it freezin' with the cold y'are? And what is that stink? Have you died and we've been too slow in putting you under the sod?"

Patrick turned from his work and looked up. His face was florid with heat from the fire, and sweat glistened on the briery stubble of a two-day beard.

"Well, speak up," she demanded, her voice rising in pitch. "And what is that mess yer brewin' in me cookpot?"

"Hide glue, darlin' girl," he said mildly. "You've been wantin' the table fixed fer some time now. A drop of this on each of the pegs will keep 'em tight forever more."

A dejection bordering on grief flattened Maggie as she looked at the glue-encrusted cast iron. No amount of boiling or scouring would rid the pot of that stink. The taint of rancid hides would be steeped in it forever. She would cook no more meals in that pot.

With an exasperated wave she quit the reeking kitchen to pluck the chickens and get in the morning wash.

The wash hung dry and motionless in the breathless heat of the yard, and she advanced on it, carefully folding each garment and placing it in neat stacks in a wicker basket. She was pressing the last piece into the basket when she heard the rider. She tried to catch a glimpse of the horseman trotting easily along Crick Road, but the leaves were too thick this time of the year.

Nobody in Chicken Alley owned a horse. Dorgan sometimes used a rented team to bring his ale kegs and plunder from town, but few people she knew had even ridden a horse. Whoever it was must be important. At last she caught a glimpse of the rider flicker by. It was enough to satisfy her that she was right. She could tell from the getup that he was quality.

Well! An aristocrat in Chicken Alley. She darted to the back corner of the house and sighted along the cleared path between their rail fence and the cottage wall. He came into full view and reined in directly below her.

The man was quality all right! With a ruffled shirt and tight breeches and knee-high riding boots, he was finer dressed than any she had seen even in town. A neatly groomed crown of red hair set off his pale face, and Maggie thought idly that the green of his velvet coat went nicely with the hair.

With a start she realized he was dismounting. With hat in hand he began walking up the path to their front door!

She nearly kicked over the fresh clothes in her rush to duck into the kitchen. Patrick was seated on the floor, the dismantled table in pieces around him.

"Patrick!" she said, grasping his arm and tugging him to his feet. "Quick! We've a caller!"

Patrick Gallagher stood there speechless, holding a glue-smeared dowel in one of his sticky hands. Maggie gave him a quick appraisal and brushed some wood shavings from his shirt. "Ooh, now! Look at you," she whispered. "No matter," she sighed, turning him with a push toward the front door. "He's a stranger—and a gentleman at that."

By this time they heard the caller rapping on the front door of the cottage. The stranger was standing to one side on the stoop with his back to the open doorway looking out over the quiet surface of the Brandywine.

Patrick was seldom intimidated by social position, having left a need for it back in Ireland, but that did not prevent his noting that the man's bearing and dress did indeed mark him as an aristocrat.

"Good day to ye," he said, watching the visitor closely as he turned to face him.

"Good day... Mr. Gallagher?" The stranger had a queer accent, and for a reason he could not fathom, that gave Patrick a measure of confidence, an edge over the man.

"The same," he replied amiably. "And what can Patrick Gallagher be doin' for the likes of you?"

"I am Éleuthère Irénée du Pont," the man began. "Your name was given to me by the proprietor of the inn."

"Oh, you mean Dorgan. Yes, he knows me well enough."

"He told me that you were an excellent cutter of stone... a mason."

Patrick was intrigued by the accent, which by now he had assumed was French, and was pleased to hear the compliment on his skill. His reply was matter-of-fact.

"That I am."

"Well, Mr. Gallagher, I am looking for a mason to help me in the construction of a building."

The possibility of a job jabbed Patrick with sudden hope. His attitude sharpened immediately.

"Come in and sit, Mr. du Pont," he said with undisguised pleasure, leading the way to the small sitting room and indicating a rocking chair. "Would y' like some tea?"

"Thank you. Yes, I would," said du Pont, taking a kerchief from his sleeve to wipe his perspiring face. Patrick noticed that his guest twitched visibly on smelling the odor in the room.

"That's hide glue," he explained apologetically. "Nasty smellin' stuff, to be sure, but strong as iron for mendin' furniture."

"Ah, yes, of course," du Pont replied.

Behind the curtain, Maggie had heard the offer of tea and was already making preparations. She kept a sharp ear tuned to the conversation of the two men.

"So what is this stone work you have in mind, Mr. du Pont?"

Irénée du Pont took a breath and, with the deliberation of one who had gone through the routine many times before, began to explain his plan to build a mill for the manufacture of gunpowder. Patrick listened intently, making no response except for an occasional nod.

"So you see, Mr. Gallagher, I have found that your stream is ideal for my purpose. I will complete purchase of the land tomorrow."

"Where will it be?" Patrick asked, breaking his long silence.

"On the site of the burned cotton mill. I will need the dam . . . and the millrace . . . part of it at least. Unfortunately the old mill foundation is of no use to me. The mill I build will be entirely of stone, with heavier footings."

"If you know about our mill fire," Patrick ventured, "then you'll be knowin' that Patrick Gallagher is out of a job."

To his credit, Patrick observed, the Frenchman acknowledged the fact without giving the slightest hint of recognizing his advantage. Instead he turned to look at the walls of the house and commented, "At the inn they said that you built this house with your own hands." He continued to inspect the masonry lines. After a moment he looked directly at Patrick and said, "It shows the hands of a craftsman. monsieur."

Patrick said nothing but nodded in acknowledgement of the compliment and smiled. The curtain behind them parted, and his wife entered carrying a tray.

"Ah, here's my Maggie with the tea."

Irénée du Pont rose to meet his hostess as she set the service on a stool between the two men. She turned to nod to their guest. "I've honey in the sideboard if y'take it sweet," she said handing him a cup.

"Mer . . . thank you, no," du Pont replied watching her as she served her husband and retreated to the rear of the cottage.

The two men sat quietly drinking their tea, observing a kind of protocol. Neither particularly wanted the drink. It was much too warm an afternoon.

At last du Pont came to his point. "Mr. Gallagher, if you are so inclined, I would like to have you help me in this project. You would be my supervisor—my foreman—to direct the construction according to my plan." He paused for a reaction from Patrick but noticed that he was waiting quietly to hear the entire offer before answering. The man's patience pleased him, as did the interest that was playing about his eyes. He went on, "You should understand that I am a man of limited means. I must watch my pennies, as you say, and for that reason both you and I will act as laborers in the work."

Patrick stood up as soon as he heard the last sentence. "Done!" he said, smiling broadly.

Du Pont was confused by the term. "I beg your pardon?"

Patrick laughed as he repeated, "Done. I mean that I'm your man. When do we start?"

When he realized that the Irishman had accepted, du Pont smiled, but he had other things to add. "We have not agreed upon a wage... nor do you fully understand your duties. You will have to hire and train..."

"Look, Mr. du Pont, I can size up a man as well as you can. You come in here with the word of a few friends who gave me references, but it was the cut of my stone that gave you ease. Well, for a man of your station to admit to bein' short of cash and willing to put some of his own sweat into the job—that's good enough for Patrick Gallagher. And as for wages, I've no worry there, I'm thinkin'. You'll pay me what is fair."

The powder maker extended his hand, and they shook on it to seal the bargain. In the excitement of the moment Patrick had forgotten completely about the glue, and the two men had an awkward moment trying to extricate themselves from the grip. It was Patrick who lightened his own embarrassment by peering at the sticky mess in the palm of his new employer and saying, "I'm thinking that this is no ordinary bargain. You're stuck with me for good and all."

"And you with me, Patrick Gallagher."

As soon as his new employer had mounted his horse and ridden off, Patrick let out a whoop and danced a wild jig. He picked Maggie up and began spinning her around, singing wildly, to the tempo of a rather crude sea chantey. At last he stopped, sweat popping from his brow, and dumped her unceremoniously into her rocker.

"Whew," he gasped and sat cross-legged on the floor at her feet.

"Well, Mr. Gallagher! Sure and it's been some time since last you've carried on with me the likes of that."

"You heard the bargain?" he puffed, trying to catch his breath.
"I did."

"Oh, Maggie girl," he whispered, "I'm going to be at my mason's trade again!"

She nodded, all broad smiles. "A supervisor!"

"Aye," he answered.

"Good fortune follows bad, Patrick." She thought of his years of drudgery in the cotton mill. "You're deservin'."

Suddenly revitalized, he jumped to his feet, caught her by the shoulders, and bent over to give her a real kiss, on the mouth. When she looked up at him, he suddenly seemed taller and more powerful. She began to rock.

"I'm off to tell Denis the good news. The others can wait until tomorrow." He stood there a moment longer, and Maggie could almost read his thoughts as he relished breaking the news to Denis and Nora Feeney. Denis was Patrick's closest friend, and the two families often celebrated holidays together, almost like kin. He bent over and kissed her again—a brushing, absent gesture—and she could tell his mind was racing the hundred yards up the road to the Feeneys' cottage. She pushed him away good-naturedly. "On your way then, Mr. Supervisor. Spread the good news."

After he left, she got up, went to the door, and called after him, "If y'see the boys, send 'em home to clean up for supper." The message was a reminder to herself to get the evening meal together, and she walked briskly to the kitchen, trying to think of something special she might add to their common fare by way of celebration. She had completely forgotten about the disassembled plank table until she nearly stumbled on the pieces lying scattered on the floor. Well, they would have to eat with bowls on their laps this night. As she stared at the clutter of heavy planks, legs, and cross braces, which made food preparation all but impossible, she had a hard time beating down an angry impatience with her husband.

"Agh, be reasonable," she said aloud to herself. "With all the excitement I forgot about the mess meself."

She was not nearly as understanding a half-hour later when Patrick burst into the house with Sean and Joseph, filthy with their play, and the whole Feeney household trooping after him.

"Set five more places, Maggie me love," he roared. "I've invited Denis and Nora to supper to celebrate the day with us!"

CHAPTER 4

Brendan Gallagher was as bone weary as a twelve-year-old can be as he hustled through his menial chores at the Wilmington Tannery. Today had been especially long, because late in the afternoon a double wagonload of green hides had arrived at the loading platform hours past schedule. There was no option but to stay on until the last of the foul, slippery things had been carried in and dropped into the first curing vats. In the sweltering heat of July, the rancid animal skins fairly crawled and cooked. By the time he was dismissed, Brendan reeked so powerfully from the messy slime which coated him that he nearly retched.

The stink was so bad that he walked a half-mile out of his way directly from the tannery to the Brandywine, and plunged in. After scrubbing as much as he could, he climbed out, still faintly ripe, and with shoes in hand began the long trek homeward.

The sun had set a quarter-hour before he came within sight of the cottage. Sounds of a great commotion wafted toward him, and he could see shapes darting in and out of both ends of the house like oversized moths. All at once the stentorian baritone of Denis Feeney opened up with an off-key ballad, and Brendan groaned. He was nearly dead with fatigue, and the prospect of coping with a houseful of Feeneys was not welcome. The piercing squall of a three-year-old slashed through the sound of Denis Feeney's singing. That would be little Timothy, he thought grimly. That brat seemed to cry every minute he was awake. The presence of the little one meant Noreen Feeney must be visiting, too, since she always seemed to have her sickly brother in tow.

Brendan seriously considered sneaking into the woods and bedding down in a pile of leaves safely away from all the racket and the maddening attention of that nine-year-old pestering Noreen. She was such a plague with her constant teasing.

Any thoughts of escape evaporated that moment as his young brothers, having spied him from the side yard, came tumbling down the walk and tackled him, one to each leg.

"Brendan!"

"It's a part—a party!"

"Dad's got a job again."

"He's a *boss*!"

"We're gonna be rich!"

As he entered the cottage, Sean and Joseph loosened their grip and galloped ahead to announce his arrival. In one corner his father stood, arms linked with Denis Feeney as the two of them made a sad attempt at a jig to the tempo of Denis's singing. As soon as Patrick saw his son, he broke off and stepped to Brendan's side.

"Have y'heard the news, lad? About me new position at the powder works?" He gripped Brendan's arms and beamed into his face. When he saw the haggard face the boy turned to his own, he gave him a hug and dropped his voice. "Here now, make way for a hungry man." He began to steer him toward the kitchen and the food that had been heaped on a makeshift table consisting of a board propped across two chairs. He had to sweep away one or two children to clear the way. One was Noreen Feeney, her back arching importantly as she lugged her crying brother Timothy in her arms and issued orders to her younger sister Blanche.

Patrick caught Maggie's eye as she reached for a bowl from the cupboard. "Here he is, Mrs. Gallagher. The only working man on the Crick, fresh from his labors!"

From behind them Noreen piped, "He don't smell fresh to me. Do you always stink like that after work, Brendan?"

Tired as he was, Brendan stung from the remark and reddened with shame despite himself. He whirled on the waspish girl. "I'd keep a civil tongue, if I was you, y'little snot!" he rasped in a low whisper. "I've noticed a tangy smell of nappies on you these days. Is it you or him what needs a changin'?"

"Brendan!" The rebuke came from Maggie and was spoken just loud enough for the principals to hear. Brendan smarted more from her soft expression of disappointment than he had from Noreen's insult.

"Sorry, Ma," he mumbled. Then, seeing her begin to ladle stew into the bowl, he added, "Don't set out for me. I can't eat a bite."

Patrick reached out to take the bowl from Maggie, giving her a signal with his head. "No, lad, y'must put something down before you hit the hay. Come out back with me. I'll sit a spell while you eat."

He had not taken three steps, however, when a small hand whisked the bowl from him, and he looked down to see Noreen press between himself and Brendan. "Please let me, Mr. Gallagher," she said, and before he could do anything about it, Patrick found himself with a whimpering Feeney baby in his arms, and Noreen was leading a protesting Brendan out the door. He looked to Maggie for support, but that mad woman merely laughed at this predicament and went into the front room to gab with Nora Feeney.

Once outside in the relative cool and quiet on the bench behind the kitchen, Brendan decided to capitulate and eat the dinner. It was the quickest way to get rid of the pest, after all. He made a noisy business of eating to discourage her talking, but throughout it all he could feel her gaze boring into the side of his head as they sat side by side on the bench. When he had scraped the bowl clean, he managed to summon up a loud belch to put her further in her place.

Without a word she took the empty bowl from his hands and reentered the kitchen, leaving him alone in the darkness. He could hear her washing the crockery on the other side of the wall as he leaned back against it, looking at but not seeing the stars beyond the outline of the eaves.

For a reason he could not fathom, Brendan felt very lonely.

CHAPTER 5
SPRING 1803

Patrick Gallagher clumped wearily up to his front door and collapsed gratefully against the doorjamb. His clothes were sweat-soaked and covered overall with a fine blue-gray powdery grit. The stuff gave his face and hands an ashen pallor.

He sat on the step motionless for a moment, then reached for the laces of his shoes and tugged his brogans off, pouring out the grit before setting them neatly by the door. He sprawled there luxuriating in the freedom of spraddled toes.

"Ahh," he groaned and closed his eyes.

The bustle of his wife's approach did not prompt so much as an eyelid's twitch. He felt her standing above him, though, and he could almost see her expression of disapproval.

"I'll thank you not to go sleeping out-of-doors when there's a good bed not ten steps from where you've flopped." Maggie tugged at his arm, clucking with disgust at the cloud of gray powder her touch shook loose. "What a sight you are, Mr. Gallagher. You look as if you've turned to stone."

Patrick gave up on any idea of resting where he sat, and with a groan pulled himself erect and made as if to enter the house.

"Wait," she said. "Let me brush you off first." With that she began to apply her broom to his clothing energetically, nearly spinning him around in the process.

"Goddammit, woman!" he roared. "Go easy with that broom! I may look like stone, but I'm the same flesh and blood I was this mornin' and just as likely to bruise."

"Come in now and I'll get you a bucket and soap," Maggie said as though he had not spoken, and prodded him through the open door. She forced him to strip in the kitchen and bathe under her critical eye.

Patrick complied, although he did not like to stand naked in broad daylight in his wife's presence anyplace but in the bedroom. These occasional bucket baths always made him feel at a disadvantage, almost like a child. She was so picky about how he scrubbed— and where—that it was embarrassing, more especially so because she appeared to be so completely unaware of his exposed manliness.

"Well," she asked as he was toweling off in a rush to get into the clean clothes she had laid out, "did you get all the stone cut like you wanted?"

"Aye. Cut and set in one day," he said with pride. "If that gang of carpenters are up to it and the load of slate gets here on time, I'll have the place roofed in another week."

Maggie regarded him closely as she stirred at the stew pot swung out on the fireplace trammel. "You all seem to be in a rush to finish that house."

"Well, we are. The Mister is eager to get it done so he can move the family out of that cramped place they're livin' in now."

She snorted with mild impatience. "Cramped place, is it now? I never thought the Broom place was all that cramped."

"You know what I mean, Maggie. They's five of them stuffed into that little place with all their furniture in heaps and piles in every room and in the shed besides."

"Have you counted the lot of us lately? I would not mind being so 'cramped,' as you put it. The Broom place always looked a bit on the grand side for the likes of us."

"It's not just the people, Maggie. That lot has more stuff in one room than we have in the whole house. Why Madame Sophie can't even rig up that grand iron stove they carted down, because it would fill up the kitchen by itself!"

"Ah, now," Maggie said with the confidence of one who had the upper hand, "does she have to make do with hook and pot like meself, then?"

The sarcasm was not lost on Patrick, and he retreated into sur-liness, "Agh, woman, there's no sense arguing with you! You make me out to be a poor provider." His eyes left hers and took in the low-ceilinged room they stood in. "Time was when this place was yer pride and joy."

Maggie laughed at him good-naturedly and embraced him with a soft hug. "All right, me love, enough of that. Don't you go on pretendin' you think me serious. You know I'll never lose my pride in this lovely home because it was you who carved it for me out of the very rock it stands on. I'll be happy to be buried from it."

When she turned back to look at him, she was pleased to see him return the look with warmth. Still, she had to clear up the point. "I know the likes of them have to have a finer place than us. They're quality people, used to such things. And he's your boss, the owner of the mill. They have to keep up appearances that will never bother us. The thing that disturbs me," she pressed on, "is that the *house* comes before the *mill*." She stopped then, unsure of what it was that piqued her.

"If it's the mill yer stewin' over, you have naught to fear there. Half the crew is bustin' their guts to get it under roof before the winter sets in."

Maggie looked skeptical. "At the rate the Mister is going, you'll be lucky to get it finished by next summer. Here it is nearly a year since the man set foot in this house with his grand scheme, and so far he has little more than a house to show for all his plans."

Patrick smiled. Women had little grasp of these things. "No, me Maggie. The hard part on the mill is already done—the millrace, the foundations. The rest will be easy work."

"You'll have to show me," she said, losing interest in the subject and turning her attention to the immediate problem of feeding her men their evening meal.

Maggie had underestimated the determination of Irénée du Pont. Before the summer of 1803 was in full heat, the great house, a barn, three stamping mills, a drying shed, a charcoal rick house, and a storage magazine were completed. Even a row of houses for powdermakers was beginning to take shape. The Eleutherian Mills, as he named the enterprise, were quickly becoming a reality and should have made du Pont happy, but they did not.

Sophie completed supervising the breakfast cleanup, gave eleven-year-old Victorine orders to play with her younger sister and brother, and went to look for her husband. She found him pacing up and down the rear veranda, his grim face a sharp contrast to the balmy sunshine of this late June morning.

Du Pont was go engrossed in his thoughts and occasional glances at the construction activities below the house that he did not notice his wife standing in the doorway until she spoke.

"Well, my dear," she ventured lightly, "I hope none of your angry thoughts are directed at me."

He started at the sound of her voice so near at hand. "I did not know you were there."

"That was apparent. But why such a grim face, Irénée? I should think the news from Father Pierre should have you bursting with filial pride. Surely his great achievement must be a cause for celebration. Or do I detect a trace of envy?"

"Envy?" He appeared confused. "Ah, Sophie, I am afraid that the letters from my father and Jefferson had escaped me for the moment."

She looked mildly surprised. "Well, your inattention to the news is not shared by anyone else in this household. The letter from President Jefferson particularly has the children nearly raving! To think that their own *grand-père* was instrumental in negotiating the purchase of Louisiana from Napoleon. Imagine! They say that the territory is larger than the whole of France itself!"

"A magnificent coup for my father; the children have a right to be proud." His voice did not relfect the fervor of his words, she noticed. "It is ironic, is it not, that my father could not arrange even a small parcel for his family three years ago? Now Jefferson credits him with a virtual doubling of American land."

"Somehow, my dear," she said quietly, "your mood seems darker than the irony warrants. What is it that so preoccupies my husband?"

He walked toward her, a sheaf of documents in his hand. "These are what steal my interest these days," he retorted grimly. "The rewards of enterprise—hah!"

Sophie took the papers from him and shuffled through them. A puzzled look crossed her face.

"I can understand the notes of interest, but they were expected. What does the letter from Biderman mean? And why the report on

Jacob Broom?" She scrutinized the last document, having some difficulty with its language since it, unlike the other sheets, was written in English.

"Our stockholders in France have apparently put pressure on Biderman to act as their spokesman in order to question our construction loans," du Pont explained. "It seems that they are worried about losing their investment. Did they think the mills could be constructed overnight? My God, I wish they would send some able-bodied assistance instead of all this genteel criticism!" He slapped angrily at a fly buzzing around his face.

Sophie put a hand on his arm, and they stopped at the edge of the veranda. "Are you worried, too?" she asked gently, her eyes searching his face.

He waved off the question with an exasperated shrug, but after a moment he looked down at her and nodded. "Well, yes, I do have my anxious moments." He looked out over the spectacular vista of the wooded valley below them. "And now this other thing." He nearly choked on the words as he tapped on the top sheet in her hands. "The good Mr. Broom!"

She looked at the document again, struggling with the legal terms for a minute, but then gave up. "I cannot make any sense of it."

He took the papers from her, rolled them into a tube, and slapped it sharply on the railing. "Oh, they are clear enough, once one gets an eye for the American language... and," he added bitterly, "the American way of treating us French." He sighed and rolled his head, a mannerism that reminded Sophie of her father-in-law.

"What do you mean?"

"It seems, my dear wife, that Jacob Broom has seen an opportunity to squeeze us for more money. He apparently was not happy enough to have forced us to pay double the price for the land we own; he now plans to press me further." Du Pont extended his arm to point to their left, where the Brandywine bent in a curve upstream. "See where the stream curves? That is the edge of our property. Broom has bought the land next to ours and is building a dam across the Brandywine just above the mills!"

Sophie's mouth dropped open. Retarding the water flow would effectively slow their mills by cutting the volume to the millraces. "Why did he not tell us that he planned to build a mill of his own when he sold us this property?" she demanded.

Du Pont laughed dryly. "He does not intend to build a mill."

"Then why would he...?" she caught herself as Broom's intent became clear in her mind.

"I am certain that Mr. Broom will be quite willing to sell his new property to us as soon as the dam is completed." Du Pont nodded, his voice grating with anger. "Of course, the price will undoubtedly go much higher."

"What will you do?"

"I will pay, of course," du Pont said quietly.

"Where will the money come from?"

He looked at her, held out the roll of papers, and let them spring open in his hands. "Here. Another note from the bank in Philadelphia. My signature is still good with the lenders."

"Oh, Irénée," she said moving inside his arms and gripping him close, "I am so weary of this strange place. I think of Father Pierre happily back in France, with friends and family, and I get so homesick." She pressed closer to him. "Do you think me childish...the mother of three, acting so?"

"You know my feelings. I think that we have both been trapped— you because of me and I because of my father."

They stood silently, sadly, and Sophie withdrew to turn beside him and look across the Brandywine at the lush foliage of the forested hills. It was so beautiful, yet so alien.

Du Pont spoke again. "God knows how much I've yearned to go back. It is truly ironic. Because of my father's politics we became refugees here. Because of his impractical business sense I have become a powdermaker. Now he is warmly welcomed in France, and we are trapped in this unfriendly land."

"But it is better than it was, Irénée," she countered. "Your workers, the Irish, respect you, and soon the mill will be operating." She forced herself to smile through their gloom. "Then you will be able to show Monsieur Biderman a profit sheet for his friends, with payment attached!"

He would not be reassured by her optimism, however, and continued looking upstream toward the bend in the Brandywine.

"We will have to wait on the mercy of Jacob Broom to count on that, my dear."

CHAPTER 6

Take them for a walk, Norrie, that's the good girl," pleaded Nora Feeney as she twisted suds from a blanket, coiling the wrung end over her shoulder as she worked toward the end dangling in the washtub. At her words little Timothy broke off his squabble with Blanche and ran to his older sister, arms up, begging to be carried piggyback.

"No, no, Tim," Nora scolded. "You'll have to walk now. I won't have you breaking your sister's back with luggin' a big boy like you all over the Crick."

"It's all right, Ma," Noreen chirped. "I'll only carry him a bit until he gets squirmy. C'mon, Blanche."

Blanche abruptly sat down on the sparse grass beside the tub. "I want to stay here."

Nora looked wistfully at her younger daughter, who was six. "Go along, Blanche. Keep Noreen company."

"I want to stay and help you."

Nora knew from maddening experience that Blanche's idea of helping would slow her down to a crawl. The thought of all the work still facing her sharpened her tone. "Don't be selfish, girl," she snapped. "Be off with you!"

"C'mon, Blanche," Noreen called. "I'll take you to see the sheep." Noreen's voice had the persuasive, bribing tone of an adult cajoling a truculent child. With Noreen it was not mimicry. Despite the fact that she was barely four years senior to her sister, she accepted the task of mothering her brother and sister quite easily. She had been at it so long that it had gone from childhood "playing house" to actual fact. She no longer had much choice in the matter; Nora had abdicated most of her position in favor of her eldest's superior natural expertise. Noreen would not rebel against her circumstances even if that idea ever crossed her mind. And it never did.

By the time the trio was out of sight of their home, Timothy was quite happy to march along on his own feet. He scampered ahead of the two girls like an eager pup, zigzagging along Crick Road from one side to the other as he investigated every rock, plant, and bit of trash that caught his eye.

Blanche was sulking. "Are the minos in pasture, or do we have to walk all the way to the barn?"

"Merinos, not 'minos,'" corrected Noreen. "I don't know that any more than you do, Blanche."

"Well, if we have to walk all the way to the barn, I'm gonna be mad," Blanche promised halfheartedly, "because it is awful hot."

"It will be cool in the barn. If they are by the barn, we can go inside to look at the lambs. Victorine let me hold one last week. Did you know they have *three* babies now? I love to touch them."

"The big ones stink," Blanche said, twisting her nose into white wrinkles. "Their fur is greasy, and they have awful turds stuck to their behinds."

They both giggled at that and broke into a run to catch up to Timothy who had rounded a turn and disappeared.

When they came out on the uphill edge of the woods, they saw that the neatly fenced pasture was vacant. Farther on they could see the new du Pont mansion standing grandly among the great oaks and chestnuts rooted in the rocky hillside. Beyond the house and small outbuildings, closer to the Crick, were the nearly completed powder mills. On the far side of a gentle, grassy slope they could just make out the cupola and ridge of the new barn.

"I just knew they wouldn't be here!" puffed Blanche petulantly, but she made no sign of stopping. She was as eager to see the lambs as was Noreen. The going was easier here, too, and they fell into a single file along the narrow cowpath that wound around the bellying slopes to the barn.

Below them to their right they could see groups of workmen

clustered like aphids on the walls and framing of the powder works. The sound of a piping whistle lazed up to them, and they stopped to watch the tiny creatures swarm down ladders and scaffolds to gather in a tight knot behind a stone building.

"Fire in the hole!" The singsong warning drifted thinly to their ears as they felt a sharp jolt in the ground under their feet. Tim's eyes widened and he scrambled to Noreen, wrapping his arms about her skirts. His eyes were fixed on the group of men below.

His ears felt funny and suddenly a black puff of smoke boiled up from the deep millrace directly below them. *Crump!* The sound came a few seconds later.

"Daddy..." Tim said softly, his blue eyes turning indigo.

Noreen patted his shoulder reassuringly. "There, Tim. Your Daddy's fine. See? They're just blasting the rock in the millrace." As if waiting for her cue, the cluster of men broke into a walk back to their stations. Wisps of male laughter and incoherent shouts mingled with the renewed insect sounds around the children. The rest of their way to the barn, Timothy clung tightly to Noreen's skirt with one hand, and he turned often to glance apprehensively at the mills.

As they approached, Noreen saw Victorine du Pont talking with Hugh Flynn, who was forking hay from a wagon into the open door of the loft above him. A stab of pleasure surged through Noreen on seeing the eldest of the mill owner's children. Her attraction to Victorine bordered on worship. She was nearly twelve, virtually a woman in Noreen's eyes, and she shared the same position of responsibility over her younger brother and sister.

"Hello, Mr. Flynn," Noreen said, squinting up at the sun-silhouetted figure on the hay wagon. "Hello, Victorine."

Victorine smiled a greeting at the Feeneys. "Do you want to see the merinos?" Victorine never referred to their sheep without using the breed name of the long-fleeced animals her father had imported from Spain.

All three of them nodded shyly and followed her into the barn, which was cool and comfortable after their hot walk. Victorine led them to a small enclosure with a straw-covered floor. "This one was born this morning," she said as she bent and slipped between the rails of the enclosure. "All the rest are down the hill in the new pasture." She picked up the newborn lamb and carried it over for them to see, an incredibly white mass of long-haired wool.

Timothy was not aware that it was alive until he felt its breath on his face and only then noticed that it had a head with glistening nostrils and eyes. He stared at it spellbound, his hands gripping the rail of the pen.

"I like the lambs," Blanche observed quietly, "but not the mothers. They stink."

"Oh, Blanche," Noreen whispered. Somehow her sister's comment seemed indiscreet.

"Here now, Victorine, you'd better let me have that little one." The voice of Hugh Flynn rumbled behind them, and they started at his sudden appearance. He slipped into the enclosure and took the lamb from Victorine, turning the fluffy creature over to inspect the bloody stump of its umbilical cord. "Ah, there, we best look to that again," he muttered.

They watched him as he reached for a pail and withdrew a paintbrush dripping with amber fluid. He applied the pungent stuff to the oozing cord, taking great pains to get none of it on the creamy fleece.

Blanche turned her head away, nose wrinkled in disgust, but Noreen climbed up on the lower rail, hiking Tim with her to get a better look.

"What's that, Mr. Flynn?" she asked.

"Iodine," said Victorine with the air of one dismissing a rudimentary question, but she too was avidly following the procedure.

"Aye, iodine it is," the stableman agreed. "Some medicine to keep the lad well."

"Is it a boy, then?" Noreen said, straining to support her brother, who was dangling from the top rail. Then she added, "How can you tell?"

Noreen was sorry she had asked as soon as the question popped out. Victorine gave her a deprecating, haughty stare, and old Hugh Flynn laughed—but kindly.

"The same as any other beast," he said offhandedly. "God has treated most of us the same."

It was not an informative answer; they had misunderstood. It was all the wool she was referring to. How could anyone ever find *it* under all that fluff? She wanted to explain so Victorine would not think she was dumb, but the whole thing had left her so embarrassed that she decided to drop it.

In her distraction she loosened her hold on Tim, whose chin was still hooked over the rail. He bit his tongue painfully and cried out as he fell.

"I think you'd better go now," Victorine said evenly. "The sheep may get upset with his crying."

Without a word Noreen gathered Tim up like an awkward wheat sack and carried him from the barn. When they were out the door, she inspected his tongue. Satisfied that he was not seriously hurt, she continued marching down the wagon ramp and out into the pasture, picking up the neatly cut cowpath leading back. Blanche followed close behind.

"Seven thousand dollars! But, Monsieur Broom, that is more than I paid for all the property you sold me last year. Surely you realize that this small parcel has little value."

Jacob Broom smiled indulgently across the desk at his agitated caller. He was enjoying himself immensely. These aristocratic French could squirm like anyone else when the screws were applied.

"Ah, Mr. du Pont, that is a view we do not share. I consider it a prize property indeed."

Irénée was dumbstruck. He had expected to pay an inflated price, but the man was trying to rob him. He fought exasperation and fury, straining for control.

"But what use do you have for the land?"

Broom pursed his lips. "For the moment, dam-building. Beyond that I have not developed any plans."

"To build a dam without a purpose seems a waste of time and money," Irénée retorted sharply. "You do not have the reputation of one who likes to waste either."

"I prefer to think of the dam as an investment in the future, Mr. du Pont."

Broom's comment was said amiably, but the glitter in his eyes convinced Irénée that he was confident of squeezing every dollar he wanted from the powdermaker. What Broom could not know was that Irénée was powerless to pay even if he had been so inclined. When he had sought further financing for the mills, he had been politely refused. As he stared at Broom he knew that further negotiations with the Quaker were pointless.

"I will not play your game, monsieur."

"Game?"

"There is a limit to my patience with greedy men," Irénée retorted. "I am not a lamb to be fleeced."

Broom smiled. "A simple business proposal, Mr. du Pont, nothing more. After all, it was you who approached me about the land in question."

Irénée stood and looked down disdainfully at the fat landowner. "Yes. And it was an error I shall be careful not to repeat in the future. One warning I will make to you, however; if you should be so unwise as to check the flow of water to my mills, I shall have recourse to the laws and courts." Then he turned on his heel and left the office.

Laws and courts, eh? The Frenchman would soon learn he had no recourse there. Broom had helped write the laws himself, and the local courts, like himself, were not friends of the foreign born— especially those damned French.

For all his assured manner with Jacob Broom, Irénée du Pont felt little confidence as he hurried to the livery stable to retrieve his horse. He had had friends make discreet inquiries into the status of water rights above his property and knew precisely where he stood. If Broom wanted to, he could build a dam high enough to make the water course beside Eleutherian Mills nothing more than a shallow mudflat.

CHAPTER 7

The cool of evening was settling over Crick Road as Patrick made his way toward Dorgan's for his ritual Saturday night draft of beer. He could make out the raucous voice of his friend Denis Feeney blending with others while still at some distance from the tavern. From the sounds of things the discussion was not pleasant. Patrick hurried in case he might have to pry Denis away from a fracas. He hoped the man was not soused.

Denis was not drunk, but he was not in a good mood either. Neither were the other men in the room, Patrick noted as he hurried in.

"It's the kind of trick a Protestant would pull!" Denis boomed.

"The same."

"Y'can't trust any of them."

Heads bobbed in grumbling agreement.

"Well, lads," Denis said in a firm tone, "somebody has got to do somethin' about it soon. If he don't, this time next month, yer wives and babes will be goin' hungry."

"And you'll be sufferin' from a great thirst, Denis," piped Dorgan from behind the bar, triggering a round of laughter.

Denis turned a baleful look at the innkeeper as the chuckling subsided. "And you will be closin' up this place, I'm thinkin', without this lot of wage-earnin' fellow countrymen you see here making you rich, Dorgan."

"Has the world come to an end then, Denis, that yer so upset?" Patrick asked as he slipped unnoticed to the bar. "Quick, Dorgan, fill me pail before I hear the bad news. Is it that the black buggers have shut down the breweries?"

Dorgan and the others laughed again at Denis Fenney's expense, but when he drew off Patrick's beer, the old man slid a full one under Feeney's righteous nose. "That's for bein' the good sport for us all, Denis. On the house."

Denis finally unbent and smiled at his own seriousness. He took a long pull at the tankard and set it down next to his friend.

"I take it, then, that you didn't get the news, Patrick."

"What news is that?" Patrick asked, aware of the silent faces waiting to see his reaction.

Denis turned away and called to a table in the dim corner of the room, "Hugh Flynn, tell Mr. Gallagher here what y' heard at the big house this morning."

The others switched their attention from Patrick to the stableman, as quietly attentive as if they, too, were hearing the news for the first time.

"Jacob Broom is building a dam across the Crick above the mills. When it's up, only a trickle of water will get into our millraces. The mills will never turn."

The news was catastrophic to Patrick. He walked across the room and sat down at the table with Hugh Flynn.

"When did you hear this, Hugh? Who told you?" His voice was tight.

"The Mister. He was upset, he was. But I seen them with me own eyes, up around the bend. All new fellows, not from Chicken Alley anyways. Oh, Broom had quite a crew. They was dumpin' ballast rock all day yesterday and today." He paused to take a sip of beer and continued, "And workin' from both sides they were. They'll close it off before the week is up."

Patrick was confused. Why would Broom start another mill upstream from the one he had abandoned barely three years before? The location was just as poor, and he would have to build a new road.

"What side is he building the mill on?"

"No mill."

"What do y'mean, man? Why would he build a dam, then?"

"For fishin' maybe," the voice came over his shoulder, and Patrick looked up into Denis Feeney's grim face.

Patrick was becoming exasperated. "Look, now, I've had enough of riddles. Are y' puttin' me on, the lot of you?"

"Aye, Patrick. 'Tis fishing he is! Fishing for gold."

When Patrick responded with an incredulous stare, Denis continued, "That Broom is the crafty one. He waited on the Mister to finish the mills, just ready to start, like we are, and he buys up that worthless piece of rocky woods upstream for a song. Then he offers to sell it to Mr. du Pont at ten times the price."

"I heard the missus talkin' to their oldest this noon," the stable hand filled in. "They was talkin' of throwin' up the whole mess and goin' back to France. Said she was homesick for the old country and might be glad to go if he couldn't get the money for Broom."

The whole room fell silent at this information, which Hugh Flynn apparently had not mentioned before. Patrick seemed stunned and sat without speaking, his pail of beer warming flat by his elbow.

Finally he roused. "There must be laws against the likes of that," he said, spitting the words.

Denis laughed hollowly. "Laws, is it? The only laws we got, man, are the ones them damned Quaker bastards set down here before we set foot on the Crick. Do you know that du Pont don't even hold title to his own land?"

Patrick waved off the sidetracking. "That's only because he's not a citizen yet. Next year the lands will come under his name easily enough." He turned back to Hugh Flynn. "Do you think the mister will be able to meet his price?"

Flynn shrugged. "I understand he's goin' to the Philadelphia bank this comin' Monday."

"Then he intends to pay Broom, you think?" Patrick fixed him with a steady look as Flynn mulled over the question.

"I'd not be too quick to bank on that. I've been working for them for some time, long enough to learn something about the way they think. Mr. du Pont don't have his heart in the business, even though he acts like a slave to it sometimes. I think he would go back to the old country, given enough reason."

Denis Feeney swore softly and turned back to the bar. He banged his tankard disgustedly on the scarred hardwood. "I've a need for a drop of stronger medicine, Dorgan."

Patrick watched as Dorgan poured a measure of liquor, only half aware that his friend was setting out on a binge.

His mind was on other things. For the first time since he and Maggie came to this country, he had felt a real sense of security. And now to face the prospect of having his hopes tumble down about his ears was dismal indeed. He got up and looked at Hugh Flynn as he sat pulling at his pipe.

"Thanks for telling me, Hugh."

Flynn nodded gravely without speaking. Patrick waved half-heartedly to Denis Feeney and walked heavily out of the tavern.

CHAPTER 8

Patrick Gallagher rarely let work matters interfere with the harmony of his home life, but this Sunday was the exception. The moment his eyes opened, Patrick's mind snapped to the great worry about the dam. He tried to shift his attention away from the gloom of the thing, but the problem would not go away. The moldering anger he had felt at Dorgan's the night before rested like sour hay in the pit of his stomach, and there was the brassy taste of fear, too, at the root of his tongue.

Not that he said anything untoward in the presence of the boys. He did not have to. All of them took note of his mood the instant they came into his presence, and wisely refrained, even the younger ones, from probing for the reason.

Maggie knew what was troubling him, of course. She had lain beside him for the better part of three hours after they had gone to bed, listening to the man rant furiously in a hoarse whisper about the troubles with the dam. Like Patrick she was also worried, but her concern was mainly for his state of mind rather than for the economic welfare of the family. Maggie had a simple philosophy that had prevailed throughout their marriage: she tried to keep her mister well fed and content; the rest she left up to him. It seemed to work. She had great faith in her husband's performance as a provider. Any worry she might have would simply add to his burden by suggesting that she had doubts about his ability.

So she had listened, a patient witness to the strained pouring of his outrage, mindful of the undertone of fear but never alluding to it. When he finally gave it up and rolled over into snores, she fell into exhausted sleep herself.

When the grim morning meal was over and he went out back to puff angrily at his pipe, the whole family breathed a sigh of relief.

"What's the matter with him?" Brendan asked.

"Your father heard that Jacob Broom is building a dam across the Crick just above the new mills to cut the water and close us down before we even start."

Brendan was indignant. The two younger boys simply looked blankly at their mother, wolfed the rest of their breakfast, and bolted out the front door to play.

Maggie waved them off and turned her attention to Brendan. The boy was a copy of his father to be sure—minus the heat, thank the Lord. Whatever charge of anger flowed through him now was quietly controlled. He's got that from my side of the family, she thought, watching her son as he chewed absently on the last of the biscuits. He was deep in thought.

When the last scrap was gone from his bowl, he pushed back from the table, gave her a preoccupied glance, and headed for the front room. "Bye, Ma."

"Where are y'off to?"

"Up to look at Broom's dam."

A stab of concern brought a frown to Maggie's face, and she called after him, "Now mind your own business, Brendan. Keep your tongue still, and stay out of trouble."

Brendan gave her a grudging nod and shambled off up Crick Road.

Maggie watched him for a moment, then returned to the kitchen to clear the breakfast table. She did not like Brendan's nosing about. He was just big enough to be mistaken for a man with an unhealthy yen for trouble. Poking around other people's property and business. It was not a good thing to be getting mixed up in.

The site of Broom's dam was little more than a half-mile from the Gallagher's as the Crick flowed. Brendan had reached an overlook immediately above the project by taking a shortcut over the hill and through the woods below the du Pont house. The stream bent sharply south as it entered the woods before straightening into its normal northwesterly path. The rock from which Brendan peered down was an easy stone's throw from the dam, and the woods at his back screened the spot from the du Ponts' property although it was only a few hundred yards to the east.

The dam proper was nearly completed. The near side stretched halfway across the stream. The workers had already begun construction on the north side, and Brendan could see an uninterrupted strip of footing stone gleaming under the green sheet of rushing current between the unconnected ends. The place was deserted in deference to the Sabbath, but Brendan could see that spanning the short breach in the dam would be but a few days' work. He counted eight idle handcarts and from that evidence estimated Broom's work force to be at least two dozen men. He wondered where they had come from, marveling that a structure of such proportions could have been built under their noses without their noticing.

The eye of a stonemason's son prompted him to snort a judgment of the workmanship. "Huh! The whole works will be carried off with the first heavy rainstorm." He noted that none of the stones had been properly fitted; instead they appeared to have been dumped in a loosely tapered berm of jumbled points and edges. He wondered if the dam would even hold back normal pressure once the breach was closed.

He had been absorbed in the dam for so long that the chill of the flat granite on which he sat numbed his buttocks. Rising stiffly to his feet, he spat a large globule and watched it arc down to splatter on the new stone at the edge of the dam.

Someone laughed, startling him so that he nearly lost his footing as he spun around. Irénée du Pont was standing a few feet away at the edge of the rock. He came forward to stand beside the embarrassed youth. "My sentiments exactly," he said in a quiet voice. Brendan was struck by his shy demeanor.

"I am sorry to startle you so, young man. You are the son of Patrick Gallagher, no? I met you at your home last year. You have grown much since then." He was fumbling with his memory, "I do not know your name..."

"Brendan, sir."

"Ah, Brendan! Well, my friend, you seem to share my dislike of Monsieur Broom's new dam, eh? I curse and spit on it also."

"My father says the dam will stop our... your mills from ever turning, sir." Brendan stammered.

Du Pont looked at the young man soberly. "Yes, Brendan, *our* mills. . . ."

They stood silent for a long time staring morosely at the works. Brendan shifted awkwardly and attempted to make conversation. "Where does Mr. Broom's property end, sir?"

Du Pont raised his arm and sighted a line across the Crick. Then, he let it fall carelessly and shook his head. "He built this precisely on the property line. The spillway ends exactly where our property begins." Anger had crept into his voice, and muttering something in French that Brendan presumed to be an oath, he continued, "To be sure to cut off our millrace, he came as close as the law allows."

The two of them stood quietly again, their gaze adjusted downstream a few feet below the gleaming new masonry. Brendan sensed a vague empathy for this Frenchman, a kinship of frustration, perhaps, which seemed to diminish their differences in station and years. But as the silence drew on, he found himself overpowered again by an awkward confusion. Their discussion seemed to be at an end, and he was at a loss as to how to take his leave.

He stole a look sideways at the Mister. The anger had drained from du Pont, and he nearly sagged. Suddenly Brendan stirred with angry realization of what the dam meant for this man, for his father, for the whole lot of them. His abashed shyness of a moment before was pushed out by a wave of true anger. He flushed red with its emotion, and each thought of Broom's affront served to kindle a corresponding loyalty to du Pont. He stiffened with resolve.

"Don't you mind, sir," he blurted. "He's not going to be stoppin' the mills. Not if me father and I put our minds to it!" Saying that, he turned purposefully and strode back into the trees.

Du Pont was startled out of his dour mood by the boy's vehement promise, and he was impelled to laugh at the prospect of young Brendan Gallagher carrying his battle to the offices of Jacob Broom. It lightened his morning considerably, but he had the presence of mind to stifle his chuckling until Brendan had gone out of earshot.

After he was well into the trees, Brendan broke into a run. He had to do something about the dam, and quickly. It was not the inevitable economic plight facing his own family that disturbed him as much as did the insulting symbol of the dam itself. For the first time in his young life Brendan felt devotion to a cause.

He ran nonstop all the way home, finally pounding to a halt next to the chicken pen, where his father was mending some broken boards. He blew like a spent racehorse.

Patrick put aside his tools and looked apprehensively at his wide-eyed son. "Well, lad, is it the devil himself that's after your hide?"

Brendan tried to speak, but he was puffing so hard that the rush of words sounded like gibberish. "The...da...dam!"

Patrick's eyes narrowed. He had been distracted from the thing momentarily, and now the sour feeling came upon him again.

Although his own frustration with their calamity was still fresh, as he listened to his son's earnest gush of concern for Irénée du Pont, Patrick felt his rage ebb. The boy was a copy of himself, surely. He found himself unable to rant in the presence of Brendan's exuberant crusade.

"So we must do something, Dad!" the boy concluded, pacing around the scattered wreckage of the dismantled chicken coop. "There must be something we can do before the dam is finished and ruins everything!"

Patrick considered his idle hands a moment before answering. It was strange how they always seemed to assume at rest their natural grip of chisel and hammer. He wondered how many hammer blows he had dealt the stone, how many hours he had gripped the tools, how many stones he had cut and set for Irénée du Pont this past year.

He led Brendan to a shady spot in the corner of the yard, and they sat together on the upturned flat side of a split log.

"Look, lad," Patrick began, surprised at his own calm, "there are some things we are powerless to fight. Your Ma and I have had our share of that, here and in the old country." He spat to underscore his point. "The likes of us, you see, must cast our lot with the fortunes of our betters. When Jake Broom's mill burned down, he lost some money and some sleep, but his table was no lighter and his house was always warm. The mill was his toy for making money, but the Chicken Alley folk earned their daily bread in it."

Brendan shook his head, objecting. "I don't think Mr. du Pont is that kind, Dad. He was very sad today... and he knew who I was because of you."

"Ah, don't get me wrong, boy. The Mister is a fair man, and one who looks to the good of his help. What I'm sayin' is that, fine as he is, if the Mister loses out and sells the Broom, all he has lost is a year of planning and some of his family money. He can move on to try something new."

"But so could we, couldn't we? What do they have that we don't?"

"Money, to start with, lad. That and the power what comes of bein' the right class."

Brendan understood that well enough, and he was suddenly depressed. But then his father said something else that gave him food for thought for many days thereafter. It tied in somehow with certain other half-formed plans concerning the dam.

Patrick had pulled out his pipe and was fussing with it as he spoke. "There is another difference, Brendan. The 'owners' of this world know how and when to step on others so as to get their way. They don't seem to mind the screaming of the smashed ones underfoot either. Sometimes I think they're partial to the sound."

Patrick had finished patching the chicken coop, and Brendan was rounding up the scattered flock when the Feeneys arrived for their ritual Sunday visit. Denis came straight into the yard looking for Patrick while the others of his family sat with Maggie and the twins in the cool shade by the front door. Denis came right to the point.

"We have to do something about the dam."

Patrick winced. "Jesus Christ, man, why is everybody out to ruin me Sunday pleasure? Twice now I've nearly put the thing out of mind, when some good soul comes up from nowhere to remind me of me ill fortune."

Denis gripped the wicker gate to the pen as Patrick bound on the leather hinge. He appraised his friend's workmanship. "'Tis a fine job you've done for your hens, Patrick. Do you think it strong enough to keep out the weasel and the fox?"

Patrick gave him a baleful look as he knotted the rawhide bindings, but said nothing.

"And will you be fixing up the rest of the place in time for Jacob Broom to exercise his note?"

Still no comment.

Denis watched as Brendan drove the sluggish fowl toward the enclosure. "Still and all, you might be able to trade your chickens for what's left on your mortgage." He let that sit for a moment and added, "Of course, you might need to eat the things yourself to keep alive come this time next month."

Patrick knotted the last tie with a vicious tug and stood eyeing his tormentor. "All right, Denis, what would you have us do? Blow the thing to kingdom come?"

Denis grinned. "Oh, that I would...for a nod."

"Well, you can forget it. The Mister will never agree to that kind of work. That is all he needs, to give that Protestant crowd reason to toss him—and us—in Bridewell and throw away the keys.

Denis frowned. "It seems about the same result whether we take some action or sit on our hands. If I'm about to lose me home and commence to starve, I think it would be more fun to give the bastard notice."

"Ah, you're talkin' reckless again, Denis," Patrick chided. "Listen to the man, Brendan. All these sappers are the same; all they want is a chance to dig a hole, fill it with powder, and blow it up." He laughed and slapped his friend on the back.

Denis give in to the jibe and smiled. "Well, that's true enough, Pat Gallagher, but I'd like to have a penny for every rock I've split for you when your hammer arm gave out."

"Ah, g'wan with you! Most of the time I let you do it because I couldn't stand seeing you there hungry to work your tamp and fuse. I swear you carry that keg everywhere you go. It makes me nervous."

Denis winked at Brendan, who was following the give and take with admiration. "Carrying explosives is the habit of a little man, Brendan. I'm not so tall, you see, and with me red hair"—he pointed to his rusty thatch—"it is a good way to discourage fights."

They all laughed, and Patrick started walking toward the house. Denis and Brendan were following when suddenly Denis stopped in his tracks.

"Just a minute!" he roared.

Patrick stopped and turned around.

"What about the dam?" He glared at Patrick. "And you can spare me the innocent look. It was leading me down the garden path you were. All that talk about... Well, I'll not be put aside so lightly now."

Patrick walked back to his friend, the two of them standing hot in the sun in the middle of the yard. For a moment as he stood in the shade of the house, Brendan thought they looked like fighters about to begin.

"There's nothing to do, Denis. Good God, if I thought there was, don't you think I'd be doing it?" He lowered his voice a notch. "If you want the truth, I don't think there is much the Mister can do about it either. About the only thing we can do is wait—and hope for a miracle."

Denis stared back at Patrick, his face purpling with frustration. Abruptly he jabbed his hand into his trousers pocket. Slowly he pulled his fist out and held it toward Patrick. "Open your hand," he demanded.

"What?"

"I said open your hand."

Patrick complied dumbly. Denis opened his fist and let a tarnished penny roll into the other man's hand. Then he turned brusquely and walked across the yard in the direction of his house.

"What's this for?" Patrick mumbled turning the coin over in his palm.

Denis answered without turning his head, "It's a reward for saving all of us from the likes of me. Find a church and buy a candle to burn for your miracle."

The coin lay like an insult in his hand, and the bile of rage burned in Patrick Gallagher's throat. He flung the copper away wrathfully. Its aimless flight carried it into the coop, and when it alighted a few hens fought over it. They gave up when it proved too large to swallow, paying homage to its dull gleam with a few desultory pecks.

Patrick looked at his palm again as if to be sure the coin was gone. Going to the rain barrel he plunged both hands into the tepid water and scrubbed with great energy.

He did not notice when Brendan slipped from the shadow of the house and hurried after Denis Feeney.

A breathless heat hung over the whole Brandywine Valley as the afternoon wore on. The humidity was a softness in the air that one

could feel like a thing. No birds sang, and even the insects were
still, the air too sodden for flight. As he rushed after the figure of
Denis Feeney, Brendan was aware of a sheen of sweat oozing over
the skin of his swinging arms.

"Oh, Mr. Feeney!" The voice brought Denis to a halt.

"What now?" he frowned. "Did your dad send you after me with
my penny?"

Brendan smiled crookedly with the guilt of his being here in light
of the insult to his father. "No, sir. He threw the penny away. I
think he was pretty mad."

Dennis nodded, still scowling. "It pleases me to know that something stirs his guts."

Pride piqued the boy. "He's awful mad about the dam, too."

Enough of this, Denis thought. I'll not be driving a wedge between father and son. He eased up. "I know that, lad. Then what
do you want with me? Not a donnybrook in this heat, I hope."

The suggestion that he might be there to square things helped
Brendan speak as a man. It was heady sensation. "I went up to
Broom's dam this morning and spoke with the Mister."

"You went up and talked with du Pont?"

"He came down to the rock while I was there."

"I see. What did you talk about, lad?"

"Oh, mostly about how he felt about... about what Mr. Broom
did."

"I suppose he was displeased."

"Oh, yes."

Denis waited for the boy to continue, but had to prompt him.
"What else, then? Did you speak of aught besides his feelings?"

Brendan shifted his feet, not knowing whether the information
he had thought so valuable moments before was of any importance.
"I asked him where Broom's property line was, and he showed me
that it was exactly below the spillway."

Denis's eyes narrowed, and he spoke sharply. "How close?"

"Half a rod or less."

"How far along the dam?"

"From one end to the other. Du Pont said he thought the idea
was to get as close as he could to the mills."

"Aye," Denis replied thoughtfully, "and to rub his nose in it."
He reached out and gripped Brendan's arm. "Listen sharp, now.

Do you remember what the bottom is like below the dam? Is it rock or soft?"

"I'm not sure because is was so deep, but the banks are mostly earth except for the big rock we stood on."

The answer came so promptly that Denis understood now why Brendan had come to him and to no other. So the boy had been thinking of possibilities himself. He winked at Brendan and smiled for the first time.

"Do you think you'd like to show me how that line lies, Brendan me lad, or is it too hot for more walking?"

"Not for me, Mr. Feeney. Let's go!" he said, and this time it was Denis who had to run to catch up.

CHAPTER 9

The following week was marked by depression. What should have been a time heady with the excitement of finishing up the string of powder mills and readying them for operation was instead a season of sour disenchantment. By now everyone connected with the mills knew about Broom's dam and how it would cripple the operation before it had a chance to start. The final phase of construction and installation of machinery went ahead on schedule, but nobody's heart was in the work.

"Like building a ship in the desert," said Hugh Flynn a dozen times to his friends at Dorgan's, and all would nod sadly and sip their beer.

The Mister was the saddest one of all. He seemed stunned into inaction. When Patrick tried to probe tactfully into the matter, the man seemed distant and unreachable. Like the others in the community he appeared to be hoping for a miracle. One thing about the man had not changed, however: he clung fast to his obstinacy. He would neither beg from Broom nor abandon the mills. Even the ceremonial opening of the millrace floodgate was still on the calendar for the end of the week, Saturday, a double holiday since it would be Independence Day.

The Crick itself seemed to conspire against the opening of the mills. All the hot weather without so much as a single thunderstorm along its course had shrunk the stream to an alarming degree. Even with the millrace closed, flow over the adjacent mill dam had slowed to a trickle. If the drought continued, there would be hardly enough head of water to drive the mills for very long.

That problem would be temporary, of course, until it finally rained, as it must eventually. The hard knot in the problem was not the temporary kind; it lay in the obstinacy of the upstream landowner.

By midafternoon Wednesday, Broom's crew had completed all the stone work except for a narrow opening in the center of the dam. This portion had to be closed last so that rising water behind the new dam would not push away the masonry as it was put in place. An eight-foot-wide sluice gate was being built in the opening when Broom and his engineer arrived on the project.

"Will you complete the floodgate today, Mr. Croft?" Broom asked as he gripped a piling and watched carpenters set timbers beside the foaming stream.

"Yes, sir," replied the engineer. Croft was wiry and deeply tanned in sharp contrast to the ponderous and pallid Broom. "We'll have to. I want to have it working in case we get some rain."

Broom pulled out a kerchief and mopped his face. "Not much chance of that, friend," he said, looking at the sun-dominated sky.

"I'd feel better, all the same, if you would let me stop her up today and dump the last of the ballast behind the sluice gate. The stream is perfect; look how low it is."

Broom laughed and pulled a printed sheet from his pocket. "No, Mr. Croft, not today. Timing is very important to this project. The creek must be stopped precisely at ten o'clock on Saturday morning." He handed the paper to Croft and pointed to a single line: "10:00 A.M. Opening the floodgate to commence operations."

After Croft had read the announcement, noting the party for employees to celebrate the opening, he folded the paper and handed it silently back to Broom.

"So you see, Mr. Croft, if we plug our dam at the same time, we can temporarily halt the flow of all water to his mills for several hours. I think that should make our point most effectively." Jacob Broom positively beamed.

"*Your* point, Mr. Broom, not mine. You are going a hard way to spoil their party."

Broom reddened. "Please spare me your squeamishness, Mr. Croft. You were not unaware of my intent when we contracted to build this dam."

Croft gave him a hostile look. "I understand that, all right. You wanted to squeeze a bit more money out of the sale. What bothers me is that you are really trying to drive him under—him and his workers."

"We have a contract, Mr. Croft. Let's adhere to that, and save your opinions."

Croft glared back but finally dropped his eyes. "It's your business. I'll plug it whenever you say."

"Saturday, ten o'clock in the morning."

Nora Feeney was apprehensive. She had seen the signs many times before. Denis was building up to a three-day drunk. It always happened following one of his sustained high moods. Just when the family had begun to adjust to his positive change of habits and treat him like an ordinary husband and father, he would go off into liquor oblivion.

It was strange. Sunday, after he had had words with his best friend, Patrick, she had come home expecting to find him in a sour mood or with his jug—or both. Instead he was delightful, playing with the children, running at the mouth about silly things, a joy to be with. She knew he had not made up with Patrick—Maggie had told her that—but Brendan had stopped by several times on his way home from work. Thursday they had gone out together in the evening for several hours, and when Denis returned she was surprised to note that he had not been drinking. It was strange, all right, and each day his mood became more buoyant.

And then there was Noreen. She was beside herself with preparations for the employee party. She had been sewing for two weeks, constantly asking for help with the stitchery, and rarely giving Nora any help with Tim or the household chores. It had been Victorine this and Victorine that.

Nora wondered if their friendship was really something Noreen had made up in her head. Oh, Noreen had seen the Mister's daughter on several occasions, but only by accident—usually when she took the others up to see the sheep. Victorine was somewhat older than Noreen anyway, and probably had other friends from the

[60]

French families up the hill on the other side of the Lancaster Pike. They were all rich ones, from what she'd heard, or looked it, which was pretty much the same thing. She hoped Noreen didn't make a pest of herself by being too pushy. Lord knows, Nora thought, I wouldn't want any of mine buttin' in where they didn't fit.

Nora believed that it was terribly important for people to know their place and keep to it. There was even a Gospel story about the Lord himself saying you should take the last place when you weren't sure, just to be on the safe side. It had been so long since there had been a mass close enough to go to that she had forgotten just how the story went. One thing she did know: the Lord said never to take the best place, because you might be asked to step down.

God help us, she thought. I truly hope that child does not go and make fools of us all at the party. She resolved to pray to the Virgin for that as an extra tacked on to her nightly beseeching for Denis's victory over the jug.

Nora had not underestimated her daughter's state of exhilaration over the opening day ceremonies. Noreen could not remember ever being so excited. Even the day she helped Ma when Tim was born with nobody around but Blanche, who was so terrified she couldn't even go to get Mrs. Gallagher. Not even that day was nearly so wonderful.

The dress she was making was not finished until Friday evening. She was making the final adjustments as the light began to fade and just had time to try it on before dark. It was beautiful, she thought; very close to the style of dress she had seen Victorine wearing several months before. Of course, that had been in cooler weather, and this dress was quite heavy to be worn in such heat. She felt perspiration pop out all over her as she stood in her parents' sultry bedroom decked out in her creation.

She grimaced and gave the ruffled cuff of her left sleeve a tug. She had made it a bit too snug, but it would be all right if she didn't bend her elbow much. The hemline of the skirt didn't hang quite even, and she tried to see how far off it was by bending over at the waist with her knees locked. It was hard to tell, looking at it upside down with her rump pulling it from the back as she doubled over. Oh, well, who would notice it anyway?

Noreen hoped the different swatches of color went together properly. That was a worry. She had had to make do with such a bunch of scraps that it had been a terrible job matching up shades that looked good next to each other, especially the faded ones.

"Ooh, it's hot!" she whispered as she began the tedious unfastening of all the assorted buttons down the bodice. With relief she slipped the garment off, folded it carefully, and danced out of the room feeling free and cool in the damp looseness of her cotton shift. Climbing up to the sleeping loft, she crawled to her cubby and slipped the new dress smoothly under the tick.

Margaret Gallagher was doing some sewing of her own and was just about to put it aside in deference to the failing light when she heard Patrick speak to the twins on his way up the path.

"Soon bedtime for you two, eh? Come in when it gets dark." His tone was friendly enough, she noted, but it lacked his usual cheer. The man was still worried about the mills.

She put down her work basket and got up to fix his plate. The rest of the family had eaten hours ago, but she had made a cold supper because of the weather. It would be a simple matter to dish up his portion.

Patrick clumped in wearily, nodded a silent greeting when she turned around with his plate, and slid into his chair with a groan.

"Where's Brendan?" he asked, spooning a chunk of cold potatoes into his mouth.

"I think he's off to the Feeneys'."

"Again, eh?"

Maggie sat down with her tea to keep him company while he ate. She watched him break off the end of a loaf and dip it into the meat liquor.

"Have you seen Denis?" she ventured. Might as well see right away if *that* mess is set aright.

He stared ahead and took another spoonful before shaking his head. "He's not even at Dorgan's—on a Friday night. Now that's a marvel."

"You were lookin' for him then?"

He looked at her sharply and half grinned. "Ah, Maggie, is it yer worried that the two of us will never kiss and make up? Put it out of your mind, lass. Denis Feeney and me have had worse differences... and we always patch it up."

"Well, you've been like a sour clam for five days. I think he hurt yer feelings."

"Me pride is what he hurt, the little bastard. Here he comes into me own yard, spouting off like the fool he is without an ounce of sense, wantin' to take matters into his own hands. He'll never change."

"He's a restless man," Maggie observed, suddenly thinking of Brendan. A frown creased her brow.

"Aye, restless it is. I don't think he cares a whit about the mills. It's excitement that one is after. He's bound to bring the law down on the lot of us."

"Is there any news from the Mister? Is he going to give in to Broom?"

Patrick pushed away his plate, the meal unfinished. "If you can believe Hugh Flynn, he couldn't pay even if he wanted to. He heard the banks in Philadelphia have cut his credit."

"Have you talked to him?"

"The Mister? Aye, this day. I tell you, Maggie, the man may be startin' to crack. He acts like he's not got a care in the world. Either he's daft or he knows something I don't."

"Do y'think they'll sell out and go back to France?"

"Mebbe." Patrick scowled darkly, thinking of what that would mean to the Gallagher fortune. "I dunno."

Well after dark that night Hugh Flynn saw the wagon approaching as he sat outside the du Pont barn with his last pipe of the day. A flicker of lightning backlighted it so clearly he could see the lead gelding toss his head in fright. He hoped the horse would not take the bit; the driver was young and inexperienced.

"I knew they waited too long to cut that fellow," he muttered. "He still thinks he's a stallion with independent ways." A low rumble of thunder agreed.

Brendan had no trouble with the team, however, bringing them neatly up the ramp and into the open barn. Hugh clucked with admiration; the boy had a natural hand with the animals. He picked up the lantern at his feet and followed the rig inside.

Brendan set the brake and climbed down. He was grinning like pleasure itself as Flynn approached.

"Well, boy, you had no trouble I see."

"No, Mr. Flynn, it was grand." He waited up beside the gelding, running a gentling hand along the animal's flank as he walked. "May I help with the unhitching...and putting them away?"

"I see no harm in that. If the Mister will trust you with his horses on the road, I won't deny you the pleasure of putting them to bed." Then he chuckled. "The sooner I'll be in mine."

They had put the horses into the stalls below when Hugh asked Brendan, "Did you bring back me shovels, too?"

"Oh, no. Mr. Feeney said to tell you we'll be through with them tomorrow. I'll bring them up on Sunday."

After he had started down the path toward the Crick and home, Brendan was glad Hugh Flynn hadn't asked any more questions. Denis Feeney had warned him to keep mum. The less said about things the better for all concerned.

The day of the grand opening of Eleutherian Mills, as du Pont chose to call them, dawned hotter than ever, with oppressive humidity. Only the passage of an occasional cloud gave the illusion of relief.

"That's an awful name for a powder mill," Blanche observed with casual negativism.

"Ell-yew-*ther*-ee-en," said Noreen to correct her sister's butchery of the word. "I think it sounds grand."

"What's it mean?"

"Victorine said it was her father's first name."

That stopped Blanche for a moment, and she continued picking at her porridge. "I still think it sounds dumb."

Nora Feeney interrupted her children in a rare show of authority. "Come on now. Finish your breakfast. Noreen, clean Tim up and get him dressed. Your father wants us to be there on time."

At the Gallaghers' the same scene was being played out. Patrick, who was ready to leave shortly after dawn, kept urging Maggie to hurry with the twins.

"Please, Maggie," he growled, "the Mister wants me there early to help out."

He went out back to look again at the lowering sky. The solitary puffs of white above the haze of morning were beginning to gather at an alarming rate. "Damn," he grumbled. It surely looked as if rain would wash out the festivities. There would be no stopping it.

The air was charged like a loaded cannon waiting for the match. Patrick sniffed at it like a hound. The rain would come by noon; he was certain of it.

For a man who had thought it prudent to skip the grand opening altogether in light of the pickle the Mister was in, Patrick was certainly behind it now. He was aware more than anyone else of his vascillating mood, but was at a loss to control it. Instead he chose to philosophize.

"It's Irish blood, Patrick Gallagher," he told himself, "Ye cannot resist takin' sides with the loser."

The loser, as Patrick called him, arrived on the scene of the day's first event after nearly everyone else had settled in a good position to witness the raising of the floodgates. For most of the workmen that operation promised small diversion, for they had seen the heavy wood panels cranked up and down many times in the course of their installation, as had their wives and children, who often brought baskets of lunch to their menfolk.

Only one of the spectators was really interested in the floodgate opening. Despite the fact that he had been in and out of the milling industry most of his life, those closed doors that were now holding back the Brandywine seemed to fascinate him.

He was, of course, Jacob Broom.

Every few minutes he would consult a gold watch, cock his eye at the darkening clouds overhead, then rivet his attention again to the millrace crew. When Irénée du Pont arrived with his family and brushed past him, he bowed deeply to the couple and smiled broadly. "Good luck today, Mr. du Pont," he said smoothly.

He was surprised when du Pont smiled back. "We will try to give you a good show, Monsieur Broom."

It may be a short one, Broom thought, hoping that Croft had closed off the dam upstream, a few hundred yards around the bend.

Croft was true to his word. He closed the dam sluice on the hour and had his men dump the readied ballast into the gap. The last step was to lever the really large stones in place behind the gate to make the dam solid on a level with the rest. It was done in a matter of minutes.

Just as the last boulder tumbled into the slot, a blinding flash of

[65]

lightning struck upstream and was followed almost immediately by a crack of thunder. A few raindrops spattered on the dam.

"That's all," shouted Croft to his crew. "Go home to yer holiday!" Croft waited until the last man was out of sight. Then he looked below the spillway toward a clump of bushes on the near side. Very slowly he removed his hat and waved it twice. Then he, too, jogged off the dam and into the trees.

Nothing stirred for a half-hour. The water level below the spillway dropped rapidly as the opened millrace downstream sucked at the channel between the two dams. Just as the muddy bottom of the spillway was exposed, two figures struggled from the bushes, each carrying a shovel and a pitch-smeared keg. Over the next fifteen minutes they made several trips out into the muck, each time with the same burden.

One was a rather large fellow in his teens and the other an older man, on the smallish side with flaming red hair.

Back at the mills Patrick kept a close eye on the water level at the race head. When the gates were raised an instant torrent of muddy water had surged into the empty channel of the stone-walled race-way. Gradually it cleared up as debris clogging the opening was swept away. When the first rush spewed over the fresh masonry bottom, a great cheer went up from the workers' families lining each side of the huge waterway. Mothers clutched their youngest to keep them from venturing too close to the quarter-mile-long, twenty-foot-wide trench. Their fears were not exaggerated, for the boiling raceway was fifteen feet deep. If a person fell into it, the sheer vertical walls would have made it impossible to climb out.

As the channel filled, rapidly at first and then more slowly as it approached the level of the stream feeding it, it was clear to Patrick that it would barely rise to the minimum depth needed to turn even the lead mill. He was the only witness to the low level, because all of the others had moved down along the race to the first mill.

This was the only completely operational unit, since the others below it were in various stages of construction. The plan was to demonstrate the overall operation using this one mill as an example. No powder was to be processed because of the hazard to so many visitors.

By the time everyone had clustered around the mill, Patrick felt the first gust of the approaching rainstorm. "Well, here it comes, too late to help and early enough to spoil everything," he grumbled. "It does look like a mean one, too." The flash and crack of lightning up the Crick endorsed his words.

He decided to join the others and suggest to the Mister that they all get inside the building before the rain struck. There would be little to see outside anyway; the way the water level was dropping in the race he doubted that the huge wheel fed by its own small sluice on the mill side would turn for more than a few minutes. As he hurried toward it, he saw the ponderous bucket wheel begin to move. They must have opened the mill valves.

He had nearly reached du Pont's side when a strange lightness came over him and he felt something push him softly but firmly in the back. He nearly sprawled at his employer's feet. Everyone was turned toward him, looking not at the slowly turning wheel, but at something rising above the tree level upstream.

Then the rippling crack of Denis Feeney's string of blasting kegs punched at his ears and set them ringing. The crowd shrank back, stunned by the force of the explosion, gazing at the distant curtain of mud and rocks hurled ragged toward the sky. After a moment, cued by the Mister's reassuring smile and nod, they began to buzz with nervous laughter.

Dorgan was the first to speak. "Well, that's the grandest Independence Day display I've ivver seen!" Then the rain began to fall in earnest, and they pressed through the narrow doorway toward the shelter of the mill.

Jacob Broom separated himself from the crowd and blocked Patrick and du Pont's way. His face was ashen with anger, and his voice trembled. "What have you done to my dam, du Pont?"

Du Pont turned to him with a look of surprise. He seemed not to comprehend. "Pardon me. What have I done...?"

"You blew up my dam! I'll have you in jail, you foreign bastard."

"Oh, no, my friend, you have me wrong." Du Pont turned to gesture upstream. "My men are simply making the river deeper... on *my* side of the line. I will give the same respect to your property as you give to mine, no?"

Broom looked at him incredulously. "Deeper? You are a fool,

man. What you need is a shallower creek bed. Deeper channels will not raise the water level. Look at your wheel. It is slowing already."

Du Pont nodded as he watched the buckets slow and the great wheel creak to a halt. He spread his arms in exaggerated acceptance of his fate. "Perhaps it will improve with time. I will look to my mills, monsieur; you look to your dam."

An idea seeped into Broom's mind—an idea he apparently did not like. Without another word he raced for his buggy and, climbing awkwardly onto the seat, whipped his horse along the road upstream. As he careened along Crick Road, he nearly ran down a young man racing in the opposite direction pushing a handcart. Another figure was slumped inside the barrow, his head lolling with the jouncing ride.

Broom paid them no heed. He drove on as far as the road led along the Crick, then jumped out and lumbered along the slippery path toward his property and dam. The rain was pelting down now. Finally he reached the rock overlook marking his boundary.

Shielding his eyes from the downpour with both hands he peered out over the stream. With a shock he saw that the dam was intact. He sagged with relief and then began looking for signs of demolition.

The downpour made it difficult because the stream was rising steadily with runoff for miles along the waterway. As he watched, it crested the new dam and began curling over the top. He could see that Croft had done his work well; the spill was perfectly even throughout its length from bank to bank.

Then the trench caught his eye. A deep trough, exactly along the du Pont property line, cut a deep cleft several feet wide parallel to the spillway. As the flood spill poured over his dam, it tore at the raw edges of the trench, eating it away before his eyes and inching backward toward the dam.

He was spellbound by the process and stood there unmindful of the relentless rain and the passage of time. The waters kept inching up until the crest at the dam lip was nearly a foot deep.

Broom felt his dam begin its collapse before he saw it move. It came as a shudder underfoot, then as a groaning in his ears, and then he saw both end sections begin to slide. The noise was loud enough to make him retreat a few steps on the rock, and the grinding vibrations were terrific.

At last the dam came unmoored, both ends bending in upon themselves with the mighty sweep of the released flood, and the whole mass of tumbling rock was swept into a useless ellipse in the middle of the stream.

Patrick did not recognize Brendan when his son first rushed into the mill; the boy was covered with mud.

"Please hurry, Dad, Mr. Feeney's hurt," he whispered.

Patrick rushed outside with several others who had overheard. He saw his friend struggling to pull himself out of the stone cart, a look of pain on his mud-smeared face. When Denis saw them coming, he gave up the struggle and lay back in awkward repose. Five or six men circled the buggy, peering down at him.

"Where be y' hurt, Denis Feeney?" Patrick demanded in a low voice trembling with apprehension.

Denis flashed them a quick grin of reassurance. "Me leg. One of them stones came down on me. Did ya like me blast, by the way?" he added. "Wasn't it a lovely shot, that? I think me knee's busted a bit."

They carried him in and cleaned him up and sent a buggy for the doctor. The knee looked ugly, but as Hugh Flynn observed after looking at it, it would mend. Hugh had treated many an injured leg. Of course most had been the legs of horses.

Someone brought Denis a jug, and that relieved his pain considerably. He wouldn't hear of leaving the celebration to be taken home, and even hobbled about, leaning on a stick they had found in a corner of the mill. When the dam broke, and they heard the rumble of it, Denis insisted on being helped to the door so he could see the wall of water sweeping down the Crick. He led the cheering when the wheel began to turn again, and the Mister went out of his way to thank him and Brendan personally for their good work.

There was dancing then, and spirits were very high even as folks made their way home through the rain. Brendan Gallagher was on top of the world, because starting Monday he was to report for work with Hugh Flynn—at a man's wages. The doctor was not very happy with Denis Feeney's knee, and he was quite angry that he had been up on it after drinking pretty heavily. He made them carry Denis home on a litter after he had fixed the leg in a splint.

Noreen was terribly proud of her father—and Brendan. She was especially pleased that Brendan had mentioned how nice she looked in her new dress and had been surprised when she told him she made it herself.

That almost made up for the fact that Victorine made a point of not speaking to her at all. One time Noreen had caught a glimpse of her pointing in her direction and laughing to her mother. She knew whatever Victorine said had not been nice, because Madame Sophie had shushed her up with a raised finger and a cross look. Noreen's feelings were hurt, all right. She was glad that Brendan said what he did, because he had not seen her tears or known how she felt.

Even so, before she went to bed that night, she put the cut-up pieces of her dress back in the scrap hamper.

CHAPTER 10

1810

Adelaide Reardon shivered as she stood in the brick-paved courtyard of St. Mary's College chapel. The January morning was unusually crisp for eastern Maryland and seemed colder, especially to one accustomed to the warmer winters of Richmond as was the Widow Reardon. Her trembling was not due to the frosty air, however. She was shivering with maternal pride.

As he walked toward his mother, the newly ordained Reverend Francis X. Reardon cut a striking figure. He was dark and tall, on the slender side of muscular, and with a perfectly fitted, fine serge cassock whipping about his legs, he moved with almost feminine grace. When he caught sight of her standing slightly apart from the cluster of other laity waiting for their newly ordained kin, he flashed her a brilliant smile.

"Mother of God, but he's beautiful!" she gasped to herself, and as he drew close she knelt on the brick pavement to receive his blessing. The lovely flow of his voice intoning the prayer with the perfect modulation of seminary-fresh Latin warmed her like spirits. She was aware of the hushed respect the others accorded the ritual meeting of mother and priest-son. A delicious pride swept away her flickering attempt at objective devotion, and she wanted to leap to her feet and parade with him, on his arm, for all the world to see.

When he concluded with a sweeping sign of the cross over her upraised face and stooped to help her up, she was choked with emotion and said for the third morning in a row, "Ah, Frank, if only your father could see us now."

"God rest his soul," young Father Reardon responded. He led her into the private refectory where they sat down to breakfast with the relatives of the other four recently ordained priests. The Reardons sat alone, only two places set at their table, which was large enough to seat six. Theirs was the smallest family unit, the others numbering both parents and a brother and sister or two as part of the group.

They did not seem to mind. Mother and son were so close they seemed not to be aware of the others. Their privacy was respected and no one imposed upon their company. It was apparent also that the Widow Reardon was a cut above the social level of the others, a fact they deferred to automatically.

Francis waited until the meal was over before he delivered the bad news. He eased into it obliquely. "What time does your carriage arrive, Mother?"

"Oh, I haven't arranged for it yet." She gave her son an arch look and smiled. "I was thinking of extending my visit."

He frowned slightly and then looked up at her. "I'm afraid that would be pointless . . . under the circumstances."

"Circumstances?"

"My appointment was made this morning."

She brightened with expectation. "Oh, Frank, where will it be— Baltimore or Richmond?"

He shook his head and wiped his mouth with the linen napkin and tossed it carelessly beside his plate. "No, my dear mother, I have been posted in . . . Delaware."

Adelaide Reardon looked as if someone had struck her in the stomach. "Merciful heavens, Frank, didn't you ask for—?"

"Yes, but the monsignor thought it would be good for me to start out assisting in a less complex post. I suppose he is right." His expression belied the words.

"Well," she whispered under tight control, "I think a letter to . . ."

Her son waved the suggestion away and smiled grim reassurance. "It can't be for long. Besides, I am, after all, a priest," he said, "and I have certain vows to keep, you know."

She nodded. "I know, I know. The Lord—"

"Moves in mysterious ways."

She fell silent for several minutes, then asked, "What part of the state?"

"Wilmington."

She started, stunned again. "What need have they for a priest there? That lot of Quakers and Scots-Irish! Is it that you'll be a missionary to the abolitionists?"

"The monsignor informs me that there is a growing community of people from Kildare and Carlow."

The disappointment was clear in his mother's face, and her attempted reassurance came out flat. "You will not be far from Philadelphia, which has some culture, at least."

"And more Quakers?" He had to laugh in spite of the situation, and when she tired to rise above her chagrin with a smile, he decided to tell her the rest. "The pastor of my church is a Pole."

"God in heaven, does he speak our language, Frank?"

"I'm told he speaks five or six fluently," he said dryly, "but I doubt Gaelic is one of them."

"Oh, you!" she gasped, exasperated, but she chuckled at his wit.

Later that afternoon he barely had time to see her off before he had to leave himself. The separation was more painful than he had thought it would be, especially now that he would be too far away to give his mother help. As he handed her up into the Baltimore–Richmond coach, he was acutely aware of severing ties.

"Are you sure you will not need help in selling... or moving off the place?"

"I've handled things mostly by myself for years, Frank. I do not see the need to collapse now."

"And the house people and field hands... are they arranged for?"

"They go with the place, Frank. All a part of the sale." Then she added for emphasis, "And the new proprietor is a kindly Christian man. He'll see that none of the families are broken up. You can rest easily; they will not be hard used." She laughed. "Some of your new Irish cottage folk will not be doing as well, I think, in glorious Wilmington."

Then she was off with a lurch of the double teams before they could say good-bye. He waved until the rig disappeared into the barren trees below the seminary.

As he trudged up to get his duffel for the trip east, he hoped the Negroes would fare well. It was a shame to have to leave them to another, regardless of his credentials. The responsibility of land-owner, son of a slaveholder, lay heavy on him now.

He sighed and resigned himself to his mother's decision to sell out and move into Richmond. Hard economics and his vocation dictated that. He bowed to the weight of both. It was the will of God.

Father Francis Reardon's trip from Baltimore to Wilmington led him more than eighty miles over roads that were bad enough in summer but extremely treacherous in the winter season. A major natural obstacle lay midway along the route. At a place that Iroquois called Conowingo, a great river named for their tribe, Susquehanna, begins its final rush into the upper reaches of the Chesapeake.

Conowingo was a ferry crossing attempted only during those times when the river was at or below its normal level. During the spring flooding there were few days when anyone cared to risk life and wagon to its currents. Since rainy periods coincided with boggy turnpikes anyway, there was usually no reason to attempt the ferry operation if the river was up.

As it approached the Susquehanna, Father Reardon's stagecoach faced no such problem. The winter had been cold and relatively dry, and, except for fringes of ice on either bank, the crossing presented no apparent hazards. Yet they were held up for several hours on the southwest side of the river waiting for the cable-drawn ferry to make its trip from the opposite bank. The chill of evening began to settle over the small group of passengers and stamping teams.

"Well, gentlemen," called their driver, puffing up the planked ramp of the dock slip, "she's a comin' soon like, 'pears t' me."

"What seems to have been the cause of the delay?" The tone of a well-dressed fellow passenger of Father Reardon's suggested a desire to vent anger rather than glean information.

"It's one of them powder wagons, I 'spect," the unperturbed teamster drawled, turning his head to squirt a stream of tobacco juice. "Luke Perkins don't much like their comp'ny on his barge." He barked a short laugh. "Nuther do the customers. My guess is the holdup was Luke jackin' up the fare to pull only one rig acrost."

When the creaking pulley stopped ten minutes later, and the ferry was secure within the slip, Francis saw only a single Conestoga centered on the long craft. A white-faced ferryman dashed about the deck, releasing tie-downs and pulling wheel chocks. Then he hurried off the boat.

Their driver guffawed watching the man's quick exit. "No, I guess Luke ain't too comfy with his fare."

They all watched the triple teams gently take up slack and begin drawing the canvas-covered wagon off the ferry and up the ramp. The driver handled the team so well that the high vehicle flowed rather than jolted over the corduroy surface of the landing. When it was close enough for them to make out the figure holding the lines, they were surprised at his youth.

"Fer a young 'un he has a nice touch," the stage driver commented.

As it drew abreast of the group, the Conestoga eased to a stop. A neatly stenciled logo was painted at the center of the wagon's side. The red letters spelled out "Du Pont's Powder."

After setting the brake and tying off his reins, the young man left his high seat and climbed down. He was thickly built, a trifle taller than average, and moved with the gait of one used to heavy labor. His freckled, lightly bearded face seemed mismatched to the overall appearance, as though the wrong head had been stuck on an older man's body, and a nervous smile pulled at his mouth as his hazel eyes flickered over the stagecoach group searching for a friendly face.

He was Irish. Francis Reardon knew that immediately, and he stepped forward extending his hand.

"Good evening. I'm Father Reardon. We were admiring your skill with those draft animals."

The younger man, who could not have been more than twenty, quickly pulled off a knitted cap and took the priest's hand.

"Hallo, Father," he stammered, a bit amazed to confront a real priest on the highway. "Me name's Brendan Gallagher."

"And where are you bound, Brendan Gallagher?" Francis smiled expansively with the full authority of twenty-six years and clerical status. "You are not planning to blow up Baltimore with that, are you?"

"Oh, no, Father. This load is bound for Federal City. I'm to give Baltimore a wide berth on me way." Brendan smiled at the other travelers and the stagecoach driver to include them in the chatter, but they were withdrawn and unresponsive.

Francis Reardon sensed it was not the gunpowder that had silenced them. It was the other thing, something more explosive, he thought grimly. He had felt it from the moment he stepped into the coach. They had known he was a priest, and although he was comfortable in Baltimore, the farther north he went the more suspicion of "papists" he would encounter. Brendan's ethnicity might be acceptable. After all, there were more Protestant Irish in the country than there were Irish Catholics. In the company of a priest, however, his Irishness became a real threat, in the minds of these Protestants at least.

"Where is your home, Mr. Gallagher?" Francis asked, looking more closely at the legend lettered on the wagon. The address in small print leaped out at him, and he read it aloud: "Wilmington, Delaware!"

"Aye, Father," Brendan answered. "That is . . . well, near there. Up Crick Road a few miles, by the mills."

"Up Crick Road?"

"We call the place where we live Chicken Alley. All us powdermen live there."

The well-dressed passenger quipped, "Right next to Duck Run, I imagine."

Brendan hastened to correct him, a bit proud of the interest in his locale. "Oh, no, sir, it's Squirrel Run you mean. Have y'been there?"

There was a round of laughter that the priest did not join and that Brendan did not understand.

The quipster ignored Brendan's question and turned to the stage driver. "Come along, man. Get us loaded aboard. It will be dark soon."

The teamster hurried to his coach and began coaxing the horses down the ramp to the ferry. When they finally settled in place, he yelled back to the others, "All aboard now folks. . . . C'mon, Luke, come outta them trees and git us acrost!"

The others in his party began to drift down the ramp, and Francis Reardon gripped Brendan's hand again. "We'll meet again, Brendan

Gallagher. I'm to be your new priest at Wilmington. Do you come to mass?"

Brendan flushed deeply and dropped his head. "Well, it's a long walk, Father. And I don't understand the old priest so easy." But then he looked up brightly. "O'course with you there it will be a different matter."

The priest raised his hand to give his new parishioner a blessing, and Brendan stood there confused as to what he should do as the Latin words cascaded over him. When the short benison was over, Francis walked a few steps toward the ferry, which was nearly ready to cast off.

"Where will you spend the night, Brendan? The nearest house must be many miles south."

Brendan laughed at the idea of pulling a wagon loaded with explosives next to an inn. "Me and me wagon are not welcome as guests for the night, Father. We make people nervous."

"Then where do you sleep, man?"

"Under the wagon. I've grub for me and grain fer the team."

A sharp hallo from the ferryman pulled the priest around and he began jogging down the ramp. He called back over his shoulder, "Be careful with your campfire!"

Brendan laughed. "No campfire, man; not even a pipe till I offload!" He suddenly remembered: "Father..."

It didn't matter. The priest hadn't heard him anyway, he supposed. He watched the flatboat pull out along the tow line until it disappeared into the murk of nightfall. There would be no more traffic this way until he was long gone in the morning. Ah, 'twas a lonely business, these powder hauls, especially at night.

When he crawled between his bedding in the fodder box under the wagon, he felt quite warm and comfortable. All the stacked kegs of powder inches from his nose did not bother him at all.

Being alone bothered him, though. And the more comfortable he became, the more he was apt to think of Noreen Feeney. He longed to be in her company, to share her wit and pleasant humor. A small constriction formed in his throat and moved like a cramp down into his chest. A most peculiar sensation—it made him feel sad and happy at the same time.

Brendan wondered if he was in love with the girl. She had seemed like such a pest until a year or so past. The thought troubled him. To find himself in such a state with a person so much like a cousin did not seem right somehow; besides, he did not feel ready for... marriage.

Thinking the word roused him fully awake from a drowse. Marriage, eh. Now that was a terribly serious thing to let a sleepy mind fool with! He played out the line of thinking, let it uncoil enough to measure the length. Well, he was old enough at twenty, sure, and there were lads younger than him at the mills with wives and babes to support.

Still, he didn't *feel* that old. He wondered if a man ever did, ever got over thinking of himself only as the child of someone else.

He allowed himself to think of the other things. There was no question of his need. Some days he could think of nothing else, a fire in his drawers and the rod rising up of its own will. There was no pleasure in that, surely. A vision of Noreen taking off her dress struggled to surface. He put that one firmly away. It would not be pleasant riding the rest of the way to Washington with stiff underdrawers. Even the relief wouldn't be worth that.

CHAPTER 11

One of Noreen Feeney's more pleasant duties each week was to shepherd the Chicken Alley young-sters to Sunday school. The classes were sponsored by the du Ponts for the benefit of their employees. Designed mainly to teach reading, writing, and arithmetic, the school also provided informal religious instruction given by volunteers from various denominations.

Few of the adult Irish were literate, having emigrated from the old country where education of Catholics was prohibited by English law. The exceptions—the Gallaghers, Feeneys, and Flynns among them—had received their instruction in the illegal and dangerous hedge schools.

Both Noreen and Brendan had attended these Sunday instructions, eager for the chance to make up for missed opportunity in their childhood years. The classes became a contest between them: each tried to master a problem more quickly than the other. The rivalry was stronger in Brendan since he was three years older than Noreen. Noreen's industry sprang mainly from a desire to avoid appearing stupid in front of Victorine du Pont, who directed the teaching program. The Mister's children had gained their education from tutors who lived at the big house from the first year. Noreen would have loved to have Victorine as her teacher in the early days, but the class difference now goaded her into a frenzied performance.

The result was that she now frequently shared the duty as teacher of the beginners.

The limited feeling of equality was short-lived, however, for Victorine soon married the son of a French stockholder and disappeared from Noreen's life altogether.

By the time she was seventeen and Brendan twenty, he rarely appeared at the weekly sessions. The long hauls with the wagons frequently kept him away over the weekend, and when he was home, he usually showed up at the school only to make sure the twins had stayed for the whole lesson and to see they went straight home to supper.

Perhaps he came to get a chance to visit with her, too, she hoped. Their conversations certainly had been more pleasant during the last year. For one thing she had learned to keep her tongue. At least she didn't contradict him so much . . . in the little things that didn't really matter.

This Sunday she allowed her charges, the Gallagher twins and her own brother and sister, to dally on the way home. It was not that there was much of a chance of meeting Brendan, since he was away on a haul to Baltimore. She just did not want to get home too early. Denis had been on a terrible drunk since the day before, and she would rather eat a cold supper than share the hostility between her parents at the table.

But it was not to be. Blanche complained almost as soon as the three boys showed signs of slowing.

"Noreen, please make them hurry. I'm cold!" Blanche hugged herself with a shiver for emphasis.

"Tell them yourself, Blanche," Noreen said tiredly.

"They won't pay attention to me, and you know it!"

"*You* know it, so they won't, is what it is."

"Huh!" A puff of vapor exploded from Blanche's mouth, and she stamped her foot. "What's that supposed to mean?"

Noreen stopped in front of her sister. She would prefer an argument with her in the fresh air to listening to another at home. "Listen, girl, you should act your age. Here y'are nearly thirteen, and you piddle about like a baby."

Blanche assumed her best outraged, before-the-tears, pose. Her jaw dropped, and she jammed mittened fists on her hips.

"And don't be giving me that hurt look," Noreen said quickly to cut her off. "In a few years you'll be looking for a husband. The way you mope and whine no man worth his salt will even look at you as a prospect for marriage."

Blanche found her voice. "I...I...do not have to listen to this!"

"Y'can stop your ears any time for all I care, darlin' sister, but you know I speak the truth."

The frozen silence between them was broken by the distant sounds of Tim and the Gallagher twins cavorting along the road. At last Blanche bubbled out a shaky retort. "I don't *want* to get married...not to some dirty stinking man."

Something stabbed at Noreen then, compassion for her crumbling adversary perhaps, but she pressed on. The warning was needed. "You plan to spend the rest of your days taking care of the one at home, then? Think about it, Blanche."

Blanche glared at her sister briefly, and then a fleeting glimmer of fear came into her eyes. They welled over finally, and with a choking sob she ran away from Noreen, never slowing her stumbling rush until she was home, up in her corner of the loft.

When Noreen arrived some time later with Tim, she was surprised and pleased to find her father neatly dressed and sober at the supper table. He was not in the best of moods, but he managed to give Tim a clumsy squeeze as they approached the table.

"Well, me lad, did you learn any more writin' this day?"

Tim nodded, keeping silent and looking at his plate. His father looked at him with a trace of irritation.

"I'm thinking it might not be a bad idea to give the boy some speech lessons, Norrie," he said pushing back his plate and getting up. "I've forgot the sound of me own son's voice." Denis reached down beside his chair and picked up a cane. It was a knob-ended length of gnarled cherry looking more like a club than a walking stick. The end he gripped to support himself as he struggled to get up was nearly as large as the fist enclosing it. With his other hand flat on the table he twisted away from his seat and limped toward his coat, which hung near the door.

After he had thrown it on, he unlatched the door and went out, calling back over his shoulder to no one in particular, "I'm off to see Patrick Gallagher."

A bright-looking youngster of thirteen answered Denis Feeney's knock. On seeing who it was standing in the cold night outside, he swung the door open wide.

"Please to come in, Mr. Feeney."

Denis swung in cheerfully, using his stiff leg and shillelagh as a pivot, "Hallo, Gallagher!" he boomed, reaching down to rumple the boy's thick hair. "Now which is it you be, lad, Sean or Joseph?"

"I'm Sean." The answer came matter-of-factly in the tone of one who was used to clarifying his identity.

Denis laughed. "I can never tell you twins one from the other, and that's the God's truth."

Sean pointed to his nose which was marked by a half-inch whitish scar. "You can tell by me nose—where I got hit by a rock from Meg Halloran. Joseph don't have a mark."

As if on cue the other twin walked in from the kitchen and stood beside his brother nodding a silent greeting.

The curtain between them and the kitchen parted, and Patrick Gallagher peered in. "Come sit by the fire, man. Me boys'll have you froze standin' at the door."

Patrick was delighted to see him. His visits over the past few years had been few enough—and frequently unwelcome when Denis was in his cups. The man had cause enough to drink, God knows, what with the pain in his leg. Ever since that stone had crushed his knee in the blowing up of the dam, he had not taken a painless step. Denis had never once complained of the hurt, not to his wife, to his children, or even to Patrick with whom he shared nearly all else in his mind.

When they came into the kitchen, Maggie made some room for Denis at the end of the table nearest the hearth and had a steaming mug in his hand before he had settled himself in the chair.

"Well, what brings you out on a cold night?" Patrick beamed at his friend across the table.

"A conference of landowners is what this is," Denis said, thumping his cane on the floor.

"Oh, that," Patrick answered quietly with a sidelong glance at Maggie.

"Aye, Patrick, that it is. We landowners need to get our heads together before any of us goes and does anything foolish."

"You're speaking of the Mister's offer to buy our houses?"

"Our land and homes, man," Denis corrected pointing his finger.

Patrick looked at Maggie, amused exasperation in his eyes. "Is it *our* homes I hear you saying, Denis? Have ye recently purchased the house you've lived in these last ten years paying rent?"

Denis dismissed the question with a careless wave of his fingers. "A figure of speech, Patrick. You know I pay rent and always will. It's you others I worry about, the ones who plan to drive down roots and have paid yer hard-earned dollars for a place to rightly call yer own."

Denis shifted his leg to a more comfortable position and leaned forward. "I hear from my missus that you plan to sell out to du Pont."

"We may."

"But yer a fool, man. Don't be giving up the very thing you came all the way from Kildare to get!"

"I won't be losin' a thing," Patrick countered.

"Your home and land," Denis repeated.

"Mine to use as long as me and Maggie live."

"As long as y'work fer *him*."

Patrick was becoming a bit rankled. "Well, the man is not giving charity, now, is he? He pays me a fair price for me house and only asks that if I want to live in it, I should work for him. He's giving me both sides of the bargain."

Denis shook his head. "It has an unpleasant, familiar smell, boyo. The Mister is a fine man to work for, I'll grant ye that, but he has an unholy liking for other people's land."

Patrick recalled the opening day celebration of six years before. "I think you have him mixed up with somebody else," and he glanced down at Denis's leg.

Denis ignored the reference. "The man has an eye on every plot of ground his side of Wilmington and on up the Crick to Pennsylvania. It's a lordship he's after, I'm thinking."

"Goddammit, Feeney, you sound the same as you did back home when you rigged up bombs for the Steelboys. It's like you can't get used to bein' in paradise. Why, man, here we are as happy as ticks on a dog."

"That's true enough. But, God, I'd rather be a hornet or even a flea able to hop off on my own. It is a curse, I think, to be beholden, to have to suck at any teat until we fall off, skinny or fat, into our graves."

Maggie felt a compassion for Denis Feeney that surprised her with its intensity. She had no time for the man usually.

Patrick shoved Denis's mug under his nose. "Here, man, drink yer tea. It'll soon be cold, and y'haven't touched it."

"So you are letting him buy you out, then?" Denis asked, ignoring the tea.

Patrick bristled again. "If you must know, Denis, yes. I'll be sellin' to the Mister. And I won't be losing a thing. I have me a job, I keep me house as long as I like—and the boys after me, if they want—and I get enough on credit at the store to clear accounts past and for some time to come."

"The company store."

"Aye. The company store," he retorted. "Don't tell me he runs a shady place, now; the accounts are true to the penny!"

"I wouldn't know," Denis observed quietly. "I've never used the place."

"Take my word on it, man," Patrick shot back hotly. Then he eased up, feeling that his argument was finally beginning to tell. After all, Denis did not have a place to sell; that made a difference. He forced himself to smile at his friend. "The way I see it, it's too good to let pass. I can have me cake and eat it too."

Denis labored to his feet and shucked on his coat. "I can't eat sweets anyway," he chuckled ruefully. "They rot me teeth." He turned to Maggie. "Thank you for the tea, Mrs. Gallagher, though I didn't do it justice."

"Good night, Mr. Feeney." She smiled. "Mind the cold, now." For a moment she felt a strong alliance with the man, admiring his peculiar strength.

At the door he turned back to Patrick. "Before you sign the paper, Patrick, just remember one thing."

"And what might that be?" asked Patrick.

"It will always be somebody else's cake."

On the way home Denis felt the cold penetrate his leg and knew it would ache well into the night. The thought of hobbling to work in the morning brought an anticipation of pain that was always terrifying.

But that was not the reason he decided to stop by Dorgan's for a jug of the creature. He did so to dull a deeper terror. For he knew that he was as trapped by circumstance as Patrick was by preference. His hands were shaking when Dorgan handed him the jug, and he had the cork out before stepping off the porch of the tavern.

At about the same time Maggie knew that something was stuck in Patrick's craw as he paced the length of the place, kitchen to sitting room and back again, like some fretful beast. When he suddenly halted in front of her chair, she dropped the darning egg out of a sock into her lap and looked up.

"Well, what do you think, Maggie?"

"You'll do as you must, Patrick. It's good enough fer me. Ye usually do; I've no complaints about the way you look out for us."

"But Denis. What he said, y'know. Is it a mistake I'm makin' to sell the place to the Mister?"

"It's not Denis's money nor his house then, is it?" She picked up a tattered sock with such a great hole that the darning egg slipped through completely.

"I don't know. There is a bit of wisdom in his words, though I hate to admit it. It's not like it's just our place we're talkin' about. There are others, too, and like as not they'll side along with me to make their choice."

"It's a responsibility," she agreed, not pushing him one way or the other.

"Aye, and a heavy one for me. Damn the luck! Why does that little snot come bargin' in to upset me thoughts just when I've laid things to rest. He won't give a man peace!"

Maggie raised her eyes from the mending. "It's not late yet. If it will set yer mind at ease, go over and prod his brain a bit. You can make up yer own mind later. Y'have until tomorra anyway."

He looked at her thoughtfully and turned to pull his coat down from the wall peg.

"I'll go to him and hear him out before I make up me mind."

Without another word he was out the door. Maggie picked up her stitch and began to rock easily. The gaping hole was filling in more easily than she imagined it would. Her fingers flew over the rent cloth, crisscrossing yarn restructuring the toe without drawing it like a purse, making a lump that would gall and blister his foot. She took the time to make it right, and when she finsihed, it was

[85]

as smooth as a new sock; only the color change marked the repair. She had just set the basket aside when the door opened and Patrick came in. He shucked off his coat and hung it back on the peg without a word.

"Well," he said, "that was a quick visit surely."

"Ah, why did I bother with him, Maggie? He was half soused by the time I caught up with him on the way to his house."

She passed him going to the kitchen and patted him on the arm lightly.

"Shall I be makin' a cuppa, then, to warm ye a bit?"

"Aye, thanks." He sucked on his pipe. "Well, to hell with him and his doomsday ideas. I don't know why I let him get into me brain. I'm sellin' to the Mister in the morning."

Noreen Feeney was not sleepy, and for more than an hour she lay awake under the heavy quilt listening to the quiet breathing of Tim, who slept on the same mattress between herself and Blanche. For a time she heard an occasional movement in the kitchen below, but that ceased with a single creak of her parents' bed cords, and she knew that her mother had turned in also. She half expected to hear her father return from the Gallaghers', and when he did not, she put the inevitable conclusion from her mind.

As she lay there staring up into the blackness, which by day would revert to the rough-sawn planking of their roof, she felt a detached objectivity that gave her thoughts a new clarity.

It was time for her to make her own plans. The thought slipped up on her with a hard conviction that had never attended any of her earlier thoughts of marriage. Those had been mere dalliance with possibilities. Daydreams. This was made of a different metal; it rang with a surety of minted fact.

"Brendan Gallagher is my man." The words came from her as loud as normal speech, and Tim stirred at the sound. She heard sucking noises as he reverted to the old habit of taking comfort from his thumb.

She could not remember ever having slept alone. The prospect seemed pleasant and somehow even necessary now. She craved the purification of solitude. The long sequence of her childhood oppressed her like a serfage to flee from. She was mildly surprised that

[86]

she, fiercely proud Feeney that she was, felt no remorse at the discovery—only exhilaration.

Plans began to form around this new awareness of self. She and Brendan would marry and move away from the Crick. Brendan would be the proper choice even if he were not so handy and a friend of hers already, because he had seen so many places on his wagon trips. She would help him build his own freight business, and they would become rich. They would have others work for them and be admired for their success in their own place, forever free from taking orders from their betters.

Brendan was a bit shy, and it would take some prodding to bring him around, but he would be fine. She had known for some time that like some other local lads he had looked her up and down more than once. She smiled to think of it. How clumsy and confused men became in heat! Oh, it would be no task to lead him on.

She could even see the two of them in bed together. The thought was nice, really. Brendan had good shoulders and a strong back, and although he was a good worker, he did not smell sour, as so many men did. Oh, she knew what he would be after, but it would probably cause her little distress. She knew from the way he acted in other things that he would be gentle and considerate with her.

The image of their lovemaking was a bit clouded, to be sure, since she was ignorant of exactly how men and women did these things, and knew no one with whom she could have talked to find out. No matter, all this would resolve itself according to the plan she now could see so clearly.

Noreen wondered if Brendan had used any women on his trips. She doubted it. She could sense something about him that told her no. She let it go at that and stretched her body straight, luxuriating in the cold spot her feet probed under the quilt. Then she pulled them back into the warmth and lay indolently with her knees spread and lazily rubbed the soles of her cold feet together.

The thought of his mounting her filled her mind again, and she began to have doubts. She wondered how big a man became. She had seen animals many times as they mated, but it was hard to visualize a man in proportion. Many times as a child she had seen in the du Pont pasture a stallion that seemed forever to be growing a fifth leg. That had been disgusting. Then there was Tim with his little thing. Once she had seen some men bathing in the Crick while she was walking in the woods, but they were far enough away for her to see only great bunches of hair.

She dismissed the problem as relatively unimportant and gave way to warm feelings of tender embracing and gentle kisses. The soft sensations were beginning to lull her to sleep when she heard the door thump open below.

Noreen knew her father was drunk even before he tipped over a chair, sending it across the room with a clatter. She followed the sound of his staggering limp across the floor and into her mother's room. The thump of shoes dropping was mixed with the soft hiss of Nora Feeney's angry whisper.

Soon the whispered sounds changed to muffled cries, then the rhythmic creaking of the bed, and finally an awful hoarse grunting. Although she had plugged her fingers in her ears, Noreen could not block all of the sound.

It was over in a few minutes, and when his gentle snoring broke the intervening silence, Noreen curled up on her side.

She was awake for a long time after that, staring into the darkness, unblinking until her eyes stung. The tender thoughts were gone for this night, but one idea locked itself in place until she finally drifted off, and it would be there when she awoke in the morning.

She had made up her mind. Her plan would not change.

CHAPTER 12

The promise of a balmy afternoon prompted the young assistant pastor of St. Peter's Mission in Wilmington to read a portion of his *Breviarium Romanum* out-of-doors. The daily required reading of canonical hours was a duty that Francis Reardon embraced with near joy. It was an intellectual escape from the more mundane chores he faced ministering to his widely scattered congregation.

As he picked his way carefully along the muddy streets near the rectory, he welcomed the chance to be alone with his recital of the prayers and lessons that had been read by countless priests before him. The haze-filtered April sun spread penetrating warmth across his shoulders as he walked north toward the King Street Bridge.

Despite the concentration his mind began to wander from the psalter, and a sense of gloom drifted over him. The depression he had fought since arriving here was not lessening. If anything, he thought ruefully, it was growing worse.

The muddy path he now trod led away from the town buildings through an open stretch of field. Clumps of grass were greening in the respite from winter frost, and the tips of dogwood branches swelled in bud. He did not notice them. He did not notice that he had reached the middle of the bridge until he found himself leaning against the wooden railing. The rushing waters of the Brandywine below were swollen rust brown with spring thaw and seemed ugly to him. He might as well face it, he thought. It was useless to try to ignore the simple truth. He was homesick.

How he longed for Baltimore, or Richmond, or any place with an atmosphere of spiritual intellectualism, of scholarship, of curiosity and pursuit of learning. He sighed. Perhaps his confessor had been right; he should have become a contemplative instead of the secular missionary this place needed. He thought sadly of the depth of his study and qualifications. Well, it was a test, a trial of his vow of obedience.

If only he could have a week or two to unburden himself to his old teachers. One day with his seminary confessor would do wonders. An *hour* in the seminary chapel to collect himself. Even a visit with his mother...

It would have helped if his pastor were more communicative, or understandable. The old priest might be a linguist as the others had claimed, but Francis had serious doubts as to his fluency, at least in English. It was true that the Polish cleric seldom made grammatical errors in his adopted tongue, but his accent and pronunciation frequently made it necessary for Francis to ask him to repeat even the simplest of their rare exchanges.

He wondered why on earth the church had assigned Krasicki to this post in the first place. There were but a handful of Poles in the area, and these were outnumbered by a half-dozen other Catholic immigrant groups. The French enclave west of town comprised more potential parishioners than even the Irish community.

Thoughts of that group prompted him to recall the meeting with the Gallagher youth. He wondered why he had not been to mass on any of the several Sundays since their meeting at the river. Perhaps he should call on the family. He had heard that there were twenty or more Irish working in the du Pont mills. He could not remember the name of the place, but he remembered being embarrassed for the young man when he was made the butt of a joke. Something to do with chickens, ducks, and...Oh, well, he could find it easily enough by taking the road along the Brandywine. It was but a few miles. Someone would know the way.

When Francis reentered the rectory, the housekeeper and cook, also Polish, explained in broken phrases that the pastor had gone out but would be back for supper. Father Reardon withdrew to his room, removed his wool cassock, and put on a black dressing gown.

He opened the window a crack, picked up his breviary, and sat at his desk. He would have the rest of the afternoon, until the pastor returned.

He wondered what the topic at supper would be tonight. Probably the old man would give him an accounting of progress in the parish; he kept forgetting that St. Peter's was technically still only a mission. There was a real church being built, slowly to be sure, but it would be complete in another year, and the faithful of St. Peter's, however polyglot their origins, supported Father Krasicki. These simple folk might not understand his English, but they rallied to his needs with intuitive spirit.

During the next few hours Francis was distracted only once. The thought occurred to him that he had time today to seek out the Gallagher fellow. He hated to interrupt his reading, though, it was going better than it had for several days. He decided to leave that for some other time.

The late winter and early spring of 1810 had been a busy season for Brendan Gallagher. It had been a relatively dry year, but very cold, and the combination of clear skies and frozen earth made for excellent freight shipping. Whole days could be saved on a fifty-mile haul as the Conestoga rigs rode high and free on the rock-hard turnpikes.

There was another reason for all the activity, but it had to do with a climate of another sort. Government orders for gunpowder climbed steadily as Anglo-American relations deteriorated. News of international affairs rarely penetrated to Chicken Alley, but Brendan sometimes picked up choice pieces of information on his travels. Nearly all of his wagon cargoes these days terminated at one or another seaport for shipment aboard American merchantmen. The tales of close calls with British warships seethed in the port cities. Not a few American vessels had been boarded, searched, and stripped of any English-speaking crew who could not prove American birthright.

The falling-out predicted by Jefferson and inherited by President Madison was inexorably developing into a real threat of war with England. This situation, coupled with the consequent loss of contact with black powder suppliers abroad, made every ounce of explosive manufactured by the Eleutherian Mills a suddenly precious commodity. Federal City in 1810 had become du Pont's number one customer.

As a result, the drivers and teams from the du Pont stables were always on the road. Brendan did not mind the hectic pace at all. It was exciting for him to vist new places in spite of the discomforts of the trip. Some nights he was sorely tempted to move his bedding downwind of the wagon and build a fire, but he never did. His cubby under the load was better protection from the wind and cold anyway, though there were some days and nights strung together when he never managed to get his feet warm. Once, outside Philadelphia, he grew so stiff while driving from the high seat of the wagon that he walked the lead team with a halter for two miles just to get the blood moving in his legs. That had been dangerous, because if something had spooked any one of the large draft animals, he would never have been able to control them without reins.

Each time he was on the deadhead run from some new place, he catalogued every experience against the telling to his family and Noreen. By the time he got home his head would be buzzing with so many new sights and events that they would come tumbling out in a nonstop torrent the moment he had a willing audience.

The Gallaghers were more than he could wish for in this respect, particularly the twins. They hung on every word, demanding that he tell everything in such detail that Brendan had developed a rather clever narrative style which anticipated most of their questions and spared interruptions in the story. But Noreen Feeney was the one he most liked to share his experiences with. She had such a quick wit and sparkling eagerness that halfway through the discourse he had the peculiar, and pleasant, feeling that she had been there too, sharing in the experiences, instead of just hearing about them.

"Oh, Brendan, do you really think it was him?"

"It was him, all right, big as life."

"But how could you tell? I wouldn't know the man if I fell over him on Crick Road."

"Oh, you'd know him all right, Norrie. He has the look of a big man . . . not size so much as the way he has of lookin' right through ye. A leader. Y'know what I mean."

Her eyes sparkled with questions. "But didn't you feel bold as brass goin' up to speak to him?"

He burst out laughing at that. "Me speak up to Mr. Jefferson? I'm not that daft, girl! Nor that pushy either." He smiled into her expectant face, radiant with excitement. "It was him that walked up to me empty wagon as I was gettin' down to check the hooves of the team. That Federal City is like a swamp, Noreen, all slurpy clay and sand. I was afraid the horses' shoes might rot off. Y'know, I told Dad they have to drive pilings twenty feet deep to build foundations on—"

"Brendan!" She stamped her foot. "It's President Jefferson I want to hear about, not the muddy Washington streets!"

"Oh," he teased absently. "Well, he's not President anymore, now is he?"

Her eyes snapped dangerously, and he retreated. "He was standin' by the rig as I got down, himself and a crowd of others, lookin' at the sign on the canvas—you know, 'Du Pont's Powder'—and he looks right at me and says, 'You work for the best powdermaker in the country, sir. He is a friend of mine, Irénée du Pont.'"

She waited for more, and he swallowed and went on. "Can you believe it? Tom Jefferson and the Mister bein' friends! Then he says, 'When you get home, tell Mr. du Pont that the country appreciates his help.'"

"My!"

"And that's not all; when he was about to leave, he asked me what me name was, and I told'm Brendan Gallagher."

"And you shook his hand."

"Aye." He grinned. "Man to man."

Noreen took Brendan's hand and squeezed it between her own. She looked him hard in the eye. "Tom Jefferson and you being friends. Now that is worth remembering!"

Brendan gave her back the squeeze and laughed happily. "Ah, Norrie, you make it seem even grander than it was, and that's a fact!"

She had a way, that girl, of unreeling thoughts from him. All that snarled-up coil of stuff in his mind that snaked out softly like braided silk when she was the listener. And it wasn't just the tales of his wandering that paid out when he was in her company. All kinds of other things came unknotted in his brain: plans that were as yet unwoven, dreams still so gossamer that they were more web than cloth, and fears, too. She seemed to get at them and have them out between them to look at without his ever feeling her tug at the loose end.

Lately she seldom said much herself. But she was the power in their talks; he knew that. Sometimes he found it hard to believe that she was three years younger than he, and impossible to connect her to the brat he had so detested having underfoot as a child. That was the most amazing thing about her. He wondered that she had changed so much, as if she were someone he had liked from long ago who had recently come back to replace another. Brendan certainly did not feel much different himself. There were occasions when he thought of himself as a man, but usually it was as if he were parading about, a child pretending at a grown-up's work.

That was what the plans and dreams and fears were all about. It all seemed so pretentious a blather in his mind, this dream of cutting out a small empire of his own and building a trade into a whole company of teamsters working for himself, these visions of dozens of Gallagher wagons scattered along routes extending hundreds of miles in all directions. He had seen other men in fine dress and heard their coarse speech. They were none of them gentlemen as far as he could tell, but they were bold and aggressive in their manner, unafraid to jump at a chance to make the impossible seem easy.

Was it possible for him? When he was on the road it seemed so. There in the isolation of the trip he allowed himself the planning, the dreaming, and there was none of the fearing. But when he got back on the Crick with all the rest, his dad, the other workmen at Dorgan's and at the mills, he wasn't quite so sure. Ah, that was an understatement! When he got home the whole thing seemed so farfetched he would have felt the fool for mentioning it to anyone.

Anyone, that is, except Noreen.

Somehow the girl encouraged his daft scheme. He was not even sure how he ever came to mention it to her, she was so much on his mind these days, but it seemed to come up every time they were together.

Other things popped out, too. Those awful times of black terror, like stepping from the rig after a long drive on a cold, dry day and feeling the crack of a static spark when your foot touched ground, knowing that probably just such a spark had sent Liam Murphy to heaven forty years ahead of time.

That story had just bubbled out of his mouth. She had reached out quietly and touched his arm in the telling, and the touch had thrilled him with a spark stronger than the one of which he spoke.

They had been on the way home from her Sunday class at the time. After he had spilled it out and she had taken his arm, he stopped as though to look at the brown current of the Crick roaring over the upper dam. But he was not interested in the spectacle, and she knew it.

"Ah, Norrie, it's a timid soul I am to be dreaming of making a big splash in the world."

She kept hold of his arm, resisting an urge to move closer to his warm bulk. "I don't see that there is any connection between having a healthy respect for the danger of gunpowder and planning for a successful future."

He was suddenly abashed by his remark. "Well, I mean by that, I think, that all these plans I speak of are easy to talk about, but puttin' them into action is a different matter altogether."

"Aye, Brendan. There is a difference between talk and action, but bein' terrified by a mindless and unpredictible power has naught to do with it. It frightens me, and I'm never near the stuff, but every time Daddy goes to the mills or you roll out with a wagon I pray you'll come back sound and unhurt."

Her reference to his safety gave him a stab of pleasure, but he ignored the reference in his reply. "You needn't fret about Denis Feeney, girl. Your dad knows more about handling black powder than the Mister himself."

She did not counter that, and they resumed walking. Their pace was slower than before, and he was happy that she chose to keep her hand on his arm. After a few steps she slipped it down into his palm and lightly interwove her fingers with his. They walked in silence minding how their fingers behaved as if they were creatures of some independent will.

"We have not spoken for weeks," she said matter-of-factly.

There was not a hint of reproach in her voice, but Brendan felt that he had been remiss. Their twined fingers seemed to accuse him of dereliction.

"Aye, Norrie," he blurted, "and I've missed y–your conversation this past month." He went on, unsure of his words. "Everybody for miles around is demanding powder. We no sooner get back to the yard than we're off again the next day. All me days off have been on the road with just the horses to keep me company. . . ."

"I'm glad to hear it, Brendan Gallagher."

"Glad to hear. . ." He looked sideways at her, somewhat confused by her slow smile. "Glad to hear what?"

"Oh, all of it," she said, being coy with him for the first time he could remember. "Glad you missed. . . my conversation. Glad you're working hard, as a good man should, and. . . glad you've only horses to keep you company on cold nights."

He could not think of an answer and decided to let it go. It was a topic he was uncomfortable with at best. If she could read his mind, though, some of the thoughts he had of her on those cold, lonely nights would take her breath away.

It was strange now that recalling his fantasies seemed coarse even to him. In her presence, touching her hand, a different feeling dominated. He felt a desire to shield her from abuse, even from the crassness of his own appetites.

"Where are the boys?" he asked, aware for the first time that she was not surrounded by the usual trio. "And Blanche?"

"I sent them packing with her in charge. Or maybe it was the other way around. I hope the poor thing lives through it. Your brothers are a handful surely."

He laughed. "I'll not deny that. I wonder sometimes where they get their wild streak." He decided to score a point. "The Lord knows they act more like Feeneys every day. I wonder if the bloodlines crossed some generations back?"

She pulled her hand away and gave him a cross look, eyes snapping. "And what is *that* supposed to mean, eh?"

He pointed at her, and they both stopped walking and squared off at each other. "See? That's what I mean."

"*What* do you mean?" she demanded, her skin paling into two almond white spots wide on her cheekbones.

He had grinned when he baited her, but the instant she reacted he regretted having started the process. It went on, though, carried by its own momentum. "It's you yourself, girl. See how your tail's up? It's the hot Feeney blood."

[96]

"Oh!" she choked and turned to walk away.

"I'm just teasin' ye, Norrie," he called, rushing to catch up. A voice inside was putting him down terribly for hurting her, and his face flamed shamefully. "C'mon, now. Y'know I was just trading insults for what you said about the twins." He had overtaken her and was walking backwards to keep her face in view.

"Aye, it was insulting is what it was!" she panted, struggling to avert her face from his.

He was skipping backwards full tilt now to keep up with her forward pace. She angled across the road to get around him.

"All right, then," he puffed. "I apologize to ye...humbly.... I do! 'Twas naught but...fun...I meant, but I'm most truly sorry, Nor—" His heel collided with a rock in the roadbed, and he fell backward like a tree, flailing his arms helplessly to break the fall. He landed with a thump, snapping his head sharply on the ground.

She was on her knees beside him immediately, anxiously trying to raise his head from the rocky muck. His hair was matted with mud, and she wondered if he had cracked his skull.

"Brendan...oh...are y'hurt?"

He looked at her queerly, eyes out of focus, then sat up and shook himself like a dog. He sat there a moment staring at his feet.

"Brendan..."

He pushed himself to a squat and made a tentative effort to stand. She stood back, worried that he might topple again.

"Whew!"

"Are you all right?"

"Well," he said without conviction, tenderly exploring the back of his cranium, "I don't think there's any damage." He looked at her sheepishly. "That was a lively dance it was. I think I skipped a beat."

She laughed with relief and approached to brush the mud from his back. He turned away from her busy hands.

"Stop now, Noreen. You'll make a mess of yourself and ruin your frock and shawl."

"You gave me a fright, truly. Did you know your eyes were crossed?"

"Were they now?" He growled and made a face at her, crossing them again. She laughed nervously with relief that he was sound, and that sent a tender regret through him. "I never meant to hurt your feelings, lass. It was a fool's jest."

"It's over and done," she murmured looking down with arms folded as they moved along.

"All the same, I'm sorry for it."

After a moment she looked at him again with her chin high. "I thought you made the crack about my father."

Brendan was stunned. He cursed himself at the realization of how deeply he had cut her. "Ah, Norrie, Norrie, how could y'make a mistake like that?"

She forced the words through her teeth. "Well, you know his temper when he drinks. I'm sure it's the talk of the whole of Chicken Alley."

He snorted. "Talk, is it? No one speaks ill of Denis Feeney in me company, nor me father's, nor any of the ones who know what he did in the old country. The man's a hero."

"That was long ago, I'm afraid."

"He's still the same inside."

"The creature's got him, Brendan. It gets worse as time goes by."

Brendan nodded. "Since the dam. His leg must give him awful pain."

Noreen looked up as the low sun slid behind a cloud, darkening the whole narrow valley. "It's more than that, I'm thinking, but I don't know what it is."

Brendan followed her gaze and studied the leaden clusters of the cloud. "I don't care what it is, Norrie. It's none of my business anyway. But I love the man. There is some great power always churning up in him. I tell you, he was meant for better things than blowin' rock out of the ground."

Noreen moved closer to Brendan, and when he held open the sheepskin coat she slipped inside as naturally as if it were an everyday habit. He dropped his arm about her and pulled her close. The walking stopped very suddenly then, and he forgot about Denis Feeney, powdermaking, and all else except the warm softness of her body pressed to him. When she raised her mouth to his, he trembled with the effort not to bruise her lips with his own. He forgot all else and thought he could stand rooted to this spot forever and a day.

When their lips parted, he thought so much of the idea that he murmured it as she pressed her head against his chest. "Ah, Norrie, Norrie. I think I'd like to stand here forever!"

She pulled slowly away from him then, stepping back and carefully fastening his coat. "Not just now, me bucko. You smell too much of horse for my taste." Then she laughed and turned off the road to run up the path to her door.

Just as she reached the door, she turned and called, "Come back tonight after you've had your bath." Then she blew him a kiss and disappeared inside the house.

Brendan could not be sure how long he stood there gazing stupidly at the closed door, but that evening, after he had had a bath, he was a guest in the Feeney sitting room.

CHAPTER 13

Denis Feeney sat on the stump where he could watch the drillers and eased his right leg into a pool of sunlight to warm the aching muscles. The sun would help, but what he really needed was a good hot draft from the jug. God, but the knee ached today!

"You there, O'Rourke. More to the left and down. Lower, man; dontcha see me mark?"

The young man nodded after a moment's searching and placed the star drill on the spot and resumed swinging his maul to the ringing spike. Little spurts of granite dust spilled from the hole as he sank the drill into the rock face of the deep millrace.

Denis admired their work. They were fast, those two brawnies; their arms so heavily muscled from the hammering that the biceps were almost as thick as their legs. And mild-mannered, too. He chuckled at the good fortune of that. In a fight with bare fists either one of them could take a man's head off with one swing.

He looked down at his own arms. Ah, he was built like a scrawny mudwasp, and that was a fact. A good puff of wind would knock him sideways. The runt of the Feeney litter, not tall enough and thistle-thin besides.

It didn't bother him much. He had learned how to compensate for short measure. It was a matter of speed, timing, and quick wits. Well, now he would have to make do without the speed. He pushed away from the stump and limped over to his kit. Thunder plunder, Patrick called it.

"That's good, lads," he called to the drillers. "Everybody out of the ditch." Picking up a pair of leather bags, he draped them over his shoulder and stooped to cradle a twenty-five-pound keg of blasting powder in his arms. He walked slowly toward the deep trench. A sapper never rushed.

By the time he had filled all the drill holes there was little more than a few handfuls of powder left in the keg. He carried it back to the ladder and climbed up slowly, counting time until he was well away from the ditch and placed it with his remaining powder cache behind some trees. Then he paced off the distance to his sheltered place behind the stump.

As he returned to the race, he calculated the time needed to ignite the fuses and make his way back to the stump before the charges blew. Each fuse would have to be a trifle longer than the next to make sure they all went off at once.

He had already cut and set the fuses and was plugging each charge with clay when he heard Patrick speak from the lip of the race above him.

"Well, Denis, do y'think ye kin slice me off a fine piece of stone? Or do y'plan to blow it all to useless rubble like before?"

Denis grinned at his work. It was a challenge to blast this way. Simply cutting a fifteen-foot-wide raceway through granite was hard enough. But the day before he had suggested to Patrick that they try to cut the rock clean so that the stone removed could be used on the spot to wall the waterway. It seemed wasteful to haul cut stone from the quarry when the same stuff was right here. The first try had failed because the charges went off in a ripple.

"You'll see, me mason friend, it'll look like a slice of cheese."

"Yer fuses look sloppy to me... and short enough besides."

"It's timing that does the trick. The longer they are the more there's chance for error. I want them all to go off at once." He turned and winked. "Don't worry, Patrick; I've enough time to make me leisurely escape. I don't want that slab to flatten me like a bug in this hole of yers."

He pressed the last plug into place and leaned back, rubbing the gummy clay from his fingers. "Now if you'll go duck yer head, I'll be about me business."

Patrick looked doubtful. "I think I'll just wait here until yer arse is out of there."

"Suit yerself."

Denis bent over his bags and withdrew a foot-long length of fuse. With a flint and steel he sparked the tip expertly, igniting it on the first try. He limped over to where Patrick was looking down from the edge and handed up the leather sacks. The fuse hissed in his hand.

"Here, then, if ye want to stay and watch. Take me kit so's I won't have to climb that ladder a third time."

Patrick got down on his belly and reached for the demolition tools. He kept a worried eye on the sputtering fuse.

Then Denis limped slowly over to the fuses, and like a practiced acolyte ignited them with methodical precision until they all flickered on the gray face of the rock. He cast the lighting fuse away and limped toward the ladder. He might have been on a casual walk for all his apparent lack of haste, but his eyes were on the ground before him picking a safe step along the uneven floor of the excavation. Patrick's heart began to pound just to watch his progress, and he kept looking back at the hot fuses as they inched closer to the explosives. Even agitated as he was, he had to admire Denis's timing. They were all exactly the same length. But, oh, they were getting close!

It was the third step he took on the ladder that was his undoing, and Denis knew he was going to fall the instant he put weight on his bad knee. With a curse he toppled backward into the muck.

When he tried to get up, the knee pained him so terribly that he could not put weight on it. He twisted his head to measure the fuses. Not much time; he would have to pull himself up the ladder hand over hand. He began to crawl toward the ladder, but when he looked up he saw it lying flat beside him in the race!

Patrick's face appeared above him on top of the wall. He screamed at Patrick, "Get away, man! It's gonna blow! Get away!"

He clawed at the ladder trying to raise it, wrenching it free of the sucking mud, but it was too heavy to lift with him down on one knee. He thought of the great arms of the young drillers and tried to will their strength into his own. The ladder rose inches, trembled, and fell again into the muck.

There was a sudden thud beside him, and he turned to see Patrick pick the ladder up as though it were a straw and prop it back against the wall. Then, his face white with fear and splotched with mud, Patrick snatched Denis up bodily, threw him over one shoulder, and clambered frantically up the straining rungs.

When they cleared the top, he tossed Denis to the ground and flopped down beside him.

A second later the ground slapped their faces, filling their mouths with earth, and a numbing thunderclap deafened them utterly. They huddled together, arms over their heads as a rolling cloud of dust bellied out of the race and a rain of stone chips pelted them like hail. They didn't move until they felt the hands of the drillers brushing off the debris.

They had to cart Denis home again in a barrow. It was a round-about trip with a long layover at Dorgan's. Denis sang all the way to the inn, even before he had a drop in him. The drillers were laughing at his antics as they took turns at the handles of the barrow.

When they got there, Denis insisted that they match him drink for drink, and refused to let them pay for even one.

"Ah, Patrick," Denis said after tossing down the first of many to calm his nerves and ease his pain, "thank ye fer savin' me hide!"

"Don't be thankin' me Denis. 'Tis Maggie ye'll be owing thanks."

"And why is that?"

"It's Maggie who has to wash me britches."

"Oh, did they get muddy with honest toil fer once?"

"Not that so much, me reckless friend. It's the brown stains in me balbriggans I'm thinkin' on."

Denis smiled. "Normal hazards of me trade. Well, tell me now, did it come off properly?"

"What's that, Denis?"

"The bloody rock, man! Have ye forgot already?"

"Oh, that. Why surely it did, Denis. Just like you said it would. A slice of cheese."

The knee was pretty bad for about four days, and it was another week or so before Denis was limber enough to report for work. During all that time off the Mister kept him on half pay. It was the talk of Chicken Alley for months afterward. The reputation of the man for such unheard of generosity spread up and down the Crick. And it spread to Ireland, too, in the letters sent home fattened with a dollar or two to ease their bad times. More than a few young Irishers were tempted to drop the little they had by way of hope in the future for a chance to improve their luck as powdermen along the Brandywine.

Another bright spot was cause for some quiet celebration by the Feeney and Gallagher clans. Denis had gone on the wagon. Since the day he was carted home from Dorgan's, he had not had a drop. Patrick touched on the subject one day when he dropped in on Denis to see how he was mending.

"Have ye lost interest in the creature?"

"Not likely." Denis smiled grimly. "Oh, the crawlies have left me, but I still twitch a bit, and the cravin's at the root of me tongue. But I'll not have another."

"What makes you so sure?"

Denis thought a moment, pursing his lips. Then he tapped his game leg with a finger. "I got to thinkin' how important it is for me to keep me wits about me now that I have to favor me pin. Like in the hole two weeks ago, I shaved it too close—didn't make allowances for the leg."

"I'll agree to that. It was too close!" Patrick whooshed a sigh and shook his head. It still gave him shivers to think on it.

"Well, then, there it is, boyo. I've got too much responsibility with that stuff to go cloudin' me mind or gettin' the shakes."

They pondered that in silence for a time. Then Denis added thoughtfully, "I think before I had to drink to... to ferget... things. Now all of a sudden it dawns on me—it took almost gettin' you killed to see it—that I have to stop sippin' at the jug so I *don't* ferget."

The next day Patrick stopped by the office to tell the Mister what a fine thing it was for him to keep Denis on pay while his leg mended. At the same time he spoke of his worry that the leg might give out again and cause the sapper serious grief. He was worried for his friend and told the Mister so, hinting for an easier job where Denis could rest often and not have to worry about tripping on rocks and such.

When Denis reported for work, he was assigned to the rolling mills to learn that operation. It was easy work for the most part. The great iron mill wheels did all the heavy toil. All the operator had to do was make sure the gears did not get hot, keep the powder mix from getting dry, and turn the mill off and on. It was a trifle boring, but it wasn't too dangerous if a man kept his wits about him. And the pay was just as good.

But after the first day was over, Denis came fuming to Patrick to tell him what had happened.

"They've stuck me in the rolling mill! Can ye feature that, Patrick? Denis Feeney pullin' a handle and watchin' the wheels turn for six hours at a time!"

"But, Denis, it's easy work, and y'can sit often to rest yer leg. The Mister is just lookin' after yer best interests."

"Best interests, is it? Jesus, man, *usin'* blasting powder is me craft; not *makin'* the grubby stuff! I'm a sapper and a good one. If I wanted to be a miller I'd be grinding wheat and rye."

It was settled, though. Denis even made an appeal to the Mister himself, but as the owner pointed out, he was only looking out for Denis's own good.

Following his short meeting with the Mister, Denis failed to show up for supper at the Feeney table. And from that day on he was again a regular at Dorgan's place.

CHAPTER 14

The day that Father Reardon chose to seek out the Gallaghers sparkled with the heady freshness of early May. Week-long spring rains ending the day before had left an occasional soft spot along the road, but the gummy clay of northern Delaware had dried into a soft loamy texture that muffled the hoofbeats of his mare and seemed to give her a more sprightly pace. As he cantered easily west of town, the landscape unrolled into gently undulating vistas of woods and farmland. The morning sun filtered softly through branches of greening oak, sweet chestnut, birch, and willow. Even the late-starting leaves of maple were beginning to spread. He reined the mare in and let her walk. He was in no great hurry anyway.

The air was fragrant with wild flowers until he turned upstream at the foot of the hill. Then a faintly unpleasant odor replaced it, and it got stronger the farther he went. He caught sight of a high brick smokestack jutting up through the trees ahead and finally realized what the odor was.

"Brimstone," he muttered, wrinkling his nose with displeasure. The mare echoed his sentiment with a long snort and tossed her head as if to rid it of the sulfur fumes.

He saw a woman carrying a lunch pail standing by the side of the road staring at him with her mouth open. When he got close he tipped his hat and smiled down at her.

"Good morning. Can you tell me where to find the Gallaghers?"

The old woman snapped her toothless jaws together and sized him up before she spoke. "An' who's wantin' t'know, if I might ask?" she challenged in a very businesslike manner.

Francis nearly laughed at the impertinence of the plainly dressed creature, and it gave him some pleasure to assert himself. "Father Reardon of St. Peter's Mission," he said.

"Ooh! *Father* Reardon, is it?" she cried and clamped a wrinkled hand to her mouth. "Yer pardon, Father, but I didn't think y'were but one o'them Protestant Presbyterians come down to make trouble."

"And you are..."

"Lizzie Dorgan. The Mister and me run the inn. You'll have to stop for a drop on the way out. Didja come in by way of Barley Mill or Risin' Sun?"

"Barley Mill."

"Go out by Risin' Sun. On the right. Y'can't miss it. Dorgan's, now."

"Thank you, Mrs. Dorgan," he said. "And the Gallagher home?"

She turned and pointed. "You're almost there. The next place you see, Father. On the left side of the road."

"Ah, yes, I see," he observed distantly.

"Well, be off now, Father. I won't be keeping you back." She hoisted the dinner pail. "I'll be gettin' this to me son, Joseph, who's a worker at the mill, God help him, pardon me, Father."

As he left her behind, Francis was perplexed by his mixed feelings. The woman was nearly a hag, her English hideously butchered, an illiterate in all probability. Yet there was something in him that was drawn to her, something generations deep. And it had nothing whatever to do with his being a minister of God's work. That was a different thing altogether. It was as if he were slipping backwards toward primitive beginnings.

"God help me," he thought. "I'll soon be smelling peat fires if I'm not careful."

It was in this guarded frame of mind that he rapped on the cottage door of Patrick and Maggie Gallagher.

After meeting the young priest, Lizzie Dorgan hurried on to the powder mill yard with her son's noon dinner hot in the pail swinging at her side. When she got to the gate, there was such a thundering rush of workmen surging toward her that she feared they might be bent on picking her up bodily and throwing her out. What was the noonday rush? Suddenly it came to her with a pinch of flustered shame. She had forgotten again and brought Joseph's dinner on a Saturday, and him heading home this moment because of the half-workday. Now what would he think of his addled old ma? She hid the dinner bucket behind her apron skirt and tried to think of a way to hide herself.

With a flash of inspiration she remembered the priest caller on the Gallaghers. Spotting her son in a knot of boisterous young men, she called to him. As he approached there was a look of exasperation on his face. She did not miss it and tried to head it off.

"Where's Pat Gallagher, Joe? There's a priest callin' for him to his house."

"Mr. Gallagher...?" The mention of the priest had redirected Joe Dorgan's thinking, but not altogether. He kept looking at his mother's right arm held under the great expanse of her apron.

"Ooh, there he stands now," Lizzie said, pointing behind her son. "Run now, and fetch'm fer yer mother. There's a good boy!"

When she told Patrick about the young Irish priest calling at his house, Lizzie had a greater audience than when she used to lead the singing at her father's pub in Belfast. That had been a long time ago, when they were still pretending to be Protestants. There had come the day of reckoning, of course, when the informer had sent them running to this new land with just the clothes on their backs and the hidden sack of coins. They were thankful for that, to have made it aboard the American ship with money to start out new.

Lizzie kept at the retelling of her brief encounter with the new Father Reardon until Joseph took her arm and dragged her back. He reached under her apron and took the handle of his pail.

"Give it here, Ma. I'd sooner eat it on the way than let it go cold." He popped off the lid and sniffed. "Is it all spuds, or do I smell a bit of lamb?"

He probed with his grimy fingers in the tin until he found the morsel buried in the stew, fished it out and popped it in his mouth. His belly growled as he chewed contentedly.

Lizzie Dorgan's gums gleamed in the sun as she happily contemplated her late-born last child feeding his face and leading her home on his arm.

Passing by in clusters of a half-dozen or so, most of the thirty Irish families of Chicken Alley managed to sneak a look at the priest as he sat near the open door of Patrick Gallagher's cottage. They were too shy of seeming nosy to come up the path and introduce themselves, but such a parade there was of people wanting to take the air along the Crick of a Saturday afternoon!

Maggie was in such a stir as she couldn't remember unless you counted the day she got married. She almost pinched herself to make sure it was not a dream she was having as he sat in the front room and she clattered about the kitchen to fix the man a proper pot of tea.

Her Patrick was not home when he came, nor Brendan, both of them still at the mills, and the twins were out raging around somewhere looking for some trouble to get into. So there she was, up to her chin in work of a Saturday morning and looking like it.

The first half-hour alone with the priest had been awful, with her just aching to get away from the man for time to wipe her face, brush her hair, and change into a clean apron. When Patrick came stomping in all out of breath, she had never been happier to see him. She barely gave them time to meet before rushing behind the curtain to fix herself up a bit.

She was just about to go back into the room with the tea when she heard the twins and Brendan storm in. She could tell by the racket they made that they did not know about their distinguished visitor.

It got quiet enough all of a sudden as Patrick made their introductions, and she decided that now was the best time to make her entrance. Brendan was shaking the priest's hand when she pushed back the curtain and marched in with the tray.

"So we finally meet again, Brendan," Father Reardon was saying.

Brendan blushed under the surprised look of his father, remembering that he had not told anyone except Noreen about his meeting with the priest.

"You've met my son before?"

"Yes, Mr. Gallagher. We ran into each other outside Baltimore. Brendan was having some trouble with a ferryman who did not like the nature of his cargo."

Brendan laughed nervously. "There's always trouble at that crossing, the Conowingo."

Maggie nodded to Sean to clear a spot on a low table. As she poured Father a cup of tea, she observed, "Now that is a strange thing for you, to stumble into Brendan for the second time."

"It is not really a coincidence, Mrs. Gallagher, I came here to find him."

Brendan kept silent, red-faced with the guilt of not following up on his promise to visit the church.

Patrick joked good-naturedly, "Ye've not come to haul me eldest away to be a priest, Father? If it's that you're after I'm afraid you've come a bit late. From what I can tell he's hot for one of the girls up the Crick."

"Patrick Gallagher!" Maggie gasped and shot him a withering look.

Father Reardon reddened and took a sip of tea, and Brendan shrank in mortal embarrassment. It was the only time his dad had said a word about him and Noreen.

"You have not heard, I take it," said Father Reardon changing the subject, "that I have come to assist at the mission in Wilmington. I am touring the outlying places to get an idea of the number of Catholics we can serve." He smiled at Brendan. "And to encourage you all to come to St. Peter's for Sunday mass."

Patrick cleared his throat. "Aye, Father, we've been... a few times since the old priest started up last year."

"I know it is a long way to go. I take it you do not attend mass regularly?"

Maggie put down her cup and smoothed the apron across her knees. "It's a long walk, yes, Father, but the reason most of us don't make it much is that the father is so hard to understand." She hesitated, wondering if that should make any difference.

"I see." Father Reardon's answer was free of accusation or reprieve. "You can come to the mass I celebrate. I do not read the Epistle and Gospel in Polish, I can assure you. Nor do I give sermons in that language."

"Oh, we will, Father," Maggie chirped. "You can bank on that."

Patrick nodded and reached for his pipe from the table. As he packed it carefully he looked the priest over. "You don't sound, if you'll excuse me sayin' so, like you come from the old country, Father."

"No. I was born and raised here... Richmond. My father came from Ireland, though. My mother is Irish, too, but like me she was born in America."

As the priest spoke, Maggie studied him closely. Why, he was hardly more than a boy. Between the two of them, her Brendan and Father Reardon, there was barely the span of six years. Every priest she had ever known had seemed so much older than she. Now here she was looking at one who was young enough to have been one of her own children. She calculated. How old was she now? The years had slipped by so fast. Was she thirty-eight or thirty-nine? Heaven help her, she wasn't sure. She would have to look it up! She didn't feel any older than she had at twenty-five. She looked at Patrick. He was beginning to show his years, but then, he was older than she and would be expected to. What was he now, forty or forty-one?

"... and for the nice cup of tea."

She came around with a start and realized that Father Reardon was on his feet and making his good-byes.

"Oh, but Father, y'must stay and have a meal with us before startin' that hot trip back to town! We've plenty in the pot, and we'd be honored to have you at the table."

"Thank you for the offer, Mrs. Gallagher, and I would be delighted, but I have many calls to make along the way."

She tried to persuade him further, but in the end he left without dinner, blessed them with the sign of the cross, mounted his horse, and cantered off.

On the way back to Wilmington Francis did take the Rising Sun instead of Barley Mill Road, but he did not stop at Dorgan's for a friendly drop with Lizzie and her family. He pressed on for the town, having done enough parish work for the day. It had been rewarding in a spiritual way, and he hoped he had not been too direct in pointing out their religious duties to the Gallaghers. He wondered if they were literate. There were signs of considerable intelligence in the family. Perhaps he would draft a letter to Baltimore to see to the education of these folk some time in the future. He would like to be in on the planning for such a model.

CHAPTER 15

The following Sunday dawned warm and humid. Shortly before six o'clock a straggling procession of a dozen or so Chicken Alley faithful made their way along Crick Road heading for morning mass. They were dressed in their best for the occasion, mainly in homemade fashions, but some of the youngsters were barefoot. Here and there a dinner hamper would trade hands as different families alternated in the lugging of the noon meal just as they had cooperated in provisioning for it. The ten-mile round trip with an hour or so for services made such planning a necessity, especially for the children. It would be well into early afternoon before they got back from the nine o'clock mass.

Maggie and Patrick were part of the parade; indeed it had been at Maggie's urging that the rest of them were there at all. "We owe it to the good father to show him that the faith is not dead along the Crick. Besides, the young ones are like as not to grow up heathen if we don't make an effort," she had said to everyone she could reach the day before.

Brendan had not come along. His explanation, accepted with some reserve by his mother, was that there were some important things he had to get done before going out on the road again Monday. She had an idea that Noreen Feeney was one of the important things he referred to and was sure of it when only Nora, Blanche, and Tim represented the Feeney clan.

For their "important thing" Noreen had also packed a basket. The night before, Brendan had left saying that he wanted to speak to her about something very important the next day. Noreen had little doubt as to what the matter might be since her basic strategy had been proceeding on schedule. If he had an idea of speaking his mind to her this day, Noreen wanted to remove any possible distractions. A picnic for two in the woods along the Crick would do nicely.

With the others away she luxuriated in a cool bath. The wooden washtub she set up in the curtained kitchen was filled with clear soft water from the rain barrel, and she decided to squander the last sliver of perfumed soap she had used with miserly caution since Christmas. She scrubbed with vigor, using an oval of sandstone to soften her elbows, knees, and heels, and saved the soap till last, standing in the tub and working it into a scented lather from her neck to her knees. Then she lifted a bucket of clear water and poured it over her chest and shoulders to rinse away the film. One splash was enough. She did not want to lose all of the perfume.

She decided to empty the tub before putting anything on for fear of getting wet. Moving about naked was the best way to dry off anyway. The late spring growth of weeds and brush would screen her from Crick Road, which ran parallel to the front of their cottage.

She made several trips with the bucket, dumping her bath water in the shallow ditch beside the house. When at last the tub was too low to bail, she tilted it on edge and rolled it on an angle through the door. Her feet had become muddied and she swished them clean in the bottom of the tub before upending it, and stood on a patch of grass to let them dry.

The sun bathed her with a warmth made pleasant by the sleek wetness of her skin, and she threw back her head to let it fall full on her face. Reaching both hands behind her neck, she unpinned and fluffed out her coppery hair until it lay like a burnished veil about her, split by her shoulders and breasts.

The still expectancy of the balmy air heightened a sense of wicked abandon, and she envisioned herself as Eve surrounded by the lush spring foliage. She, too, was blossoming. She felt life like a powerful thrust within her sending vibrant ripples along the surface of her skin.

A light breeze began soughing through the tops of the trees riffling the new-green leaves and lifting her hair with a cool breath. Musky earth smells from the Crick blended with the fain perfume rising from her own skin, and she breathed the scents in deeply, filling her lungs with one long draft.

The words of an old Irish song ran through her mind, and she began humming the melody, tapping her foot lightly to keep time. The grass tips tickled her feet, and she began to dance a tight circle in the middle of the yard.

She did not notice a male figure watching her from within the shaded kitchen. His mouth gaped as he took in the wonder of this vision of naked womanhood dancing nymphlike in full light of day.

At last he dropped his eyes and quietly withdrew. A little smile broke out on his lips, and he muttered, "Ah, she's ripe for the picking. And that's the truth!" He wondered when he would tell her that there had been a witness to her gambol, if ever he would. Some things are better left unspoken, even between those who are so very close.

In the midst of her whirling abandon in the yard she suddenly remembered that Brendan would soon come by. Snatching up her hairpins, she dashed into the kitchen and threw on her clothes. A look at the clock in the front room served notice that she was well behind schedule in putting up her hair. In fact, Brendan should have been there by now. Just as well that he was not; she would need all the time she could get.

She had just put the finishing touches on her hair and was picking up her bonnet when he knocked. She put on a mild expression of reproof as she went to the door.

"Yer a bit late, I'm thinking, Mr. Gallagher."

He smiled as though he had a secret when he answered. "Oh, I thought you might need some extra time... it being so early in the day for callin', if y'know what I mean."

She apparently didn't, or did not want to say so.

She pointed to the hamper by the door and began tying on her bonnet. "There's our dinner. Pick it up and let's be on our way."

Brendan looked happy to have something to occupy his hands, and he hefted the hamper as though it were empty.

For their outing she had picked a place they had never been to before—together at least. It was a rock outcropping shaded by over-hanging trees with a narrow band of wild grasses sprouting from the loamy slope on three sides. The projecting shelf of the great granite slab jutted over the Crick itself, making a promontory eight or nine feet above the water.

The stream was noisy here, dashing white and foamy over the tumbled rocks that had once been Jacob Broom's ill-fated dam. Brendan had been to the rock many times since meeting Irénée du Pont at the dam. It was his favorite place for solitude. But as Noreen led him to it, pointing out the charms of its lovely setting, he thought it better not to mention that. So like a little girl she was, nearly bubbling over in her delight of everything. He couldn't spoil that.

He even let himself be surprised when she showed him how close it was to the collapsed dam. He pointed downstream to the bushes where he and Noreen's father had lain in hiding, waiting for the signal to set off their charges.

"Ah, that was the most exciting day of my life, Norrie. We got the mills off to a proper start that day, we did."

Noreen nodded, but he noticed she had sobered at the memory, and he could have kicked himself for his one-sided recollection. What had been glorious to him and security for the millhands had been purchased at the cost of great misery for Denis and his family.

He turned away from the stream and looked uphill into the thick woods. "Anyway, 'tis a handsome place you've picked for us."

Noreen took the basket from his hand and set it on the rock. "Come down here," she said brightly, taking his hand and leading him to a natural stairlike jumble of stones. "Let's sit next to the water. I'd like to wet me feet."

They found a rock close enough to the roaring current to sit and dangle their legs without falling in, and suddenly they were at each other like children, pulling off each other's shoes, pretending to toss them into the Crick, teasing with threats to push each other in, clothes and all, and finally coming to rest side by side, watching their feet being sucked sideways in the rushing water.

Noreen had gathered up her skirt and tucked it between her legs. Her feet kept skipping to the surface of the surging water and lightly grazing his as she struggled to hold them against the current. Each time her tiny foot touched his, a spark traveled up his spine. It was a marvel to him. The touch of her toe! He must be daft to be so pleased with someone's foot. But it was a darling foot, it was. He tried to keep up a reasonable conversation with her, but her foot consumed most of his attention, the dainty whiteness of it, so perfectly attached to her ankle, itself a wonder! And her legs. Once in a while he caught a glimpse of knee, and he found himself staring at the folds of soft fabric she held pressed between...

"...the teams of horses? Have you though of that?"

He pulled his eyes away. "What did you say, Norrie?"

"Honestly now, Brendan, sometimes I get the feeling that you're off someplace else when we talk. Or is it that you're growing deaf?"

"Oh, yes. The teams," he said finding the strands of their conversation at last. "Well, we'd have to have an arrangement with the liveries in each of the towns. I think we might do well enough with just the wagon and one good team for local hauls. We could rent others along the route both goin' and comin' for longer runs." He stared across the Crick into the emerald woodscape on the other side. Out of the corner of his eye he could see her foot barely missing his under the water. He was beginning to get a cramp in his left leg just with the effort of keeping it within range.

"Could it be done, do you think?"

"Oh, aye," he said with conviction. "Others I know are doin' it all the time. It is a fine way to get started when y'have but little money."

That seemed to satisfy her, and they sat in silence, mesmerized by the flowing water.

He cleared his throat, and realized with a start what he was about to say. "Norrie, there is someth—"

"Oh, Brendan, look!" She had scrambled to her feet. "Look at the size of him, wouldja."

He got up and looked downstream where she was pointing. A great fish, nearly a yard long, flashed silver and blue in the furious current. It was angling up and across the rapids toward them as it hunted for green water in the seething tumult over the rocks.

"What kind of fish is that? He's too big for the Crick," Noreen gasped as the struggling creature exploded up and over a spuming cascade, and continued upstream of the obstacle.

They could follow its progress clearly, for it swam, black-tipped fins raking the water, like some wild predator just under the surface.

"It must be a shad," Brendan said as he studied the approaching fish. "And I think yer right, Noreen. It's a he shad, not a she."

"What's he after, do you think?"

"They come in from the ocean every year to spawn."

"Spawn?" Was she smiling? No, but her eyes taunted him.

"Aye, spawn. The males and females head up rivers to where they was hatched years before to lay their eggs in the exact spot they started from." His voice was taking on the ring of authority.

"Blarney."

"No, 'tis true, Noreen," he protested. "The buck shad go upstream first, a week or two before the females, to find the right place and get it ready. Then the others come up and find them and lay the eggs."

Noreen laughed. "Is it a cottage they build, that it takes so much time?" She looked away toward the fish and gently squeezed his upper arm. He felt his bicep soften under her fingers.

The shad suddenly decided to test the current again, and shot from his resting place directly into the rocky flume beside them. They held their breath as he approached, fighting the tremendous velocity of the narrow chute with desperate wriggling lunges of his long body. Then a pulsing desperation drove the shad into rippling thrusts of advance until with one final wrenching flip he cleared the narrows and shot like an arrow into the slow deep water above the rocks and disappeared.

They stared at the spreading ripple where the black fin had submerged until it was swept into the tumbled rapids and the water above had flattened calm again.

"He was a lovely one, that fish," she said quietly. "And a fighter, too." She took her hand from his arm and picked up her shoes. "Come help me set out our dinner. Are you hungry?"

"I'm hungry," he said with emphasis and scooped up his own shoes to follow her up the stones.

After they had set out the picnic stuff on a cloth she had spread on the grass, he surveyed the array with amazement. From the light basket she produced a real banquet. There were boiled eggs, cold lamb, cheese, boiled chicken and potatoes, a whole loaf of bread, and even a small jug of tea. He was suddenly ravenous.

They began eating, talking between bites. All the while he was waiting for the right time to ask her the question, but every time he was about to speak, she would launch into something new, and he would have to bide his time.

When the time finally came, the words were out of his mouth

before he fully realized it. He had just swallowed a lump of chicken and then blurted it in a rush. "Will you marry with me, Noreen?"

The way she looked at him made him wish he had taken the time to phrase the request more carefully. A more romantic time might have helped, too, damn the luck. He was the fool surely to pop the question all the while feeding his face.

Noreen finished chewing, swallowed, and wiped her lips carefully with her fingertips. She looked him straight in the eye as she answered. "That's me plan, Brendan Gallagher."

"You will, then?"

"Aye, but you have to ask me first," she said casually and began to put the food back into the hamper.

"But I just did, girl!"

"You were asking my opinion of the future, what I was apt to do, and I gave me answer."

"Well, I don't know what y'mean, but I'll ask again. Do you want to marry me?"

The vessels of food were disappearing quickly into the basket. She paused in the work to look thoughtfully into the trees. "That depends."

"Depends on what?"

She folded the cloth before answering. "It depends on how you feel about taking me to wife."

"How I feel... oho, I see. Well, then, *please* say ye will be my wife, Noreen!"

She snapped the cloth into a final fold. "You're gettin' close."

"My God, woman," he muttered hotly, "you know how to put a man to the test. Jesus, Mary—"

"No need for blasphemy, I'm thinkin'," she interrupted.

"You already know how I feel. I'm sure y'do!" He began to pace around her angrily. "Here I am just about out of me bloody mind with wantin' you... thinking of you night and day to the point that I can do naught else for the distraction. Wild I am to be with you, and when I'm here it's all I can do to keep my hands to meself until I'm away from you again." His face was getting red, and his lip trembled. "And now you say you want to know how I feel about it all? Well, I'll tell you... in plain language. I'm nearly daft with love for you."

"*That's* the word!" she said, stepping close to him. "And now that you happen to mention it, I love you, too, my darlin' man, and I want to marry you to save you from losing your mind." She laughed, watching the color changes in his face and the softening of his angry eyes.

Brendan was not sure if he was delighted, relieved, angry, or all three at once. He stood like a stump. "Ah, Norrie," he said like a man spent, "if y'only knew how these hands have ached for me to put them on you...."

"Oh, Brendan mine," she whispered holding up her arms, "put them on me now."

Her coming into his arms that moment would be the touchstone of joy for the rest of Brendan Gallagher's life. In a searing flash of prescience, he held the conviction of immortality, the boundlessness of love, the welding of souls. At first all he could think of was holding her closer; she seemed to melt within him, her lips, the softness of her everywhere filling in his aching void. His heart pounded, ringing in his ears, his hands crying out for the soft delight above her ribs....

There was a hard pressure in the center of his chest. He was being torn away, and he opened his eyes, his fingers still gripping her waist. The palms of her hands were against him, stiffly holding him at arm's length.

When she spoke, her words were gentle but firm. "That's all for now, me hot-blooded suitor. The dessert will be served at a later time." But he saw the yearning in her eyes even as she pushed him away.

They picked up the basket then and stepped down to the edge of the rock to gaze out over the water once more before turning into the woods on the path for home. A late afternoon breeze riffled the sheen above the ruined dam.

"When will she come to him, Brendan? The shad's mate?"

"A week, they say, or maybe two."

"How far up will he go?"

"I don't know that; it could be miles."

Noreen sighed. "I hope she finds him."

"Oh, she will. It's instinct." He nodded. "They always find the place."

"And the shad return to the sea again after they spawn? They never stay up the Crick?"

"They would die if they did, Noreen. They're meant to live in the open sea."

"What about all the other fish, the smaller ones we catch all the time? They seem to be happy enough to stay."

Brendan laughed. "The ocean scares them a bit, I'm thinkin'. All that wide big place with lots of things to bite. No, the small fry like to live out their lives in a nice place like the Crick. It's not very exciting, but it's safe all right."

"I see," Noreen murmured thoughtfully. Then she added, "Tell me again how we plan to build the freight line."

CHAPTER 16

The announcement by Noreen and Brendan came as no surprise to either family, and both the Gallaghers and Feeneys were pleased, though Patrick and Maggie showed it more. It was all they could talk about. They wanted to get started on the planning in a grand way. Why, this would be the first marriage between the Irish powder men's families on the Crick... and a union of Gallagher and Feeney to boot.

As soon as he saw Brendan off on a fresh trip from the packing house the following Monday, Patrick made it his business to call at the company office. The newlyweds would be needing a house, and he checked to see if any of the company houses were coming up vacant.

He did not have much luck. With the increased business and production of the last few months all the houses were filled, and there was a waiting list as long as his arm. He found out that many of the workers boarded out, and those with families were forced to double up until new homes could be built.

"But there's not much chance for that this year," the clerk had commented. All of Mr. du Pont's credit was being taken up with the buying of saltpeter and brimstone to meet the demand for gunpowder. "If y'want my opinion," the clerk whispered confidentially, "I think the Mister would be hard put to honor our credits on the petty ledger if we all asked fer 'em in a bunch."

Patrick never gave the bookkeeper's opinion a second thought. He was quite happy to let the company do his household budgeting for him. He seldom drew more than a few dollars each payday, leaving the rest as a credit against his account at the company store. True, the dollar a day he earned barely kept pace with his charges, but the ledger was fattened considerably by the two-hundred-dollar credit he banked after selling the house to the company. And they were living better than ever before, with meat on the table three times a week and fish on Fridays.

But as he went about his work that day, he was troubled by the lack of housing for Brendan and Noreen. It was well into the afternoon when he hit upon the solution. So the others were doubling up, were they? Well then, the new married couple would move in with Maggie and him!

And it would not be any cramped doubling up. They would have a room of their own, with space to add for the grandchildren when they came along. He would build the addition with his own two hands.

Patrick was so excited about the idea that he could hardly wait for the day to end so he could tell Maggie. Through the long afternoon he soothed his impatience by building the entire structure in his mind, and by the time he reached home, it was all complete, down to the last measurement, mortar joint, and dowel.

It was understandable, then, that he was disappointed by the reception she gave him.

"Yer asking for trouble."

"What trouble?" he demanded.

"Meddling in their business, for one."

"*Meddling*, is it? For me to try to smooth the rocky road for them a bit?"

Maggie was careful not to let her own temper match that of her husband. "You are not only deciding where they're to live in their marriage, but you even have made the measure of the bedroom."

"Agh, woman, y'make me out to be a string puller. 'Tis but a gift from us, a wedding gift is all. I think they will be tickled with me idea."

"Better it should be *their* idea."

Patrick laughed. "The two of 'em are so mush-brained in love, I doubt they're thinkin' of aught but what's in each other's pants."

She bristled. "You've a pretty narrow mind on love yourself, then."

He reached out for her hand, but she pulled it away and went to the cupboard to begin setting the table. He walked up behind her. "Aw, Maggie, you know me better than that. I was only jokin'."

"A cheap joke on your son and that lovely lass is what it was."

He took her by the shoulders and turned her around. "Look at me, girl. I've not forgot me love for you, and all the different turns it takes. You should know that."

"Well, then, you should know easy enough that it's not just poppin' into bed that takes the measure of love between husband and wife. The Lord knows we had a lot to learn and took a long time in the learning."

He smiled at her. "That's true for me, thick as I am; I always lagged a bit behind your lead. In fact, I'm still learnin'."

"We're *both* still at it, and will be till the day they cover us up for good and all."

He kissed her lightly on the neck. "Ah, but it was sweet and wild, it was, that early bit of learnin'!" he whispered in her ear. "Just the two of us in that wood bin of a house; shameless scholars we was night and day in the marriage bed."

She drew back and looked at him meaningfully. "And lucky we were to have that time alone."

"And that's me point!" he exclaimed. "This room, y'see, will be off to the side with a thick wall between." He paced to the wall and slapped the stone masonry for effect. "And with a good solid door that I'll make. You'll see, Maggie; they could set off a keg of blasting dust in there and we'd barely feel the thump."

Maggie gave up. It was useless to argue with the man once he had his mind set on a plan. "One thing," she charged, shaking a finger. "Be sure to ask them what they think first. Don't be going your own way until the last minute and then dumpin' the thing on them so's they can't refuse."

He looked surprised that she'd presume he could be guilty of such an oversight. "Of course, woman. What kind of tyrant do y'think I am? I'll be glad to get their ideas before I build."

A few moments later, however, she saw him pacing off a parcel on the side of the house and scratching marks in the dirt with a stick.

When Brendan arrived home at the end of the week, he barely had time to say hello to the family at the supper table before Patrick seized him by the arm. "Now, lad, go get Noreen and bring her back here. Your ma and me have a surprise."

"It's *your* surprise, mister, not mine," Maggie corrected him.

After he returned with Noreen, Patrick led them out the back door and around to the side of the cottage. A freshly dug rectangular trench was connected at two points to the foundation of the house. A first course of neatly cut stone was already in place.

"There it is!" said Patrick proudly. "Yer new room. A weddin' present from Maggie and me."

Noreen looked to Brendan who seemed as dumbstruck as she. Something was going awry; she sensed it in the ticking silence.

Patrick laughed with delight. "See, Maggie? I knew they'd be pleased. Both lost the power of speech, is it?"

Noreen knew they were losing something, and it was not the ability to speak. This had to be set right—now, before it became more complicated. "Oh, Mr. Gallagher, such a great lot of work you've done, and it's a lovely idea, it truly is . . . but we can't take it. We can't."

She looked at Brendan for support, and was rewarded with a nod. "You see, we have our plan, Mr. Gallagher . . . our freight line. Brendan has set it up for when we save a little more money. We'll buy a team and wagon and start out on our own."

"The Gallagher Freight Company," Brendan said softly.

"But what about yer job at the mills, boy?"

"I want to be me own master, Dad." Brendan's quiet explanation thrilled Noreen, and she slipped her hand into his. "We'll be movin' out of Chicken Alley," Brendan announced soberly.

"What's the need?" his father boomed. "Y'can stay with us and still have yer business. Y'do need a bed and roof."

Noreen explained, hating to hurt this kind man who wanted desperately to keep them close, "But it's too far, you see. The best route for us to start on is the New Castle and Frenchtown Turnpike. We have to live in one place or the other."

"I saw a vacant house to start in," Brendan said to Noreen. "On my way home yesterday. The owner said he'd wait for us if we want it."

"Where?" Maggie's voice sounded more apprehensive than she wanted it to.

"New Castle, Ma. A small house with a stable and barn. It's a bit run down, but the rent is cheap."

"New Castle!" Patrick snorted. "That's halfway to hell and gone."

"Not fifteen miles," Brendan corrected.

"Might as well be a hundred. We'll never see you two again."

The four of them stood in awkward silence until Maggie prodded Brendan toward the back door. "Get in with you both; I've set a place for you and Noreen. Yer dad and me will be in after."

When they had left, Maggie folded her arms and watched as Patrick paced around the trench line. After he had walked completely around twice, she spoke. "Are you comin' in, or are you going to tramp around in circles all night?"

"Damn!" he rumbled and kicked a clod off the new masonry. "Now what am I gonna do with all this?"

"Forget it. Shovel the earth back in and forget it."

"No," he retorted sharply. "No, I think I'll finish it anyway."

"Suit yourself, Patrick. But I think it a waste of money and muscle. The family is gettin smaller, not bigger."

Brendan's next haul was a three-day run he had traded Joe Dorgan for because it covered precisely the route he planned to open with his own line. Brendan had to drop part of his load in New Castle and deliver the rest at the other end of the turnpike in Frenchtown. He could not have been happier with the timing. The half-day in New Castle would give him time to set up a schedule with several warehouse owners, importers, and small businessmen interested in a regular daily delivery to points along the pike. At Frenchtown he would have the same opportunity the following day. On the return trip he would have ample time to inspect the house and barn and make a list of repairs they would need, particularly the barn-stable, before he could use them as a base.

Things could not have turned out better. There was more than enough interest in New Castle to justify the daily run, and he even had firm promises of trade if he jumped before someone else got the idea. Frenchtown was not as promising, but he could see from the various activities already in progress that once the shuttle was in operation it would get heavy use.

He offloaded at Frenchtown early in the day and gave himself several hours to inspect the vacant homesite. The small house looked worse than it was. A few days of patching up would set things right. It would be better to let that go and plan to attack some major structural defects in the barn. It would have to be sound. He could not risk losing a whole loft of feed to the elements.

The owner was delighted with Brendan's offer to repair the place in exchange for most of the first year's rent, and he agreed to set a firm price beforehand should they ever want to buy. Brendan had decided that the sooner he and Noreen married the better. As he urged the triple team of draft horses onto the dusty New Castle–Wilmington road and set a quick pace for home, he recalled with pleasure that there were definitely other reasons for getting on with the wedding.

Noreen had been watching the road for him. When she saw his figure approach through the dusky twilight, she rose from the stoop and ran to meet him. Their embrace was intense... and brief.

"Phew!" she gasped and pushed him to arm's length. "You *are* gamy, my love. I have second thoughts about tyin' the knot with a driver, after all. You must have slept with the horses this trip... or under 'em, more likely."

He laughed groggily, then outlined the great accomplishments of his trip. He saved the best part for last. "So why don't we get married right away? I'll draw out the sixty dollars from my company credit, buy the team and rig, and off we'll go."

She was taken aback and responded hesitantly, "How soon is right away, Brendan?"

"Why, in a week or two. We have to tell the priest, I guess. And there'd be some plannin' for the party after." He thought a moment. "Why not a week from this Saturday?"

She hesitated, looking away. "*Two* weeks from Saturday would be perfect. Give me two and a half weeks, Brendan."

"But, Norrie, we have to move quick on this. The merchants are all primed for the service. I don't want to wait so long they forget."

"Please, Brendan. It's important."

He was somewhat deflated but decided that another week would not make any difference really.

"Okay, Noreen Feeney, two weeks from Saturday you change your name to mine!" He held out his hand, and she took it with a laugh shaking it like a businessman closing a deal.

"Now, go home, y'smelly beast, and take a bath. I'll see you in the morning."

He walked backward a long way to keep his eyes on her until she vanished in the dusk. Oh, how she made him ache, that girl, but two and a half weeks would not be long to wait.

CHAPTER 17

Brendan and Noreen decided they should go to church the next Sunday and tell the priest their plans. Both families made it a point to go, including Denis Feeney. He was on his best behavior. He had not taken a single drink the whole week long, and he was dressed better than anyone along the Crick could remember.

They all sat together throughout the mass, and after the service, stood back to watch as Brendan introduced his intended to the priest.

The conversation between Brendan and the priest did not seem to be going as well as they had expected. Father Reardon appeared to be trying to explain something to the couple, which they either did not understand, or were not quite willing to accept. At any rate, there was much shaking of Brendan Gallagher's head, and he was red in the face.

At last the father shook his hand with a smile, waved them good-bye, and turned back into his church. Noreen and Brendan walked slowly back to their folks. Brendan was frowning, and Noreen looked worried.

As soon as they got close, Patrick stepped out to see what was wrong.

"He won't do it next Saturday is what it is," Brendan explained bitterly. "And not the week after, nor the week after that."

"Well, why not, for God's sake?" Patrick demanded.

Noreen piped up in the smallest voice Brendan had ever heard her use. "It's the banns," she said. "They have to publish the banns of matrimony."

"They make the announcement on the three Sundays before every marriage," Brendan explained angrily. "That makes a whole month less a couple of days if y'get married on Saturday, just to make sure somebody ain't out there who knows one of the two of us was married before."

Maggie tried to lift their spirits by looking on the brighter side. "Well, now, it isn't all that bad. We'll just have a bit longer to look forward to it all." There were some nods, but nobody said anything, and Noreen kept looking at the angry, worried face of her fiancé.

Back in the temporary sanctuary of St. Peter's Mission, Francis Reardon tried to collect his thoughts. Why had they made such a fuss about the banns? What business would be that pressing for a simple teamster? Could it be that the girl was already with child? He rejected the idea as it formed in his mind. It was repugnant to him. Noreen Feeney. She was a beautiful... person. There was an intelligence about her that was startling. Her eyes, blue-green gems in the perfect setting of that face... well, they missed nothing, hid nothing. Remarkable. When she looked at him it was as though she could read his thoughts. It had been distracting, the frankness, the absolute absence of dissembling about her.

She was proud, too, and that alone convinced him she was still a virgin. He had an idea that if she had slept with Brendan she would have worn the knowledge like a badge.

Father Reardon sighed, blessed himself with the sign of the cross, genuflected before the Blessed Sacrament, and walked slowly up the aisle of the makeshift chapel. Except for the rows of rough-sawn benches, with the altar at his back the place looked every inch the warehouse it had been converted from. How he missed the atmosphere of a real church. In this place his own calling to Holy Orders seemed temporary, unreal, the acting out of some role upon a rustic stage. He yearned for the music of a solemn high mass, the full panoply of the liturgy, the odor of incense, and yes, he could admit it, the aesthetics of magnificent architecture. Thinking about it sent a shiver up his spine.

Later that evening he had an idle thought that if he had not gone into the priesthood, and chosen instead to marry, someone like

Noreen could have been his choice. This time he was thrilled with a pang dangerously close to regret.

There was little to do but wait.

Brendan had to visit the livery stable in Wilmington and inform the proprietor that he could not pick up the team he had bought until next month. He had hoped the horses could be kept in service in exchange for feed and stabling, but the man had already replaced the animals with a new team and had no use for them. Brendan was forced to accept the fact that the horses would do nothing for a month but stand idle and consume grain—at his expense.

He kept busy hauling powder for the mills, a string of long trips west and north, and not once could he arrange a run along the New Castle–Frenchtown route. At one point he was tempted to quit his job then and there and start the freight line alone. But there were so many last-minute things cropping up over the wedding; he was afraid to make commitments to his customers and then have to skip a few days while he ran home for one chore or another.

When there was but one week left before the wedding, Brendan decided to take a day off between hauls and visit New Castle to confirm the starting of service on the following Monday. It would be a working honeymoon for the Gallaghers, but Noreen was even more eager than he to get about their move.

While he was gone, Noreen decided to bring her wedding dress over to Maggie for advice on some of the more complicated finishing touches. They still had their heads together over the garment when they looked up to see Brendan coming through the door. Maggie quickly covered up the dress with a length of sheeting and demanded, "Men trampin' through the house all hours of the day. What are you doin' home so quick?"

He neither answered nor looked at them, but went straight to the cupboard, took down a small jug, uncorked it, and took several long pulls. The stinging whiskey racked him with a fit of coughing, and when he recovered, he stoppered the vessel and slammed it to the table.

Noreen's face went pasty white, and she turned away from the wildness of his bloodshot eyes. Maggie got over her own shock and found her voice. "Are y'drunk?" she demanded. "Have you been at the creature all day?"

"Better that I was," he spat with a bitter laugh. "The jug at least is time away from grief."

"That's fool's talk, and you know it," Maggie snapped. She looked apprehensively at Noreen.

Brendan followed his mother's glance, and the look of fear in Noreen's face redoubled his own pain. Suddenly he slammed his palm against the jamb so violently that the cupboards rattled.

"Our plan, Norrie, is ruined!"

"Ruined?"

"Aye, smoke in the wind."

His mother moved beside him, searching his face. "What do you mean, ruined?"

"Our house is gone, and the route's been taken up by somebody else."

"Oh!" Noreen pressed a hand against her chest.

"I was gone too long... and spoke too freely to the wrong people," he added grimly. "One of the New Castle companies took our idea and started with it."

Noreen moved toward him. "And the house and stable?"

Brendan laughed through his teeth. "Huh! That was the twist of the knife, it was. The New Castle Company bought the place, hung out a shingle, turned the house into an office, and started hauling." He shook his head in disbelief. "It was the man I trusted most who bought it. An importer he is, a wealthy man. He kept tellin' me I had a fine idea... that he would be the first in line for me contract."

Noreen bristled. "Did y'see the scalawag?"

"Aye, I seen the bastard. He was all milk and honey, said he couldn't wait... thought I'd given up the idea, so he started the line himself."

"Let's take him on!" Noreen stood before him, eyes flashing, tiny fists at her sides.

He melted then and almost laughed. Oh, but she was a darlin'! But he shook his head. "No, Norrie, I thought of that, but he's too big... four outfits already rolling. And he's rich enough to undercut us till we starve."

Maggie watched their pain with anguish. How much harder it was to see her young ones hurt than to bear it herself. "What will you do?"

Brendan put an arm around Noreen and grinned crookedly at

his mother. "Well, Ma, he offered me a job at eighty cents a day—almost as much as I'm makin' now."

"The scum!" said Maggie.

"Why can't we start someplace else?" Noreen blurted. "There must be a hundred other places just as good."

Brendan shook his head. "I'm sure of that, but we have to find them first, see what kind of business they deal in, where they need to ship, what other kinds of transport we'd have to work against."

"But we could do that."

"It takes time, Norrie, and money. I'm a wee bit short of both these days."

When Patrick came home from work, he listened with a scowl all through supper without so much as a word as Brendan explained what had happened. Noreen had stayed for the meal, but she barely touched her food, she was that upset. When his son finished, Patrick pushed back his plate, rose, went for his pipe, and stood by the hearth packing it thoughtfully.

"Time and money, eh?" He blew a cloud of smoke at the ceiling and coughed. "Well, all is not lost, me young lovers." He grinned and winked at Noreen. "What do you think of this proposition? We'll go on with the weddin' as planned."

Brendan started to interrupt, but Patrick waved his pipe to cut him off. "No, no, now let me finish first. You two get married and move into the new room there. It's finished but fer a coat of whitewash on the walls. Brendan keeps on workin' fer the Mister awhile."

Noreen stiffened. Patrick noticed and looked at her warmly. "Now, hear me out, lass. It's not what y'think." He took another draw on the pipe.

"In me company account I have a credit fer the sale of this house." He looked at Brendan. "It's to go to you and the twins after your ma and me is put to rest. I'll lend you half of it, a hundred dollars, when you save that much on your own. By that time you'll have a dozen places picked to start the freight business, and enough money to begin with a fine rig and to tide ye over lean times." He paused to let the words sink in and then resumed with increasing pleasure. "When ye gets rich enough with your haulin' empire, y'can pay me back. If ye goes bust, well, then you've spent your inheritance is all. And here's another thing. Sean and Joseph have been thinking of moving in with Murphy's widow. The poor thing can use the board to keep her house, and we can use the room."

Maggie had not heard about *that* idea. Her voice was sharp. "You'll not be pushing my sons out before their time, Patrick Gallagher; they're boys yet!"

"Full grown, Maggie," he countered mildly, "and they want to do it. I talked to them and Missus Murphy today." He looked at Noreen, "So all ye have to do is move in, fer as long or short as ye please."

Noreen looked at him and then at Brendan, who seemed stunned with relief. She spoke to Patrick. "'Tis a generous thing you've offered, Mr. Gallagher, and tempting surely, but I think Brendan and I should talk it over before he gives you an answer."

Even before they talked it over, Noreen knew that they would accept. It would have been brass in her mouth to turn the man down a second time. Besides, there seemed no point in postponing the wedding again; she could feel the peaking urgency in Brendan. They needed to be together, to get over that distracting hurdle and get on with their plan. It shouldn't take long—a few months, a year? Then they would be off on their own at last.

Noreen could not have known that they would have to sell the wagon and team at half the price Brendan had paid for them, that she would bear a child within the year, that life with the Gallaghers would be so pleasantly secure, or that their credit on the company account would never seem to rise.

The weeks and months drifted by into years. With each promising plan came a new delay—postponement for a while until the baby was a little older, until her mother got over the fever, until the 1812 war was done with.

Oh, that war was an exciting thing for the country and especially for Chicken Alley. The arguments raged over the glorious foolishness of taking on the British Empire. But whatever the bad effects on trade and the American economy, nobody could deny that it was good business for the Eleutherian Mills. And wasn't it grand for the Irish of the Crick to get in a few licks at their ancestral oppressors! Of course the fighting never got close to the Brandywine, except for a weak threat to destroy the mills. That incident came to little more than an exchange of cannonballs between some British ships and a shore battery at Lewes, more than eighty miles away.

Brendan and the other drivers were terribly proud that it was the gunpowder they rushed to Lewes that repulsed the English force, and the Mister was so pleased that he thanked some of them personally.

When the White House and Capitol were burned, there was some fright, but in the end the world knew that Americans would not sit on their hands and take it on the chin—not even from a power like Britain. Of course economic times turned very bad after the war. Because of all the war restrictions, trade with Europe was a shambles, and domestic business sagged with the weakened banks. People were out of work all over. It was very comfortable to have a steady job with Du Pont, a company that never laid off a worker, even when times were lean. The company mills never shut down.

Noreen was patient but restless with Brendan on trips most of the time. Sometimes she would take walks through the woods or down by the Crick with the baby in tow. One time by the dam she saw another shad. It was as big as the one she and Brendan watched that day from the rock. But this fish was bloated, floating on its side. She could see by the cuts that it had been caught in the turning mill wheel.

A number of other fish were nibbling at the floating carcass. They were smaller than the shad, a different species with no yearning for saltwater oceans. They never left the Crick.

PART TWO

1815-1816

CHAPTER 18

A seriously troubled Irénée du Pont returned home from Philadelphia in March 1815. This time it was not anxiety about his many loans that troubled him, but news he had heard from France. Napoleon had returned from exile on Elba with an army behind him, and Irénée was concerned about the fate of his father. Pierre du Pont de Nemours was seventy-seven, and he was still in France. In spite of his brilliant handling of the Louisiana Purchase more than a decade earlier, he had become an outspoken enemy of Bonaparte.

As Irénée told Sophie the news in their gloomy parlor that rainy afternoon, he could not muster the optimism to assure his wife of Father Pierre's safety. And it was she who voiced his dread. "*La guillotine!*" she said, shuddering.

Irénée patted her hand absently. "The time may have run out already. My information does not reach beyond the middle of February, when Bonaparte set foot on French soil again. Oh, how I wish we had more to go on." He went to the window and stared at the streaming panes.

"You must send word to Victor, my dear; perhaps he could..." Her voice trailed off. At one time Irénée's brother might have had some influence, but by now the elder son was little more than a dependent of the family.

"Yes...yes, of course I will tell Victor, but somehow I must reach Jefferson...or James Monroe."

Sophie du Pont's face lighted at the prospect. Jefferson was an old friend, and Monroe, now secretary of war, had worked with her father-in-law to secure the Louisiana Territory. A moment later her hopes dimmed. Two months had passed since Napoleon Bonaparte had restored himself to power; it would take months longer for diplomatic intercession to reach France.

They would send messages immediately to Washington, but both knew that the odds were against the outspoken old man. Father Pierre would have to fend for himself.

For the next several weeks a pall of apprehension settled over the big house. The du Ponts had shared the ominous news with their older children, and the servants learned almost immediately. In due course most of the mill hands and their families found out. The suspense became almost too much to bear. Every parcel of mail was immediately searched through for any letters that might hold news of Pierre du Pont, and any unexpected visitor was received with hope...and dread.

Such was the case when a strange carriage came unannounced to the Eleutherian Mills residence a month later. Sophie du Pont watched from her bedroom window as an elegantly dressed young man stepped down from the vehicle. He appeared to be speaking to someone still inside. Then she saw Hugh Flynn hurry over to help the other passenger alight. As he emerged into the April sunshine, she recognized the old bald head of Pierre du Pont. Calling out to anyone who might hear, she rushed out to embrace her limping, beaming father-in-law.

The news flashed through the mills like a burning powder trail. The old grandpa had come back safe and sound after all, just one jump ahead of that crazy Napoleon who, they say, was itching to lop off his head just to shut him up. At Dorgan's when they were passing the story around that night, someone swore that the old man had just run up the gangway of the first ship he came to at Le Havre and said, "I'm du Pont's daddy, boyo! Set sail and take me back to the Crick!"

Hugh Flynn said he doubted the exact words, but it sounded like something the old fellow would say. The powder men decided finally that it was the God's truth and had a drink on it anyway.

The balmy greening of late spring along the Brandywine tantalized Noreen almost to the point of affliction. She had never felt the fever so intensely as she had this year, not even when she was a budding girl. Now here she was, a mother at twenty-two, with a four-year-old son, mooning about like some lovesick girl of fifteen!

It nearly had her daft, this honeymoon weather, the nights heady with fragrance of spring blossoming and almost as pleasantly warm as the velvety afternoons that begot them. She could not sleep at night and moved in a drowse through the day. He was on the road with that team so much these days. Lugging a wagonload of powder to God knows where. Off to the ends of the earth, it seemed. The trips were so long—days and weeks at a time.

This time he had been gone for over two weeks. She had awakened with a vague peevishness that had carried over from the day before. She knew it was mostly irritation with his long absence, but her feelings were confused.

Noreen wanted him back almost desperately, but that hunger was undermined by a conflicting feeling. His homecomings were never quite up to expectations. Ah, they were less than that if she owned up to the truth. More like bitter disappointment was what they were.

She stared over her pile of dirty dishes at the sink and wondered if it would have been so were they on their own and not stuck here still with Patrick and Maggie. Probably not. At least he would have been home more often. And they would not have to share their muted quarrels with his parents. Not that they ever interfered, but it wasn't the same as having their own place where they could be out with hurt feelings at once. It was a hard and hurtful thing to have to wait until night to share harsh words in the marriage bed.

It was not that he had not been attentive to her during their reunions. Indeed, he gave every indication of his own hunger for several days after returning from the long hauls. But it was never quite up to what she had imagined it would be in his absence. Perhaps she was in love with an idea and not in love with him at all. She longed to talk to someone who could reassure her that she was not daft.

Well, it certainly was true that the man gained all the carnal pleasure out of marriage. Sometimes she thought otherwise, but on those rare occasions when she felt strongly drawn to him, almost with an animal lust, it had not worked. Once when she thought she was almost... there... Brendan had drawn back dumbfounded at her strange behavior and lost *his* desire. She blushed at the memory.

An abrupt thump at the back door broke into her reverie, and she looked up from the tubful of breakfast dishes to see her son marching sullenly into the shed kitchen. He stood there stiffly, hands clenched at his sides, and she realized that he was beginning to cry.

"There, there," she whispered in his hot ear. "Tell Mummy what's wrong."

"Mama-Maggie is mad at me," he blurted.

"Oh, Kevin, your grandmother could never be angry with you." She laughed lightly, relieved that the problem was no more serious.

Kevin looked at her sheepishly but nodded to emphasize the point.

At that moment his grandmother turned the corner of the cottage, puffing with the exertion of walking up the incline from the front of the house. As she approached, she gave Noreen a look of mild reproach.

"Down at the Crick he was, pokin' at the tadpoles with a stick," she puffed. "I was sure he'd slip in and drown, what with all that slippery mud along the banks." She drew up to them and stopped, pausing to take a labored breath. "All alone he was. It was luck I saw him on my way back from your mother's."

Noreen paled when she realized that her four-year-old had been left unwatched for the better part of an hour. The Crick had claimed its share of toddlers—one she could remember herself when she was six.

"Maggie, I thought he had gone with you," she said, but blamed herself for having been so preoccupied. She opened her arms to let her mother-in-law take the child, but he hung back. "I think he's afraid that you are angry with him," Noreen explained.

Maggie worked her charm on Kevin for no more than thirty seconds before the child forgot his mood and ran giggling to his grandmother.

"Oh, I nearly forgot with all the fright," Maggie said to Noreen. "Your ma said would y'look in on Blanche up at the big house.

They sent word that she's down with an ailment." She began to walk toward the kitchen with Kevin in tow and looked back. "Don't worry about this tyke; I'll keep a sure eye on him till you get back!"

"Is she very sick?" Noreen felt a pang of remorse that she had not even looked in on her younger sister for the six months she had been working as a domestic at the du Pont house.

"No," Margaret called over her shoulder. "At least they said it was nothing serious. Her stomach finds it hard to get used to all that French food, I'm thinkin'."

Noreen stood alone in the yard trying to decide whether to dress up for the visit to the house on the hill. It goaded her a bit to think it necessary to put on airs for the benefit of the mill owners.

It wasn't so much that the family put on airs themselves; to tell the truth they were strange masters, working elbow to elbow with their help. And they were always on the lookout for the powdermen and their families. It was the beholding that rankled Noreen so. There was a bit of shame in all that for the folks in Chicken Alley, almost as if they had not grown up into men and women.

Well, maybe she was just more sensitive about it. She had cause, and that was the truth. The memory of her mother's going up to the big house to plead with them to send Denis Feeney's pay direct to her so she could dole out money for his drinking only on Saturday nights...That galled Noreen more than it did her father. She burned with the humiliation.

She shook her head with annoyance and went to the rain barrel again to fill the wash bucket. She would bathe and put on the dark blue muslin she had ironed yesterday. The dress was hanging in their bedroom, ready in case Brendan got back from his trip in time for them to go to mass together on Sunday. Was she slipping into the pattern of putting her best foot forward in deference to the family on the hill? Or was she being defiant?

She smiled as she lugged the heavy bucket toward the back door. She would be defiant, then; let them think what they would. She would not be caught skulking about *their* house rigged out in homespun like just another servant.

Like her sister, Blanche, she thought miserably.

After a late breakfast Louis Jardinere relieved himself in his room and replaced the cover on the porcelain chamber pot before tucking in his drawers and buttoning up the front of his doeskin breeches. His finely chiseled features twisted into a frown of disgust. The odor of the vessel untended since the day before offended him mightily, and he resolved to have a word with his cousin Sophie about the servants. One of the girls, that raw-boned Irish wench who tended his room, was ill, and since she had taken to bed the domestic service in the house was awry.

He walked to one of the windows of his second floor guest room and opened it wide, breathing in the welcome scent of lilac heavy on the late May morning air. He could see why du Pont had picked this place on which to build his house. In some respects it was more beautiful than home. A bit more primitive than his country estate at Montchanin, but then that was the difference wherein lay the charm of this place. In France, even the woodlands had been tamed by centuries of civilization. Here there was a primeval rawness even the noisy mills could not overwhelm.

Louis sighed. It was overpowering, all right. My God, the heady fragrance of lilac was like a drug. He thought briefly of his wife thousands of miles away, but the erotic vision of her softness was dispelled by the idle thought that she was probably at this moment approaching the childbed with their third baby.

A two-week old memory of an exotic creature in Philadelphia slipped into focus, and he allowed himself to luxuriate in the sensual images he had collected during their four-day rendezvous.

Abruptly he turned away from the window and cursed quietly. It would be days, probably weeks, before he could arrange things so that he could get away again. One thing was certain: there was no woman hereabouts worthy of pursuit. Besides, even if there were, his host and hostess would not be likely to understand.

These émigrés to America were rather stuffy in such things, he thought regretfully. Probably tainted by the Calvinists farther north. It was too bad du Pont had not chosen to set up his business in New Orleans where they were more open-minded.

Blanche looked up from her cot on the third floor through dazed eyes. "Mother of God," she croaked, "I thought for a minute you were one of the family. Aren't you dressed up now, for callin' on the sick!"

Noreen laughed mirthlessly. "I thought I *was* calling on family. Or have you gone and disowned us folks in Chicken Alley?"

"You know what I mean, Norrie. Oh, thanks for coming. It's awful to be sick and not in your own home."

"What is it you've caught, girl?"

"Nothing all that bad. Just the chills and fever—and bein' green in my stomach. I think the worst is past; the fever broke last night, but I'm feeling awful weak."

Noreen held up a wicker basket covered with a towel. "Ma and Maggie Gallagher sent some things." She placed the basket on a small table by the cot. "From the weight I'd judge there is enough to feed you for the week. I nearly strained my back lugging it up the hill."

Blanche laughed weakly, obviously pleased by the visit and the gift. They spent an hour together, chatting away the time as Noreen helped Blanche bathe and then served her some lukewarm broth and tea. By the time she left, with the promise to call each day until Blanche was well, Noreen was satisfied that her sister was truly on the mend. She is more homesick than anything else, she thought. A few more visits and she'll be good as new. Noreen felt the return of protectiveness toward Blanche; something she had forgotten when they had both reached womanhood.

She had to admit to a feeling of chagrin that she had not encountered any of the du Ponts, and now her finery served to mock her as she descended the stairway to the lower rooms. The family had left for a shopping trip to Wilmington, according to Hugh Flynn, whom she met in the kitchen on her way in. He, like Blanche, had raised an eyebrow at her dress, and she decided to leave by the front door in order to avoid seeing him.

Just as she stepped off the last step of the curved stairway and turned into the hall leading to the front door, Louis Jardinere strode out of the parlor to her left, and stood blocking her way. Bowing graciously he greeted her in French then straightened with a smile, watching her reaction with covert amusement.

Noreen halted abruptly, and her fright neatly covered up any embarrassment she might otherwise have felt at meeting one of the household in the family rooms. She knew immediately that this was not one of the du Ponts, for she had seen them all at one time or another over the years, but it was obvious that he was very much at home here. She very definitely felt otherwise herself.

She had the distinct impression that he had not walked into the hallway coincidentally, and somehow his use of French irritated rather than intimidated her. She felt the color come to her cheeks, but her blue-green eyes flashed anger.

"You've nearly frightened me to death, sneaking out that way," she snapped. "And I do not speak French!"

Louis was immediately the epitome of contrite chivalry. "I'm truly sorry," he said in perfect English, and took the basket from her hand before she could react. Then he had her by the arm and was steering her to an upholstered bench set against the wall. "Here, madame, please sit. Can I get you something? A cool drink, perhaps?"

Noreen felt her resentment flowing away and experienced a floating detachment as she allowed this handsome dandy to minister to her. It was nearly comical, so much attention lavished on a patently contrived charade. Yet she found herself fiddling away the next few minutes in meaningless chatter with the man. Somewhere in the banter they had exchanged names, explained mutual connections with the du Pont family, and gone on to other things.

He was so interesting, she decided. So charming. So . . . unaffected. What could he see in her? Was it really true as he had claimed that he thought she might be one of the many du Pont friends dropping in from Philadelphia, New York, or *London*? She had a vague feeling that it was blarney, but for some reason that didn't matter either.

It was when she stepped from the sunlit lawn in front of the big house into the cool gloom of the woods leading to Chicken Alley that the reality stung her. For the first time in her life she had fallen for a man. So this is what Brendan must have felt, she thought. The comparison was so analytical and caused her so little concern that she was amazed at herself. She was already looking forward to tomorrow's visit with Blanche.

Back in his room Louis watched from the window as Noreen crossed the gentle slope and slipped into the woods on her way back to the Brandywine. He caught occasional glimpses of her auburn hair and blue gown until finally the greenery swallowed her up. He marked the place where the path wound through the trees, and he began to hum softly.

There was little to occupy him until the du Ponts returned, so he picked up a book of English verse, found the place where he had left off the day before, sank into a chair by the bed, and resumed reading.

After a time he snapped the volume shut and sat there with a smile, savoring the delightful bouquet of lilac that eddied in tantalizing snatches past his nose.

Later that evening as Maggie and Noreen were cleaning up the supper dishes, a mule driver stopped his rig in front of the Gallagher cottage. Patrick ambled down to see what the man wanted. After they heard the rig moving on again, Patrick returned to the house and walked back to the kitchen.

"That was Dorgan's boy, Joseph. He says the gang had to leave Brendan at Baltimore. Seems an axle split and he has to wait a few days until it gets repaired. He won't be back till day after tomorra."

Maggie gave a snort of exasperation and turned to Noreen, who was up to her elbows in wash water. "Well, it's been a long wait, but at least we know he's well and on his way. Another day or two can't do any harm."

Noreen did not look up and kept her silence. Her mother-in-law interpreted that for disappointment, but Noreen felt nothing at all. Again she was amazed at the sense of detachment that seemed to envelop her. She began to think of how she would dress tomorrow when she visited Blanche.

The next day she took her leave of the big house by way of the kitchen, for there were family about. She did not let herself admit that she really was disappointed that Louis had not seen her, but her mood darkened more with each step away from the mansion. She was deep within the woods when he stepped from behind a tree directly in front of her.

This time she cried out in real fright, dropping the basket, and stumbling to a halt. Louis lunged forward to prevent her from falling, and in the process both went tumbling into the soft greenery beside the path. She clutched at him as she fell, recognizing him as a tormentor and savior in the instant of her fright. They rolled once

[145]

in the brush and stopped with Noreen astride his hips, her hands clutching at his chest. She glared down at him as he lay there on his back, head partly submerged in a pile of dead leaves. A contrite smile was beginning to form at the corners of his mouth.

"You devil!" she whispered hoarsely when she got control of her voice.

"Yes," he answered and pulled her down to kiss her gently on the lips.

She was up on her feet in a second, brushing the leaves from her gown. Her lips burned with the kiss, though, and brief as it had been, she knew that she had returned it. When she had enough control to look at him, she managed a cool smile. "Well, sir, the next time you are in such desperate need of a kiss, please let me know. Where I come from there's little need for a grown man to knock a lass about for such a soft peck on the mouth!"

Louis lay back on the leaves, one arm behind his head, gazing up at her. He was silent a long time before he answered.

"I must confess to being desperate, my dear. And I do apologize for 'knocking you about.'" He paused, running his glance over her in a way that was strangely upsetting. "But I am not sorry for the kiss; indeed, I crave another."

Noreen stepped backward to the path, retrieved her basket, and left without another word, fearful she would hear him crashing through the brambles after her. She rushed all the way to the end of the woods, listening for his following footsteps, but he did not pursue her. In her confused frame of mind she was both relieved and disappointed.

The following day she decided it would not be necessary to visit Blanche. Instead she washed and ironed the blue dress to wear at supper in case Brendan got home in time.

When Brendan finally arrived late in the evening, the family was preparing for bed. He wanted to see Kevin, who had been asleep for an hour or more, and in the process of kissing the child, stirred him wide awake. The reunion lasted until nearly midnight while Brendan regaled them with stories of his escapades on the road. At last Maggie and Patrick said good night and went to their room. Kevin was in no mood to go back to sleep and kept tugging at his father's arm, prattling at great length. It was apparent that it would take some doing to get him settled for the night.

Brendan looked at her apologetically. "I'm sorry I woke the boy, Norrie. Had he been asleep long?"

"Long enough."

Brendan swept the child into his lap, hugged him squirming in his arms and whispered to his wife, "'Tis a shame, now. I was kinda hoping we might have a little party of our own tonight."

"Daddy... please *down!*"

Noreen laughed softly, and reached out for her son. "Here, Brendan, give me the child before you crush the life out of him." She led the toddler off to their bedroom in the shed wing of the house. He wailed angrily as she tucked him into the trundle bed in the corner. "Hush now, Kevin. See, we're going to bed, too. It's late, and your daddy is weary from his long trip."

Brendan leaned against the doorjamb watching her as she tried to quiet the child. It was true that he was bone tired after fourteen hours behind that plodding team, but he had a new energy surging within him now. How he wished he had not awakened the boy.

He spoke softly to her. "I'll see to the lamp while you try to get him settled." His eyes gradually adjusted to the gloom, and he could see Noreen sitting by Kevin's bed humming a barely audible lullaby. He crossed to their bed, stripped off his clothes, and crawled naked under the covers.

After an interminable wait Noreen at last moved away from the child. He was breathing in the easy rhythm of sleep at last. Brendan watched hungrily as she disrobed in silhouette beside the single window. When she finally slipped in beside him, he reached out to caress her eagerly. His breath came in hot shallow bursts.

"Slowly, my love," she whispered into his ear. "Give me some time to catch up." Taking his hand she drew it to her breast, feeling the first tingle of arousal at his touch. She felt him grow rock-hard against her thigh, and began to slide into a soft lassitude.

"Mama."

The child's call snapped her back, and she pushed Brendan away slightly to answer.

"Go to sleep, Kevin."

"Is Daddy there?"

"Yes, dear. Now go to sleep so you don't wake Daddy."

Brendan drew her back to him, pressing insistently, fumbling with misdirected caresses. She whispered in his ear, "We should wait.... He'll be asleep in a few minutes. Maybe if I rock him..."

But the passion was upon him now, and he mumbled, more gruffly than he intended, "I can't.... Now.... It's been three weeks." And the decision made, he plunged roughly into her to the rhythm of the complaining ropes under the mattress.

She yielded to him, riding out the brief assault, and even managed to kiss him lightly when he was spent. She lay there waiting for his quiet snoring to begin, then rose to cleanse herself in the privacy of the darkened kitchen. When she returned to the bedroom she checked to be sure her child was asleep and got back into bed.

She lay awake for a half-hour or more before the silent tears came, and then she, too, slept.

CHAPTER 19

It was nearly nine in the morning before Brendan roused himself and shuffled from the bedroom into the adjoining kitchen. His father had already been at work for three hours, and the breakfast cleanup was over. Noreen and Margaret were sitting on the front stoop peeling potatoes for the evening meal.

Kevin was making mounds of dust in the deserted roadway in front of the house and pelting them with stones. He never quite connected with the target, and after several tries he gave up. With a squeal of frustration he swooped down on one of the dust piles, scooped it up between his hands, made an explosive sound with his mouth, and tossed the powdery dirt into the air. It made a little cloud above his head and rained dirt down into his hair.

"Kevin!" Noreen stamped her foot in exasperation. She had scrubbed him clean not fifteen minutes before. Her mother-in-law chuckled, enjoying the relative immunity of a dues-paid grandmother. It was nice to be able to enjoy the antics of a four-year-old without having the corresponding responsibilities for his care and cleaning.

Again the child threw dirt into the air. "Boom, boom!" he shrieked. This time Margaret kept silent, but another chuckle sounded from behind her in the doorway. At the sound, Noreen flushed and looked up at her husband's amused face. Eyes blazing, she tugged Kevin into the house past his father. Brendan reached for her playfully, but she shrank from his hand as she passed.

"One child at a time is quite enough play for me, thank you!"

Brendan scowled darkly in his wife's direction and muttered in a voice still thick with sleep, "Now what's got into her all of a sudden?"

When he got no response from his mother, he ran a hand through his hair, roughly smoothing the wiry black curls, and stepped down from the stoop. "I think I'll report in and see about the next haul."

Maggie looked up from her peeling. "Don't you want something to eat before you go?"

Brendan shrugged off the question and continued on his way. After gaining the road he picked up a brisk pace and began to whistle, apparently dismissing whatever squabble there might have been between himself and Noreen.

Maggie worried about the minor flareup, though. There had been too many tight moments between those two during the last few months. The problem was connected to his long trips; that was obvious. What troubled the older woman was that the homecomings, instead of mending the pain of their separations, seemed to bring out a hostility. She and Patrick had never had that problem. When he returned home after those rare occasions when he had been gone for more than a day or two, they were after each other with such intensity that she feared for scandalizing the children.

She caught herself smiling at the memory. As if to dismiss such dalliance, she grunted and got to her feet with a bucket of potatoes and an apronful of peelings, and shuffled through the front door.

"His highness is off to work," she muttered wryly. "I'm taking the skins to the chickens. Maybe they'll pay me with an egg or two."

Noreen's frown eased somewhat at the oblique criticism of her husband. She toweled Kevin's wet hair absently and looked after the departing figure of her mother-in-law. At least she had an understanding ally. Maggie would never come right out and criticize either Brendan or Noreen in an argument. But somehow she had a way of letting Noreen know how she felt.

She wondered if Maggie had ever had such a problem with Patrick... or if she would admit it. Noreen doubted that anybody ever did talk about such matters. What a shame, she thought ruefully. They could speak in unabashed detail of other private things, but when it came to the intimate needs of a wife for her husband, there was a well-defined barrier to discussion.

Noreen wondered if she might be abnormal somehow. Maybe it would pass. She hoped so.

Abruptly she thought of Louis Jardinere.

By the time Brendan returned home it was past three in the afternoon. Maggie had seen him when he was still some distance from the house, and she could tell from his gait that his mood was darker than it had been when he left. Kevin was down for a nap, and now would be a good time to make herself scarce. She picked up a piece of unfinished embroidery from her work basket and spoke to Noreen on her way out.

"I'm over to your ma's to see if she can teach me that fancy stitch of hers." She added, "He's comin' up the road now—not too cheerful from the looks of him."

Noreen realized the errand had been contrived for her benefit. A faint smile crossed her face, and she caught Maggie's eye.

"Thank you, Maggie," she murmured.

Brendan banged his way into the house, walking heavy-footed all the way to the kitchen where he poured himself a drink of water.

Noreen kept silent, standing with her arms folded waiting for him to explain in his own time.

"I have to go out again in the morning."

Noreen was stunned. "So soon? Why, you haven't been back a day, and he's sending you off again?"

"Not the Mister," he countered, anxious that she not misunderstand. "It's that Dorgan. He's decided to quit hauling, he says. Not enough money to risk bein' blown to kingdom come, he says. Gonna work for his daddy at the inn, he says." Brendan's voice had taken on a sarcastic falsetto lilt.

Noreen spoke before thinking, "Well, I think he's wise. It *is* dangerous, and if there is a choice it is better, I think, to be your own master."

"*Wise*, is it? To leave his friends in the lurch? Here I am supposed to be his friend, and he sticks me with a ten-day haul—one that should be his, by rights."

She reached out for his hand. He was stiff with anger, and she knew that although most of it was directed at Joe Dorgan, a trace

[151]

of his irritability was somehow meant for her. Had she been too waspish with him this morning?

"Couldn't the shipment wait? Why must it go out tomorrow?"

"It must," he replied tersely.

"If you had your own drayage rig, they would not be asking you to dance to their music, I'm thinking. In a way Dorgan *is* the wise one. He knows that he and his father will always be the ones to set their own rules, and not be waiting on the likes of the du Ponts to tell them when to come and when to go."

"Aye, my own master, you think. How many drivers have had the same idea in fat times when they could hire out easily? When slack times come, they are the ones to go hungry and sell their teams at a loss to put food on the table. No, I'll not take the chance. It's foolhardy, woman, when I've not lost a single day of work— with pay—through good times and bad with the Mister."

"'The Mister,' you say," Noreen retorted with more heat than she intended. "I hate the term we all use when speaking of them, *Mister* Irénée and *Madam* Sophie."

Brendan looked at his wife directly for the first time since he had stepped into the house. He felt demeaned in the role her words suggested.

"He *is* the boss, Noreen," he said evenly. "They do own the mills, after all. Would you have me callin' him du Pont and herself Sophie?" He snorted good-naturedly with half a smile—his first pleasantry since reentering the house. "I don't think my job would last long after that."

Noreen poured tea into both their cups. "The mill's not the only thing they own, I'm thinking."

He bristled. "Now what is that supposed to mean?"

"We all treat them like the lord and lady, the whole lot of us. Is this so different from the world our parents ran away from? 'The Mister' sounds little different to me than 'His Lordship,' I'm thinking."

"Aye, there's a difference," Brendan replied, thumping his open hand on the table for emphasis. "The difference, woman, is that we've had nothing but fair treatment and good wages from du Pont, and the sure knowledge that he'll take care of us and our loved ones in any calamity."

Noreen stood facing Brendan as he drew fire into the packed bowl of his stubby pipe.

"There are two things that bother me," she said. "It is true I know better than most about the generosity of that family. I have watched my own father shrink to a drunken half-man most of his waking hours. The only time he is sober is when he's on the job. That seems like loyalty to the wrong people, if one is forced to make the choice." She paused. "The other is that those calamities you speak of are *their* making. The profits for the chances we take go into their pockets."

"They take chances, too, Norrie. Many's the time I've seen his lads pull their weight with the rest of us, and no shirking from the danger either."

"You think that a wonderful thing, don't you, Brendan?"

"Indeed I do," he said earnestly. "It's a fine thing to see folks of quality not afraid to blister up their hands."

Noreen knew with dread calm the impact her words would have even before she began to utter them, but she said them all the same. "The aristocracy is what you mean, then, Brendan mine, but I tell you though the whip they use be as gentle as a spring breeze, you hop before it more willingly than to the lash. And it will strip your manhood from you more surely than the cat-o'-nine-tails. Get out from under the du Ponts and be your own man again!"

Brendan blinked at his wife's attack as though he had been doused with cold water. He stood like stone for so long she feared that when he moved he might strike her. She heard the snap of his teeth as they broke through the pipestem and watched the clay bowl fall from his grim mouth to shatter on the stone hearth. He spat out the crushed stem and walked stiffly to the front room and out the door.

There was no loving that night. By the time he got back from Dorgan's he was too far gone in his cups.

When she awoke the next morning he had already left with his team.

CHAPTER 20

Throughout the early morning hours of the day Brendan left, Noreen rushed briskly about the house seeking to erase the hurt with work. Maggie had given her daughter-in-law a wide berth since breakfast, but she couldn't keep out of it any longer. "Slow down, lass. You'll be making me look like a slattern in me own house with all your industry."

Noreen's trembling lip threatened to get out of control, and she turned away, crossing her arms tightly over her chest.

Maggie clucked sympathetically. "Don't waste your anger on the worthless bugger, Noreen. He's actin' like a spoiled child, that's sure. Save your energy for later when you can swat him proper with some crockery!"

She saw with satisfaction that Noreen's hunched shoulders loosened perceptibly. "Look, girl, you need to get out of the house for some air. Go for a walk. I'll take care of the little one. Surely you've left me nothing to do in this house for the rest of the day anyway."

Noreen suddenly turned and embraced—almost clutched—the older woman. Maggie was so startled that she took a step backward. Noreen recovered herself and withdrew into stiff embarrassment. She laughed nervously. "Thank you, Maggie, I think I *will* go out."

Even before Noreen had gained the road, Maggie cursed herself for taking that involuntary backward step. She knew that she and her son's wife had never been closer then they had in that instant.

Noreen would have opened up, surely. The thing that had been gnawing at her would have come out.

By the time she had reached the coolness of the woods behind Chicken Alley, Noreen felt the hurt and frustration ebb. Birds twittered behind leafy screens, a gray squirrel scampered up the trunk of a massive chestnut and scolded her from his vantage point in a crotch high above, and the long buzz of a cicada gave promise of a warm afternoon.

Halfway through the trees she decided to continue on to the big house and look in on Blanche, whom she had not thought of during Brendan's brief homecoming. She was glad that the tears had not flowed; otherwise there would have been curious looks from the kitchen help at the du Pont house. She could do without that, she thought.

The visit with Blanche depressed her more. Her younger sister was not above whining over trifles, and she had taken some offense at having been ignored in her illness. Noreen did not mention either her row with Brendan or their father's most recent debauch. It would have served little purpose to pass on the information. Besides, bad news might lower her spirits further, prolonging her illness.

Stripped of substance, their stilted conversation lagged. As she half listened to Blanche's listless rambling, Noreen felt a twinge of humiliation. What a fine name the Feeneys must have earned with the du Pont family: two employees who were more of a burden than they were worth. Taking their charity was worse than being on the public dole.

Gloom descended upon her as she negotiated the narrow servant's stairway and left the mansion through the deserted kitchen. Suddenly free of the need to keep up a controlled exterior she gave free rein to her feelings. The opulence of the big house, the whining of her sister, the shame of her father's drinking all welled up as she crossed the sunny lawn toward the path in the woods.

But above all it was the memory of Brendan that did her in completely. Not their spat—that could be patched up. It was the other thing, his using her that last night the way he did. And she had felt such loving tenderness... such yearning.

Without warning the passion gripped her again, and she was so confused by the hurt and this unsought burning desire that she feared for her sanity. The second she reached the shade of the woods, her face collapsed into sobs, and she was not at all surprised this time when Louis Jardinere stepped into the path and took her into his arms.

The dam of her reserve broke in his embrace. The great strength of his arms and chest drew out resentments hardened in her breast, and she sagged against him. His soft, reassuring words caressed her mind, and light kisses on her brow and cheeks blotted away her pain. She felt his hands gently massage her back and shoulders. She bawled like a child, hot tears blurring her eyes, stinging her cheeks. Burrowing her face in the soft, perfumed lace of his shirt-front, Noreen surrendered completely to her miserable grief.

She felt him sweep her up easily and carry her off the path to a secluded mossy clearing beside a large rock. He sat down still holding her in his arms, leaned back against the flat planes of the granite outcropping, tucked her head under his chin, and began crooning a lovely song whose words she could not understand. She lay like a child in his arms. Her tears subsided, the shuddering ceased, and she squirmed closer against him.

"You must think me separated from my senses."

"Not at all," he murmured. She felt the breath of his words riffle the hair at her temple and felt comfortable in the deep rumble of his voice.

"I'm sorry you caught me acting like a child," she said quietly, but she made no move away from him.

"I'd hardly make the mistake of considering you a child," he said, pulling out a lace kerchief and handing it to her. She looked at it doubtfully, wondering if she could foul such a fine thing by daubing at her tears and runny nose.

"Go on... please," he insisted.

She hesitated, then with a shrug of resignation, blew her nose with a sodden toot. When she felt him chuckle, she flushed and balled the wet cloth tightly in her fist.

She made a tentative effort to get to her feet, but he restrained her gently.

"Rest for a moment, little one. You should not always be in such a rush."

"But I feel so silly lying here, so... helpless!"

"I was beginning to think you were all stone and no feathers.

Frankly it is reassuring to discover that you are not always in such stern control."

Noreen was enjoying herself in a peculiar way. She had always been the one leaned upon. It was nice to have someone baby her for a change.

"I don't like to let myself go like that," she said in contradiction of her thoughts. "It's a weakness, surely, to be giving in so easily to blubber and tears."

Louis had begun to caress her arms, working upward from her elbows to her shoulders. He spoke easily as he worked. "Ah, that is the problem. You are the oldest in the family... the one on whom the work is laid. Do you not also have the responsibility of looking after younger members of the family... your parents, too? *Chérie*, you must realize that none of us is made of iron." He began to knead the muscles along the top of her shoulders and at the nape of her neck. She felt nothing like iron at the moment. His hands were marvelous! She rolled her head back in rhythm to the stroking of Louis's deft fingers on her neck.

"Ah," she groaned with pleasure and laughed softly, "I shall have to hire you each wash day to rub away my kinks." She felt his warm lips touch the base of her neck and move up lightly to her ear in a simple variation of the matching motion of his hand—exciting and pleasant all at once.

Even when his free hand slipped from her waist to her breast, she accepted the transition easily. Oh, there was a wee tug of conscience at the moment she turned to seek out his lips with her own, but she dropped it as easily as she let go of the crumpled ball of handkerchief and embraced him.

He did not rush her. Each step of their undressing was a dallied progression of delighted exploration more delicious than the last. Noreen felt the lassitude of his compassionate massage being replaced by a mounting urgency she had never experienced before. She was in a trance of excitement, and yet she felt an exulting power of control. She matched him move for move, touch for touch, delighting in his losing fight for dominance, and all the while she, too, raced against her pounding need.

Finally it was she who ordered the finale, "Yes, yes, Louis, now!" and exulted in his hot compliance. Great rippling paroxysms of pleasure swept her uncontrollably. Yet in the grip of her own passion she felt the deeper sense of orchestration. Euphoria flushed through her slowly like the release from some excruciating pain. She was numb with well-being, hungering in the fullness of satiety, awestruck yet knowing.

They slept. Noreen awoke with a dreamlike slowness, aware of muted greens and browns and flesh tones, light filtered through gauze, the musky scent of the bruised mossy earth on which they lay. She was softly pleased with her own nakedness and marveled at her lack of shyness as she dressed under his unblinking gaze.

"I will see you again?"

There was a faint plea in her lover's voice, and that gave her pleasure. That there should be any question of her meeting him again astonished her, and she nearly said, "Of course." For some reason her reply came out more matter-of-fact. "Yes. Tomorrow."

When they had dressed she approached him with mock formality, curtsied grandly, and spoke lightly, "Now would y'give a lass a goodbye kiss without knockin' her down?"

Then she left him, darting quickly through the screen of foliage. She fairly floated over the fallen leaves and soft earth in a trance that stayed with her the rest of the way through the woods until the path fanned out into the weedy border of the houses along the Crick.

Something warned her to be wary of her mood. She knew she was suffused with secret delight, and instinct cautioned her to protect her treasured aura lest it be noticed and ripped away.

When she reached the door, she was greeted by Maggie with a finger to her lips, to warn her that Kevin was asleep.

"Keep your voice down, Noreen. The tyke has run himself out with playin' this day. And me, too!" she added with an exaggerated groan. "And how was your day, lass?"

For the first time in her life Noreen had the odd sensation of being an onlooker as she listened to herself prattle on excitedly about her visit with Blanche. She observed with some anxiety that she was not as morose as she ought to have been under the circumstances so she supported her good spirits with other details. "And I had such a nice walk. It did not seem as hot today as it has been. It was quite lovely and cool on the path through the woods."

"Ah, yes. It's a pity that we don't take time to enjoy the lovely things right under our noses," Maggie agreed with a vigorous nod.

As she listened to Noreen rattle on happily, she was amazed at the remarkable change in the girl's mood. It made her furious to think of her being unhappy when it took so little to please her.

That evening at supper, Noreen found out from Patrick that Brendan was delivering a special shipment of powder to Maryland and would be gone for nearly two weeks. She was both angered and delighted by the news. The length of his trip, coming as it did less than forty hours after his return from a longer assignment, really galled her. At the same time Brendan's acquiescence to the demands of the company made her feel less guilty about yielding to the seduction of Louis.

Had Maggie Gallagher realized her part in the affair it would have killed her, but without her constant urging to get out of the house Noreen's meetings might not have continued beyond the first. However, urge her she did, nearly every day of Brendan's absence.

Louis had similar good fortune in explaining his afternoons away from his host's residence. The du Ponts were pleasantly surprised that he had apparently developed a sudden passion for the natural scenery of the estate. To satisfy this interest he had resumed a childhood hobby of sketching plant life. He insisted on taking long walks armed with his pad and pencils to secluded woodland places along the Brandywine. Sophie noted that Louis did not always manage to find anything worth sketching, and those drawings he did complete were rather poorly executed, but the walks did him a world of good. When he returned in midafternoon his usually acid disposition was positively buoyant and his appetite at dinner ravenous.

On the day of their first prearranged tryst, Noreen and her lover slipped into the trees from opposite ends of the woods. While he was still a hundred yards or so from the massive granite boulder that was their point of rendezvous, Louis caught a flash of blue moving through the dense summer foliage. He reached the rock first and stood leaning against its cool massiveness as she burst into view. She was breathing heavily, more from excitement than from the exertion of her walk, and a flush of color high on her cheeks accented the glinting copper tones in her tightly coiffed hair and set off her blue-green eyes.

On her way to the rock Noreen had grown more excited. The immorality of her behavior was little more than a passing shadow burned out by the brilliance of her desire. Perhaps the absolute dissimilarity between the attachment she had felt for Brendan during the years of their marriage and this novel passion she had for the Frenchman was the reason for her lack of remorse or restraint. She did not *love* Louis at all. That was what was so strange, that she had virtually no interest in him as a person. There was a feeling of power, too, in seeing the ecstasy she was able to arouse in him.

She was only dimly aware of walking to their secluded bower, of wordlessly disrobing. But she throbbed with his embrace, yielding to his gentle, unhurried caresses. The place where they lay between the rock and the spring-fed run was thick with moss and dotted with mushrooms. The odor of the crushed fungus blended with their own essence filled her with a carnality that suffused her completely. She enveloped him until, finally exhausted, they slept.

After they awoke, she bathed in the run, gasping with the tingling shock of the cold water. They dressed without a word, strolled together to the path and stood facing each other.

"Tomorrow, *chérie?*"

"Yes," she said easily, as if discussing the weather. "If I can get away. If not tomorrow, the day after."

He nodded and bowed gracefully as she turned and began walking down the path toward home. Louis watched her until she disappeared around a turn; then he, too, turned and began climbing the pathway to the open lawn of the estate.

"*Mon Dieu!*" he muttered softly.

CHAPTER 21

Francis settled himself comfortably in the caned rocker on the du Pont's veranda and sipped a glass of excellent sherry as he waited. He twirled the glass slowly and peered through the amber clearness of the wine as it magnified and distorted the far tree line across the Brandywine.

"*Révérend Père?*"

The voice was so near and unexpected that Francis started, spilling a few drops of wine. He turned to see a man standing at his elbow, tall, athletic, with an indolent carriage that hinted of insolence.

"I am sorry, Father... Reardon, is it not? I did not mean to startle you." The man smiled, and Francis had the distinct impression that it was mirth he felt, not contrition. He had to work at controlling his feeling of irritation as he extended his hand in greeting.

"My clumsiness... daydreaming on this lovely veranda ... Francis Reardon, at your service, sir.... And you must be Mr. du Pont's guest from France.

"Louis Jardinere." The other smiled, releasing his hand and giving Francis a slight bow, "at *your* service, *Révérend Père.*"

Louis gave his fingers a discreet shake to remove the few drops of sherry that Francis had transferred from his own in the handclasp, and again Francis had the distinct feeling that this fellow was enjoying his discomfort.

"Am I to call you Francis or Father? I must confess that I expected the village priest to be an older man." Louis pulled a chair closer and seated himself in a fluid movement. He waved Francis back to the rocker and sat facing the priest with his back to the greenery of the Brandywine, as though sitting for his portrait. His bearing was strangely intimidating.

"Please call me Francis if you like. After all, we..." He could not for the life of him formulate a reason why this man should feel above deferring to his clerical office, but then...

"Ah, then it shall be Francis and Louis, eh? Good! It clears the air, does it not?" His eyes were sharp, with a glitter of concentration that made Francis feel gimleted like a specimen on a pin.

"Louis and Francis, yes. Why do I feel that we have solved some great business problem?" He laughed, more relaxed now. After all, their backgrounds were similar.

"Sophie and Irénée will not return until later. They asked me to make their apologies for missing your social call. Some business matters with the mills."

"Oh, I see." Francis was suddenly deflated. "It doesn't matter, Louis. I was making pastoral calls in the neighborhood anyway." He was not really. This was his only mission today.

"And you will have to reconcile yourself to me as a... lesser substitute," Louis observed, but there was no self-deprecation about him at all. Francis was irritated by the transparency of his banter.

"And what brings you to America, Louis, business or pleasure?"

"A little of both." He chuckled at a private memory. "One should call my visit speculative as to business and particular as to diversion. You see, Francis, it is my hope someday to settle here as my cousins have. At the moment I am assessing various business opportunities in which to invest."

"Then you would like to join the du Ponts here on the Brandywine?"

"I'm afraid not. Not here. I do not have the nose for alchemy, my dear Francis, especially on such a grand scale." He wrinkled his nose and twisted his head disdainfully in the direction of the powder works. "Something along the lines of a profitable estate would better suit my aesthetics."

"I see."

"You disapprove of my aversion to manufacturing?"

"No. I can understand that."

"Ah, yes, and well you could, Francis. The call to the priesthood, eh? We are of similar minds."

Francis had not meant that at all, but Louis rattled on.

"You see, my family for generations has controlled a more bucolic enterprise. The Jardinere estates have been the envy of all France." Louis frowned, for the first time, Francis realized, and the facade dropped from his face like a mask. "The envy of rather powerful factions, I might add. Scoundrels waiting for the right opportunity to take what has been ours for over a century."

Louis's mood was positively black. The man certainly had another side.

"I can fully appreciate your loss." Francis responded in a softer tone. "Our plantation in Virginia—"

"Ah... a plantation! Cotton, I imagine? Or sugarcane?"

This Frenchman was in over his depth. Sugarcane in Virginia! How his mother would howl over that.

"The crop is tobacco, Louis. The area is quite famous for a pale leaf prized worldwide."

Louis suddenly laughed. "My apologies, good *Père*. I did not realize that I was speaking to a fellow member of the gentry."

The recognition rang hollow with Francis, but he accepted it silently and sipped thoughtfully at his wine. It galled him to have protested his claim to "quality."

"Do you visit there often?"

Louis's question brought him back. "Not as often as I'd like. It is rather far, and my duties here..."

"Yes, yes," Louis smiled. "*Noblesse oblige?*"

"Holy Mother Church would not put it quite that way."

Louis brought the conversation back to the Virginia plantation, and spoke with animated interest. "You have an elder brother, I suppose, who will carry on after your father retires?"

"My father is dead."

"Ah..."

"And my mother carries on alone. I am the only child."

Louis was confused. "I do not understand. If you were the only son... why take the cloth?"

His mother's words drifted out of the past again, against the quiet backdrop of his father's disappointed face: "Not a word to stifle his vocation, not in my house. He has chosen the better thing, as the Lord said. My own son, a priest of God."

He looked at Louis and was not sure this Frenchman would understand the deep conviction of his spiritual calling. "It is not the same in this country, Louis. It is a calling that cannot go unheeded, a supernatural mandate, if you will."

"An honorable alternative to inheritance, yes. But do you not have an obligation to your line, Father?"

"It is the will of God."

"*Mon Dieu.*"

This time it was Louis who turned to stare at the greenery on the far side of the river. Insect sounds whirred into the silence.

He turned back and leaned against the balustrade. "Then it is your mother alone who oversees the plantation?"

"We have had to put it on the block, I'm afraid," he muttered glumly.

"On the block..." Louis caught the idiom. "Ah, sold? That is a cause for sadness, my friend."

Francis squirmed uncomfortably. "It is not yet sold, but soon will be."

Louis smiled. "The thought is distasteful to you. It is not the end of the world, eh? You and I are two of a kind...dispossessed aristocrats."

Francis could not quite make out the nature of Louis's expression. Was his smile one of commiseration or of disdain? He watched the young Frenchman closely as the conversation worked its way through a series of questions about the location of Skibbereen, the size of the plantation, the number of slaves, and a host of other details. At the end he was reasonably secure in the feeling that Louis was truly interested, but he could not shake a certain sense of being out of place here, of being somehow above his rightful place, lounging with his betters.

When he finally took his leave, he was nearly to the door before he remembered to mention the reason for his call. "Louis, I was hoping that sometime in the near future I might say mass here for the powdermen and their families. Most of them are Catholic, you see..."

"Splendid! A wonderful idea. I am Catholic myself." Louis put a finger thoughtfully to his lips. "The du Ponts are not, of course, but I am certain they would agree to having a mass celebrated here on the grounds. The weather is ideal, and I should imagine your parishioners would consider it a great holiday. I shall put it to them this evening on their return, eh?"

As Francis drove his buggy slowly down the gravel drive, Louis Jardinere went directly to the study and picked up a quill. He wanted to get down the name of that real estate broker Father Reardon had mentioned. Richmond, Virginia. The name had a nice ring. Perhaps it would be possible to negotiate a transaction with the limited capital he had available.

After he had scratched down the name, he held the paper carefully, waiting for the ink to dry, and then folded it once and took it with him to his room upstairs.

CHAPTER 22

Nora Feeney managed to get her husband sobered up enough to report for his Friday shift. Since the mill hands worked from sunrise to sunset, Denis faced the prospect of putting in a tremens-riddled fourteen hours before the long summer day was over. He had to be able to keep his wits about him, too. As operator of a rolling mill he controlled one of the more dangerous steps in the fabrication of black powder.

There were nearly a dozen rolling mills stretched along the Crick from the original Eleutherian section to the newer Hagley Yard. Each was run by a single workman who rarely had occasion to meet with any of his fellow operators in the adjacent mills, because they were spaced apart to reduce the scope of catastrophe in the event one of them exploded.

Each mill was about twenty feet square, constructed massively on three sides of granite walls several feet thick. The fourth wall, on the side next to the Crick, was a flimsy frame affair barely strong enough to keep out the weather. Inset below the top of the stone walls was a shed roof of overlapping iron sheets. If the mill were to explode, the force of the blast would be directed out and upward over the stream and away from other installations in the yard. The iron sheets of the mill roof were just heavy enough to deflect the explosion before being themselves blasted across the Crick.

Each rolling mill was powered by a system of gear-turning shafts connected to a water wheel set in a millrace. Several mills could be run off the energy developed as sluice gates were opened to release water into the raceway from the pressure of the damned-up Brandywine.

Denis's first act on the job was to check that the bearing blocks supporting the power shaft to his mill were getting a good supply of water. This was essential lubrication for the bearing, and equally important, it kept the rotating shaft from getting hot. Overnight the sluice had collected a handful of leaves and tiny branches carried downstream on the typically high early summer waters of the Crick. Denis carefully removed the trash before moving on to the building itself.

He noted with satisfaction that the carters had delivered the first batch of ingredients for his morning work. The wooden tubs of saltpeter, sulfur, and charcoal sat in a neat row under an overhang next to the only doorway into the stone mill.

Next he entered the cool room and checked the floor to make certain that it was free of traces of the explosive granules from the day before. The interior of the mill was dominated by twin cast-iron wheels over six feet high with smooth treads a foot and a half wide. These were mounted side by side on a central driving pinion and rolled in an endless circle within a round dishlike track nearly twelve feet in diameter.

Denis took great pains to inspect the wheels and their mating track to make sure no sliver of stone, granule of sand, or other substance had found its way into the machinery. One spark at the wrong time could spell the end of the mill and the operator as well.

Satisfied that he could begin, he carefully measured out his ingredients, spread them evenly around the track of the huge wheels, stepped outside, and pulled a huge lever to mesh the gears of the driving shaft. With an ominous rumble the huge wheels began to move, crushing the chemicals beneath their weight as they rolled.

After a few minutes he reentered the mill and began the tedious process of raking the powdered black mixture so that it could be blended equally and reground again and again into a finer texture. To do this he had to walk in a circle to keep ahead of the inexorable progress of the groaning wheels, raking carefully as he limped along.

About midmorning the ague struck him, and he trembled mightily, craving a drink to quiet his twitching nerves. He forced himself to settle for cold coffee from his lunch pail, and after some moments he was even able to choke down a few lumps of cornmeal mush.

By noon the shakes had subsided, and when the bogeyman came with a handcart for his first tub of freshly made explosive, Denis was able to swing it on the rig expertly, despite his crippled leg and his hangover.

Once during the early afternoon Tim Feeney dropped in on his father on the pretext of checking to see that he had had lunch but actually to see if he would be able to make it through the day. Tim's job at the cooperage permitted him time off occasionally to "see to the old daddo," particularly since the foreman in charge was an old crony of Denis Feeney's. On two days during the past year, in fact, his boss had looked the other way to allow Tim to fill in at his father's rolling mill. Most who knew Tim would admit that, although he was not really trained for the mill task, he was a quick learner and was a safer bet than trusting Denis with the black stuff when he was in his cups.

Denis greeted his son gruffly when he turned to see the smiling boy standing in the doorway.

"Well, now, how is it that you can loaf when the rest of us are workin' ourselves to an early grave?"

Tim smiled awkwardly, unsure of his father's mood. "Ma told me to make sure you had something to eat."

"I've et," he retorted perfunctorily and limped past his son to pick up an empty powder tub. "Now then, be takin' yourself back to the cooperage before they fire ye or I blow us both up tryin' to scoop up this infernal stuff with your distracting yakkin'."

Tim nodded and took his leave.

He had gone quite a distance from the mill when Denis reappeared in the doorway. He followed his son's progress with bloodshot eyes until the figure disappeared at a bend in the roadway. He stood there a moment hunched over awkwardly as he massaged the tortured muscles of his twisted leg. Incongruously a smile lit his face, and as he turned to recommence his work he muttered, "Ah, Timmy, my lad, you're more a credit than I'll ever deserve, God help me."

CHAPTER 23

The priest is goin' to be saying mass at the Mister's," Maggie said, bursting in on Patrick and Noreen as they sat in the front room enjoying the fading twilight of a comfortable July evening. "And they've invited all of us who want to come." She nodded enthusiastically. "This coming Sunday."

Patrick took his pipe out of his mouth. "Is it the Reardon lad?"

Maggie clucked with disapproval. "'Tis *Father* Reardon, of course. You wouldn't be thinking that his grace the bishop of Mary-Land would be making the trip for the likes of us."

Patrick winked at Noreen and spoke with feigned chagrin. "It's not for the likes of us *Father* Reardon is comin' either, by the looks of it. It's to the big house, you said, not the home of Patrick Gallagher, modest cottage that it is."

"Mr. Gallagher," Maggie snapped back, "that is a silly thing to say when you know this room would be full to standing with a half dozen people."

"Well, then, why not in the cooper shop? Sure there's space enough and more in that barn of a place."

"Barn indeed! Is it in a filthy place like that you think the priest should offer the mass?"

"In the old country, when times were dangerous, I recall we weren't so particular."

Maggie rocked back in her chair and shot Noreen an exasperated look. "I think the man's gone soft in the head. Here is a generous rich man offering his home to the likes of us so that we can celebrate the mass with some decency, and he's complaining!"

"The home of a Protestant, my girl," Patrick said softly, and Noreen detected for the first time an edge in his voice. "When it comes to choosing between rich and poor, I'm still a bit leery of a priest who is cozy with the rich."

"But, Patrick, darlin', that was a long time ago, in a different land. We can let it go now, thank the Lord." She leaned back in the chair and continued to rock.

Patrick gazed out the window. For him the matter was closed.

"I'll not go with you," he said. "It may seem poor reasoning, but I'd not be easy in that house, even in the presence of the Lord God Almighty."

Noreen met Louis three times that week. In the times between he seldom crossed her mind. Her newfound sensuality had its place carefully compartmented into the early afternoon hours. She did not let it intrude otherwise. She marveled at her own detachment. It was, she thought, as if she were two people who shared their most intimate secrets with each other.

She had fallen into a state of numbness toward Brendan. It seemed as if the man she married had evaporated and a disappointing man had assumed his identity. The longer he was gone, the more she began to think of him as a stranger. Was it possible that they had been married for five years without her ever noticing what he was really like? Perhaps she had deceived herself into thinking that this childhood friend could be her lover and husband as well.

One morning when she was doing the washing she had the fleeting sensation that she was beginning to forget what he looked like. She closed her eyes tightly and willed a picture of him into her thoughts. It sprang before her instantly. She could see him seated on a wagon seat, smiling and looking lordly as he always did when driving a team. She could see him wave, and she watched as a frown crossed his face. She concentrated intently as he changed subtly into the unpleasant person she had come to remember, and then suddenly he and his wagonload of powder disappeared in a red flash.

The vision was so real that she started, popping open her eyes.

She had some difficulty letting go of the daydream even after she had washed all the clothes and hung them out to dry.

By the time Saturday afternoon arrived, the whole of Chicken Alley was astir with the prospects of going to mass at the big house. The company employee roster numbered a little under one hundred. With the exception of people like Patrick Gallagher, who had private reasons for not going, nearly all of them would attend. The relatively short trek to the du Pont estate would be a welcome relief from those nine-mile round trips to town for mass. Besides that, nearly everybody was looking forward to the chance to see the interior of the big house.

The du Ponts had decided to use a newly completed side terrace for the ceremony. Summer weather was unpredictable in Delaware, and the makeshift altar was set up just inside wide French doors leading to the dining room. Should it rain, it would be a quick matter to swing the altar around and squeeze the congregation into the house.

But it turned out that there was no need to worry, for the day opened hot and dry. The locusts were singing from the first rays of sunlight, and the skies were cloudless. Maggie and Noreen arrived at the edge of the estate with the first cluster of a few dozen neighbors. In due course others arrived, forming a rather large assembly standing awkward and hushed in the hot morning sunshine. At last a fashionably dressed woman appeared at the front door, and someone in the crowd identified her in a whisper as "the missus herself." She called to someone inside the house, and young Terry Flynn came clattering out, running awkwardly toward them, all adolescent knees and stiff new brogans.

"C'mon, everybody. Behind the house is where we go, on the new terrace!" There was a real pride in the young man. This was the first time any of his friends would see inside the grand place where he had begun to work as a handyman just a month before.

Father Reardon smiled genially as they came around the corner of the mansion and shyly mounted the steps leading from the rear lawn to the terrace. Noreen had become separated from Maggie as they maneuvered into a ragged column of twos and threes marching behind the Flynn boy. Then the brim of her bonnet caught Noreen's eye, and she spotted her in the very front row standing behind a group of chairs that were occupied by family members. She saw someone rise to offer Maggie his chair. That was nice! Her heart went out a little to the finely dressed gentleman who had been so considerate. He was wearing a silly wig that seemed too formal and out of place here, and she followed him with her eyes as he moved away from the chairs to stand at the side of the terrace. When he turned around, he looked her squarely in the eye.

It was Louis Jardinere.

Noreen's legs buckled and she fell to her knees, cracking one of them painfully. No one turned to look because by now everyone save the older folk were kneeling. She fixed a stare on Father Reardon's back and tried to erase Louis from her mind, but it was futile and she knew it.

Seeing Louis in the company of family and friends, in attendance at the Lord's Supper, suddenly released in her the crushing self-recrimination that she had been able to ignore until this moment. She was nearly suffocating with an appalling guilt. This was the grossest blasphemy. She was shocked to realize that the guilt had not struck her before this.

Following services Father Reardon disappeared into the dining room to change out of his vestments. As soon as he was clear of the terrace, the small congregation broke into knots of excited greeters, milling about with animated whispering and subdued laughter.

Noreen nearly fought her way to be the first out of the place. Only after she had reached the top step did she turn to see if Maggie was following. Her jaw dropped aghast when she saw her marching directly to Louis. She was thanking him profusely for having offered her the chair. Now he had taken her arm and they were walking toward her!

Noreen turned her back and tried to descend the steps and flee. She would wait for Maggie at the gate. But the way was blocked by the entire Halloran clan, who had stopped on the bottom step to listen respectfully to Terry Flynn's beaming lecture on the layout and plantings of the sweeping rear lawn. Before she could squeeze past and make her escape, she heard Maggie call.

"Noreen! There she is. Noreen, wait darlin'!"

She pretended not to hear, feigning apologies to the Hallorans as she edged past them, but Maggie was too quick. She felt a hand on her arm, halted, and forced herself to turn around.

"Mr. . . ." Maggie faltered with the introduction.

"Louis Jardinere," he prompted, smiling with good humor at Noreen's obvious distress.

"Mr. Gardiner, I'd like to introduce my daughter-in-law, Noreen."

"Of course, but we have already met."

Louis paused just long enough for his comment to produce bewilderment in Maggie and white-faced apprehension in Noreen. "Ah, please do not say you have forgotten our meeting, Madame Gallagher." Here he bowed, taking Noreen's hand to brush it lightly with a kiss.

Noreen recoiled from the gesture. She was painfully aware of the open-mouthed stares of the Hallorans. Louis turned to Maggie with a genteel laugh. "She had come to visit her sister, who was quite ill, and as she was leaving I blundered into her, giving her quite a start, I'm afraid."

Maggie chirped away happily without the slightest sign of social intimidation. Secretly she was proud of the fact that Noreen had had the salt to dismiss a casual meeting with this aristocractic dandy while visiting Blanche as not worth mentioning. Even as she blathered on she noted with glee that the girl was practically ignoring this Frenchie with all his frumpery.

"And how long will you be stayin' with the Mister, Mr. Gardiner?" she continued, mispronouncing the name again.

Louis glanced at Noreen who stared coldly past his shoulder. "Ah, Madame Gallagher, that depends on business. . . how do you say it? . . . affairs that I am presently involved in. One never knows about these things."

"Well, we all wish you good fortune, and we hope you enjoy your stay," Maggie rattled on.

"You cannot imagine, madame," Louis said, while beaming at Noreen, "the great pleasure I have had here during the past weeks."

Maggie glanced at her daughter-in-law and saw her reserve begin to crumple into a hot flush of distracted embarrassment. Well! Enough of this small talk. The man was becoming impudent. Noreen was pretty enough to turn a man's eyes surely, but this scalawag was taking a few too many liberties with his.

"We must be goin'," she snapped peremptorily reaching for Noreen's arm.

A voice stopped her. "Good morning, Mrs. Gallagher."

They turned to see Father Reardon walking up, stiffly clerical in a neatly tailored cassock with a biretta of the same black cloth resting squarely on his head. A few errant, gray-flecked locks curled incongruously from under its severe crown, giving it the effect of a costume rather than the clerical garb of a priest.

"*And*, Mrs. Gallagher," he added with a nod to Noreen. "I see you have already met Monsieur Jardinere," he observed. "Brendan must be away on another of his journeys, I take it. And how is young Kevin these days?"

Noreen fought the hot flush that had spread to her neck, and managed to mumble, "Fine, thank you, Father."

"My Patrick is lookin' after the lad this minute,"Maggie interjected, thankful for the chance to sidestep the priest's *next* question about her husband's whereabouts this Sabbath.

Apparently the priest took little note of Patrick's absence, for he continued in the same vein. "Noreen's was my first marriage, Louis. She and Brendan are very special in my ministry."

Something in the cleric's eye arrested Louis. Instinctive rivalry seized him, and he was thrown into a disquieting mood of jealousy. He was amazed at its suddenness and its irrationality. For no apparent reason he sensed this priest was somehow a competitor.

Maggie was tiring of the conversation. She noted that most of the others had left and was thinking of the long walk to Chicken Alley in the rising heat of midday.

"Well, it was a nice mass. Thank you, Father, but we must be steppin' on our way." Without further ceremony she hooked Noreen's arm, and they followed the stragglers away from the terrace.

Left alone together, Father Reardon and Louis found nothing to say to each other. The priest excused himself, saying that he had to make his thanksgiving. Louis bowed and drifted inside the house.

Father Reardon tried to formulate his prayers by gazing out over the clipped expanse of lawn, but Noreen was again the distraction he had fought so many times before. At last he gave up any hope of spiritual concentration, leaned against the stone balustrade and savored the grainy coldness of the carved sandstone against the soft flesh of his palms. Finally he closed his eyes and began murmuring a personal litany of memorized prayers that would, in time, erase her tantalizing vision from his mind.

CHAPTER 24

The following week was tense for the du Pont household. As the days progressed, their guest became more and more irritable. Once, in fact, he lashed out so at Blanche Feeney over a minor inconvenience that the attack brought tears to her eyes and a stern rebuke later from du Point.

Louis apologized to his host at once, but the others were painfully aware that something was upsetting him—the tedium of isolation from city life, or perhaps the lack of news from his wife. His solitary walks through the woods seemed to augment rather than allay his temper. They would all be happy to see him leave, but the business arrangements he was involved in could not possibly be resolved for another month.

Louis had other things on his mind. By Friday his patience was exhausted. He had found out quite easily from Blanche exactly where her sister lived. That information had been elicited neatly without the girl's even being aware that she had passed it on in a sprinkling of other gossip.

Shortly before noon his midday walk took him along the path as usual, but this time he continued all the way to Chicken Alley. He arrived at the house of Patrick Gallagher to greet a startled Maggie as she was sweeping out the front room.

"Good morning, grand-mère Gallagher," he said from the open doorway, and without ceremony let himself in.

Maggie was fumbling for his name, which she had not been able to pronounce even when she heard it. Her tone was tinged with exasperation. "Well...what can we do for you, sir?"

Louis was smiling, but there was something about his eyes that made her distrust him. She had said so in as many words to Noreen several times since meeting him after the mass.

"I have a message for your daughter-in-law, madame," he said easily, bowing formally to her.

As he spoke both of them could hear Noreen enter the back of the house. She could not see Louis from the kitchen, and pausing only to place a water bucket on the table she burst in on them.

"It seems we have a caller, Noreen." Louis could not have missed the flatness of her announcement. Noreen stood rigid with her mouth drawn in a tight line.

"Ah, Madame Noreen," he greeted her. "Your sister Blanche has some messages for you and your parents. I took the liberty of offering to convey them to you personally."

Noreen was seething with anger at the impertinence of this visit. She knew that Blanche would never in a hundred years presume to ask such a favor, nor would Louis offer it.

She waited for him to speak.

Louis took in the roadway below the house. "Perhaps—since I have to hurry back for an afternoon appointment—perhaps you could walk with me a short distance so that I might convey Mademoiselle Blanche's confidences to you."

Noreen was terrified that the whole sordid truth would slip flippantly from his lips, and she was desperate to leave the house to keep Maggie out of earshot. Somehow she managed to keep up a cool exterior, however, giving her a sharp look.

Maggie caught the expression and, satisfied that the girl could handle the situation by herself, strode to the kitchen. "Humph!" was the only comment she could muster.

"Good day, madame," Louis called after her.

Noreen walked briskly from the house without a word, crossed the narrow dusty roadway, and descended the sharp riverbank, stopping only when she reached the water's edge. Then she turned and stood stiffly with folded arms, glaring at Louis.

His eyes were bright with conspiracy as he approached, and he stopped several feet away from her, aware that they could be seen clearly from the front of the Gallagher home.

Noreen demanded, "How *dare* you put me in such danger to my reputation!" Her mind churned with fears for Kevin, Brendan, Maggie...

Louis answered coolly, "*Ma chérie*, I think you were more than willing to risk the danger on several occasions. Which encounters, by the way, I grow more desperate to resume. You have been unfaithful to our rendezvous, and I am deeply distressed."

"Unfaithful!" The word was a rebuke of her wedding vows.

"Please," he went on, "do not let me upset you. My words perhaps do not express so well the way I feel. If we could meet... in less public circumstances..."

"I think *that* is ended," she said, feeling as though she were in a waking nightmare.

"Oh, but it is not at an end. We must meet again, my sweet one, and soon."

"No, Louis. God in heaven, I still do not know how I got myself into this mess, but I do know that it must stop—now—before my life is ruined for good."

He snapped a mulberry branch from a bush beside them and began stripping it absently of its leaves.

"You must see how it is with me," she went on. "I was daft to have had anything to do with you from the start. I have a husband and child to think of." Her tone had softened to one of conciliation, and she pressed the point. "It was at the mass on Sunday that the ugly truth struck me first. Just seein' you there with all the rest of my family and friends in the sight of God and Father Reardon woke me up."

At the mention of the priest's name Louis stiffened and gave her a black look, but Noreen mistook it for nothing more than bleak disappointment.

"So it's over, Louis. I'll not see you again."

The branch gleamed long and wetly naked in his hands as he scraped off the last of its green-brown skin with his thumbnail and turned to look at her again.

"*Oui*, madame, you will," he said with a hard smile. "We shall meet again tomorrow. Do not disappoint me."

She was dumbstruck at the command and bridled. Her old manner returned and she shot back angrily, "You'll be having a long wait, I'm thinking!"

"Oh?" he said with eyebrows raised in question over eyes that had turned brittle. "If you do not, I will have to make do with whatever wench who comes along."

He paused long enough for Noreen to show her lack of interest in his proposed sexual escapades. Then he added, "Mademoiselle Blanche is recovered and looking quite well. She has resumed her duties, one of which is to attend to my chambers."

Noreen absorbed the words like a blow to the solar plexus. She stared at Louis, unable to speak.

"It is a most convenient arrangement, really," he continued. "Her room is on the garret floor just above mine—just a few steps away."

He inspected the slender white shaft of mulberry, looking closely at its end. Very deliberately he straightened the single tender bud at its tip then pinched it off. It fell to the dirt at her feet.

"Until tomorrow then, *adieu*," he said softly and, switching lightly at his boot top, walked away.

Patrick Gallagher's current job of supervising the new millrace construction had definite advantages. It was less than a half-mile from home. That meant he could eat lunch with Maggie, Norrie, and the boy. He might as well take advantage of being this close to home while he could. The masonry work on the race would last until spring, but in bad weather during the winter he would be shunted off to other jobs around the mills. Besides, that grandson of his was growing fast. By next year he might not think his grandpa so much fun.

He was blowing hard when he climbed the front stoop, more from the heat than the exertion. At the sound of his step a staccato thumping raced toward him, and he stooped just in time to gather his squirming grandson into his arms.

"Where's Norrie? Gone on one of her walks, is she?"

"I'll want to talk to you about that," Maggie answered curtly.

Patrick looked at his wife for further words, as yet unused to the idea, after more than twenty-six years of marriage, that she never elaborated unless plied with questions. He waited the usual length of time. "Well, woman, I've not stopped up me ears."

Maggie still kept silent, but at last she raised her eyes to his and spoke. "She is on a walk, but to town this time."

"In this heat? Has she the need to do penance?" he joked, but his face showed concern for the girl's health.

"She's no need for that, poor thing. But there's another who should be wearin' a hair shirt."

"Who should be—and why?" Patrick demanded.

Maggie waved the question aside. "She said she wanted to look into some of the stores. Maybe find something—a small gift for Brendan for when he gets home." She shook her head as if Noreen were still there for the disagreement. "If the truth were known, it's Brendan should be buying gold for that girl, good little thing that she is!"

"Is it my son, then, who needs the hair shirt?"

Maggie shook her head slowly. She stood and swept Kevin out of his chair. He was grubby with spilled food, but she looked at him ruefully for a second and sent him out the back with a pat on his behind, "Go and play for a minute till I send your grandfather back to work."

She walked to the doorway and waited to be sure the child would stay within sight, then turned to blurt it out. "It's that friend of the Mister is the one I'm talking about. I knew there was something I did not like about him at the mass. He's a bad one."

"You mean the one staying at the big house? The business friend from France? What's he done?"

"I think he's after your daughter-in-law!"

"Because he passed the time of day with you after the mass?"

"He came *here*, today, to see Noreen herself—on some excuse to give her a message from Blanche." She began to clear off the table with quick nervous gestures. "It was all blarney. Even after he left, and Noreen said it was how Blanche was upset about Denis and his drinking and her being homesick, I knew she was fibbin' to spare me."

Maggie's lip began to tremble. "Oh, he was sniffin' around like an eager hound. You can be sure of that! The poor girl must be terrified."

When she turned away from him to stand at the sideboard, he walked over to her and hugged her roughly from behind. "There, there, Maggie girl. You've no worries on that score. I'll talk to the

[179]

Mister about the bastard before this day is done. He'll take care of the whelp."

At a loss to help matters further, he popped outside to say goodbye to Kevin, reentered, and passing through the kitchen saw that Maggie had recovered enough composure to face him.

"Now don't you be doing anything silly, like you might have years ago," she said, a new alarm spreading across her face.

He laughed at that. "No, girl, I'll let the Mister clean out his own house. I'd not want to be out of a job and a home besides."

On the way back to the job site, however, Patrick felt a white anger hot in his chest and he toyed with the idea of breaking the Frenchie's delicate neck.

CHAPTER 25

After the five-mile walk through muggy July heat, the cool, dark interior of the new St. Peter's Church should have felt soothing. For Noreen, however, who had made the solitary trip to Wilmington's only Catholic church, the fears of her pending confession allowed no comfort.

As she waited Noreen hoped desperately that when the door to the sacristy opened, it would be Father Krasicki who would walk through. Although it would be bad enough, God knows, to confess her sin to an old man, it would be far less humiliating than to have to tell Father Reardon.

Sitting there she blushed terribly just thinking about it. The man had been almost a family friend since he came to visit five years ago. She had confessed to him so many times before, all those faults that, compared with this mortal monstrosity now blackening her soul, seemed childish and trivial. He had married them, worried that they might not be quite ready for the responsibility. (God help her, how true that seemed now!) He had baptized their Kevin, absolving that sweet, pure thing of the sin of Eve and Adam.

The sacristy door opened, and although he kept his eyes averted from her as he walked to the single confessional, Noreen knew that before she even opened her mouth in the darkness behind the screen, Father Reardon would recognize his penitent.

Patrick's noon meal had soured in his stomach by the time he reached the new millrace. After issuing brief instructions he continued on to the upper yard and turned off on the path leading to the office building below the big house. It was a quarter past one. He knew du Pont would be at his desk. The man was more punctual than most of his employees.

"I'd like to talk with the Mister," said Patrick to the young clerk who answered his knock.

"Come in, Pat," called a pleasant voice from the dim interior of the small building. He recognized du Pont's greeting with a smile, and stepped inside.

Du Pont rose from his desk and extended his hand. "Come, sit down. How have you been? I have not seen you for more than a month. How is the work on the millrace coming along? I looked it over last week, and the stone work shows your usual fine touch, eh?"

They talked briefly about the masonry, the crew, the schedule.

"And how is your family? They are all well, I trust."

At the mention of a subject close enough to bring up the reason for his call, Patrick shifted uneasily in his chair. "Ah, they're quite well, thank you," he began, "but there's somethin' I'd like to talk to you about."

His manner was signal enough for du Pont that the matter was private. They left the office and sauntered to a few benches sitting in the shade of an old maple. The two men sat facing each other.

Patrick got right to the point. "Y'see, it's concerning my daughter-in-law, Noreen Feeney, Brendan's wife. She had a caller this mornin'. The man's a guest in your house, I take it, and me wife Maggie seems to think that he was makin' improper advances."

Du Pont's eyes darkened, but he said nothing.

Patrick went on, "Now, I don't know for certain that he was really bein' a pest, y'know. He might have come on real business, something about her sister Blanche, who's working here as a maid...."

He stopped as du Pont nodded to cut off the explanation. "But my Maggie says that he was nearly flirtin' with the lass Sunday at the mass here, and then today he took her outside to have some words in private."

Patrick was not quite sure of his ground. It was obvious that his employer was becoming very upset.

"Now, I know the womenfolk sometimes make more of a thing than they should, but the missus is not one to gossip, and she has a good eye for spottin' mischief." He allowed himself a rueful laugh. "I can speak with authority on that, I can."

Quickly serious again he concluded, "I would go to the man himself, but I thought it better to let you in on it from the start, since the man is your company, and you should know him best."

Du Pont spoke softly, but his eyes blazed. "You did the correct thing, my friend. I will attend to the matter today."

"I hope I didn't start trouble in your—" Patrick began, but du Pont cut him off.

"No, no. It is I who must apologize for the behavior of my guest. Please convey my regrets to your ladies, and tell them that Monsieur Jardinere will not disturb them ever again."

Patrick thanked him awkwardly for his understanding, and they parted under the tree. On his way back to the roadway Patrick could see that the Mister made directly for the big house without even stopping at the office.

The confession did not go well at all. Noreen managed to unburden herself of the sin, but it was torture. The admission would have been bad enough in itself, but she was doubly tried by the confessor's detailed questions about the act, its frequency, the marital status of her partner, whether he was kin of hers, and other questions she found difficult or impossible to answer either because she was ignorant of the terminology or, as was with the number of times she had lain with him, she simply could not remember.

Her face burned with humiliation at that admission.

"It was... many times, Father," she whispered in a dry croak.

Once all of the particulars of her guilt had been established, she was able to affirm quite easily that she was indeed sorry for what she had done. There remained a third requirement to satisfy before she could be absolved: "a firm purpose of amendment." Noreen knew what that meant, that she would sincerely try never to commit the sin again.

"Then you will not see this man again?" The question was gently put, but there was an imperative tone in the priest's voice.

"Oh, no, Father," she said huskily.

"Very well, then my—"

"Oh, but I will have to see... I mean, I won't do anything...." she blurted, remembering that she would have to see Louis to persuade him not to carry out his threat.

"But you cannot meet him without the risk of sinning again," Father Reardon said, surprising himself with the sharpness of his comment.

Noreen was confused. At this moment the prospect of further intimacy with someone who had taken on the aspect of an ogre was repulsive to her. In the silence following the priest's warning she murmured, "I've no fear of that happening again."

Father Reardon sighed. He was struggling with a need to be objective, to forget the closeness he felt to this woman, to forget how dashed his spirits were on being made privy to her frailty. How he wished she were an unknown penitent.

"But you must protect your immortal soul. You must promise to avoid the *occasion* of sin whether you fear it or not. Mother Church knows how frail we can be and how clouded is our vision when tempted by the prince of darkness."

"It will be all right, Father," she said. "I won't let anything like that happen again."

"Then you will not promise not to meet this man again?"

"I have to see him again."

"Can you promise to meet him only publicly, in the company of others, to avoid temptation?" he urged the compromise on her.

Noreen was horrified at the prospect. "No," she whispered sadly, "I have to see him alone."

Father Reardon was silent a moment, and when he finally spoke his voice was as crisp as a barrister's. "Then I must refuse you absolution until you can promise to avoid the company of this partner in sin."

She knelt there, dumbstruck, not knowing what to do next. The seconds went by, and she measured them by listening to his shallow breathing. At last she heard his chair scrape back as he rose and left the confessional. His footfalls echoed hollowly in the empty church, and the door to the sacristy boomed once as he closed it after him.

Noreen even forgot to genuflect before turning her back on the altar in a headlong rush for the vestibule. The late afternoon sun blinded her as she stumbled down the stone steps and began the long walk back to Chicken Alley. Inside she was trembling, but gradually her deep humiliation and confusion gave way to a rising sense of injustice and anger. Against whom she was not quite sure, and it did not completely erase the gnawing, lonely guilt.

Tomorrow she would see Louis again, to reason with him. Maybe he would understand. She would worry about that when the time came. Right now she was trying to think of a plausible reason for leaving the house again tomorrow.

Her emotional turmoil so preoccupied Noreen that she had passed the limits of the town before remembering the pretext on which she had come in the first place. She had to retrace her steps to the market to purchase something to justify her trip. The thought of buying a gift for her husband under these circumstances was a mockery of her real mission.

She knew precisely what to purchase, however, and bought it without a second's hesitation. It was a saddler's knife that Brendan had admired on so many occasions, in much the way that one would ogle at any work of art, with no thought of ever owning it. It had been a source of light humor between them. When dreaming the workman's dream of sudden riches Brendan would mention the knife, with its exquisite design and inlays and intricate tooling, a symbol of wealth now within reach.

She squandered heavily in buying it, profligate in a generosity inversely proportionate to her mood. She did not even consider whether Brendan would scold her for foolishness and refuse the extravagance. She really didn't care.

When she arrived home, she was exhausted. All she wanted to do was bathe and crawl into bed.

"There y'are!" exclaimed Maggie as she came in from the kitchen drying her hands on her apron and trying to avoid stumbling over Kevin, who was hanging like a monkey to her skirts. "Now get right in there," she puffed, pointing to their room," and get out of them hot clothes."

"Mama, Mama, Mama!" Kevin yelled when he saw her. He let go of his grandmother to gallop to Noreen.

[185]

"Now, lad," Maggie scolded sharply, "leave your mama be. Come, Noreen."

When she entered the bedroom and closed the door, Noreen saw that Maggie had already set a pitcher and basin next to the bed. A cloth-covered tray and a handful of wild flowers stuck in a vase were on the chest. She uncovered the tray and found a light supper served up on Maggie's best dinnerware.

Noreen opened the bedroom door and looked out. Across the room, settling Kevin in his chair, Maggie caught the movement. She looked up and smiled. Noreen looked gratefully at her mother-in-law, blew her a kiss, and obedient to Maggie's waving hand, retreated again to her welcoming sanctuary.

CHAPTER 26

When Patrick and Maggie discussed the meeting with du Pont, they decided not to tell Noreen. Now that the matter had been taken care of, there was little to be gained by upsetting her with the details. Better to let the poor thing go on thinking that neither of them was aware that she had been pestered by that fool of a Frenchman. After all, Noreen herself had tried to do as much for them.

After breakfast the following day, Noreen showed her purchase to Maggie, who was flabbergasted.

"Mother of God, Noreen. Is it Christmas, and have you found a goldmine on one of your walks?" she exclaimed. "Oh, that knife will make him sit up and take notice." Then she added as Noreen repackaged the gleaming tool in its oiled paper wrappings, "But it's too nice a thing for the likes of him, after the way he's treated you recently."

"Later this morning I'm going to the woods to see if there is any poke still soft enough to eat," Noreen commented matter-of-factly to change the subject. "I think something green on the table would do us all good."

"Well, I wish you luck in that, but it's a bit late in the season for pokeweed. Most of it will be hard and gone to berries, I'm thinkin'." The two women worked in silence at the dishes for several minutes. Then Maggie added, "Be sure not to cut too far down the stalk. I have no wish for us to poison ourselves. The roots are death to eat, y'know."

Shortly before noon Noreen left, armed with a paring knife and a small basket. She was about to enter the woods when Maggie called after her with yet another warning.

"Watch out for copperheads! Look before you thrash around in those boggy places."

The thought sent prickles up Noreen's back and made her scalp crawl. Well, she thought wryly as she plunged into the clammy cool of the woods, the serpent I'm looking for will not be hard to find.

After she had gone a few hundred yards along the path, she decided to begin searching for the spear-shaped herb on her way to the meeting place. It would appear strange to Maggie if she returned later empty-handed. She found enough finally to flavor the pot, but the search cost her the better part of a half-hour. Conscious of the time, she regained the path and rushed toward the large rock.

She could see him, or rather could get a glimpse of flashes of his clothing through openings in the leafy screen. She prayed she would be able to reason with him about the hopelessness of continuing this sordid affair.

She had to duck her head to clear the last bush, and when she raised it and stepped into the mossy clearing, her eyes fell directly on the face of Irénée du Pont.

"Oh, Mr. Irénée" she blurted in confusion, using the subservient form of address she disliked so much.

"Madame Gallagher," he responded softly.

"I..." She was blushing furiously. "You startled me. I didn't expect to see you...that is, anyone..."

Du Pont spared her the further humiliation of pointless fabrication. "Please, madame, I have spoken with Monsieur Jardinere about his improper advances, and I took the liberty of waiting here in the hope that I might meet you privately."

Noreen swallowed hard, her dry tongue useless for speech. The fact of his presence here at their precise rendezvous implied how complete had been Louis's admission of their meetings. Dear God, how much had he told? She was sick with the possibility that he might have boasted of his conquests.

"Let me assure you," he went on, "that you have no fear of his bothering you again. Indeed, at this moment he is on his way to Wilmington and from there to Philadelphia to await passage to France." His tone was conciliatory, even kindly, the attitude of a man who was sparing a child the threat of a recurring nightmare. There was something else. He assumed an air of personal responsibility, as though he was holding himself accountable for their actions.

"I see," she said thickly.

"I realize how upsetting this must have been for you, madame, and for that I most humbly ask your forgiveness for the actions of my guest. You can be certain that he will not be afforded the hospitality of my home again."

She smarted with the thought that the man was playing the role of gentleman protector of her virtue, all the while knowing that there was precious little virtue in her to defend. He undoubtedly thought that she was here to satisfy Louis's lust once more. How she longed to declare her present innocence, to give her real reason for being in this now unlovely place. But she could not. He would have found her story hard to believe anyway. She bowed her head in spite of the frustrated anger welling inside her, in spite of the fierce pride that rankled at being so compassionately put down.

Du Pont cleared his throat to cover this awkward moment and added earnestly, "I deeply regret any embarrassment he may have caused you, Noreen. Is there anything I can do to make amends?"

Noreen spoke without raising her eyes to his, "Thank you, no." The words were almost a whisper but clipped and businesslike nonetheless.

"Well...then I will go." To ease the parting he attempted a light change of subject and pointed to the basket she clung to tightly with both hands. "Be sure to drain off the first water when you cook that poke, madame. Otherwise you could bring sickness upon your family."

When she did not respond to his unsought advice, he nodded amiably and left.

On arriving at the hotel in Wilmington, Louis Jardinere curtly dismissed Hugh Flynn without so much as a thank you. He paid for his ticket to Philadelphia, found out that the afternoon coach would not leave for two hours, and returned to the street. After a few minutes of idly looking into shop windows, he paused and checked the time registered on a clock jutting from the corner of the bank building. Suddenly alert he asked a passerby for directions to St. Peter's Church.

The three-quarter-mile walk to St. Peter's took him through a portion of the factory district and shanty quarters of the workers. He drew stares from families sitting clustered in patches of shade trying to escape the oppressive heat of their crowded houses.

When at last he reached the church and its adjacent rectory, he was let in by a brusque housekeeper and shown to a modest but comfortable study. He sank indolently into the most comfortable chair to wait for Father Reardon.

As he rested, Louis bitterly reviewed the unpleasant confrontation with du Pont the day before. He had been taken off guard, and, unfortunately, had covered his confusion by giving out too much information, trying to appear more flippantly blasé than he really felt. He wished now that he had not been so reckless, freely admitting his escapades, giving details designed to embarrass his host, going so far as to describe the heady beauty of the spot where they met.

If he had known at the start that the girl was not the one who had told, he might have been able to carry off a protestation of innocence. That would have ensured his status of houseguest of the du Ponts for the remaining weeks of his stay in America and virtually secured the cooperation of the girl, whose favors he craved more than he liked to admit. It must have been the priest, then. He should have caught it that day after the mass. There was no question that the girl meant more to him than the usual parishioner did. He had seen it in the man's eyes. He wondered if the worthy cleric had ever taken her to bed. These things were not all that unusual. Had he not himself seen proof of lechery by that sort of a curate while he was at university in Orléans? He nearly laughed aloud with mirthless humor. That was the best disguise of all, an apparently impenetrable spirituality, an indifferent, aloof chasity. How that would turn a girl's head.

Where was the man? Louis rose to his feet irritably and looked at the homely clock hanging on the wall over the mantelpiece. In little over an hour he had to meet that wretched coach. He considered forgetting the whole thing. There was little to gain by talking to the priest anyway. He knew he was simply indulging his jealousy and spite. Well, if the cleric did not arrive soon, he would leave.

As if waiting on cue, the study door opened, and Father Reardon burst into the room smiling broadly at Louis and extending his hand in friendly greeting.

Several hours later as he bumped along with his fellow passengers in the crowded coach, Louis Jardinere felt curiously refreshed. He was thinking with intense satisfaction of the remarkable confession he had just made to the priest.

It had been the most complete purging of his sins that Louis could remember. In explicit detail he had told of every sexual encounter he had indulged in with Noreen. It had been an exhilarating experience, only slightly less satisfying than the acts themselves. In the end he had identified her by name, relishing the protesting gasp of his confessor that it was improper to name other parties in confession.

By the time he had gone to the church with Father Reardon, he was convinced by the man's transparent surprise at his sudden departure that he had had no part in his incrimination. That did not matter, really. He knew there was something between Noreen and the priest, and even if it was one-sided, the prospect of slipping the knife to his little unrequited *amour* was perversely appealing.

CHAPTER 27

For Francis Reardon the week ended at the lowest point in his short ministry. He had heard two confessions, and both of them had been tragic. He had refused absolution to Noreen Gallagher as a result of what he now felt was a misunderstanding, a misapplication of his superior grasp of canon law. If ever there had been a time to temper his judgment with human compassion it was during that poor girl's painful confession. Had he by his misguided ministry plunged her into the deeper culpability of despair?

The longer he dwelled on her the more he felt compelled to rush from the church, harness Father Krasicki's mare, and whip the beast toward Chicken Alley to amend his wrong. But he knew he could not. The veil of Penance, that inviolate seal of the confessional, forbade it. Even though he knew her, and she knew that he knew, the protection of the sacrament prevented him from making any reference to confidences between the penitent and her confessor. He was compelled by his vows to put even his memories of the confession out of his mind unless she brought the subject up in a future confession.

He would have to have faith in the omniscience of the Holy Spirit to guide her. There was nothing he could do. It was in the hands of God, and he tried to find comfort in that fact.

When he thought of Louis Jardinere he was nearly swept into rage. Long before the man let Noreen's name slip into his indecent listing of adulterous acts, Francis had known that the confession was a sham. There had been no contrition in Jardinere's voice. He had actually seemed to be enjoying himself!

The fact that Francis had allowed this blasphemous charade, had been a party to it by intoning the rote prayers of absolution and blessing in his own astonished numbness, now filled him with horror and shame. What the man had hoped to gain from the mockery of the sacrament he could not imagine.

Suddenly he realized it was Louis who gave him the information that changed the color of Noreen's confession. It was then he saw the trap Louis had sprung on him. It was almost as if the man could read his mind. Why else would he have gone to such pains to commit so sacrilegious an act? He could not have known that Noreen had confessed to their sin in vain. Did he have some prescience to realize the effect the telling would have on his confessor? Could that perverse man somehow have seen into the secrets of Francis's soul?

At that moment a hissing crackle filled his ears and a jarring thunderclap exploded above the church. This time the brilliance of the flash lighted the church dead white, and a pungent smell filled the room.

"Mother of God!" Francis Reardon gasped and dashed to the holy water font, splashing his fingers in the basin. He crossed himself with the droplets and stood breathless as the cloudburst drummed on the roof above his head. "So, it's Lucifer himself has come to try me," he whispered, marveling at the thought.

Father Reardon was still quite young, as clerics go, and when he opened the door to watch the rain coursing down, he did not realize the touch of pride he felt at being thus singled out for testing.

"Maggie! Maggie!" Patrick Gallagher's voice boomed through the house as he banged through the sitting room without bothering to close the front door after him, and puffed into the kitchen.

"Where is everybody?" He darted off to the side room, peered in the open door. He crossed back through the kitchen and tried looking in the yard. Nobody.

Damn! Here he was with the grandest news in a year and nobody to tell it to.

Just then the piping laugh of his grandson drifted from the front of the house, and he looked through the open door to see the three of them—Kevin, Noreen, and Maggie—ambling along Crick Road. The two women were lugging a bucket between them as Kevin skipped ahead in the dusty roadway.

Ah, now , this was more like it. The both of them together.

He could bust the news to them at once. The excitement began to build up in him again, and he sauntered out on the stoop to meet them.

He lifted the water bucket and waved them all toward the door. "Inside now, the three of ye. I've somethin' to say."

"Well?"

He turned to face them, Maggie seated at the table and Noreen standing with the child in her arms. He cleared his throat importantly and gripped the back of a chair.

"The Mister called me in today."

He paused for effect. Maggie seemed unimpressed. Well, that was her way, wasn't it? But Noreen, why, she almost turned pale. He wondered if somehow she had guessed the good news.

"And he told me somethin' that'll turn ye both around."

"Come on, man, out with it," Maggie demanded. "Don't be keeping us in a stew."

"It's our Brendan. The Mister has transferred him permanent to the yard . . . the chief dispatcher job, supervisin' all the shipments everywhere. No more nights and weeks away from home! And a dollar more a week from when he starts! Can y'believe *that*? Why, it's a dream, it is. More pay, less work, home nights, and no more worry that he might go up in a flash like poor Murphy three years past."

Maggie clapped her hands like a child, gave Noreen a quick hug, and trotted around the table to kiss Patrick full on the lips. "Oh, you darlin' man, such a fine bit of news!"

But Noreen was the one! Patrick could not get over how much the news affected her. Why the poor thing got white as a sheet and bolted from the kitchen. He and Maggie could hear her sobbing from the bedroom.

"Maggie, is it tears of joy, or was it that dumb remark about the wagon goin' up?"

"No, don't fret on it. Like as not it's relief she feels at last. Let her be."

They ate in silence for some time before Patrick paused and smiled to himself. "'Tis a wonderful thing to see yer own flesh and blood comin' along in the world. The Mister told me himself what a good lad Brendan was, that he owed it to him to make sure he was home nights for a change."

He took another spoonful of the cold porridge and swallowed it thoughtfully. "He's a good man, the Mister is, lookin' after us almost like we was his family. I tell ye, Maggie, as long as it's in his power that man will never see us want."

"He's a fair man, Patrick, better than most, I'll admit." She looked at him directly. "But don't be makin' him out to be a saint."

"Aye, aye. I don't mean that, woman. Well, you know my meaning. . . . I'm just grateful is all."

He twisted around in his chair to listen for a minute, then whispered across the table, "She's probably just wound up with the sudden good news. That's all, don'tcha think, Maggie?"

Maggie shrugged and then nodded with a smile. She would not tell Patrick that she knew there was more to it than that.

But just what it was she wasn't sure. It was not all good either; she *was* sure of that.

Brendan made it back the day after his father got the news of his promotion. As soon as Patrick heard from the gatekeeper on his way home after work that the wagons had come in, he hurried up the road to Widow Murphy's to invite his two younger boys to the house for a celebration. The idea of having all his children under his roof again made this summer day seem like Christmas. He missed the boys, seldom saw them at work because they were true powdermen, unlike himself, a stonecutter, but it was a good thing they were doing, providing an income for Murphy's widow by boarding out at her place. The poor woman would have been shifted off to tighter quarters if she couldn't fill the house.

He spent a good ten minutes talking with the old lady about inconsequential things after first making sure she would tell the boys to come home for the gathering. The conversation was by way of making up to her for taking his sons away and leaving her to spend the evening alone. It was a small thing. He did it out of habit. It was one of the reasons people liked Patrick Gallagher.

All during the celebration that went on from the time he came home for supper until nearly midnight, Brendan tried to get close to his wife. It was impossible. If she wasn't busy with the cooking, serving, or cleanup, he was busy answering questions from one of the others, who were more excited than he about his sudden rise in the company.

What made things worse for him was that Noreen seemed so sad and reserved—almost as if she were in the company of strangers.

How he wished he had made it home early enough to take her for a walk along the Crick so they could have had a time to talk in peace and quiet. There were so many things he wanted to tell her. Most important, of course, was to ask forgiveness for the bad way he had treated her between trips. He wanted to apologize for getting drunk, but more than that, he wanted to get at the reason for his drinking in the first place. He had done a deal of thinking behind that team these past two weeks, and he realized that she was right and he was wrong in that argument they had had.

And there was more. He needed her to tell him what it was she wanted, because that had to be what he wanted, too. The sharing was what was missing, what was needed to give them what they had missed so sorely, what they never had before. He had believed that happiness was theirs, but it had been a mean, one-sided happiness based only on his pleasure.

It was more than just the job, too. He was sure of that.

By the time his brothers had left and the other three were bedded down, he and Noreen were too tired to do anything but collapse into bed. Brendan decided to let his talk with his wife wait until a better time. He also decided, with the memory of their last bedding still sharp in his mind, that it would be reasonable to postpone any tender gestures beyond a kiss. Something told him that the loving would go better once the other things were off their minds.

After he had gone to sleep, Noreen lay beside him in turmoil. When Patrick had come in with the news of Brendan's transfer, she was dumbstruck with rage and fear. How could that man du Pont have the gall to interfere so with their privacy? It had been like a slap in the face for her. So he would solve their little problem for them, would he? A simple matter of keeping the woman satisfied by sending her man home each night. She burned with the shame of it.

Of course there was also the terror that the story of her sin might slip from his lips and become known to all. Had he told Madam Sophie? Dear God, she would never go near that awful house again. Blanche could die screaming for her and she would not take a step in her direction.

Overriding all her anxiety was the simple fact that lying here beside Brendan she felt soiled and unworthy of him. He who had so abused her just a few weeks before in that mockery of love now seemed the paragon of romantic purity compared with her in her state of debauchery.

And she was confessed but unabsolved. Would her sin be somehow transferred to him as the sin of Eve was visited on all men and women? Oh, she was miserable in her ignorance. Her guilt engulfed her.

One of the concessions granted Brendan in switching from long-haul driver to supervisor of shipping was a two-day rest period with pay. This was unheard of along the Crick, and the yard was buzzing with Brendan's good fortune. The arrangement for pay without work was supposed to be confidential, but it slipped out, and Brendan took on the aura of a minor celebrity.

Noreen recognized du Pont's allowance not as a reward for extra hours on the road but as an opportunity for the Brendan Gallaghers to strengthen their marital bonds. All the same she was quick to take advantage of it. At Brendan's suggestion that they take a long walk down the Crick in the early morning, she nearly jumped to her feet.

The air was still cool here along the shady banks, and for a time they enjoyed it in silence, walking hand in hand. The smells of the Crick enveloped them. Waterlogged timbers, damp stretches of sandy loam, and rotting leaves fairly steamed in puddles of yellow morning sunlight, but they were homey, comfortable odors, quickening the senses with their mild pungency. They inhaled deeply once in perfect unison, caught simultaneously with the simple joy of breathing, then laughed together at the timing.

When they were far downstream from the house, he led her to a rock sloping out of the eddying current. They sat listening to the purling water.

At last he began to speak—a quiet torrent of words made urgent by his new awareness of her during this last separation. She listened, attentive to his every phrase, savoring the outpouring with an almost greedy absorption. The words fell like cool drops on her parched affection, quenching dry pockets like a balm.

He talked for quite a long time without letup, until he had covered every aspect of the discovery he had made about himself, then looked to her for comment. But she said nothing.

Brendan was confused by her silence. He read good things in her eyes, but wondered if he was making any sense.

"I'm not putting it well, Norrie. That I know. I'm not even certain of what I mean myself," he finished lamely, again looking to her for a response.

"You're doing quite nicely, Mr. Gallagher," she said.

"Well," he went on, "what I was hoping for was that you could help me out a bit by giving me your opinion. Here I am tellin' you how it's been me all along who has been forcing my ideas on you, and so far that is all I've been doing—telling you my thoughts." He looked expectantly at her. When she still did not reply, he added, "I don't know what else to say."

Noreen ran her finger along a worry wrinkle on his brow and gave him a light kiss on the mouth. She spoke softly. "We should have had such a conversation a long time ago."

She plucked a stem of wild rye from beside the rock and began to pluck grains from the bursting head. "Please don't misunderstand me," she said. "I am as much to blame for not sharing my fears and hopes with you." She tossed her head. "All my life I have felt trapped by things. Oh, I was happy enough as a wee one, although my mother's sadness always dimmed the fun. And I loved Papa. I still do, even when he hurts us all with the drink. You know I raised the small ones as much as Ma, because she was always looking after him, keeping him out of trouble as much as she could." She paused.

"I don't want to hurt you, now or ever, but I think part of my wanting to marry you was just to get away. Having you meant having my own little ones and my own house, and my own chance to be myself."

Brendan shrugged as if to indicate that it really was unimportant, but she could see a trace of hurt in his eye.

"I know how you felt about me, Brendan. Honestly there were times you turned my head the way you made your feelings known. And I love you for that. But I didn't understand it, you see. I mean, I didn't understand what all the heat and bother was about." She flushed with embarrassment to be speaking so directly to him.

Brendan was listening intently now. He had no idea where this conversation was leading, but it certainly was enlightening.

"Lately I have come to have some of those feelings myself," she continued. "At first I thought it was a disgrace for me to be thinkin' such things and entertainin' such feelings. They would come in the night and day when you were gone, and I found myself wanting... your having me so much I feared for my mind. Then when you came home it always worked out wrong somehow."

This was a revelation! All through his married years he had presumed that she, like all wives, was simply putting up with his needs. He had heard, naturally, in some of the more wildly graphic yarns spun by other drivers on the road, that there were some women who had itchy pants, but he had always assumed they were scarlet types. His own experiences had been exclusively those he shared with Noreen. Now he had the uncomfortable feeling that she was about to teach him the facts of life. He was not sure he liked the idea, but he was all ears.

She went on, "I feel sometimes that you're just using me. For a long time I felt that there must be something about all this bother that was more than making babies, something lovely for us both, and now I know..."

She tripped on that, realizing with horror what she was basing her knowledge on. "I just know," she rephrased, "that if you took the time to think of what is happening to me... well, it would be... much nicer for the two of us."

She had finished lamely, and he appeared more confused than ever. But she was unable to go further; her cheeks were hot with what she had said as it was. Perhaps time would bring the answer.

They sat together for several minutes in an awkward silence. At last he stood and helped her to her feet. They continued along the stream, deeper into the greenery. The air was becoming sultry with late morning heat and humidity.

"You haven't said much about my new promotion," he observed.

"I think you deserve it," she replied. "The Lord knows you gave that man faithful service."

"That's not my drift, exactly," Brendan persisted. "Have your feelings changed at all about my staying on with the company?"

She stopped walking, forcing him to halt also. "I have not changed, Brendan."

He frowned slightly. "You'll have to admit 'tis a good job with good pay."

"I'll like having you home at the end of each day like a normal husband, that's true. And I'm proud that you were picked, but that doesn't mean I like your working for that family. As to the pay, you know it's no better than you'd get anywhere for equal work."

"Seven dollars a week is what he said; I'm earning' just as much as my dad."

"That's my point, Brendan," she said. "Your father should be making more than he is. The du Ponts owe him a share of the profits if you ask me. Why he practically built every one of those mills himself."

"He doesn't think he's been ill-used. Mr. Irénée never stops praising his stone work to anyone who listens, and my dad will always have a job—and a roof over his head."

"But it's not *his* roof any longer," Noreen observed sadly.

"Well, it's as good as his anyway."

She shook her head. "No, not nearly; it *belongs* to du Pont now, and your father can use it only as long as he works for the man."

"He wants to work for no other." Brendan smiled.

"The point is—he has no choice in the matter, and when he and your mother die, neither will you. The only legacy he has left is to will you the same trap he is caught in himself."

The air was oppressive. "I'm thinking we should go back," she said.

Brendan pointed to a narrow sandy spit leading from the woods into the gentle current. "Would you be wanting a dip in me private bath?" he grinned.

Noreen looked apprehensively up and down the stream.

"There's nobody within a hundred rods," he reassured her. "We'll have complete privacy." He pulled off his shoes and stripped to his underwear.

After some hesitation she followed Brendan's lead, and in a moment they were both gasping hip-deep in the cool water. With a yell he grasped her around the waist and stepped off into the deep current. They sank together over their heads relishing the shock, then swam easily to the surface, exploding up together with laughter.

Finally tiring of horseplay they stretched out to dry in the sun. Lying beside her on his stomach, Brendan reached across Noreen's upturned face and gently brushed wet tendrils of hair from her forehead. She lay there, eyes closed against the sun, smiling contentedly. A great tenderness came over him, and he eased closer, moving his face directly over hers. The shadow of his head fell across her eyes and she opened them. He looked at her longingly but made no move until he saw acceptance in her eyes, then gently kissed her.

Suddenly she twisted away screaming, crawling frantically on her hands and knees toward the water. Her head was turned back toward him, and her eyes were fixed in terror at something near his feet. He followed the stare and recoiled himself when he saw the snake slithering away.

He was on the point of picking up a rock when he realized that it was a harmless blacksnake. Noreen crouched in the water trembling with her arms crossed, hugging her shoulders.

"It's all right, Norrie," he said and stamped his foot to drive the snake away. The reptile suddenly veered away and slid into the water. With its head arched above the surface it began a rippling course directly for Noreen.

Her eyes widened with horror, and she plunged into deeper water, thrashing desperately to escape the creature. So violent was her swimming that the snake immediately changed direction and made for the safer brush along the bank.

Noreen did not know this as she plunged farther from the shore, nor did she hear Brendan's reassuring calls. She pumped her legs harder and harder, thrashing her arms in a desperate effort to get away. She was twenty yards from shore before she stopped from fatigue. A curious perch nibbled at her ankle and she tried to scream again, but choked on a mouthful of water. It was then she felt the cramp.

It spread quickly up her leg, locking her toes and calf, then her thigh muscles in a spasm of immobilizing pain. She tried to call out for Brendan but the earth-smell of the Crick was in her nose, burning the membrane, gagging her as she sank.

Just before she lost consciousness she remembered that she was still in sin, and the weight of that tugged her down. The water grew dark and cold, and she wanted desperately to cry out with sudden loneliness and fear.

She did not feel any pain at all when Brendan roughly seized her by the hair and towed her to the pebbly shallows along the bank. She awoke slowly to the sound of his weeping and the hoarse rasping sounds in his lungs as he carried her to the bank.

Much later after they had started home, Noreen told Brendan that she would have to go into town the next day. For some "things" as she put it. He hardly heard what she said, but he was holding her especially close as they slowly made their way along the Crick.

She would feel much better about everything after getting the priest's absolution, Noreen decided.

CHAPTER 28

Noreen could hardly contain her high spirits the following afternoon, and she nearly skipped on her way back to Chicken Alley. How wonderful that old sweet man had been! She might have been talking to the Good Lord himself instead of to Father Krasicki. He had been so kind and understanding, helping her over that terrible confession, giving her the words when she floundered, making her feel that she really wasn't such a tart after all. He kept repeating that she must think of herself as good— good!—and what had happened was more a mix-up than a crime.

She was breathless remembering how her bad times with Brendan even came tumbling from her lips, and how Father Krasicki had said to be patient but to talk about it with her husband without shame. Men are sometimes dense in these things, he said. Ooh, what a saint that old priest was! She wondered how he came to know so much about man and woman stuff. Maybe the Polish were more open about such things.

The last thing Father Krasicki said to her was "Now go and be good, my little one." She smiled remembering his awkward expression. "And put these mistakes from your mind. They are now like they did not ever happen. Only good things remember."

When she got home the whole household was infected with her good spirits. She remembered the present she had hidden away from

Brendan, brought it out, and presented it joyfully to him. He was dumbfounded at such a fine and expensive gift. The household chattered on happily until bedtime, and in all those hours Noreen never once recalled her "mistakes."

But later, when she and Brendan were lying in each other's arms, the good things she did remember.

Several weeks later as the heat of summer was fading into early September and the sun was beginning to lose its contest with the longer chill of night, Patrick and Brendan were hurrying to work in the predawn half-light.

"It's a beautiful morning, Dad," Brendan observed, scooping up a stone without breaking stride and sailing it toward the misty surface of the Crick.

"Y'must be gettin' old, then," rumbled his father.

"How's that?"

"Well, it used to take a prybar to separate you from yer blankets. That is the way of it. Young people snooze their time away like it makes no difference. Old folks the likes of meself are beginnin' to add up the number of mornings left."

"Old? You should tell the mason crew! Every time I see Mickey Dougherty he's complaining that they can't keep up with you."

Patrick absorbed the compliment in silence. He would not protest, because he knew it was true. There wasn't a man on the crew who could beat him, and not a one of them was a sluggard, either.

Brendan began to whistle, turning his head to look at different things as though he had never been this way before.

"If yer not gettin' old, then it must be in love y'are."

"What is that supposed to mean?" He spoke harshly but his mouth gave way to a self-conscious grin.

"You're acting more like a bridegroom this past month than ever y'did on your weddin' day. Have you come to like marriage after all this time, is it?"

Brendan laughed. "Why, Daddo dear," he scolded, you've not been peeking in our bedroom door at night, have ye?"

"Here now, none of that! You're not so big I can't yet take my razor strop to your behind."

Patrick slowed his stride. "I've been meaning to talk with you about this very thing," he said, suddenly serious. "It came to my mind months ago that things between you and your wife was not as good as they might be." He cleared his throat. "Y'know, Brendan, the women need a tender treatment... in the loving, I mean. Their lives are not all wrapped up in babies, cookin', cleanin' house, and such." He found the ground marshy going, but pressed on. "You know that bedding a wife is not just for the comfort of her husband, if you get my meaning."

Brendan stopped dead in his tracks and waited until his father stopped and turned to face him.

"Is it instruction in the ways of making love that you plan to fill my brain with, Father?"

"That I am!"

"Aren't you about five years late?" The question implied no rancor, and Brendan smiled softly.

"Better late than not at all, they say."

"Hooo, then! You better give me a minute to collect my wits."

They resumed walking. "Can you keep a secret, Dad?"

Patrick nodded, wondering how he was going to commence the "instruction" phase of their little talk. He did not feel all that qualified himself.

"Noreen tells me that she thinks she may be with child again."

Patrick looked for a sign of teasing in his son's face but found only a delighted smile. At last he gripped Brendan's shoulders and kept repeating softly, "Fine, fine, fine!"

As they walked through the gate to the lower yards, Patrick had his arm thrown over Brendan's taller shoulders. The prospects of a second grandchild occupied him completely.

When they came to the parting of their ways, Brendan spoke soberly, "About that other thing—the instruction that you mentioned. You were right about my being dense in that." He smiled. "But I don't think you'll need to teach me after all, much as I hate to disappoint you. I already have a teacher, and if it's all the same with you, I'd rather learn the art of loving from her."

After Brendan left, Patrick could not tell if the wonderful feeling he had was in knowing about the baby coming, hearing that his son's marriage was on the mend, or realizing that he had been spared the awful job of enlightening his son in such delicate matters. Abruptly he thought of the two younger boys. God in heaven, being a father to sons was a cruel task, it was!

CHAPTER 29

Pierre Samuel du Pont de Nemours might have been plagued with gout, ingloriously expatriated, and approaching eighty years, but his enthusiasm for life and controversy was undiminished. He had definite ideas on the way a society should be run and took pains to impress them on everyone within range of his voice and pen.

Thomas Jefferson was his most celebrated correspondent, and the letters between these two men were frequent and intense. Soon after the old man's narrow escape was generally known, he had prominent visitors from Philadelphia and Washington with whom he regularly exercised debate. His favorite target was his own son, Irénée, not because he was a willing combatant, but because he was readily available under the same roof.

Irénée also represented the antithesis of his father's "Physiocratic Ideal," wherein all good things sprang from a completely agrarian society. To be within sight and smell of his son's factory enterprise was deliciously compelling. It did not matter that Irénée never returned an argument. The Eleutherian Mills were themselves all things anathema to natural human activity: they stank of brimstone, they were noisy, and they trapped owner and worker alike in an environment threatening life and limb at any moment.

"It is not that I do not think you have the welfare of your workers at heart, Irénée," he said one afternoon as they lunched with Sophie on the terrace. "You house them, feed them, clothe them better than are the 'liberated' workers at home. But the danger—"

Sophie interrupted, "They are free to choose, are they not? As independent men they are not obliged to work here."

"Ah," Pierre went on, happy that Sophie at least was rising to the bait. "Just my point. How can they make the correct choice in their ignorance and need? Is it not the obligation of the enlightened to protect the masses from ill choice?"

Sophie realized she had fallen again into the old man's trap. She looked at Irénée who shrugged the challenge away. He would not be tempted.

"In this country, dear Pierre," she went on, "we cannot presume to make choices for free men. If they decide to cast their lot with us, they will enjoy the blessings and endure the risks."

Pierre laughed happily and pointed at her. "Sophie, you sound exactly like Jefferson! He, too, considers the masses to be adult and responsible. Well, I do not share your delusion."

She rankled a bit, but she realized he was simply baiting her again. Thank goodness she could escape into the kitchen. She rose with a light smile. "I must tell Blanche about dinner."

"I must leave also, Father," Irénée said, rising. "The bank notes must be signed again in Philadelphia."

Pierre was miffed at losing both respondents. "Then you will be gone until tomorrow?"

"Late tomorrow afternoon."

Pierre sighed and made to get up himself. "Well, my son, I will make do with looking after your mills until you return. I may disagree with your enterprise, but that will not allow me the pleasure of abdicating the responsibility our station in life demands."

Irénée smiled. His father's digestion always improved after delivering an acceptance speech. He left for Philadelphia without seeing his father that afternoon, and he was well into the journey when the charcoal sheds caught fire. It was not until he reached his Philadelphia hotel that he was told about the blaze and about Pierre du Pont.

The last workman to leave the mill yard saw the smoke belch from the roof of the drying sheds. One of the charcoal ricks had reignited and set the whole thing afire. When the workman began ringing the fire bell, not only the powdermen came running back, but some of the women and children, too. Soon there was a long bucket brigade reaching from the millrace upslope to the fire. All of the du Ponts were there, swinging water buckets with the rest, and at the head of the line, choking on the smoke and singed by the cascading embers, was old Pierre.

Sophie pleaded with him to step out of line, but he refused, gasping that Irénée had left him in charge. He kept at it until, hours later, the last ember of the inferno was quenched. His face was blistered from the heat, his hands raw and bleeding, and his white hair singed black. When he tried to walk, muscle spasms seized his arms and legs, and he tumbled to the ground.

They had to carry him up to his bed, and it was there that Irénée found him in the morning. He died three weeks later, the first du Pont to be buried on the Brandywine. It was a small parcel of land called Sand Hole Woods. Not Pontiania by a long shot, but du Pont de Nemours had finally set the roots of his American colony.

October's rage of color lay in a short walk from the rectory of St. Peter's, but Francis Reardon took no joy in it. As he struggled with the wording of yet another letter to Baltimore, the futility of his request for transfer redoubled his depression. How alone he felt, and how empty of spiritual fulfillment had been these past years. He gave up on the letter, wiped the quill carefully, and closed the cover of his silver inkwell.

Francis studied the delicately engraved silver vessel, a Christmas gift from his mother, and let himself slide into reverie. Visions of Skibbereen floated into his mind and mixed with memories of the seminary, a blending of soft summer evening parties with graceful dancers, lavish gowns, waltzes, cool echoing stone cloisters, evening benedictions pungent with incense, and library shelves stacked full and high.

He sighed deeply and stepped away from the desk. His eye caught the narrow vista of wooded hills above the distant Brandywine. For some inexplicable reason he thought of Noreen Feeney. Noreen Feeney. He could not think of her as Noreen *Gallagher*. Why in God's name couldn't he rid himself of these plaguing thoughts! Her confession came to mind again, and with it the lascivious tongue of Louis Jardinere... and the images, again.

He felt his breast surge with the desire to hold her in his arms, to tell her she had been long forgiven for her sin, that he...no, He would guide and protect her with...loving embraces...

"Holy Virgin, Mother of God, Virgin most pure, House of ivory, House of gold, Comforter of the afflicted, pray for us... sinners...now."

He simply had to get out of this place, back to where he could regain control. Away from the dullness of his pointless servitude. Away from the endless apprenticeship to that tired old man downstairs.

Perhaps when the old priest retired...It would be soon; he was so infirm these days and speaking of a niece in New York. Perhaps Francis would be appointed pastor.

Francis turned the possibility over in his mind as he had so many times before. Well, it was not his first choice, certainly, but it could lead to the other. Besides, the office would provide the chance to demonstrate his worth...and it would give him direct access to his superiors in Baltimore.

The brilliance of the sunset was dying now. His hand fell on the Breviary lying open on his desk, and he picked it up automatically. The light was weak, but he read a few pages before the soft rap of the housekeeper interrupted him.

The stern-faced Polish woman struggled as usual with her English. "You, Faddah," she said pointing downstairs, "he wanna see...now."

"Thank you, Anna. I'll come right away."

As he followed the woman down the steps into the dim hall, Francis wondered what had prompted the pre-dinner conference. Usually his superior chose the evening meal as the time to gossip about parish affairs. Their other conversations were awkward and formal...and infrequent.

Was it possible that he had been transferred? Or had he been appointed the new pastor of St. Peter's? The possibilities made his heart leap, and when he stepped into the little study to confront the old priest, his palms were wet, and his throat tightened.

The pastor was seated in a rocking chair with his shawl draped across his knees. He was holding an open letter in his lap. "Ah, Francis. Thank you for coming down." He waved to the only other chair in the room. "Sit, please. I have news from the bishop."

Francis tried to make a comment, but his brain seemed frozen. He barely managed to find the chair, perched on the edge of the hard seat like a trained animal waiting to be tossed a morsel.

"You have waited a long time for news, my young friend," Father Krasicki began, his face foretelling nothing. "Well, I must not keep you longer on the point of the needle. So...I am to leave soon to New York." He spread his hands and shrugged a quick dismissal of his lifetime service. "To live now with my family till I am dead. It will be a peaceful time for me, I think."

"You have earned the rest, Father; I pray you are blessed with a long and happy retirement with your niece and her family." Francis was surprised at how smoothly he had spoken. His heart was racing, desperate to hear *his* news.

"Thank you, Francis, but not too long, I hope. An old man gets in the way of the young, eh?" He paused a long moment, letting his eyes play over Francis's face. "But there is the news for you. They want you to go to Coffee Run." He held out the open letter.

"Coffee Run...Do you mean the log cabin? The chapel west of town?"

"Yes."

Francis was incredulous. He took the letter and held it in both hands, his eyes racing over the single page. He could not concentrate enough to make sense of it and had to read it three times before the truth dawned.

"But that is not even a church, Father!"

"You have said mass there, my son."

Francis laughed nervously. "Well, yes. And so have you...a few times a year to keep the faith alive among the farm folk."

"And the powdermakers."

"Few of them. Why it is farther for them to go to Coffee Run than it would be to come to town."

"But you will make it their church. They will come to you, and you will go to them."

Francis swallowed hard. "Am I to do that and run this parish as well?"

"No, Francis." The old priest seemed surprised at the question. Then he understood. His voice was gentle and his eyes compassionate as he added. "Another priest will replace me here. It is there in the letter. A Father Keene."

Francis dropped his eyes to the letter, pretending that it held his interest, but he was fighting to control his shock. A full minute passed before he was ready to look his pastor in the eye.

"Naturally, I had thought, with your retirement..."

Father Krasicki smiled, "Naturally."

Francis Reardon went on, stumbling as he tried to regain his composure, "Such a small parish, really, and although I am young for the post, it seemed a logical..."

"Young, yes."

"Well, not *that* young. After all, Father, I have been here for some time now."

The old pastor nodded. "True, Francis, but time... is merely time. Were you thinking of experience, perhaps?"

"That, too. Certainly a parish as diverse as this—the mixing of different races and nationalities, for example. The distances I've had to cover alone should account for something." He spoke rapidly, then ground to a stop. "I was certain that they would agree with your recommendation."

"They did." The old man's voice was hushed but kindly.

Francis bolted to his feet with sudden anger before he had a chance to absorb the shock. He was embarrassed by his own reaction, which made him feel like a spoiled child denied an expected gift from an indulgent parent. What made matters worse was his own conviction that he had been unfairly cast in that role. He retreated into hauteur. "Then you were the one responsible for the denial of this post. Would it be asking too much to inquire what specific faults you have assessed in my character that I might be about mending?"

Father Krasicki cocked his head slightly and raised his eyebrows at the sarcasm in this young cleric's tone. He nearly clucked reprovingly at the pouting arrogance of his charge, but compassion overrode combativeness, and he merely smiled.

"Of course I will give you my reason. But first, please sit down. I am afraid I will get a stiff neck looking up at you."

Francis managed a curt nod to his superior and sat with elbows propped against the arms of the chair, folded hands stiffly pressed against his chin and mouth.

The old priest said nothing for a while. The silence piqued Father Reardon further until he withdrew his folded hands from his lips revealing a mouth pressed into an angry line, and flicked irritably at a speck of lint on his cassock. At last the words came.

"Francis, when we are young, the hardest thing to accept about the priesthood is giving up our independence. The trouble is that we do not realize that the giving up of independence—the taking of vows—is in itself an independent decision. The real test of our obedience, our submission to the will of God, comes much later." Father Krasicki paused to let his words sink in. From the look on the young man's face he was not making much of an impression. "You see, Francis, leaping over the wall is only the entrance into submission. It is not true service, true obedience. Real submission begins when we give ourselves over to direction by others... and I have to say now, by others who seem to be inferior to us, capable of making poor decisions."

He could not miss the sharp look Francis Reardon shot at him. Well, good, he mused, perhaps he was listening after all. He pressed to the heart of the matter. "The reason that I recommended you to a post other than the one you had set your heart on, was because you need it, for now and for later. I know you imagine yourself becoming a great theologian and teacher in the church. No, no, it's true." He waved aside Father Reardon's protestation before he could voice it. "I have watched you carefully as you preach, and I am a close student of your behavior. You have a great love of oratory and a deep pride in your control of the minds of others."

"We are all teachers of the Word, Father." The comment had a debater's edge.

"You see, Francis? You cannot resist the chance to make your point. Well, that is good. It is a good tool. But... it is not good as a way of life for a servant of the Lord."

He waited for another rejoinder and getting none went on. "I am sending you among your people, the Irish, because they need you now, and that is more important. But you also need them. You need them to listen to, to find out what life is, the Church Militant, before you go on to teach others how to minister."

"Could I not find out about life just as easily in an established parish here, or in Philadelphia or Baltimore? Surely there are as many people, *more* certainly, to listen to than there are along the Brandywine."

"Yes, too many more, I am afraid. You would be lost from them, Francis. They become a church full of audience for you. Too many for you to get to be one of them. Among the powdermen and their families you will be able to share your life with them. They will be people with names, and fears, and joys, and hopes."

As he looked at the wrinkling brow of his protégé, Father Krasicki felt that he was making some headway. He took a breath and gave his last argument. "Also, Francis, out there you will not be tempted from your study of the true priestly calling. You will be removed from the temptations of the other branch of the Church Militant."

"And what is that, Father?" asked Francis Reardon with real curiosity.

"I call it the Church Politic, for obvious reasons. There will be time for that later, perhaps. Not now. Now you must put aside letters to influential offices and princes of the church. Attend to your stewardship, Francis, and let these other duties come if God wills it so."

Father Krasicki was heartened to see a smile cross his listener's face and was positively delighted with his reply. He could hardly have hoped for more.

"Thank you, Father," Francis Reardon said, "You have turned me around in my thinking. I can see the wisdom of your decision."

Later the old priest wished that the conversation had ended on that high note. But it was not to be. His buoyant mood was dashed by Father Reardon's last question as they rose to prepare for dinner.

"How long do you think it will be, Father, before they reassign me to Baltimore?"

Although Francis had said mass twice in the log cabin chapel at Coffee Run, he had never met the Widow Toussaint who lived in the residence adjacent to the church. Both times the place had been closed up while that lady was off attending to private affairs. From what Father Krasicki had said, Francis inferred that the widow was a person of considerable enterprise, having substantial business dealings with merchants in Wilmington. Why she would be interested in living as a caretaker so far from her source of income was a puzzle to Francis, but he was not interested beyond idle curiosity and the question slipped from his mind soon enough.

Despite the lowly station of his new assignment, he was eager to get on with it. Within two weeks he had packed, made his farewell sermons, and was ready to start.

The day he chose to begin his new ministry at St. Mary's started out pleasantly enough, but before he had traveled half the ten-mile distance to the log cabin structure in his fine new parish buggy, the day had turned cold and miserable with November rain. Although the high-wheeled trap was roofed with bowed canvas, he had decided against tying on the side curtains and lap sheet before he left, and now the slanting rain had soaked him to the skin.

When he drew close to the church property, he saw firsthand why the place was called Coffee Run. The roadway led directly across the stream bed, and Francis heard the rushing sound of the run before he saw it, a rod-wide torrent so thick with topsoil it looked precisely the color of overboiled coffee.

"Whoa," he called, reining in his horse. Francis gave the crossing a wary look through the heavy rain. "Oh, well, we're wet anyway, you and I, old girl. Let's go!"

He slapped the reins over the mare's back and gave her her head. The animal half-reared and then plunged headlong into the swirling current. The sudden lurch tipped the light carriage sideways, and Francis sawed at the reins fighting to redirect his horse out of the swerve. For a moment he nearly had the tilting buggy righted, but the mare lost her footing and went down. The rig flopped on its side and dumped Francis into the muddy water.

The roiling stream was barely a foot deep over an equal depth of mushy bottom, and as he struggled to his feet he realized he was covered wih an umber slime.

His animal reached the bank just as he did, dragging the overturned buggy on its side. When she finally got it clear of the water, the axle hub dug into the bank like a plow, bringing the whole sodden outfit to a dismal halt. It was not difficult to set the vehicle upright, but he had to look up and down the banks of Coffee Run to locate all of his spilled duffel. Everything was sodden and caked with mud, and he never did manage to find one missing shoe. Fortunately the tin box holding his vestments and the precious vessels for communion—chalice, ciborium, and pax—was still lashed securely to the wagon bed. As far as he could tell, they had not been submerged.

He limped up behind his sorry-looking horse and swung into the soggy cushion. Taking the reins he snapped them easily on the mare's spine.

"Let's try again, Thunder. Get up," he spoke softly.

The old mare swung her head around and began plodding down the road. Francis huddled on the seat and began to feel the chill for the first time. Each bump of the road sent a cold squish of muddy water from the seat into his crotch. More than anything he hated losing the shoe. He had another pair packed away, but these were his best. His teeth began to chatter, and he knotted himself against the wind-driven rain. It had begun to get dark, and he peered anxiously ahead for a sign of light from the mission. He hoped the housekeeper had built a fire.

The road angled left through a lumpy patch of brier and led directly to a spit of virgin timber at the crest of a low ridge. Francis recognized the lane immediately and squinted through the murky twilight for the squat outlines of the mission church. The house lay a few hundred feet farther away, but he could see nothing through the blurring rain. They were well beyond the chapel, passing it unseen, when he smelled wood smoke and caught a flare of sparks from a chimney directly ahead. Thunder must have smelled a barn, too, for she picked up to a trot and nickered. An unpainted picket gate stopped her as the carriage drew abreast of a sloping porch set on the side of the house. A small shed was dimly visible to the rear. There were no lights. The interior of the porch was inky dark, and Francis could barely see the outline of the one-story building.

"Come in, Father, out of the rain."

It was a female voice, strongly French accented.

"Thank you...yes," he stammered through chattering teeth. "But is there a place I can take my horse?"

Laughter tumbled musically from the porch, warm and rich. "I'll see to that. Come in. I have supper and a fire." She laughed again, a light crooning laugh that sounded foreign but oddly familiar to the priest. He liked the sound. He climbed stiffly from the buggy, unlashed his metal trunk and, hefting it and the sodden bag of clothing, felt his way to the nearly invisible steps of the porch. His stockinged foot was numb with cold.

The figure on the porch suddenly materialized as she pushed open the door to a small room brightly lighted by a new fire blazing in a corner hearth. She came closer to reach for the sopping canvas bag, and as Francis released it to her he saw that she was black.

"'Allo, Father Reardon," she said. "Look at you!" She dumped the bag beside the door and looked him up and down. Then shaking her head and clucking, she took him by the arm and pushed him into the room.

Francis stumbled in. He was having trouble reconciling her accent with the fact that she was Negro.

"Here," she directed, pulling him closer to the fire and pointing to a spot on the planked floor. "What happened to you, man? You will have to get out of them clothes quick!"

She darted through a doorway leading into another room and came back carrying a huge tattered quilt. She dumped it at his feet, and marched out to the porch. Before she slammed the door shut, she ordered, "Get out of all your clothes, and wrap up in that comforter—every stitch now. I will see to the horse."

Francis dearly wished for the privacy of his own room as he stripped obediently to his goose-fleshed nakedness, but the warmth of the fire was enough of a prod to get by his squeamishness. He wondered where the housekeeper might be, and who the old Negress was. Father Krasicki had not mentioned that anyone but Mrs. Toussaint was to live in the rectory.

The black woman was gone for such a long time that he began to wonder if she had been able to manage unhitching the horse. She was quite old, how old he could not tell. Some of the people at Skibbereen had been ancient, and he had never been able to guess their ages.

She burst in at last, in time for him to be dry, warm, and doubly embarrassed standing before her naked except for the ragged comforter. She grinned and laughed.

"I'll find you a shirt and pants."

Francis could hear her thumping around in the darkness of the adjoining room. After some moments she came back with an armload of clothing. "Come with me and I'll show you where you sleep. You can get dressed while I serve out our supper. Humph. Unless it is all cooked dry in the pot."

"Whose clothes are these?" he said, following her. "I thought the Widow Toussaint lived alone."

They were in a short hall barely lighted by the flickering fire at their backs. The woman unlatched a door at the end, opening it on a spacious bedroom illuminated by a single oil lamp set on a rather well made chest of drawers. The high bed was covered with a new version of the quilt Francis was wearing. The bed's four corner posts gleamed like cherry candlesticks, satin finished and intricately carved. Across from the chest, a matching armoire stood against the wall. Francis was impressed. The finery of the room seemed a gross contrast to the severe simplicity of the kitchen–living room.

"They used to be Pierre Toussaint's before he died."

Francis wondered if the Widow Toussaint might not be upset to have this black handing out her husband's clothes to someone else. "I'm not sure I should use his clothing."

The old woman gave him an impatient look and snorted, "The dead leave everything to us living. Don't worry, Father Reardon, he will not bite. Hurry now and get dressed. You need to eat... and so do I," she snapped, and left him, closing the door behind her.

The clothes were a trifle oversized, and he had never worn workmen's clothing before. It was strange, but comfortable enough. He liked the thick socks especially.

Dinner was on the table in front of the fire when he came out. And after he said grace, they sat down together to eat. He was so ravenous that they were halfway through the meal before he realized that he was sitting at the same table with a Negress! It was a jarring realization, so novel that he nearly laughed outright. The food warmed his disposition, and he broke the silence.

"Do you work here often?" He wondered if she might be a slave. Probably not. Most Negroes in this part of Delaware were freed blacks. "What do they call you?"

She looked at him boldly. "You can call me Maddie, Father."

"Your accent is strange," he observed. "Were you brought from some other place?"

She laughed harshly. "Some other place! Yes, all of my people come from some other place, all right. Ah, yes, I know what you mean." Her voice softened. "I am from Haiti. Many years now." She paused to reflect and added, "It is very warm and lovely there, you know."

"That explains the French melody in your voice, the. Did Monsieur Toussaint bring you here?"

[217]

"Monsieur?" Then she laughed gently, "Oh, yes. Pierre."

Father Reardon thought it rather flip of this woman to speak so casually of the man who had brought her to America and probably freed her as well.

"And Madame Toussaint has kept you on?"

"What?"

"Madeleine Toussaint, my housekeeper. By the way, where is she tonight? I expected her to be here so that I could go over her duties with her when I arrived."

"Ah, my young Father, your old curate did not explain the situation here, eh?"

"What do you mean?"

"This house, your 'rectory,' does not belong to the church."

"I'm sorry, but I do not understand," Francis said. "Why all of this property..."

"Belongs to the Widow Toussaint," Maddie said evenly. "And she makes a gift of it for the new curate as a guest in her house... rent and board free."

Francis was startled. How could he have misunderstood? He felt suddenly like a beggar. And here he sat decked out in the castoffs of his landlady's deceased husband!

"I must arrange to have my wardrobe dried and brushed clean. This will not do at all." He stood up from the table and looked down at the old woman. "Maddie, do you think you could clean up and press some of my clothes? I realize it is late, but I would certainly not want her to see me like this under the circumstances."

The old woman looked away into the collapsing embers of the fire. She was fighting some inner agitation Francis could not quite figure out. When she looked back at last, she pointed to his chair and spoke with quiet restraint.

"Finish with your meal, young Father," she said. "there is no need to be worried about the clothes. I will care for them tomorrow when it is light and the sun comes out again."

"But when will Madame Toussaint re—"

Maddie shook her head to silence him. Her look was mixed with sadness and pride as she put him in his place.

"You are *my* guest in this house, Father. I am Madeleine Toussaint."

CHAPTER 30

Maggie Gallagher stood at the front window swabbing the soot from the chimney lamp as she peered anxiously into the gloom outside. "And now it's snowin' is what it is!" she grumbled, turning her back on the window and snapping the chimney over the guttering flame of the lamp. She gave the wick a swift twist to adjust it lower, and carried it to the kitchen table.

"They'll be all right." Noreen smiled. "They're both big boys, y'know."

Maggie looked down at her daughter-in-law as she sat working with a needle and thread on a torn shirt.

"Aye, 'tis *boys* they are, true enough, and that's what has me worried. Pickin' the worst day of the year to go traipsin' through the wilds with that musket of Denis Feeney's."

"I wish I could have gone with them," Noreen said. "It would be exciting, I think. Different."

Maggie snorted, "Now *that's* daft, girl. Who ever heard of a woman luggin' a gun through the woods to shoot at God knows what? And you five months gone with child. Is it affectin' your brain?" She chuckled and shook her head.

"I don't know," Noreen said seriously, "but sometimes I think I should have been a man. . . . Of course, there are exceptions," she laughed, patting her swelling abdomen, "like this. I don't think I would trade this for the excitement the men have."

"Well, girl, I'm glad those days are over and done for me, and that's the truth. God help me if the devil prompts me tongue, but each one of me babes was misery to carry and a terror to birth, and that includes your dear Brendan."

Maggie felt like biting her tongue, then. Oh, me and me big mouth, she thought, to put the bad luck on her when she has one in her belly this minute! But it was too late to pull back the words. "Agh, don't be listening to this old woman, Noreen! None of it counts anyway when they're in yer arms at long last wailin' and suckin' away like little pups. It's a miracle that puts the discomfort to rest, or should, forever out of mind and heart. I didn't mean it like it sounded . . . just the foolish blather of a woman worried for her men."

"You shouldn't. . . . Worry about them, I mean. With them out there having a good time in the woods."

"Well, I hope they didn't spend the day shootin' holes in trees. The powder and shot cost three days' pay. They better bring home meat bigger than a squirrel, I'm thinkin'!"

"Daddy wanted to go with them, you know. He was glad to lend Brendan the musket, but he would rather have been toting it himself. I'll bet he comes over later to see if they had any luck."

"Well, if Denis had gone with them, I would have reason to worry the more, now wouldn't I?" Maggie chirped, "You've eased me mind, Noreen."

Noreen's eyes darkened. "Daddy has not been drinking nearly so much as—"

"Oh, Noreen, that's not what I mean," Maggie said, cutting her off. "It's his game leg, I mean."

"It's all right, Maggie. Drink or bad leg, it's all the same. The poor man's a mess. I was only thinking how much the excitement would mean to him . . . the freedom to be unlocked and rambling somewhere without a road or path that led to Dorgan's or the mills."

Maggie pulled out a chair and sat at the table next to Noreen before she answered. "You put it right, girl; yer father never took to harness in all his life. When I was just little, I used to wonder if he would ever live to manhood, with the whalin' he used to get from his daddy. The chores, y'know, he never got around to them, it seemed. Always playin' tricks on people bigger than himself."

Noreen broke the thread and tied off her last stitch. Folding the muslin shirt carefully, she placed it on the table and looked directly at Maggie. "What happened to him in Ireland?"

"You mean about the prison?"

"No," Noreen spoke thoughtfully. "Well, maybe it was that, too, but there was something else... something he and Mother know that they never talk about."

"Well, he was well thought of, yer dad, in some places." Maggie laughed nervously. "Different ways of doin' things for the Cause, y'know."

"I've heard of that, too. Not from him, of course, but Mother tells us things. The English keeping him in jail for blowing up a building when he was very young."

Maggie said nothing more, and after a moment Noreen pressed on. "You knew him as a child, didn't you?"

"Oh, I did that. Both of them. Yer daddy lived in a cottage I could see the roof of from my own. Yer ma was a bit farther away, but, yes, I knew 'em both from when we was kids."

"Well?" Noreen prompted. "Was there anything else? Sometimes I swear I can see a hurt in his eyes that almost makes me want to cry myself."

Maggie shook her head, but Noreen could see that it was not an answer. The older woman's eyes had clouded over with the memory of something unpleasant.

"Your face is as clear as the page of a book, Maggie. What is it that you would have me not know about my own father?" Her eyes held Maggie's as she put the question again, and this time she saw not pain but agitation and a trace of fear. Finally Maggie looked away. Her voice trembled in a whisper.

"Your father was little more than a lad when he set that bomb at the English armory. You know about that. A young firebrand he was, the local hero. Aye, but it was just another prank to him, even if the ones who set him up to do it was grim enough about the business. But he was the choice, bein' so clever as he was with fooling around with that infernal stuff.

"The others wanted him to blow up the barracks where all the troops were sleepin', but Denis Feeney would have none of that.... It wouldn't be fair, y'see. Besides, he wouldn't hurt a louse, that boy, and he said to all those older men in the revolt, that he would blow up the armory with all the guns and powder instead, even if it meant crawlin' half the night under the noses of the guards. So they had to go along with the lad.... After all it was himself that was doin' the thing, so how could they tell him how to risk his own body and soul? And he had the priest on his side, too. From what I heard, the father raked them all over the coals just for plannin' to take another life, even if they was all English black buggers, all of them."

Maggie's face was beginning to lighten with the telling of the story, all of it familiar enough to Noreen. She began to wonder if Maggie was protecting her from details she didn't know.

"Yes," she injected, being careful not to seem impatient, "the story has been told to me by others."

Maggie looked at her sharply. "But never by yer dad, nor in his company, I'm thinking."

"No, that's true. Daddy never wants to talk about it at all."

"Small wonder, poor man," Maggie murmured and slipped into her gray mood again. "Ah, girl, it's like a knife cuttin' into me breast to drag it all out."

"Mama Gallagher, there's nobody here who can hurt Daddy for what he did against the English years ago in the old country. In fact, the way things look these days, most Americans would think him a hero, too."

Maggie shook her head. "It's not bein' hurt by any living man that bothers Denis Feeney. And he can't be hurt any more than he already has." She shook her head again, clicking her tongue, and went on.

"Well, he did it, all right. He set his bomb right under their noses and blew that whole magazine full of guns and powder into dust. There was a hole in the ground where it stood that was as deep as a man's waist. And him high-tailin' out to the hedges and miles away before they got their wits together to go after him."

Noreen added, "And that was when they captured him and sent him to the prison."

"No. He was never captured, girl. He gave himself up to those awful men."

"He surrendered?" Noreen had never heard *that*. "Why would he turn himself in?"

Noreen's whispered question was insistent enough for Maggie to give up any idea of not spilling the whole mess, now that she had gone this far. The lard's in the hearth, she thought grimly, and there'll be fire before 'tis out.

She reached across the table and took Noreen's hand in her own. "He turned himself in to save his brother, God rest his soul."

"My Uncle Mike, you mean? Daddy's older brother?"

Maggie shook her head. "No, child, his brother Tim is who I mean."

"Tim?"

"Denis Feeney's twin, your Uncle Tim."

"But I have no uncle named Tim."

"Not living, no; but your uncle all the same."

Noreen was perplexed. "You mean that Daddy had a twin brother, truly? But why keep it such a deep secret? Nobody, not even Ma, ever breathed—"

"Small wonder, girl," Maggie murmured, cutting her off. "I sometimes forget meself, and that's a blessing, though 'tis a black thing to forget the dead in prayers."

"But what did he do? Was he that bad a person?"

"Ah, cut yer tongue, girl! He was the sweetest young man in all Kildare, kind and gentle, tall and strong as a bullock, he was, but never took advantage in a fight."

"Then why all the dark secrets? I feel that I've been cheated of my kin."

"That y'have, God help us."

A clump of snow tumbled down the chimney flue and plopped sizzling on the fire. They watched the white fluff melt into the blackened embers and hiss into a ribbon of steam lacing easily upward through the yawning vent back into the night. In a moment the charred wood glowed red again.

Maggie got to her feet and pulled a gnarled log from the wood box. Her Patrick would not be pleased with all this talking about Denis Feeney's private business with his own daughter. She probably shouldn't even tell him about the conversation with Noreen, but she knew she would. It was the way they were.

"Denis had been to hiding for a week by the time they got word to him," she went on with the story. "It was terrible news. They had picked up his brother, Tim, and put him in the dungeon. It had been a mistake, y'see. They had just gone out to the Feeneys' place and picked him up."

"Was Daddy's brother in on the bombing?"

"Oh, no. Tim would have none of that. There used to be the sayin' that Denis was the imp and Tim the angel. Denis would commit the sin, and Tim would pray that his brother wouldn't be snatched off to hell." Maggie smiled at some remembered prank, then sobered and went on, "Oh, everybody swore Tim wasn't the one, and there was an awful row, with them with guns and us with clubs, and somebody might have got killed if Tim had not told all of us to be still, that he was goin' quietly and all would be well, just to wait and see."

"But how could they make such a mistake even if they were twins? Daddy is so short and thin; if his brother was as big as you say, it would be easy to tell them apart."

"Ah, Norrie, y'don't understand the way it was. We was nobodies to the likes of them. Just dumb brutes workin' their lands, and them with the guns to keep control."

"What did Daddy do?"

Maggie smiled at Noreen. "You know what he would do, don'tcha? He just gave that funny laugh he has when he loses a bet, like it was nothing very big, and started off to clear up the mistake. Of course, they was all at him not to go, because it would be his neck if he did, but he just stood there lookin' at them and sayin', 'Is it me brother that should hang for my doing? Is that what ye want?'"

"So he turned himself in?"

"Aye. Marched right up to the place like he owned it and told them bold as brass that he was the one who blew up their powder and guns, and they must turn his innocent brother loose and be quick about it."

Noreen grinned at the audacity of her father's act. How they must have retold the story in Ireland. "How do you know, Maggie? I mean did Daddy tell—"

"The priest. The priest was there through the whole thing." Maggie's face was beginning to take on an ashen color. "They told Denis that they would be turning his brother loose but that they needed him—your father, I mean—to be a witness. Then they dragged him out into the courtyard of that place and made him climb up the steps of their gallows. It wasn't till he got up on the platform that he saw Tim standin' there with the rope around his neck."

Noreen's eyes widened, and she felt her own cold fingertips on her throat. Maggie was hunched over the table, hands folded before her. She had forgotten for the moment that Noreen was even there.

"He screamed, Denis did, screamed that they were makin' a mistake. The priest tried to reason with them. But all they said was that they would not be fooled into releasin' a ring leader in exchange for a nobody."

"Oh, Daddy . . ."

"Then Tim just looked at them and said, 'It's all right, Denis,' and they pulled the trap."

"Mother of God!"

"Denis was wild. The priest said he jumped off the scaffold and fought to get at Tim's body hangin' there, and when they took the rope off the poor boy at last, Denis put it around his own neck and begged them to hang him, too. But they said that only one had done the blast and they had taken care of him. In the end they made him haul the body home to their mother's door."

The two women sat in silence for a long time. Maggie leaned against the table, her arms folded tightly against her chest, staring at the sputtering flames wrapped around the decayed log. Questions whirled through Noreen's head so fast she could not formulate even one before another spun into place. Finally Maggie spoke again.

"After that your dad was like a madman, off to do whatever wild thing the others would set him on. I don't know how much devilish work he did, but whenever a powder keg went off in Ireland, it was him they said had lit the fuse." She sighed and looked squarely at Noreen. "He courted your mother during those wild years, and they married. For a time he was able to settle down in a town far away in the west country, where you and Blanche were born. But soon those rebel lads were after him again with plans. . . . It was no good. It was Patrick who talked him into comin' here with us. Denis was just waitin' to be asked. Your mother was at wits end by then, o'course. The romance of marriage to a hero is thin stuff when you've got little ones to feed."

There was a commotion at the back door, and Brendan came

tumbling in with Patrick, both of them covered with snow and soaked to the skin. They were jubilant over their good news: a fat whitetail buck with enough meat to last both families for weeks. Even the long afternoon's work of lugging the deer through miles of snowy woodland had not dampened their spirits.

"We have to dress him out," they announced joyfully, bustling out into the swirling snow and lugging the carcass to the old elm in the backyard.

Maggie set about dishing up the supper while the hunters cared for the deer, but Noreen continued sitting until they came in again, yielding finally to Brendan's insistence that she come to the door and look at their prize. He would never know why she turned away from the sight of the drawn stag, twisting slowly at the end of the rope around its neck. For the rest of her life she never really liked venison.

Later that evening when the men had retired and she and Maggie had finished the last of the kitchen cleanup, she kissed her mother-in-law on the cheek.

"Thank you for telling me, Maggie," she whispered. "I know that you were trying to save me from the hurt, but maybe knowing why will help me to understand him . . . and make his life easier in some way.

Maggie nodded, looking as exhausted as if she had dragged the deer home singlehandedly herself. Noreen saw the fatigue and added, "And I know that my father is just your friend, but the memory must have been painful for you, too, and I want you to know that I understand and give you thanks for that."

Maggie sighed and shook her head sadly. "No child, I don't think you do—not the whole of it, I mean. It goes too deep." Then she brightened. "Anyways, now y'know the truth, and as they say, the truth never hurt nobody. Now, to bed with ye."

As she turned down the lamp and began letting down her hair to snuggle in beside her snoring Patrick, Maggie reflected that a bit of the truth sometimes was best left unsaid. After all these years there was no point in mentioning that Patrick Gallagher had been her second suitor.

Tim Feeney had been the first.

CHAPTER 31

After the first few weeks at Coffee Run, Francis had managed to adjust to the primitive appointments of his log cabin church. He was even able to see a measure of romance in assuming the role of country pastor. He was his own boss, and Maddie, who seemed to be not only capable but also surprisingly well lettered, anticipated and cared for his every need.

There was one big problem: he had nobody coming to Sunday mass.

Well, that was not completely true. Maddie always came, and a few farm people dropped in. But for the most part the church was treated as a temporary outpost that the handful of Catholic families visited infrequently. To them it was a kind of spiritual fort that they inspected occasionally to make sure it was there and ready to shield them in case of some surprise attack by Satan or impending death— or both.

Although he did not like to admit it, Francis rather enjoyed the solitude. It was like being cloistered without a library. After he had adapted to the need to wear practical clothing, particularly a pair of heavy boots, he began taking long walks in the woods and fields surrounding the place. But after a month he realized that it would not do, and when Maddie prodded him to his priestly duty, he knew he had to face up the responsibility of encouraging church attendance with personal contact.

"They won't come if they are not invited, Father Francis," she said, making no attempt to gloss over her accusation.

"But they know I'm here," he protested, feeling a bit like an errant child. "I would think their faith should be enough encouragement."

Maddie shook her head. "No, it is not enough. These people have been without a church for a long time. They have other things on their mind: getting food on the table, working through the long days of the week, fixing the roof, caring for the old ones and the sick children. You cannot keep yourself in a box like some shining jewel waiting for them to find you."

Francis did not like the comparison. "It is not I who is the 'shining jewel.' I am but an instrument who serves."

"Ah, and how do you serve? Is it the mass that you say to God? This mass that is a private little thing you keep for yourself and him?" She turned her wrinkled brown face up and rolled her eyes to the ceiling.

Francis felt his ears grow warm and began to think he had let the matter get out of hand. He had to struggle to keep his voice even. "I shall pray for guidance to be a better inspiration."

Madeleine Toussaint raised her narrow shoulders up to her ears in exasperation. "Pray, pray! That is all you do, I think. Pray and read! Go out and find your people; that is what I mean."

She could tell from his face that he was hurt, and she decided to drop the matter. As spoiled as he was, she liked him. He was filled with a goodness she could feel, and that overcame his ignorance of practical things.

"Oh," she said, suddenly remembering, "there was a letter for you today in town." She rummaged through her deep satchel until she located a thin packet bound with a blue ribbon and sealed with wax.

He reached for it eagerly, breaking the seal with shaking hands. Maddie gathered up her satchel and left the room.

He read the letter quickly:

My reverend and beloved son,
    This will be but a brief letter since I am between coaches at Fredericksburg on my way home to Baltimore. I have been to Skibbereen to negotiate the final papers of the sale. It is com-

plete, thank God, with the money safely banked. At least you can jubilate in the knowledge that your widowed mother will not be destitute in her old age! The monies are adequate for me to maintain the new place in Baltimore where I shall be among old friends until the Lord takes me to your father, rest his soul.

I could not bear to visit with the "people" on the old place. It would have been too hard on them, and me, to endure a second farewell. The La Roche couple from New Orleans seem to be capable of running the plantation, and they have plans to put it on a profitable basis. I am sorry to report that they were not agreeable to conferring documents of manumission to the servants as was your wish, my generous son, but Mr. La Roche assured me as a gentleman that the families would be kept intact, and the matter of conferring freed slave papers would be decided favorably some time in the future.

Perhaps, it is better that they stay on for a while. The poor things would come to certain misfortune were they given papers and tempted to launch out on their own. In their present circumstances they are fed, clothed, sheltered, and protected from being preyed upon by scurrilous rascals luring them into disaster.

Upon arrival in Baltimore I shall seek another interview with the monsignor to plead the matter of your transfer to a more promising post.

Remember me in your prayers.

I am always your proud and loving

Mother

He read the message twice before refolding the sheets and placing them in his coat pocket. A wave of melancholy flooded over him, and he felt truly unmoored from the past, more than when he had first left for the seminary years before.

Francis made a sincere effort to gather in his flock, and made a number of trips to the Brandywine to encourage regular attendance at Sunday services. It was discouraging work, though. Hardly any of the Irish had transport. Unless he could talk a few of the local farmers into putting their heavy wagons and teams to work, mass attendance was going to stay as it was. It would be hard going to convince these working folk that they should exercise themselves further on Sunday with a fourteen-mile walk.

He had approached one farmer about using his wagon, but the man was direct and firm in his refusal.

"The team needs the Sabbath rest more than me, Father," he had said. "I work 'em to the limit as it is. Why, I'd have to give 'em Monday and Tuesday off to rest up."

The only bright spot in his day had been the visit with Patrick Gallagher's family. Maggie and Noreen had invited him to stay for noon dinner, a timely invitation he had more or less arranged by calling upon them at eleven-thirty, and although the men were away at work, the visit had been rewarding.

He was surprised to note that Noreen was with child again, surprised and pleased. In the months since that unfortunate affair in the confessional, he had had more than a few days of doubt as to his capacity as religious counselor. He had seen her at mass only once since that time, but she did not have the aura of the unrepentant sinner. And now she appeared radiant. Perhaps she had set the matter right and confessed to the old pastor. He dearly hoped so.

The old dark feeling came over him again, the man-boy warring with his spirit. What was the terrible yearning that he felt each time he saw or even thought of this woman? He must study his feelings the better to disarm them. Was not that the best way to fight temptation?

"No, no. Drive it out of mind the instant it glimmers lest it take hold. The demon is shrewder than thou."

"But the feeling is no crude pleasure of my male appetite. It rings of the longing I have for Thee! I do not lust after the flesh. Are we not all one in Christ? And is she not among your loveliest creatures?"

Lovely, yes lovely. In any state of womanhood she was lovely— virginal, married, with child as she now was. In a filled church, with his face to the tabernacle, he would feel her presence. This noon as he was letting the horse amble along Chicken Alley, he had felt her nearby before she stepped out of the springhouse near the Halloran place and he had called out to give her a lift to Gallaghers. He could feel her breathing from across the room, the fragrant warmth radiating from her graceful body. . . .

As he made his way back to Coffee Run, he barely caught his arm before laying on the lash again.

"Poor beast, poor Thunder. I'm sorry old girl. The whip was meant for me. I'm the one who should be wearing the reins."

When he turned off the main road beside the church building, Francis noticed a saddled mare tethered at the front gate of Madeleine Toussaint's house. It was in a lather and still blowing. Someone had been in a hurry to get here.

"See that, Thunder. Consider yourself well-treated."

He hurried with the unhitching and turned his horse into the shed. He noted with pleasure that Maddie had forked the manger full of hay. The woman was a marvel of efficiency.

When he swung around to the front of the house, a young man in a naval officer's uniform was preparing to remount. Francis had the distinct impression he was in a hurry to leave, but on seeing the priest, he turned from the horse and approached with a casual salute.

Maddie was on the porch, and she stepped down between them.

"Father Reardon, may I introduce Mr. Craith? Mr. Craith is in the merchant sea trade."

"Ah, then your ship is in Wilmington?" Francis really wanted to ask what a seafaring person was doing in Coffee Run, of all places.

"Yes, Father. Tied up at the terminal there, and putting out tonight."

"I see."

"He's in a hurry to catch the tide, Father," Maddie prodded.

"I see." Francis smiled. "Well, don't let me hold you back. And have a safe voyage."

"Thankee, Father. I'll be off, then. Good day to you both." He mounted and spurred the hot animal down the lane, disappearing in the dusk before he reached the road.

"So, Madame Toussaint, a gentleman caller from the high seas?" Francis made an exaggerated bow and gestured for her to return to the porch. "Let's get inside before we freeze."

Francis did not pry, and they ate supper speaking mainly of his own difficulties with getting the powdermen's families to the church. When she was about to retire for the night, however, Maddie satisfied his curiosity . . . partly.

"Mr. Craith is one of the people I do my business with. He arranges for shipping goods, and carries letters sometimes."

"To Haiti, I suppose?"

"Yes, and other places."

"What does he import?"

"Oh, sugar... things like that. Sometimes rum, too." She laughed, "It does not make me rich, but Toussaint will not starve, eh?"

Francis shook his head. "I wonder that you do not live closer to town. Wouldn't it be much easier to run your little business if you were near the commercial section?"

She frowned, but her tone was philosophical. "It is not good for people see a black woman doing business. It is better for me to stay out here. The money is the same, eh?"

"I suppose you are right, Maddie."

"Ah, but you *know* that I am right, young Father. You most of all."

Francis looked up, mildly surprised at her comment. She was watching him closely.

"Your family has slaves in Richmond. Is it not so? Before you were the priest, you owned slaves."

Francis was stunned. Had she read a letter from his mother? What had Father Krasicki told her? Suddenly he felt suspicious and guilty at the same time.

Maddie smiled and spoke softly, "It is no great mystery. We can tell, can we not, from the first. There is a mark on both of us that we cannot hide from each other. That first day you came in here, you knew me for what I was because you were the slaveowner. And I, I knew you for what you were... because I was a slave."

"But..." Francis flustered, "but we freed our people, I saw to that...."

"Oh? Well, then, you freed your blacks, and I freed me, eh? So we are even.... Almost." She gave him a penetrating look and turned away. "Good night, young Father."

Francis sat staring into the fireplace long after there was not a single ember to see. He had caught himself in a reckless, unnecessary lie.

His knees were numb before he allowed himself the miserable comfort of crawling into bed. There had been poor solace in the prayers.

Madeleine Toussaint drifted off to sleep after some turning of her own. It was too early to tell, but she would have to be very careful in the future. She wondered what the young father would think... or do... if he knew that the tiny basement of his church was a station for the Underground Railway.

CHAPTER 32

The long winter of 1817–18 was weathered better by the powdermen and their families along the Brandywine than by their less fortunate neighbors in nearby Wilmington. A flood of manufactured goods from Europe, particularly by an England anxious to regain the American market lost in the war years of 1812–15, threatened to bankrupt many industries begun at the turn of the century. Although the du Ponts were not without their own financial stress, their problems were largely due to the cost of expanding operations at the mills.

With expansion westward increasing feverishly, there was a steadily increasing market for rifle and blasting powder. Canals were being dug, highways were being built, and farms were being cleared out of the great forested regions west to the Mississippi Valley. Whenever a rock was too large to dislodge, or a stump too deeply rooted to pull out, du Pont powder was measured out to shatter the obstruction in seconds. Hunters were employed by the construction companies, and using high-quality rifle propellant from the Eleutherian Mills, they brought down enough game to feed droves of hungry workers.

After the New Year began, Irénée du Pont seemed to be in a continual state of agitation. He had little time for his family, and this grieved him mightily. The industry that he had hoped would give him wealth and leisure was ironically depriving him of both because of its success. He was forever at wits' end trying to produce new explosive and to remanufacture a veritable mountain of surplus war powder repurchased from the government.

The costs were staggering. Every week he was obliged to ride on horseback thirty miles to Philadelphia to attend to banking negotiations. His liquid assets were nil, and he had a payroll of nearly one hundred workers to meet as well as new construction costs besides. Profits were almost within reach. He could see the golden prospects, and so could his lenders, but in the meantime he was at their mercy.

For twenty-year-old Tim Feeney the winter was most satisfying. The pressures of the cooperage to produce enough kegs to hold the increasing volume of manufactured powder gave him the chance to learn the trade and advance from sweeper to apprentice cooper. By January he had a reasonable collection of tools, paid for out of wage credits at the company store, and he was nearly as adept at swinging his curved adze as the veterans were. At day's end his pile of finished staves was a trifle smaller than those of the others, but the workmanship was as fine or better.

Other prospects were bright as well. Had not Meg Farrell as much as said that she would take kindly to their keeping company? It was a bit early to plan on anything permanent, but Tim was careful to check his small savings on the paymaster's ledger and add something each week. It would be nice to start off married with a nest egg.

The only thing, really, that marred his life these days was his father's habit. It was getting worse by the month, he thought, despite his mother's optimistic statements to the contrary. More than once she had had to plead with the Mister to keep the old man on. It was a shame. He would never think of bringing Meg into his parents' home as a bride as long as his father was a slave to the jug.

The first day of March dawned clear and brittle cold. Patrick Gallagher chafed with impatience as he and Brendan made their way to the yards. Ever since the onset of bad weather, he had been idle at stonemasonry and had to fill in at odd jobs in the packing house, the drying sheds, or the powder magazine. All the while he was dreaming of getting the foundations started on a new series of buildings that were scheduled for construction as soon as the frost was out of the ground.

Patrick spat in disgust. "I shoulda been an Eskimo. They build with blocks of ice, I'm told. C'mon, lad, we have to swing by the widder's place. I promised Sean and Joseph we'd pick them up."

"Are you working in the magazine, then?" Brendan asked, since it was some distance inside the yards and his two brothers had regular jobs there storing kegs of finished powder.

"Aye." He raised his lunch pail. "I think it's the company of yer Ma's cookin' they want to keep—not meself. I don't see 'em from one hour to the next, but at the noon bell they gather about me pail here like two flies."

The following day was warmer. A light rain fell in the morning, and everyone along the Crick woke to the groaning of the ice breakup and the roar of muddy water cascading over the lower dam. Patrick was ecstatic. A week or two for things to dry out, and he would be directing the slip operators and pick-and-shovel crew as they opened the ground for his foundation work.

Brendan was nearly as happy with the change as his father. Soon shipping would be active on the Delaware, and he could begin moving out some of the powder orders that had been dangerously backlogged since fall. He didn't like to dwell on the potential power of all that explosive stored so near his work—and so close to all their homes for that matter. The big house itself was so close to the yard that Irénée du Pont frequently shouted orders to workers through a speaking trumpet from his back door.

The morning of March 19 dawned clear and calm, with no sign of the blustery winds that had swept the Brandywine for a week. The spring was not coming late after all. In fact, this Thursday dawned with the promise of being balmy. In the Gallagher home, everybody had been awake early. There was something in the air that stirred them, and the breakfast table buzzed with such animated conversation that it might have been a Sunday supper. When it was time for the men to leave for work, Maggie handed them their lunch pails with a smile. Patrick hefted his own and looked quizzically at his wife,

"What's all this, now? Is it dinner for my whole gang?"

Maggie looked blank for a moment and then sighed. "Oh, I forgot you'll not be working with the boys today. I fixed a bite for the two of them."

"All right, woman, I'll lug it over to them though it will cut into me own eating time sorely." Then he laughed to cancel out the gripe.

He and Brendan were in high spirits as they marched down the rutted roadway, which was already showing signs of drying out. Today Brendan would finally be able to begin loading the Conestogas at the magazine and sending them toward the Wilmington wharf at half-mile intervals. The spacing was another precaution they took to avoid a multiple calamity in the event something went wrong.

The mood at Tim Feeney's home was not nearly as bright. His father had been up all night drinking. About the time other workers were rising, Denis was collapsing. Nora turned to young Tim, urging him to fill in "just once more" so that his dad would not be let go. The Mister had made it clear last time that if Denis's mill had to shut down because of what Nora euphemistically termed his "illness," it would be the end of the man's career at Eleutherian Mills.

Nora did not have to plead. Tim was a good lad, loyal to his daddo, and a loving son to his ma. So on the morning of the nineteenth he made only a brief stop at the cooperage and proceeded to Rolling Mill Number Three at the far end of the old upper yard works. The few powdermen who greeted him were not surprised to see him. He had filled in for Denis so many times lately that he was becoming a steady replacement. The operators in the adjacent mills no longer even bothered to check up on his work to make sure he was doing things correctly. Tim was a quick learner, though too shy to ask for help, and he would be safe enough to let alone.

He got Mill Number Three rolling on schedule after carefully following the inspection ritual and taking pains to spread precise proportions of the chemicals on the marble pan. One thing he did not check was the grating in front of the drive-shaft bearing. It was badly clogged with trash carried down by the high water from the night before, but there was still enough flow to lubricate and cool the mechanism. It would be fine if he remembered to check it in the next hour or so before anything else came along to plug it dry.

Back at the Gallaghers' Maggie followed Noreen's bustling, clumsy movements with affectionate amusement. The girl was big as a house from the ribs down, but she was in a frenzy of cleaning up the place. The baby had dropped, and that made her efforts even more awkward, but it did not slow her down much.

Maggie followed her as she hurried out the back door and propped the corn broom against the wall of the kitchen.

"Is it company we're havin' this morning? Or has the fine weather got you into an early spring cleaning?"

Noreen laughed and leaned back in an effort to ease the knotting ache along her spine. "It's silly, isn't it? I'm weary to death of this burden, but I get so fidgety at times that I can't sit still."

Maggie appraised the rounded contours of her daughter-in-law with detached expertise, then looked her warmly in the eye. "By the looks of things ye won't have much longer to wait."

"A month, I think. Perhaps less."

"Less than that. I think you'll come to childbed within the week."

Noreen's face brightened at the thought. "Ah, Maggie, I do so hope you are right!"

Buoyed with this expectation she turned back into the house and was soon attacking the encrusted sides of their cast-iron stewpot. She worked with a vengeance, and within the hour it swung from the fireplace crookneck gleaming with a black luster it had not known for years.

Work at the new construction site in Hagley Yard was not going well for Patrick. There was some confusion about the survey of one foundation ditch, and the Mister, who had gone to the bank in Philadelphia, was not available to verify what Patrick's sharp eye had seen as the needed correction. He decided to work around the problem, but that meant staying on top of the project, giving step-by-step directions to the excavating crew. Before the noon break he knew he would have to spend his dinner time measuring for the afternoon dig while the crew was eating.

At ten minutes to twelve he remembered the crammed dinner pail and sent it off to the packing house to Sean and Joseph under the arm of the young journeyman. He shouted after the departing mason, "Eat with them, lad, and bring the pail back to me after. I'll make do with the leavings." Why he had not switched pails with Brendan in the morning to avoid the inconvenience was an additional irritation.

Several hundred yards upstream Brendan was carefully checking harness and running gear of the first loaded wagon standing by the packing house loading platform. After a last look inside the canvas-covered rig, he nodded to Joe Dorgan to climb up to the high seat and begin the slow six-mile trip to the docks. As the load began to move away, he caught a glimpse of his brothers waving to him from the doorway of the building. They were flanked by rows of squat kegs of explosive stacked higher than their heads. He returned the wave and let out a low whistle. It would be weeks before he could ship enough to get that gigantic backlog down to normal inventory levels. A look at the sun told him it was too close to noon to begin with another load. Turning on his heel he headed toward the cramped freight office and his waiting dinner pail. The excitement of being productive had made him ravenous.

On the other side of the yard next to the chocolate-colored current of the Crick, Tim Feeney was also feeling the stab of hunger. Inside the rumbling mill he would not be able to hear the clang of the noon bell, but he knew the time was close. He was through with this batch anyway. Time to shut down and clean up for his break.

Moving with the deliberate slowness of a cautious powderman, Tim trudged to the door of the thick-walled mill and reached for the gear lever. In the relative quiet outside the rolling room he was able to hear the unfamiliar high-pitched whine for the first time. As he moved the handle it stopped. For a split second he froze there, both hands still gripping the long wooden handle. Then he remembered, even before the acrid smell of glowing iron reached his nostrils, before he turned to stare horrified at the ruined bearing collapsed around a cherry-red section of its mating drive shaft.

He panicked and lunged for the stopped-up grating. At every step a cloud of powder settled into a trail behind him. He covered the dozen feet to the stoppage before he could think and began clawing away the leaves and branches jammed against the iron screen.

The released water surged into the sluice, enveloping the super-heated bearing block and shaft. For an instant he felt relief, but suddenly the submerged metal exploded, showering him with bits of glowing metal. The powder on his clothing ignited, sending a sheet of flame upward from his feet. Gagging on the sulfurous smoke and writhing with the terrible heat, Tim ran blindly away from the mill. He had taken only a few steps when he collided with a low wall, cracking his shins and tumbling headlong into space. He was screaming in pain as he plunged headfirst into the turbulent waters of the Brandywine.

Inside the mill a hungry red mouth hissed malevolently and inched along, consuming a zigzag trail of black leading to the stone threshold and the dusted floor beyond.

No one saw or heard Tim Feeney in his agony, but when the timekeeper watched the hand of his old clock click off the last minute to twelve and tugged on the bell rope, the thunderous crack of Number Three blowing its roof drowned out the chime.

The concussion knocked Brendan to his knees, and the shock kept him there staring dumbly upward at the cascade of fiery rubble from the sky. He was in an open area bordered by the rolling mills on one side and the packing house on the other. When his sense returned he scrambled to his feet, anxiously plotting the landing spots of flaming bits of wood that seconds before had been the flimsy roofing parts of the blown-out mill. He was relieved to see that most of the debris was falling into the stream.

Men began to appear from every building in sight. All of them were running away from the smoking shell of Number Three. They pounded white-faced toward him, toward the loading space beside the magazine. A few began to man the pump beside the race, but when the wind shifted some sparks back toward the three intact mills, they, too, ran to join the cluster behind him.

Brendan was appalled. There was less danger by the mills. Even if they blew, the shock would be absorbed and deflected toward the Crick. The magazine and packing houses were like a mammoth bomb, a thin-shelled mountain of explosive.

He yelled to them to follow as he raced for the idle pumps, but no one budged. The men were still too stunned. Not more than a minute had gone by; in a few more seconds they would come to life, realize the danger, and scatter to safety.

They were not given the extra time.

Just as he crossed the millrace bridge and reached the pump, an ember sifted into Number Four, and it blew. This time Brendan was so close that the blast knocked him unconscious. He came to, still standing, pawing blood from his nose and ears. He was staggering in circles trying to remember what he should be doing, what was going on. Fireworks seemed to be showering from the sky, dropping all over the ground, on the crowd of men, setting fire to the wagon canvas. He thought he saw his brother Sean stamping at a smoking piece of wood.

Then there was a dazzling flash that lifted him bodily, and he lost all sense of being.

Patrick was a quarter-mile from the mill when it exploded. His first thought was for Denis Feeney, and he was out of the ditch and running toward the upper yards when the second explosion buffeted him like a silent wind before the sound of the blast reached his ears.

"Almighty God!" he gasped, feeling his knees weaken. "Two!" He was in full dash now, dead branches weaving past him as he thumped along the sodden track. Just as the packing house came into view, it was obliterated before his eyes; a great red-white fireball dotted with building stones took its place. The shock wave caught him in midstride and knocked him flat backward. A roar like nothing he had ever heard before actually rattled his teeth, and he could hear the building stones crashing like cannonballs into the trees around him.

"Jesus, Mary!" he gasped. He was not swearing this time, but the prayer would be of little help. When he got slowly to his feet and tried to look at where the upper yard had been, he was glad that tears were blurring his vision.

On the other side of the demolished yard Maggie and Noreen were stumbling along the roadway, which was filling up with other women whose faces were as white as theirs. Some were bleeding from cuts, and others were bruised dreadfully. One whole row of houses had been flattened by the blast, but miraculously they had all escaped with their lives. Maggie struggled to keep up with Noreen, but she was half-carrying Kevin, who was weeping with terror.

When they got to the gates, the desolation was so complete that nobody was there to keep them back from the grisly place. The horror of it all finally slowed them, though, and by the time they got to the blast site they were moving about in pathetic little bunches, averting their eyes from the horrible tattered things dashed and hanging grotesquely everywhere.

A few had tearful reunions with men as they came rushing in from other places in the yard. Four women found recognizable remains of their men. A few were taken to where surviving wounded lay. The rest, Noreen and Maggie among them, huddled tightly near the center of the yard, recoiling from the awful evidence that lay in the periphery of that macabre place.

Noreen stumbled on a torn piece of yellow painted metal, and when Maggie looked at it, she recognized a fragment of Patrick's dinner pail. The shriek that ripped from her was a long and piercing keen. It sent a chill through the dull survivors, and they began to weep quietly. Noreen clutched at Kevin's hand and looked wildly around for Brendan. She felt Maggie sag against her, nearly knocking her over.

Just then someone rushed up and took the older woman in his arms. Noreen hardly noticed until she heard him speak softly and recognized the voice of Patrick Gallagher.

"Come, Maggie love, Norrie child, I'll take you to Brendan."

Father Reardon arrived and was taken to the cooper shop by Hugh Flynn. A cluster of women and children shuffled about the doorway, glancing back occasionally toward the smoking ruin of the mills. They murmured a disjointed chorus of greeting as he approached, and some genuflected and blessed themselves, opening a pathway for him. He clutched at his small case of holy oil and tried to concentrate on the ritual words of Extreme Unction.

Hugh led him into the building, which was crowded with knots of people gathered around makeshift litters resting on the sawdust-covered floor. An odor of wood shavings mingled with the rusty smell of blood. Francis fought with a sudden image of a butcher shop and choked down his nausea.

He went directly to the first stretcher, and surprised himself as the words of absolution and healing reeled smoothly from his lips. He tried not to look too long at the fright-filled eyes of the man, white eyes bulging from a powder-blackened face.

He finished quickly with the anointing of head, breast, and feet, and moved on to the next man, oblivious of the tugs on his cassock as the women touched him in passing, oblivious of the bleating moans of thanks and supplication.

He was halfway through administering the sacrament to the fifth casualty when he realized the poor man with no arm was Brendan

Gallagher. The smooth flow of words stumbled, resumed, stumbled again, and stopped. Then a cool hand rested lightly on his neck, comforting him, and he turned to look at her face, ashen white but dry-eyed in her grief as Noreen knelt beside him, looking steadily at the unconscious form of her husband. Somehow his tongue began to work again, and he listened to the sounds of his own voice like some paralyzed observer. He felt her hand move, sliding off the stole draped around his neck, and heard her voice drifting in like soothing music, "Thank you, Father. He will be well." His eyes found hers, saw her lips move. "There are others who need you more."

And then he was beside another form that was rattling into death even as he swabbed the oil. And then another. Francis was no longer aware of rising from one pallet to walk to the next. It as as if he were floating on his knees. Once he caught himself angrily motioning for someone to pull down a blanket so that he could complete the anointing of a dying man's feet. The powderman's eyes glittered brightly, and he was speaking of ordinary things to his wife, who cradled his head in her lap.

"I must anoint his feet."

A hand gripped his arm as he made to pull the bloodied cloth back himself, and someone whispered in his ear.

"They's naught from the waist down, Father."

He was up then, looking for more, when a dizziness made him stumble and he felt arms guiding him to the door. Brilliant sunshine hurt his eyes, and the cool air chilled his sweaty face.

"Thanks, Father. Your coming calmed them."

Francis looked at the man who had him by the arm. He was in shirtsleeves, a few spatters of red on the white ruffled cotton.

"I'm the surgeon, Father. Are you well enough for the other place? Not dizzy now are you?"

"Thank you, Doctor," Francis said unsteadily. "No...no, I'm fine."

"Mr. Flynn will take you, then, if you're ready."

"Ready for...?"

The surgeon mouthed the word, "Morgue."

Lizzie Dorgan saw the priest being led along by the arm to the wagon sheds at the end of the yard. Maybe he would know! She swung the heavy dinner pail carefully as she scampered after him so as to keep the stew from spilling over the other nice things she had packed. But, oh, it was getting late, long past the noon hour, and the things were surely cold as stone.

"Father, oh, Father there," she puffed, catching up. "Have *you* seen him? That scalawag is hidin' from his old ma again."

"Hello...Mrs. Dorgan..."

"Ah, Lizzie," Hugh Flynn interrupted, blocking her from the priest, "Now, Lizzie, your husband is lookin' all over for ye. Please now, Mrs. Dorgan, go to him. He's at the gates."

"It's me son Joseph I'm after, not me husband." She held up the dinner pail. "Look! He's not had a bite this day, so much he cares for his health, and me searchin' the world around for the likes of him while it gets cold for all me trouble." She grinned a grotesque contortion that warred with the empty desperation in her eyes.

The two men looked at each other, and Francis spoke to her, as gently as he could. "Mrs. Dorgan, you know of the terrible thing that has happened. Your son...Joseph..." He looked at Hugh Flynn, who gave a curt little nod. "We think that poor Joseph—"

"No!" she spat the word out of her mouth like an obscenity. Then suddenly she turned mild and begged in a small voice, "They say he was sitting on the seat of his wagon at noon." She pointed toward the center of the yard where a flat crater was dished out of the ground. "See, he was right...here...or here. But he's gone... gone...."

Her voice trailed off, and she wandered away, head rolling from side to side as she searched, her bonnet cocked askew, her hair wild.

Hugh Flynn tugged at Francis's arm. "Let her be fer now, Father. The others will look after the poor soul."

They ducked under a canvas screen that had been tacked over the gaping doorway of the wagon shed and stepped into the makeshift morgue. A few men with kerchiefs knotted over their lower faces moved aside respectfully when they saw the cassock. Hugh Flynn stopped just inside and let Francis proceed along to the center of the hard earth floor. Francis could make out about a dozen white-draped pallets. He steeled himself for the task of uncovering each and anointing whatever horrible wreckage he would find underneath. He turned back to the masked workers.

"Please, will one of you help with the sheets?"

Finally one man came forward and went to the first pallet. Francis fumbled with the case and began the ritual, more swiftly now with the already dead. When he reached the last corpse and touched its blackened forehead with the oil, the severed head rolled back and off the low stretcher, coming to rest with its nose against the packed earth. Francis spun on his knees and retched beside the litter.

"Oh, I'm sorry, Father," a muffled voice said in his ear, breaking into sobs. "We done the best we could."

Francis wiped his mouth with a trembling hand and struggled to his feet. He patted the shaking back of the weeping powderman, and walked unsteadily toward Hugh Flynn. He had to swallow many times before he could speak.

"That is all, then, Mr. Flynn?" he whispered.

Another kerchief-covered face came close and muttered in his ear, "Excuse me, Father, for not knowin', but is there anything to be done with that over there?" The man pointed toward the shed wall. "I mean, do they get blessed, is what I mean."

Francis made out a row of shallow wicker baskets, each neatly covered with a square of canvas.

"Do you know who each of them is? I mean... is each...?"

"Heaven help us, Father, we don't even know *what* most of that is. It's all that was left of what was picked up here and across the Crick."

Francis was numb with horror now, and he nodded, giving the little row of baskets a sweeping blessing.

It was late afternoon by the time they got Brendan home. He was unconscious most of the time and weak from loss of blood, but he clearly knew that he had lost his arm. Once while they were still gathered about him at the yard in that awful place of dead and dying men, he raised the bandaged stump and pointed to it with his good left hand. After that his head fell back with such resignation that Noreen knew he wished he had been killed instead.

Their collected grief was too much to comprehend, let alone cope with. Both Sean and Joseph were gone, vaporized in the blast. So, too, was the journeyman mason Patrick had brought along so well, who had carried the dinner pail to his death. A host of others had died—friends, neighbors, fellow workers. Even Mistress Sophie had been wounded in her fine house and was gravely hurt. In all, thirty-six men had died in one second and four more were torn up so badly they would not last the night. Half the men and half the works of Eleutherian Mills were gone. It was even more horrible than a nightmare.

When Noreen found out that her brother Tim was also gone, only her concern for Brendan kept her from full collapse.

CHAPTER 33

Not tonight! Not a word to her tonight!"

"But she has to be told sometime."

"Sometime. . . . Not now."

Patrick looked at his wife's face, flushed with weeping and sagging with grief. God, but she had aged this day.

"Better to have it over with all at once," he pressed. He remembered the dinner pail for Sean and Joseph, and had the wild hope again that somehow they had been spared, that they would come rolling in drunk from a day in town, looking guilty that they had bagged a day of work. A great spasm of grief constricted his throat and chest.

Maggie seized his arm with a frenzy that turned her fingers into talons. He savored the pain.

"Aye," she whispered, "all at once is right. D'ye want to lose her and the baby, too? Merciful Jesus, man, she'll learn soon enough." The scraping of a chair from Noreen and Brendan's room made her pause. She looked at the closed door to make sure Noreen was not coming into the kitchen before she went on. "I know she looks calm and collected, Patrick. She has that way of taking awful hurts in her stride, but I know better. She's like her dad in that, bleedin' inside all the while."

The twins' faces swam into Patrick's mind again, and he choked out the words, "I'd like to break the rum-pot's neck!"

"Don't, Patrick!" she said softly. "Don't put this awful thing on Denis."

"It was his hand that killed my boys, and his only son..."

"No! He wasn't even there."

"And maimed Brendan in there and two score besides."

"It was an accident, Patrick."

"He was drunk."

Maggie looked him straight in the eye and fought for calm in her own tangled grief. It was too much, this. She should be wild with rage at Denis herself, and marveled that she was not. Her babies ripped from her just as they had grown into men. Now she had to fight to stop another tragedy. She had to bring reason back into Patrick's thick skull.

"All right, Denis was drunk and in his own bed when the mill blew."

Patrick glared back but said nothing.

"Young Tim should not have been in the mill, I know," she went on soothingly. "But did Denis send him? Why not put the blame on Nora? What about the coopers? And what about the powdermen in the other rolling mills? They knew Tim was fillin' in for Denis, didn't they?"

Patrick shook his head. "Y'can't get past the fact that this whole thing was started by him and his goddam jug."

"It was no jug of poteen that destroyed us all today, Patrick."

He wrenched himself away from her and walked heavily to the door and opened it, staring out into the deepening twilight of the backyard, seeing nothing.

"You're takin' great pains to protect the bastard, I'm thinkin'," he muttered. "Mebee he hasn't caused ye as much grief as me."

The cruel words were brass in his mouth, and a sudden guilt hung like a lead bob in his chest, but he would not turn to take them back. It eased his mourning somehow, cutting into her like that. They were so close it was like slashing himself to distract his mind from the pain.

When she spoke, her voice was so calm that at first he thought she might not have heard him.

"You forget how close it was I came to being another man's wife except for Denis Feeney. You think I would not now be like to slip into the same black hatred of the man for what he took from me today?" Her words chilled the back of his neck as he listened, remembering that awful day years ago.

"It was the same this day, Patrick. The same. Denis Feeney takin' the whole guilt of it, judged by the very ones who set him up to be the goat."

He turned around to face her, hating her defense of that Jonah. How could she throw up her old lover in his face after all these years?

"It was not Denis who hanged his brother back then, Maggie. It was the English, pure and simple, who made the mistake, God damn their black souls."

She regarded him coolly, her arms crossed over her breast. "It was not a mistake that they put the rope around Tim Feeney's neck and dropped him through the trap. That was no accident. The mistake was in picking out the wrong brother. The deed was as ugly either way."

Patrick shook his head. She was making no sense at all.

"But you hated Denis for that, Maggie; it was years before y'could put it to rest. Now this—"

"You're wrong, Patrick," she murmured. "I might have hated the sight of Denis all that time, before we... before you..." She stumbled in confusion, and the old look glowed briefly in her eyes. "But it was the sight of him alive instead of the one who was so dear to me... then." She caught the hurt in his face, but pushed on ruthlessly. "The truth is that it was *all* of you I hated. All of you that pushed Denis into that black business, cheerin' him on like it was another child's prank, and your secret meetings, and making him the hero when he was still just a boy yet."

He nearly boiled over at that. "A *boy*, is it then? You call that two-score-and-five drunk a boy still?"

The sharp rise in his voice alarmed her, and she turned to look again at the closed door of Noreen and Brendan's room. It was madness, this argument. She suddenly felt the stiffness of her reserve turn to mush and heard herself pleading. "Ah, Patrick, y'know what I mean. Don't pretend not to understand."

She slid into racking sobs, and Patrick put his arms around her and began to stroke her. They stood together in the kitchen for a long time until her spasm of grief had passed. She did not want to let go of him, afraid of starting a new cycle of pain, and she burrowed her face deeper into his neck, feeling the slippery wetness of his tears against her forehead.

Maggie knew who should be taken to task for their calamity, but she would never voice it. Patrick would probably never even think of it. To admit it would have made them all party to the crime of forty killed. It was their choice, after all, to take the danger with the pay, the steady job paid for with the risks.

All the same, it was the Mister who owned the mills and took the chance of storing all that powder. Takin' chances with people's lives to get a bigger profit. Well, it came home to roost this time. His own fine house had lost all its windows, and the missus herself had been hurt by a flying stone, they said.

"There, now, my girl. Feelin' better?" she heard Patrick whisper hoarsely and felt his hard body shift. She abruptly turned toward Brendan's bedroom. How long had it been? Noreen might need her help.

"I better check on them." When she raised the latch gently and eased the door ajar, the bedroom was so dark that she could see nothing. "Bring the light."

She motioned Patrick back, and they withdrew, closing the door behind them.

"Could ye tell if he was breathin'?"

"He was."

Patrick set the lamp on the mantel and stretched, pushing in at the small of his back. He watched her pick up a small bottle and hold it up to the light, squinting to measure the level.

"How much can the boy take?" he asked.

"What?" She seemed confused.

"The opium. How much did the surgeon say he could have?"

She pulled the cork and dribbled a small quantity into a mug. "Once more tonight, if he needs it." She stoppered the bottle and added water to the mug. "There, that's ready now, if he wakes up ravin' with the pain. God knows, I hate to be feedin' the evil stuff to me own son."

"I wish there was something..." His voice drifted off, and she saw him looking down at his own hands, working them into fists. "Y'know I'd give both of these for the boy to have his arm back,

Maggie." He shook his head, thinking about the enormity of Brendan's loss. "His whole life to look forward to without an arm. What will the lad do?"

Maggie answered with a confidence she did not feel. "Oh, Patrick, he'll do fine. He's stubborn like yourself. He'll not let the loss of an arm keep him back. Thank the Lord we have him at all." A flashing image of the twins danced behind her eyes, but she swallowed the lump in her throat and went on. "A few weeks and he'll be almost as good as new. You'll see."

Patrick looked her squarely in the eye for a moment before answering. "Aye, Maggie, 'almost' is what it is."

He had barely spoken when the sound of sobbing startled them. The door burst open and Nora Feeney staggered in. Her hair was let down, wildly framing a face blanched with fear. She rushed to Patrick and cringed before him as if in fierce pain.

"Oh, Patrick, it's Denis! You've got to come quick. Dear God, he's tryin' to do away with himself."

"Nora..." He checked the harshness of his tone. "Nora, now be reasonable. God almighty, you've lost your son this day, and we've lost two of ours, with a third lyin' in there maimed. And you expect me to smooth the drunken nightmare of the man who caused it all...."

"Oh, Patrick, please come. He's cold sober, as God is my witness, and... and he's in the backyard under the tree... standin' on a keg with... with the rope around his..." Nora Feeney broke off her frenzied plea and looked as if she was about to vomit.

Maggie watched her husband suddenly go pale and rush for the kitchen. He was carrying a knife as he raced down the steps and onto Crick Road.

Patrick's face glistened with sweat as he pounded down the center of Crick Road, his thick arms drawn in tight against his heaving chest. He was dimly aware of running, of the flashing knife blade in his hand, of the tumbled rubble of collapsed houses along Chicken Alley. Then the tree in the center of the Feeneys' yard was just ahead, and he burst through the last of the thicket, smashing the pickets and rail of their fence with his knees. A great splintery shaft of wood plunged deep into his right thigh, ripping the flesh and sending forth a pumping spurt of blood. But he felt nothing.

And then he saw Denis Feeney.

The sight stopped Patrick as though he had run flat into a stone wall. The figure hanging from the tree seemed to be doing some kind of wild dance, a soundless jig with his arms and legs flailing about as he turned slowly in the murky darkness. No music, no song, no tapping foot. The only sound came from Patrick's throat, the sobbing rasp of his own breathing.

He stood rooted by the spectacle, his brain reeling. Even in the dark it was terrifying. Denis's eyes bulged white in the distorted face, and his tongue swelled hugely above the jaw clamped against it.

The rope creaked....

A bellowing roar ripped from Patrick, and he flung himself at the rope, slashing it with the knife. Denis dropped like a sack, and Patrick clawed at the knotted hemp as he worked it free of the engorged neck.

At last it was off, and Denis lay motionless, the light of the rising moon flooding his body with an unearthly light.

"Breathe!" Patrick pleaded. "Breathe, y'runty bastard!" He knelt beside his friend and pushed once with his hand on the flat belly.

He felt a twitch under his palm, and then a shuddering gasp rattled from Denis Feeney's gaping mouth. His head rolled from side to side, and he was suddenly twitching weakly with aimless jerks of his arms and legs. Patrick felt his own heart pound, and he fought for control of his voice.

"There now, brawnie, go easy with it. It's Patrick here now," he soothed. "Mind yer tongue, boyo.... Don't be swallowin' yer tongue, fer I'll hafta dig it out with me fingers." He watched, jealously counting each new breath.

"Kin ye hear me, Denis? No...no, don't be tryin' to talk; jist press me finger a little with yer hand... if ye hear me."

He placed his finger in Denis's clammy palm and felt the slender fingers clutch his own and hang on. Patrick gave in then. With a great animal groan he gathered up Denis Feeney in his arms and sat there in the dark, weeping and rocking the other man like a child. Later, when he could trust his voice again, he whispered in the wretched man's ear, "You were the fool tonight, Denis Feeney, to do what y'did. And God forgive me, I think I truly came meself to spill yer guts."

The sound of Nora Feeney's weeping carried down to them from Crick Road, and Patrick helped Denis to his feet.

"All right, it's into the house with us now. I'll want you in yer chair, lookin' cozy when yer missus arrives. But first promise me not to try that trick again."

Denis Feeney nodded weakly, and they stumbled into the house together.

About an hour later Patrick left for home by way of the back door. He had to fetch Maggie's kitchen knife, but before leaving the tree, he pulled down the rope and cut it into very short lengths. He gave the lighted window one last look and tossed the fragments into the weeds.

On the way home he felt the stabbing ache in his leg. It was then that he noticed the wound for the first time. The blood was dried now, a crusty scab already humped over the tear.

It was close to midnight when Patrick gratefully climbed the steps of his own front stoop. When he opened the door, he saw that Maggie had lighted another lantern in their room, and she was bustling in from the kitchen.

"Is Denis all right?" she asked, looking at him closely.

"He'll live," he mumbled, avoiding her eyes. Better to let it go at that. He didn't want to relive the past few hours—not tonight, at least.

"Well, thank the Lord yer back at last," she snapped almost as if he had been carousing at Dorgan's instead of enduring the trial he had just been through. "And don't just stand there, man. We have to do this all ourselves this time. God knows Lizzie is in no shape, nor any other on the whole Crick."

"Do what? Fer God's sake, woman, it's *done in* is what I am."

She shoved a stack of folded muslin into his arms, and turned to get something else from the kitchen. "Take those into our room... quick now... and mind the way you act around Noreen."

"Well, what the devil for..."

"It's her time." She came back with a bucket and more cloths and prodded him with an elbow. "And from the looks of things you and me will be up the rest of the night."

"Her time, ye say?"

"Aye, dunce, the baby's comin'."

"Are ye certain?"

She gave him a tired smile as she led the way into their room. Dropping her voice to a whisper, she added, "And bundle little Kevin there in with his dad. After what he's been through this day, I don't think more commotion would do him any good."

Patrick peeked around Maggie and saw Noreen in their bed. She seemed to be asleep.

"Poor lass," he murmured. "'Tis sad timing for a birth."

"Cut out yer tongue, Patrick Gallagher," she whispered mildly, "and thank the Lord for sparin' us some of the black of mourning."

Brendan tried to scream for help, but he could make no sound. Everything was cotton stillness. He could feel his throat ache with the shouting, but nothing came from his parched mouth. His arm lay on top of the stone stuck fast in the mortar, and he could see the massive block of granite straining at its rope sling as it dropped toward him. Why didn't his dad see him? My God, there he was puffing at his pipe, blowing ashes all over the powder kegs, jawing away with the Mister as he turned the windlass and lowered the stone.

It was inches away from him! He strained to pull his arm free, but he could move only his fingers. Sparks from the pipe started burning on the ground. He saw Sean stamping at them with his bare feet. Sean was laughing, shrinking into a child again before his very eyes. Now he was calling Joseph . . . the two of them blowing on the sparks, building a castle with the kegs, pouring little streams of the black stuff on the ground, watching the sparks ignite them and whoosh along. The kegs began to pop, little puffs of fire and smoke. The twins shrieked soundlessly with delight.

Suddenly a searing pain sprang from his arm, and he saw the great stone mash it flat in the mortar joint. He felt sick with the pain, wondering if he could vomit with his mouth so dry. His dad came over then to undo the sling. The Mister pointed to his arm under the stone and said something to his dad. They both began to laugh.

"Brendan!"

Now he could hear again, and it was his father's voice in his ear. Oh, why didn't he lift the stone!

"Brendan . . . Son . . . can y'hear me, lad?"

"Arm . . ." He had to push the sound out.

"Aye, I know it hurts. Listen, Brendan, can ye come awake now?"

At last the dream released him, and he opened his eyes with a sudden joy. Only a nightmare! For a few seconds he felt ecstasy, then he saw the mounded bandage where his elbow used to be.

"Ah, there y'are." It was his father's voice. Brendan lay there without answering. He forced himself to look at the bandaged stump. It was hard to focus his eyes, and he closed them again, letting the full weight of despair crush down upon him. It was greater than the pain, and that was monstrous.

"Brendan..."

His father at his ear again. He knew what that meant—cheery words to buck him up. Well, he would have none of it; not now with the fire of his...arm...and the worse feeling of knowing it was gone for good...gone for good. Oh, God, when he was awake it took all the rest of him to endure the thumping torture of it.

"Brendan," the voice coaxed, "look here, lad, I've somethin' to show ye."

Patrick was kneeling by the bed holding something in a blanket. It was hard to see. Something moved; there was a strange noise coming from the bundle. Suddenly it twitched and a soft wail came begging. Confused, he looked into his father's face.

"It's yer daughter, Brendan." He beamed. "Another Gallagher woman to keep us steppin'!"

Brendan lurched and tried to sit up. A searing pain rocketed into his armpit, and he groaned. But he propped himself on his good elbow and pushed the hurt out of his mind.

"Let me...see it," he gasped. "A girl...did y'say a girl, Dad?"

"Aye," Patrick crooned as he undid the blanket and held the child up for inspection. "Ain't she the lovely lass, now?"

"How's Norrie?"

"Fine. Fine!"

"You're sure?" He was all over the child with his eyes as he spoke of Noreen.

"Sure I am. Me and yer Ma took care of that all the last night and half of the mornin'. She's restin' good now."

Brendan searched the baby over again, hungry for the sight of her. He wished she would open her eyes.

"I can't see too good yet, Dad. All fuzzy still. Is there aught wrong with her? The baby, I mean."

Patrick began to swaddle the infant clumsily, clucking possessively. "With this one? Why, she's perfect, o'course. She's a Gallagher, ain't she?"

"With her..." Brendan was not sure of his concern exactly. He eased back down into the bed. "I mean, does she have all her toes and fingers... and...?"

Patrick had a hard time answering. "All her arms and legs are there, too. And hooked on in the right places," he rumbled gruffly. "Now I better get her back to yer ma. I'm only good at this fer a short spell."

Brendan's face was slick with sweat, and the pain was crowding him again. He closed his eyes to ward off a dizzy, fainting slide and waved his father off with his left hand.

After the door closed softly, he gave in to some soft wailing between clenched teeth. It helped a little to take his mind off the pain.

But his child was perfect. Nothing missing there. All her arms and legs in place. Brendan was not quite certain why it was, but from that moment on he was sure he could make do with only one arm himself.

Throughout the day Maggie sat dozing in her rocking chair holding her granddaughter. She was the most beautiful child she had ever seen. She had always regretted not having a daughter of her own to raise, but this one made up for it, surely. She would have golden red hair and a beautiful face like her mother, and delicate fingers. Now that was a blessing. None of those stubby Gallagher fingers on this one.

Noreen slept like the dead, poor thing. It had been a hard labor, though not hurtful, thank the Lord. She would be up quick. Maggie just prayed her milk would come in strong; after all the frightful things that had happened, it would not be surprising if she had some trouble with that.

She need not have worried. Behind her closed eyes, Noreen often lay awake. Several times she looked through half-open lids and saw Maggie asleep in the chair, holding the baby close against her. With each look at her child Noreen could feel the tingling sting as the milk let down and her fullness grew.

One thing troubled Noreen about this girl-child she had borne, and she knew it from the moment she first held her to the breast. The child's hands and ears were unmistakable.

Louis Jardinere was her father.

Looking back at the past week it seemed to Patrick more like a year. He shook his head with the memory. It still seemed more like a bad dream than a reality.

Thank goodness the Mister was going to rebuild. At least their jobs were not up in smoke, too. The man had guts, surely, to stick it out even after his missus got hurt by the flying rock, and every room in that fine house heaped with broken glass.

Every single windowpane smashed and half the casements splintered, but the walls had stood the blast without shifting a hair. He took some pride in that. He had cut and set every stone himself, from footing to eave.

Well, the man deserved the best he could give. Five widows and twelve kids without their daddies after that awful crack, and the Mister giving them all pensions and a house to live in the rest of their days, or until they married again.

His eyes flickered over the collapsed roofs and sagging walls of a row of workers' homes at the bend in Crick Road. When the new batch of men arrived next month, he would have them pull the whole mess down for rebuilding. While he was at it, he would suggest to the Mister that the walls be built thicker this time.

Not that they were expecting another blast like that one. God forbid. All the same, it was good to be ready.

Just in case.

CHAPTER 34

Two weeks after the great Brandy-
wine disaster a Quaker farmer on the outskirts of Philadelphia opened
his barn one morning to discover a vagrant sleeping on a mound
of straw. One look at the fellow was all it took to realize that he
had been through terrible times indeed. His clothes were in tatters;
on his face and hands there were scabbed-over patches of ugly
peeling skin. Places on his neck were still raw. The boy was ill with
the cold, and he was nearly skin and bones.

After his wife had given the boy a good breakfast and cleaned his
wounds, the farmer rummaged through a trunk to find him some
clothes.

"Pray, lad, what misfortune hath befallen thee?" the Quaker asked
after helping his unexpected guest into the fresh garments.

The boy seemed too shy to answer at first, but finally he blurted,
"I was burned."

"But how? Did thy house catch fire? Wert thou alone?"

"I . . . was in the woods. . . . Some gunpowder got . . . spilled into . . ."

"Ah, thy campfire!" The farmer clucked sympathetically. "A terrible misfortune. My wife and I would make thee welcome here as
long as thou want to rest and heal."

The young man gulped and thanked his benefactor. "Thankee,
sir. God be good to you."

The accent made the Quaker cock his head, and smile amiably. "Thou art Irish, are thou not?"

"Aye, that I am."

"And thy name?"

"Tim, sir. Tim Fe..." The boy's eyes clouded, and his mouth snapped shut. "The name is Fenn. Timothy Fenn. I'm a hard worker and trained as a cooper."

"A cooper."

"Aye. Barrels and kegs."

"I see." There was something he liked about this young man, something that seemed of more value than the thing that had made him lie just now. "Well, Timothy Fenn, thou will not have call to fashion kegs on this farm, but if it suits thy mood, there is much hay to pitch...and manure...and other like chores to earn thy bed and board. He looked closely at the angry wounds. "But now thou must rest and heal. This house is thy house."

Tim thanked the man again and carefully tugged a homespun shirt over his head, wincing as the fabric dragged over the raw wound on his neck.

"There, now," the farmer said and stuck out his hand. "Call me Garrett. Later at supper thou will meet my son Thomas. If thou decide to stay and work, it will please Thomas very much." He smiled and winked. "My son feels hard used on this farm. He will be happy for thee to lighten his load."

They put him up in a small room in the attic of their great farmhouse. He slept through the whole day and would not have awakened even at nightfall if someone had not roused him for supper by jiggling the bed frame and shining an oil lamp in his face.

"I hate to wake thee, Tim," a voice said, "but my father says that thy supper is ready."

Tim's eyes blinked open.

"He says that thy strength depends on eating."

"You're Thomas, I guess," Tim said, twisting his head to look at him and enduring the pain as the skin of his neck wrinkled.

"And thou are Tim. Thou looks a sore tatters, friend!"

"The same," Tim muttered. He didn't like the tone this Thomas Garrett was taking. He felt like asking what *he* would look like if he had been blown half out of a powder mill and tumbled twenty rods over boulders in the Crick.

"Thy flask of powder must have been full to scorch thee so."

"Full enough."

"And thy hunting piece, was it left behind with the duffel at thy camp?"

"Aye." Tim began to edge away toward the doorway and the darkened stairs.

"If thou can tell me where it is, I will fetch it in the morning." Thomas was hovering near Tim's back, holding the lamp high to light his way down the steps.

"I can't." Tim's reply was muffled, gruff.

"Can't?"

"It's all a blur, man. I can't remember aught after the flash that cooked me good."

Young Thomas Garrett kept his peace. The subject would be closed until Tim decided to open it up again. As he watched the wracked figure below him labor down each painful step, he decided that he liked this Tim Fenn, or whoever he was. He was sure that it was the du Pont mill disaster that had caused him grief. The great thunderclap of that blast had been heard for miles around, and he himself had read of it in the post.

Why this man chose to invent another reason for his grief was his own business. The fact that he was so strong in his adversity was a thing to be admired. Why, he must have dragged himself through the woods for miles without food or drink in the very ecstasy of pain. That took raw courage, indeed.

Even as they entered the kitchen to take their places at the table, Tom Garrett knew he had been sent an ally and a friend.

It was an act of providence.

PART THREE

1837

CHAPTER 35

The mark of a stonemason was unmistakable in the hunched gait of Patrick Gallagher as he trotted excitedly through the busy shipyard of the Wilmington Marine Terminal toward the berth of the *Quaker City*. The four-master had just arrived, and Patrick could hear the hoarse shouts of the deckhands as they warped the vessel to the dock and made it secure. He was puffing now and, mindful of his advanced years, he slowed to a walk, mopping his streaming face with a red kerchief. As he rounded the last shipway he could make out the *Quaker City* clearly, and he saw with relief that the gangway was just being settled into place. He would not be late after all.

The dock was clotted with small groups of people who, like himself, were here to welcome friends or kin to the New World. They were all Irish, since the ship had taken on its only passengers at Dublin on the return trip from Liverpool with a cargo of heavy machinery for the Eleutherian Mills.

Patrick had just begun to scan the thirty or so figures looking down from the side of the tall vessel when a shout caught his ear, "Uncle Patrick!" His eyes snapped in the direction of the sound, settling on the serious face of a man who appeared closer to thirty than the twenty years James must be.

Patrick waved, and the young man smiled briefly and disappeared in a lineup for the gangplank. It was fifteen minutes before he appeared again, making his way with the other passengers down the slanted ramp to the dock. They shook hands warmly, and Patrick noticed that up close there was no mistaking James's youth. What made the boy look older was plain starvation. The bones of his face stuck out like poles under a tent. Most of the new arrivals clustered nearby were just as thin.

"Well, Jamie," the older man boomed, "they took their time in lettin' you off. I was worried y'might have had second thoughts and decided to go back to Kildare."

James smiled grimly. "No, Uncle Pat, I'm here for good—or at least fer a year. The captain made sure we signed the passage papers. It seems your friend du Pont owns me for a twelvemonth, until the passage is paid off."

Patrick patted his tall nephew on the back. "We'd better start for home, lad. We'll have a seven-mile walk unless we can catch Dorgan's wagon at the brewery." They turned away from the dock.

"I wouldn't worry about them papers, lad. The company is light with its debtors, and the du Ponts are fine people to work for. Fair wages and easy labor. They respect a man. You'll see."

"Well, it's done, and having struck the bargain I'll not be breaking it. You'll understand, Uncle Pat; we have reason to be squeamish when it comes to making deals with landlords and the like."

Patrick nodded and changed the subject. "Your daddy wrote that you were a big lad, but I'm thinking your Aunt Maggie will have to stuff you some to fill the lean places. The ship's cook must have served terrible grub. The other passengers looked a trifle thin to me, too."

James's laugh was hard and cold. "I've no quarrel with the ship's table. It was the best food most of us have had for months...years. No, you have been here long enough to forget what it is like back there. Or maybe it was not as bad years ago. If it's fat you're looking for, you will find it on the backsides of the English lords and Anglican ministers. It's for them we Irish sow and reap. And it is getting worse by the month."

Patrick looked at him closely. "That bad, eh?"

"Aye, that bad."

Suddenly Patrick reached over and yanked the duffel bag from James's shoulder. "There!" He pointed. "That's Dorgan's wagon now, pullin' out from the brewery. Run after him, lad. Tell him to wait for two thirsty powdermen who need a lift to Dorgan's Inn!"

Dorgan's was already teeming with powdermen weary from the twelve-hour workday by the time the beer wagon team plodded into the yard with a full load of kegs.

"Step lively, Jamie boy. Come in and meet the gang!"

James Gallagher followed his uncle through the doorway into the noisy, musty taproom.

Patrick marched him up to the bar, and shouted over the din. "Two pails of yer finest brew, Dorgan me lad. I've brought you a thirsty customer from Kildare!"

In the excitement of arrival, Jamie had not noticed how dry he had become, and he had drained off nearly a pint before pulling the mug away from his parched lips.

Patrick laughed. "'Tis like a thirsty horse y'drink, boy. Slow it down, now. I'll not be takin' you home to your Aunt Maggie the worse for wear."

Turning to a knot of workmen whose conversation had died of the curiosity generated by their entrance, Patrick introduced Jamie proudly. "This is James, my brother's oldest, who has traded Protestant generosity for a go at the Crick!"

There was a mild laugh of his joke, and each man came in turn to shake the boy's hand, wishing him well and, if they were from Kildare, asking questions about long missed loved ones still in the old country. They smiled their greetings, but quick eyes took in his thin frame, then darkened with the knowledge that hunger stalked the tables of kin they had left behind. The mails would be swelled with neatly folded dollars on their way across the Atlantic for the next few weeks, until gnawing consciences faded once again.

Jamie was well into his second pail and feeling a bit lightheaded when he felt a fierce tug at his arm. The ale in the tin mug splashed against his chest, and he turned, mildly annoyed, to see the man who was clutching at him so.

His face was shriveled and gaunt, his hair yellow-white and wild, his beard a hoary two-week stubble. The voice was a hoarse whisper. "Don't go to the mills, lad. Jesus Mary, stay away from..." The whisper faltered and collapsed into a sob. In a moment the figure was gone, limping out the doorway into the deep summer twilight.

"Don't be mindin' the likes of him, James," Patrick said. There was a trace of compassion in his tone. "Come, now. Maggie's keeping supper for us down the road."

As they were walking through the humid darkness, Jamie asked Patrick who the man was.

"That's my old friend, Denis Feeney. You mustn't mind him. His mind is nearly gone, I think, poor soul."

"What happened...?"

Patrick looked wistfully at the youngster striding easily next to him. "He lost his only son in the blast of 'eighteen. That was the one that took my two younger boys. You were just a babe."

Jamie didn't answer. He really had not known much beyond a rumor that some of his cousins had been killed in America long ago.

"You see, lad, a boy was fillin' in because his father—Denis Feeney—was too drunk to show for work. The boy didn't know the ropes, and he let a shaft get hot. Four mills went up, and forty Irish went across the Crick."

"Across the Crick?"

"Aye, boyo. It's powderman's lingo. The River Jordan is a long way from the mills."

CHAPTER 36

Noreen Gallagher stood in the dimly lighted kitchen of her father's house surveying the supper table and wondering if she should plan on Denis Feeney's return for the meal. It seemed pointless, but she shrugged and set his place anyway.

As she went about the ritual of supper preparation, she felt herself begin to slip into melancholy. How long had she been fighting these daily bouts with herself? she wondered. Of course everyone thought her strangeness had begun with the losing of her month-old twins to the fever in that awful hot summer of 1829, but she knew the blackness of her spirit had somehow begun before that.

Even after all this time—was it seven years or eight? no matter— she would never lose the terrible wrenching that knotted her breast each time she thought of those small varnished boxes so deep in the rocky soil of Chicken Alley.

She caught herself gazing out the window, the bowl she had been stirring locked in the crook of her arm. The thought of her mother standing so in the very spot flashed past her mind. Noreen had seen her there so many times, staring out the same window like some sad statue with stooped shoulders and vacant eyes, that she seldom thought of Nora Feeney except in association with this one place. When she died in that awful year of the blast that took Tim and so many others, the great shock to Noreen had not been her passing but the fact that Nora Feeney looked quite the same in death as she had while living.

They had put her in the open box on trestles in the front room, and aside from the fact that she had never slept there when alive, she appeared no different to Noreen than she had the day before.

"Ah, sudden it was, eh? No sign of illness, then?"

"Aye, not so much as a headache!"

"Just went out in her sleep."

"Aye, took a nap yestiddy noon and just stopped breathin'."

"Well, she's better off, if y'ask me. The poor thing has found peace at last."

"Aye, now that's the truth."

Noreen had had the curious feeling all through the wake that they could have lifted her mother from the box, set her on her feet in the kitchen facing the window, and nothing would have changed.

Except her father. His Nora's death had shaken Denis as much as the thing with Tim—more than that; it had broken him. Noreen had known it from the instant he had stumbled into Gallagher's that afternoon and croaked out the news of her mother's death. He had been like a child, all the wildness, the lovely wildness, gone from his eye, all the fierce pride she had savored in his spirit even in the days after Tim, snuffed out like a drenched fuse.

He would have to be watched. Not from any fear of violence to himself, like before, but nurtured into living lest he simply let himself die, too.

So they had moved in, back to the house she had left with such high hopes. Noreen was not sure at all that moving in with her father was good for him. Perhaps the wretched man would have been better off withering away to follow her mother. But that was unimportant anyway. She had begun to see the pattern of life that had been set out for her from the time of that first attempt to get away from this house and the failure of their dreamed-of freight line. And she had bound herself—and Brendan, too—forever more with her escapade in the woods. It was not meant to be, that freedom and independence so recklessly pursued by Denis Feeney and his daughter, and now they were to atone together in a mutually sustained purgatory.

"Mother, why are you standing in the dark?"

The voice startled Noreen out of her reverie, and she jerked her face around at the sound.

"I'll see to the lamp," the voice went on.

The sudden light made Noreen blink, and as her daughter turned to face her, she tried to cover her awkwardness hurriedly setting the bowl on the table.

"Here, let me finish with the biscuits," the girl said, taking the spoon and applying it vigorously to the drying contents of the bowl. "We'd better get these on quick if we want them for supper. Daddy and Kevin are late. I wonder if they stopped by Grandpa Gallagher's on the way home." She flashed her mother a quick smile. "I do hope the boat came in like it was supposed to. Kevin said Grandpa was going to town to see for himself. He took the whole day off."

Noreen went over to inspect the stew pot. "Where *are* those two?" she murmured, automatically excluding her father from consideration. "We will have to get along with things if we ever hope to get over there tonight." She turned to Kate. "Do you want to change into your Sunday best?" Her tone was flatly curious with a trace of urging.

Kate laughed and shook her head. "No, Mama. After all he's me cousin, not me suitor. I'm thinkin' I should save the pretty dress to use on serious game."

A little after eight that evening Brendan Gallagher led his family of four along Crick Road. It was full dark, and the evening air had a chill that seemed unseasonably sharp even for late February. Noreen shivered and pressed closer to her husband, skipping to keep up with his longer strides. Brendan put his good arm around her shoulders and shortened his step as they sought a comfortable rhythm.

"What did you think of him, Kevin?" Kate asked suddenly.

"Who's that?" her brother teased.

"Oh, Kevin! You tire me, and that's a fact. I want to know what you have to say about our cousin."

"Well, I barely saw him for five minutes, now, did I?" Kevin grumped. "Hardly time enough to make a lasting impression if y'ask me."

"Oh, Kevin, I know that. All I mean is . . . what does he seem like? Is he pleasant and all, do y'think?"

[269]

Kevin laughed. "All right, Kathleen, I'll tell you what I think, but I don't think you'll want to hear it after all."

Brendan slowed down. "You didn't like James, then? He seemed like a good enough lad to me."

"It's not that I didn't like him, Dad. It's more like he is a bit too stern for me. He looks like someone who needs to laugh but won't. I don't think he'll be much fun to be around."

"That's not fair!" Kathleen blurted. "To make such a judgment on our cousin when you've hardly—"

"All right, you two pups," Brendan rumbled, "break it off now, or you'll be bickerin' still when we get to Mom and Dad's."

Noreen looked up as they rounded the turn in Crick Road and the lights of the Gallaghers' house glowed in a warm spill into the chill night. She could hear snatches of Patrick's happy voice through the closed windows as they approached. The others were in good spirits, too. As for herself there was no change in mood. The arrival of another worker along the Crick was always a bit sad for her. Just one more person caught in the web.

Maggie Gallagher kept getting up from her rocker and fussing about the house all evening, forever asking James if he had had enough to eat, offering to refill his cup. Oh, but she was delighted to have a youngster in the house again. This place that she had complained of being too cramped when the children were small now seemed like a great barn with just herself and Patrick rattling about in the four lower rooms. She listened contentedly as Patrick and James sat at the table talking.

"A hundred forty and seven as we sit here, Jamie, and tomorra when I sign ye up, it'll be one hundred forty and eight! A far cry from when me and the Mister started years ago. O'course he don't work like he used to."

"So du Pont's retired?"

"After Madam Sophie died—she was hurt herself in the blast that took yer cousins—well, he never got over it, poor man. She was struck by a rock that came peltin' through the window. She lived on for ten years, but they say she was never the same after that."

"Who's running the company now?"

"Oh, his boys are. And a fine lot they are, Jamie. Every one of them worked the mills from the time they was just lads. They're powdermen through and through." Patrick beamed as though talking about his own family. "And not afraid of work or danger either."

The rattle of the latch interrupted them, and they rose to greet Brendan's family.

"Here, now, Jamie," Patrick shouted as he rushed to the door. "Meet two of the loveliest women ever to give my Maggie competition." Pushing Brendan and Kevin aside he planted himself between Kate and Noreen, hooked his arms into theirs, and pranced into the center of the room.

"Oh, blarney." Noreen laughed, but she kissed Patrick on the forehead. Then she looked straight into Jamie's eyes for a long moment before adding, "And you are Cousin James from Kildare."

Her look gave him a warm, calm feeling—a sensation of comforting safety. Then, as quickly as he had been stirred by her eyes, he felt their soft hold on him relax. "Kate...Kathleen, meet your cousin James."

"Hello, James, or should I call you Jamie?"

The voice floated to him from the loveliest face he had ever seen.

"Jamie...ah, Jamie or James as y'like."

"Well, I like Jamie better. I think it suits you. James is such a stern name." Her laugh caressed his ears. "So, Jamie Gallagher, I'm yet another cousin. Kathleen Gallagher at your service, but call me Kate." The beautiful creature then curtsied grandly and came forward to kiss him on the cheek.

He stood dumb as a tree, unable to speak. God in heaven, she was a vision! He watched paralyzed as she tugged at a ribbon under her chin and shook her head free of a gingham bonnet. Waves of red-gold hair framed her face like a soft halo drawn loosely into an upswept crown. As she swept past him to embrace Maggie, his eyes locked on her. Part of an ear peeked from under the mass of wonderful hair. It was pink with the cold, and he liked the soft curve of the lobe where it joined her cheek.

But, Jesus, Mary, that hair! He had a wild desire to walk up to her and slowly withdraw the bone pins, watching it cascade down over her shoulders. It would reach her waist surely.

Finally he managed to draw his eyes away from her. Everybody seemed to be talking at once, and he was glad that all the activity had covered his confusion. He looked covertly from one to another to see if anyone had noticed him staring at Kate. Just when he was about to look at her again, feeling like a lad bent on pilfering forbidden sweets, the solemn eyes of her mother arrested him. She held him in her gaze like a bug on a pin. He tried to slide away with a blink, but she drew him back. They stared across the room at each other.

The strange calmness came over him again, submerging his anxiety, and he yielded to her probing sense with a trust so complete it awed him. At last she released his eyes and looked at Patrick with a faint smile. "He does favor you, Papa Gallagher...and Brendan, too. The chin and yes," she said.

"Aye! There," Maggie chimed in. "Now didn't I say the same meself not an hour ago? The chin and eyes, it was...and the wild Gallagher whiskers, o'course." She laughed and came over to cup James's chin in her soft hand. "There it is, sproutin' like black briers already, and himself only still a babe."

They all laughed at his expense, and so did Jamie, glad for the distraction from his befuddlement. He was able to manage well enough after that, answering questions mostly, filling them in on what had been happening in the old country.

Most of the questions came from Kathleen Gallagher. The girl seemed to have a bottomless curiosity. An answer was barely past his lips when she would ask for another.

"And you've never had a job?"

"Not for pay."

"But if your family is so poor..."

"There is no work to be had," he tried to explain, part of his pride wanting to shield their poverty.

"But what did you do all day?" Her tone was openly curious with no hint of impatience.

He despaired of ever making her see, but after thinking a moment he answered. "Well, one day me dad and I dug all mornin' and afternoon to find three potatoes missed in the harvest. That was work."

The whole room fell silent after that, and he was sorry to have brought up the unpleasantness of it all. Kate kept his eye steadily, however, unwavering in her directness.

"Your dad will miss your help."

"Oh, no. I won't be missed," he retorted, a bit more sharply than he intended. "I think he's glad I'm gone."

"But why? If things are so bad, an extra pair of hands can put more food on the table."

Jamie shook his head. "Not hands. Me mouth is what they're pleased to do without. Y'see, I ate one of those potatoes."

He expected her to be shocked, but she simply nodded a grave sign of understanding. Was there a trace of compassion in her eyes? He yearned for it, some signal that she felt for him, yet he feared that he might find instead a look of pity. It was impossible to tell, and now he was tumbling under the distraction of her beauty again.

"I think we should go home now. You must be worn out, James." Noreen Gallagher's voice jolted him into realizing that all the others had been listening silently to Kate and himself. He had forgotten anyone else was in the room.

Brendan began pulling on his coat. "Will you be takin' him to the yard in the morning, Dad?"

"Aye," Patrick boomed, "first thing."

"Well, he'd better get some sleep." Noreen came over, squeezed James's shoulder and kissed him lightly. "Good night, James, and welcome to America." Her voice was so soft that the others appeared to take it as a cue. They began to file to the door with low voices almost as if he were already asleep and they were afraid of waking him.

He had a sudden disconcerting wish that his cousin Kate would kiss him good night as her mother had done, but she was already out the door, and the thought made him feel foolish. Just as she moved to the edge of the stoop, Kate turned to wave, her head and shoulders briefly caught in a sliver of lamplight, and she smiled.

It was nothing more than that, a friendly smile from a pretty cousin, but Jamie spent more time recalling that than anything else as he drifted into sleep that night.

And on the way home when Kevin asked his sister what she thought of their new cousin, she did not mince words.

"I should have worn the other dress."

CHAPTER 37

Patrick Gallagher's eyes were not what they used to be, but had he looked sharply at the other passengers on the *Quaker City* earlier that afternoon he might have spotted a familiar figure standing somewhat apart in the first-class area. The man was dressed rather elegantly for shipboard travel, even for an aristocrat.

Louis Jardinere had not lost his taste for finery, nor had he lost his visual acuity. There was no question about it. The man had aged considerably, but he knew Gallagher as Noreen's father-in-law from the moment the old mason stepped on the wharf.

So they were still here after all these years! He wondered if she was still living with them. Probably so. That class usually attached themselves to a good thing and lived out their lives connected to it. And from the talk in France, Irénée du Pont apparently was indeed a stable employer to attach oneself to.

Louis allowed himself a moment's reminiscence as he visualized her. He wondered what ravages the years might have wrought upon her. She might appear quite young. She *was* still young, really, and she had had that quality, a beauty that time seemed not to touch. No, she would not have changed much. He would probably still find her the stunning wood nymph. Mature, of course, but that could add to the charm.

Did he dare seek her out again? The prospect of winning her favors one more time was as stimulating as a swallow of cognac. He saw her again coming to him out of the sun-dappled woods, fresh and radiant with her own longing. The thought spun vivid behind his eyes, making him catch his breath and causing his blood to surge. He could even see the pale blue gown she had been wearing that first time. She flowed into his arms, a fragrant gossamer vision, her soft mouth open to his own. . . .

"Mr. Jardinere?"

Louis spun around, blinking stupidly in the direction of the voice.

"Sorry, Mr. Jardinere," the first officer growled. "I didn't mean to startle you out of a nap. It's been a hard passage, eh?"

"Oh, Captain Craith!"

The burley officer nodded. "I have good news for you, sir. Good news on both counts—the money exchange and the valuables. In Wilmington there is a dealer in precious stones who has the reputation of being honest. He has told me he will appraise your stock and arrange purchase. As a courtesy, he promised to exchange your currency for American."

"Excellent! When can I meet the gentleman?"

The officer pointed to a gig at the end of the wharf. "That fellow will take you to the store. It's very close to the inn, and I've arranged to have your baggage sent along with you."

Louis Jardinere was amazed at the efficiency of the ship's officer. He had singled the man out and made his request after having seen Craith's leadership of his crew at sea. Apparently he performed as well on land. Louis pulled a wallet from his coat and began to extract a bank note. The man should be rewarded.

Craith frowned, firmly pushing the money away. "That will not be necessary."

"But you have gone to considerable trouble. . ."

"A favor between gentlemen," the officer observed crisply, his tone a bit defiant.

Louis put the note away. Gentlemen indeed! What posturing these bourgeois did sometimes ape when they had tasted power.

"There is another thing, Mr. Jardinere," Craith added. "Your stagecoach for Richmond leaves first thing in the morning." He extended his hand. "Safe journey, sir. I hope the roads are better than they used to be."

"Ah," Louis said distastefully, "so do I. Your highways were somewhat primitive on my last visit."

Hours later when he had completed the sale of certain pieces of jewelry and had retired for the night, Louis thought again of Noreen Gallagher.

The thought of seeing her again was tantalizing. He could delay setting off for Richmond. What harm could come of postponing his plans?

A thought of Irénée du Pont intervened like a cold breath from the past. He had heard reports of his growing power. To risk another wrathful confrontation with Irénée in his stateless position was an unpleasant thought. The specter of another forced return to France was absolutely chilling. Another appearance there would certainly mean the Bastille... or worse.

He rolled over in the bed and dismissed the reunion with Noreen Gallagher as a bad risk... at least for now.

In the morning he ran into Craith again, barely recognizing him in the crowded dining room of the hotel. The officer had changed from maritime blues to a rather loud civilian dress, which diminished him considerably in Louis's eyes. The seaman's gait and commanding voice, which had set him apart as a leader during the long voyage, now seemed strangely out of place. He might be any one of the dozen or more drummers passing through town, quick-witted and noisy, flashy in appearance but rather crude. The cut of such people definitely did not appeal to Louis Jardinere's sensibilities, and he felt a strong embarrassment when Craith called out to him and threaded his way through the crowd of diners to join him at his table.

"Ah, Mr. Jardinere," he said, loud enough to pull a dozen stares from others in the room. "Lucky I caught ye before pulling out. Did y' have a good sleep on dry land in a steady bed?"

Louis dabbed at his lips with his linen napkin. It was apparent that Craith had enjoyed himself the night before and long into the small hours as well. His weathered face was puffed and florid with heavy drinking.

"I thought our business was finished," Louis said evenly, tossing the napkin next to his unfinished breakfast plate and making as if to rise.

"Hold fast, there," Craith grunted hoarsely, his eyes glinting at the rebuff. "I've information that may be of interest to you."

Louis settled back in his chair with a haughty nod. "Information?"

"Aye, information that can save ye time and..." Craith rubbed his finger and thumb together meaningfully.

"Well?"

The officer hunched forward and lowered his voice. "You said some time ago that y'were looking for an investment...a proper investment that would return a good profit."

"And?"

Craith withdrew a slip of paper from the inner pocket of his frock coat. He handed it to Louis, who took it with an air of indifference, glancing briefly at the single name scrawled in pencil.

"Look up that man when y'get to Richmond," Craith said. "He's in the bank. Tell him who sent you, and just say that you're interested in the place owned by the Frenchman, La Roche. It's called Skibbereen."

"Ah, Skibbereen." The word popped out of Louis's mouth before he fully remembered.

"That's the name."

"Was this plantation owned by an Irishman at one time?"

Craith looked at Louis sharply. "I do not know about that. Perhaps it was."

"Who is this La Roche? Can he be trusted to—"

Craith waved the question aside. "I don't know, but *he* will. He's a friend of mine...the banker...and he lets me know from time to time about good deals that come across his desk. He puts together mortgages for the landed gentry thereabouts. Once in a while a small amount of money is all that's needed to keep a farm...a plantation...from going aground and breaking up. These days the market can be a rocky place." He winked at Louis. "A man with a little cash can sometimes pick up salvage rights to a nice little plantation, if you know what I mean, own a piece of the aristocracy and live like a gentlemen farmer with blacks to do the work."

Louis began to hedge. The deal seemed a bit too pat for his comfort. "Why did you not tell me of this during the voyage?"

"It was in me packet of mail waiting here at the inn. When I saw that one of his prospects was a Frenchman like you, well, it seemed like something you ought to know."

[277]

"How well do you know this... banker?"

Craith took no pains to cover his impatience. He leaned over the table and spoke with quiet control. "He's square; you can count on it. He comes by it natural, and besides that, he knows better than to queer a deal with me." Craith paused. "Another thing. In this country, a Frenchman is still thought of by some as just another goose fit to be plucked. I think you would do well to ship on with your own kind until y'learn the ropes."

Craith tugged his waistcoat down over the top of his breeches and looked at Louis with a trace of amusement flickering across his face. "I may be wasting my time and yours, Jardinere. I don't even know if you have the capital to swing the deal. More than that, you may not even need protection from the investment sharks in these waters. Somehow you strike me as a bit of a shark yourself." He laughed. "Or a wolf, maybe. I somehow wonder if the money you have came from some poor bugger's fleecing. No, I won't trouble myself with concern for your survival. Good day, sir."

Craith did not wait for a reply from Louis, but made his way to the door. He had a week's leave before the *Quaker City* was due to sail from Wilmington, barely enough time to complete the round of business and pleasure he had promised himself these past months at sea. By the time he had reached the street, he had all but dismissed the exchange from his mind. He stopped once to jot an entry in the small private log he always carried, but beyond that he put the matter of Jardinere and the Richmond banker to rest. Any further concern he might have would be in the form of a commission if the deal went through. It was that simple. His banker always paid promptly, and well, for an agent's service.

As for the other thing, the plan with Garrett's people, well, he would have to let them know. But there was ample time for that. He would call on Madeleine Toussaint after hearing from Richmond that the deal went through.

By midmorning Louis was boarding the Wilmington–Richmond stage. He had no misgivings about not staying on to satisfy his curiosity about Noreen Gallagher. A practical decision.

His whole attention was concentrated on investing the small capital he carried in his bulging wallet. There would be enough to build the sum into grand things if he manged it shrewdly. Oh, yes, he would be very careful. The alternative was to begin working for a living like some classless immigrant. The possibility was frightening.

Still, as the distance between the coach and Wilmington grew, the fear of insolvency... and of E. I. du Pont... began to fade. In its place floated the loveliness of the woman.

David Craith did not hear from his banker contact in Richmond for nearly a month. When the word, and a sizable commission, arrived at last, he gave orders for the day to his crew and made a leisurely trip to Coffee Run.

When he arrived, the priest's trap was gone. Madeleine Toussaint told him that the cleric would be gone for most of the day and invited him in for something to eat. Craith refused the meal but accepted a cup of her coffee, which he knew would be sweetened with something stronger than sugar.

"Well, you can rest easy about the people on the priest's place... for a while at least," he told her.

Craith slurped noisily at the rum-laced coffee, then set the mug on the table and continued. "I made arrangements for a fellow to invest in the place, buy up shares to keep them afloat for a while longer. He went after the deal like a shark to a bleedin' sailor."

"Then they will not sell any of the people?"

"Can't be sure of that, Madame Toussaint. Never certain what those French might do."

"But was the investment large enough for us to make plans easily?"

He slurped again from the cup. "It was a good sum, according to my banker friend down there. A good sum."

She was becoming impatient. "But will they hold all the people for enough time to put the plan into effect? That is what I wonder."

"Past the harvest, I guess. They won't sell an able field slave until that crop is safely stowed. And after that, well, you know how soft the market for slaves is in the winter. I expect they'll keep 'em through the winter so as to bring a nice price in the spring."

Maddie made to refill his mug, but he waved it off and rose to leave.

"Who is this new one—the investor?" she asked.

"Some old aristocrat pried loose from a soft line, I expect. You know his type, all soft clothes and smelly perfume. He came across on the *Quaker City* last month."

She nodded, satisfied. "Then he is of no concern..."

Craith slowly cocked his head, and a perplexed look crossed his face. "I'd not be too quick to say that, madame. No, sir. He's a crafty one, he is. Snooty, too. And he's no stranger to Richmond or Wilmington; seemed to know his way about the place, like he'd been here before...some time ago, maybe."

Craith played with his cap a moment, spinning it loosely in one burly hand. When he looked up again his eyes hardened with something he remembered. "Another thing...when I mentioned the name of the place, he almost jumped, surprised like, and he repeated the name perfect. 'Skibbereen,' he said, as easy as that, like he had heard it before. He acted almost too excited, come to think of it. And he asked if it was an Irish plantation, as if that would be the normal thing for the La Roches to call their place."

Maddie gave him a sharp look and steered him toward his waiting horse. "Tell Garrett we have to move sooner than we thought." Without waiting for an answer she stepped back inside and closed her door.

Richmond's gentle March eased softly into April, and Louis Jardinere took stock of his luck. He had indeed stumbled upon a good thing. At the stroke of a pen (and the surrender of most of his assets) he had netted a quarter ownership in a respectable tobacco plantation, complete with a working force—all slaves—a grand old mansion, and, most important, the address of a gentleman.

It was true that the place had fallen prey to economic disorder, and it would be some time before it would realize any profits. But, after all, the money, or to be more accurate, the jewelry, had not been his to begin with. Officer Craith probably suspected that, though it certainly did not deter him from providing the name of a discreet merchant who was willing to buy up all he had at a bargain with no questions asked. Craith undoubtedly received a commission from the pawnbroker as well as from the banker.

Well, let him reap a gleaner's profit. Louis was relieved to be rid of the plunder. He had not stolen it—well, not precisely. He supposed that a case could be made for blackmail, but he preferred to consider the stones a kind of commission, too, for favors rendered. Each bauble in his cache represented sizable contrition from the less than beautiful but wealthy wife of a powerful Parisian.

By the time the loss of the jewelry and Louis's identity had been discovered by the furious husband, he was already on his way to Le Havre—and the *Quaker City*.

Louis sighed with relief mixed with regret. He took a certain pride in the way he had so skillfully managed his escape from prosecution. Still, there was his preference for France and the galling degradation of having been forced to leave a comfortable place twice in his life. His eyes hardened as he recalled the dressing down he had received years earlier from du Pont. A vision of Noreen again flooded his senses, dulling the harsher memory of his expulsion from the estate. He toyed with the idea of seeking her out someday after he had established himself.

In the meantime there were lesser, but more tangible pleasures to consider. He decided that the balmy weather of Richmond was definitely more to his liking than was the harsh climate farther north. The whole atmosphere of the place was appealing. There was an unmistakable elegance, a genteel pace, an extravagance of polish that he had found lacking in the northern cities.

Yes, he would come to like this place very much.

But the most delightful feature of all, an irony that capped his new acquisition, was that it was Skibbereen, the very family estate that the priest had forsaken for his saintly calling. Ah, the artistic beauty of life! He chuckled with self-satisfaction. The revenge was complete.

The memory of his last meeting with the priest—Reardon ... Francis Reardon—flashed back with the sharpness of an event that occurred weeks ago instead of the confession of nineteen years past. He relished the details of that "baring of his soul" with the same passion that he might recall an amorous conquest.

The priest's eyes had smoldered with the images, and the girl. Again he wondered if there had ever been anything between them. Of course there was *something* that burned beneath his clerical serge. But how far had it gone? In the intervening years ... anything?

Something down deep told him that Francis had never betrayed the cloth, but the conviction did not allay an attack of jealousy. Unrequited love, eh? He could almost see Francis feasting on her with his eyes, forever constrained from the slightest thought of consummation.

Louis argued within himself that he and Francis had both lost. But was it really a draw as he had claimed to himself all this time, or had Francis won the prize with his own perverse self-restraint?

Suddenly the cold glitter of his eye gave way to a dry laugh. The plantation more than made up for his other loss. How intimate, he thought to have taken the priest's family place as the master of Skibbereen. Well, that was a clever turn of fate, the ultimate seduction, eh? The wages of sin! Francis Reardon's birthright purchased with the proceeds of a cuckold. The thought was most satisfying.

Again he thought of Noreen, dallying only long enough to quicken his pulse. Too much of that kind of fantasy would sour him in the end. It had happened far too often in the past. How that woman's memory persisted. It was a curse.

Louis wrenched himself away to consider more immediate issues. He assessed his new position philosophically.

That his partner was also a French émigré softened the discovery that Louis did not especially like either the man or his wife. They were a trifle too coarse for his liking. Definitely middle class. However they did share the commonality of national birth, language, and... well, Louis smiled as he considered the truth... greed.

Why not admit the truth after all? Wealth was the goal of every successful man he had met. And that included the local Richmond gentry. For all their easygoing manners, they realized with the instinct of generations of planter breeding that money was the foundation of power.

Louis slipped into the mild climate and genteel society of the Virginia countryside with indolent grace, and the La Roche couple noticed that his aristocratic manner seemed to ease their own acceptance in the community. Louis's Old World polish could open doors that had been shut against the new proprietors of Skibbereen. That fact more than any other gave Louis stature with La Roche, and it was the reason he indulged Louis's obvious dislike of labor.

La Roche drove his workers hard and was his own overseer. That way, he reasoned, the work would get done with no excuses. He soon found out that Louis would be no help with the field slaves.

The man had no knowledge or feel for planting and apparently had never directed any work force. Louis had a role, however, one that emerged as the toil became more intense and the slaves began to try to break for freedom.

Retrieving runaways was a time-consuming and costly operation. La Roche could not afford the drain on his thinly funded operation. When the first black male made for the North, he assigned Louis the task of bringing him back.

Louis considered the work disagreeable, but he was ever the manipulator and managed to capitalize on social obligations to get the work done for him. Local planter families were charmed by his graceful entreaties, and soon all he had to do was spread the word of an escape to get dozens of slaveholders in on the pursuit and eventual capture.

Few of the Skibbereen runaways got more than a few miles into the countryside before they were caught, trussed up, and delivered to Louis Jardinere's wagon.

Not all of the escapes were easily handled, however. Occasionally a slave would make it to a hideaway and be assisted along the route to freedom. Then it was necessary to pay for information and try to intercept the fugitives before they reached the comparative safety of northern Delaware, where a black was presumed to be legally free unless proven otherwise. Once into Pennsylvania the property was virtually lost. Then the tracker had to resort to the unpredictable and costly practice of hiring a professional kidnapper.

Louis had to make two of these trips in the first few months at the plantation, the first to retrieve one of his own slaves, the second to act as an agent for one of the other slaveowners of Richmond. Although he agreed to the second trip as a token repayment to the community for all the help he had received, the owner had insisted on paying his expenses as a matter of honor. This experience started Louis thinking of the possibilities of starting a business of his own: the very lucrative enterprise of returning runaway slaves.

He approached his partner La Roche with the idea and was surprised by his response.

"Yes, certainly. It is a good plan," La Roche said. "From the looks of things, there will be much demand for such an agent."

"But I do not wish to leave you shorthanded here."

La Roche laughed. "Miss your labors? Come now, Jardinere. I'm pleased to release you into some line of work that will be productive. Go to it! I hope you become skillful enough to make a few dollars on your own and learn more about tracking down our niggers when they run."

La Roche went on, "If you plan to take on the business of hunting runaways, you should be warned of the dangers. It is one thing to parade around Richmond with the help of a score of planters, but you will find things more difficult the farther north the search takes you."

"I have noticed that," Louis commented dryly. "I am not fool enough to travel unarmed."

"A pistol is small protection against the gangs you will meet in some quarters."

"What do you suggest? That I conscript a private band of body-guards? That would wipe out any profit and make discreet investigation impossible."

"No. But I think you would be less conspicuous dressed as an ordinary businessman traveler. Look at your clothing. Any dolt can see that all your finery marks you as an aristocrat."

"Are you suggesting that I costume myself as a spy and set out in tatters?"

La Roche checked an impulse to end the conversation. This popinjay with his haughty airs and sarcasm was more than he could bear at times. But he could smell profit. A man could endure much in the hope of profit.

"Tatters?" La Roche laughed. "Somehow the idea of you in rags is too comical to entertain, Jardinere. No, rather you must give the appearance of someone out of luck, trying to make a fresh start. Decent dress, you see, a carefully sewn patch here and there, but tidy. The world trusts a man who is both short of cash and neat in appearance."

"Why is that?"

"Why, because such people are harmless, you see, and useful."

The sense of intrigue began to appeal to Louis, but the idea of charade seemed implausible in the business of catching fugitive slaves. He was doubtful. "Of what use would such an impersonation be? I do not see the point."

"You could get information more easily... information that would be kept from you otherwise."

"Why would anyone with that kind of information be interested in talking to a nobody such as you describe?"

La Roche warmed to the possibilities of the plan. "You would be a drummer, Louis. A traveling shopkeeper without a shop." He leaned forward to press the point. "Everyone talks to a drummer. They are filled with tales of distant places. They're traveling libraries of uncommon information."

"But it is I who will be seeking information."

"The very point, Louis. Each listener in turn becomes a font of information himself. No man delights more in knowing that *his* secret store of knowledge is being broadcast to the world from the lips of some harmless drummer. It gives him importance, you see, a kind of power."

Louis could see how it might be plausible. "So, during my rounds, I begin by seeding the conversation with tales of escapes and then let my clients fill in with real names and places of their own!"

"Just so."

"It might work, La Roche. What sort of merchandise should be my specialty?"

A slow smile creased La Roche's face. "Why, that should be obvious, my dear Jardinere. You will be a dealer in female underthings, of course."

Louis smiled, too. "I think I may enjoy this charade a bit more than the other hunts."

In the weeks that followed Louis threw himself into his new work with an energy that amazed La Roche. His searches apparently took Louis far afield, because he was frequently gone for days at a time. La Roche humored his partner by allowing the absences with little criticism. After all, the dandy was of no use around the plantation. If he could earn his keep by recapturing runaways, so much the better. Besides, the expenses were offset by his reward payments, and when he was gone, La Roche and his wife had the place to themselves again.

Louis never confided in La Roche regarding his clandestine activity, and La Roche never asked. He was strictly a one-man operation. The intrigue alone was a stimulus to Louis, but the deeper he probed into the whole issue of runaway slaves, the more he realized how lucrative his work could be. The Underground Railway might become a source of personal riches if he mastered its operation. And kept it strictly to himself.

Something about the drummer caught David Craith's attention as he turned the corner of Second and Tatnal streets. He was not quite sure what it was, but curiosity prompted him to canter his mount past the house he had planned to visit and continue on as though he had business elsewhere.

His face was a mask of preoccupation as he rode past the salesman and his wagon, but he caught the quick turn of the man's face out of the corner of his eye, and in that instant the captain of the *Quaker City* knew: the man in drummer's garb was the Frenchman. From the looks of things he was trying to press a sale on one of Thomas Garrett's neighbors. Now what in the name of blistering hell was *that* one doing selling goods from a wagon?

The answer flashed so suddenly on him that his jaw dropped and he swore. "So Jardinere is our leak! Bold as brass at the very doorstep of Thomas Garrett."

He wanted desperately to ride back to the corner of the alley and see if the Frenchman was still in sight, but he could not risk being seen. Well, something had to be done. He wondered if the others had any inkling.

He would have to warn the black woman at Coffee Run, but that would take time, two hours at least. He would attend to that later. Now the others would have to be contacted. He wondered if Timothy Fenn was in town.

He spurred his horse into a gallop down the dusty alleyway and turned south on the lane that ran behind the Garrett house and led directly to the iron merchant's warehouse. If Garrett's driver was anywhere about, he would be holed up there. Fenn was like a ghost; he rarely showed his face in Wilmington, and then only at night. With the exception of Garrett's family and the black woman, Craith doubted that anyone in town even knew that Tim Fenn existed.

Craith hoped desperately that Jardinere was still working at his sale. As he approached Second Street again, he breathed easier. The street was clear, and the doors to the warehouse stood open at the end of the weedy alley. Craith slowed his mount to a walk to keep down the dust and did not rein in until he was well inside the building.

It was a huge building that served as a stable and warehouse under one roof. The front was a wide dock loaded with iron implements of all types. Three wagons, minus their teams, were backed into the platform. Two of these had lettering on the sideboards: Thomas Garrett Company, Quality Iron Products. The third, a heavier rig with a deeper box, carried no logo whatever.

Two Negroes were busy transferring a great pile of goods from the platform to the largest wagon. As Craith approached, they stopped working, and the older of the two approached him.

"H'lo, Cap'n Craith," he said softly and smiled down from the dock. "I hear you got your own ship now. You're the master, huh? Congratulations."

"Hello, George. Yes, I'm in full command after all these years."

"Must be nice . . . to be boss."

Craith laughed. "Nice is not the word, George. It's everything. More work, more worries. . . . It gives me a bad stomach sometimes."

The old black grinned. "C'mon, Cap'n, it ain't so bad."

"Well, it's better than taking orders from somebody else like I've been doing all my life, it seems." He paused to look around the nearly deserted building. "But you should know about that, George. You've been giving all the orders around here since I can remember."

"Mr. Garrett is the boss here; he owns the store."

Craith looked the balding man in the eye. "Ah, George, you even give *him* orders; I've heard you myself."

George swung down on one arm to sit with his legs dangling from the dock. He chuckled. "Only when he starts in to do somethin' foolish. Then I tell the man, yes. But he owns the place and gives me pay."

"There, you see? It's the same with me. The owner of the *Quaker City* pays me, too. I give the orders, but he owns the ship. All I own are the worries."

The old man laughed, then asked, "Can we fix you up with somethin' special, Cap'n?"

Craith's tone turned serious. "There is something, George. I think we may be troubled with a dragging anchor. The ship might not be as secure in a harbor with shifting currents. Bigger flukes, maybe, or a trip chain."

George got to his feet. He jerked his head toward the rear of the building. "Go on back, Cap'n Craith, suh. Maybe you can find help back there."

Without another word, Craith tied up his horse and went to find Garrett's "conductor," Timothy Fenn.

Several hours later Craith emerged from a deep thicket that stood well off the road to Coffee Run. He drew his horse up at the edge of the roadway and looked back the way he had come, toward Wilmington, to see if he had been followed. There was no sign of the Frenchman.

He spurred his horse and cursed out loud when the miserable animal slipped gait. Craith was not a horseman; he simply desired a quick and comfortable mount. This was neither. He groaned with the ache of his thighs and the stinging between his buttocks. Too much time aboard ship between rides. He had grown tender and knew he would be greasing gall on his own arse come bedtime. He rose in the stirrups to give his cheeks a rest.

When he dismounted at Maddie's porch, he was relieved. In spite of the stinging in the seat of his pants, he was smiling. He was wondering how he could explain to the black woman that her spy had turned out to be a Frenchie aristocrat who hawked ladies' pantaloons from the back of a wagon.

It was well after dark before he returned the horse to the livery on King Street and made his way to the hotel. By that time he was reduced to walking with a crablike manuever, and he left instructions with the innkeeper to have his meal sent up to him.

Craith ate supper in his room standing over the tray, which he had placed on the washstand. After he had finished, he undressed and tended to his blisters with a generous coating of gall grease. Then he lay on his stomach in the darkened room, waiting for sleep to release him from his discomfort.

About the time that David Craith was drifting off to sleep, the tall doors of Thomas Garrett's warehouse swung open quietly on greased hinges. In the moonless dark of the alley, a white blouse seemed to float from within the building, hang disembodied for a moment, and then raise one of its ghostly arms in a beckoning gesture. There was a muted creak of leather harness being taken under load, and a double team of horses emerged from the black interior of the warehouse and appeared to float into the dusky alley. A high-sided wagon followed, creaking like a ship under its sheeted top. Occasionally the muffled rattle of cloth-wrapped singletree chains added to the hushed passage of the heavy freighter.

When the last canvas-covered bow of the Conestoga cleared the doors, the shirted figure disappeared inside and the massive doors swung together and latched with a wooden clunk.

The wagon continued up the alley, swayed gently into a turn onto Second Street, and faded into the night. A faint clattering of the iron-shod team trickled back as it crossed the harder surface of Tatnal Avenue, and then that, too, was gone.

A few minutes went by. At the end of the alley there was a small commotion in a clump of bushes bordering the street. The shadowy figure of a man moved clear of the foliage, snapping a branch and rustling the leaves. He hurried in the direction of the wagon, making little sound as he moved toward the cross street. As he passed a lighted window of the house adjoining Thomas Garrett's, the man stooped and darted through the illumination.

The briefest flicker of light washed over his head and shoulders. Just enough to illuminate the face of Louis Jardinere. He was smiling.

CHAPTER 38

The invitation from the du Ponts lay among a scattering of other mail on Francis Reardon's kitchen table, and he snatched it up eagerly. He recognized the bold flourish of Irénée du Pont even before he glanced at the signature under the request for the pleasure of his company for dinner on the twenty-sixth. That would be a week from tomorrow, he calculated. Tuesday. Strange day for a dinner invitation. No mention was made of the occasion being celebrated, nor was there any hint of who the other guests would be.

Occasionally persons of international reputation had been guests at the out-of-the way mansion. Was it possible, even remotely possible, that he was being invited because he represented the local Catholic clergy?

Since all members of the family now were established firmly as Episcopal churchgoers, the inclusion of a Catholic pastor might mean that the guest of honor was an important Catholic states-man...or even an official of the Chancery itself. What an opportunity that would be! To plead his case directly to the hierarchy of Philadelphia or Baltimore!

Francis Reardon dared not hope for such a possibility. He tried to put it out of his mind as wishful thinking, but before taking supper that evening he dug deep into the chest stored in his bedroom to unpack the fine cassock his mother had given him. It was several years old, but he had worn it only a few times, and it still looked as new as the day it had come from Italy.

When the day finally arrived, Father Reardon was prepared. As he set out in the polished buggy, he cut a figure that a monsignor might envy. The shabby mission chapel and his own lowly quarters with the widow slipped from his mind as he let his horse amble toward the Brandywine. The closer he got to the big house, the more he had to resist a rising hope that at last he would be given the chance to leave this place of exile.

When he reined in at du Pont's door, however, no other carriages were in sight, and the neatly raked gravel of the drive showed no tracks except his own. It appeared he was the only caller, and he had to fight off a deep disappointment. A young man came rushing up and held the horse's head as Francis stepped down.

"Good evenin', Father."

"Good evening," he answered without enthusiasm. He managed a smile. He had seen the youth at mass many times, but could not remember his name.

The boy began leading the animal toward the barn, then stopped suddenly and called back to the priest.

"What's his name, Father?"

"Thunder. Thunder the Second."

"A fine name, Father. It fits him. That it does."

Francis laughed outright. "Well, it suits him better than 'Lightning' all right. The animal is no racer." He paused, trying to place the fellow. "And your name?"

"Liam, Father. Liam Flynn. Nephew to old Hugh before me."

The young groom had begun leading the horse again as Francis approached the door and twisted the bell crank. The muted sound of chimes from inside the house continued for a time after he had released the handle, and he stood back to study the lighted fan arch above the door. Finally, the heavy door swung open, and Blanche Feeney was standing in the vestibule.

"Oh, Father, do come in! I'm sorry to keep you waiting, but I was downstairs in the kitchen."

"No apology needed, Blanche." Francis smiled and handed her his hat.

"The Mister asked me to make you comfortable here in the library, Father."

[291]

Francis looked about the broad vestibule before following her into a comfortable but sparsely furnished study. A few shelves of books, a pianoforte, an open secretary littered with papers, a settee, and several chairs were the only furnishings. As he entered, Francis's heels clicked on the varnished floor, setting off an echo in the hall.

"Is there no one home but you, Blanche?"

Blanche giggled nervously. "Yes, Father. I mean...no, not really....The Mister is home, but he is still in his office be...by the mill. Young Liam is on his way to fetch him this minute we're speaking."

"Then none of the others will be at dinner, I take it."

"Just the two of you, Father. The others are in town for one reason or another."

More bad news. Francis resigned himself to a tedious meal alone with Irénée du Pont. This was no social occasion, then; du Pont must have some particular business in mind.

Blanche left him, and he eased back on the soft chair seat, folded his hands in his lap, and waited. The chair was nearly in the center of the study, and as the minutes dragged by, he wished that he had chosen the bench by the pianofore. He felt like an island in the sterile room, a captive awaiting questioning. If he had been at the piano, he might have tried it. It had been so long since his fingers had touched a keyboard. But the longer he waited the more ridiculous the idea seemed. The quiet house censured his thought, rooting him to this spot.

"Ah, there you are, Father Reardon."

Francis snapped around, half leaping from the chair.

"I'm sorry. I must have startled you, Father."

"No...well, yes. I was admiring that lovely piece...."

"The piano? Ah, yes. It was my wife's. She loved it. It was the first piece of furniture we bought for this room after we built the house."

Francis extended his hand and suddenly became aware of how frail Irénée du Pont had become. Sophie's death must have hit him hard, he thought as he looked at the man closely.

Du Pont turned from the priest's intent look and walked to the piano. He depressed the first key, producing a muted metallic clink, and shrugged.

"It is badly in need of tuning. The children will not touch it."
He flashed Francis a quick, shy smile. "I think they are afraid it
would be painful for me to hear music without Sophie in the room."

Francis expected him to go on, but du Pont suddenly switched
moods and, taking the priest's arm, led him out of the study. "I
must offer regrets that we are dining alone, Father Reardon. The
others are at a political meeting in the city, and the ladies decided
to go along for the party that will follow."

"I understand," Francis offered, without understanding at all.

As they entered the dining room, du Pont led him to a long table
set for two, the place settings directly opposite each other in the
center. As he indicated the priest's chair, the older man quipped,
"If we sit in the middle, we can talk without shouting from either
end."

Barely a word passed between the two men as they ate. This was
not because du Pont relished eating so, but because of his difficulty
with chewing. The man's teeth were nearly gone, and the sheer
exercise of dining left him little time for speech. Francis did not
press conversation, once his host's difficulty manifested itself; indeed, he concentrated all the more on his own plate and tried to
ignore as best he could the poor man's labors.

When Blanche Feeney had cleared their plates at last, both men
were grateful to quit the table and retire into the drawing room.

"Would you like to continue with wine, Father, or will you join
me in a brandy?" du Pont said as he ushered his guest into the softly
lighted salon.

"A brandy, please, Mr. du Pont."

Du Pont waved him into a deeply cushioned chair, and Francis
took his place, silently watching the man pour two brandies at a
table beneath a large tapestry. Francis noticed a rolled document,
nearly a yard long and tied with a ribbon, leaning against the wall
beside the table.

As he offered Francis his glass, du Pont raised his own. "Your
health, Father Reardon."

"And yours, sir. My thanks for a delicious and pleasant dinner."

They sipped the liquor in silence for a few moments. Then
Francis leaned forward in his chair.

"How can I serve you, Mr. du Pont?"

The abruptness of his question surprised the old man, who looked at him with an amused smile. Putting his glass down, he rose and walked slowly back to the liquor table.

"Not at all, I think. But I would like to serve you, Father Reardon . . . or perhaps to serve your people is the better way of putting it." He stooped to pick up the roll of papers and brought them back to the priest.

Standing in front of Francis with the tube gripped across his legs he seemed suddenly at a loss for words.

"Serve my people?"

"Yes. We were speaking before dinner of the powdermen, their families, the devotion they have for your church. . . . Well, I have long wished to give them a token of *my* devotion."

"But Mr. du Pont, everyone knows of your pensions for injured workers, and widows . . . and the Employees' School."

"I was thinking of something beyond that," the mill owner went on. "Look, Father Reardon, I do not wish to pry, but attendance at your mission church is not heavy, eh? And small wonder, my reverend friend. One cannot expect your flock to walk so many miles to mass each Sunday over bad roads in terrible weather."

Francis wanted desperately to agree; that had been his own rationalization, after all, but somehow it was unseemly to take refuge in it.

Du Pont appeared to be reading his thoughts. "Ah, Father Reardon, you must not assume the responsibility. It was not you who picked the location of your little church."

"That is true."

Irénée du Pont tapped the roll of papers against the flat of his palm and then strode to a settee at the far end of the room, slipping off the band of ribbon on the way. "Come over here in the good light. I want to show you something."

When they were seated together, he unrolled a large sheet and spread it out over their knees. Francis recognized it as a map of the entire du Pont estate. He followed du Pont's finger as he traced it along the southern boundary of the family's holdings. It stopped and tapped on a penciled square near the bottom of the map.

"Here," the old man whispered. "Here is where it will be. Do you know the place?"

Francis craned his head for a better look. "Yes, I think so. That would be the top of the hill above the Barley Mill Road, wouldn't it?"

"You have a quick eye for charts, my friend. Yes, that is it precisely . . . a ten-acre parcel."

"I've been past there a hundred times on my way to your mills, Mr. du Pont. It is a lovely flat hilltop."

"It is yours."

"I beg your pardon?"

"My gift to your people."

Francis stared at du Pont for some time before the words registered.

"You mean you are making a gift of this land to the church?"

"To the Catholics of the Brandywine, yes."

"I . . . I don't know what to say! Such a gift . . ."

"There is something else." He dropped the first sheet and spread out another. "Here is a rough sketch of how the buildings will appear. The rectory is the smaller building, and the church itself is—"

"You want us to build a church . . . ?"

"Ah, well, not so, Father Reardon. Your people are not wealthy, eh? And there will not be enough money in the Wilmington diocese to finance such a project for some time. I have thought of that." He dropped the second sheet and held up a third. "Now, here is a rough idea of the floor plan of the church. Only sketches of course. You will suggest the refinements to more detailed drawings."

"My head is spinning, sir!"

"Now to the plan," du Pont went on as though his listener were not on the verge of shock. "There is little money, of course. But we have many workers, and the stone is in the earth ready to be blasted out. The company will provide the workmen—they are your people, you see—and my family will donate the materials with which we will build this church on your new land." With that he dropped the plans and looked to Francis for approval. "Well, good Father, what do you think?"

Francis shook his head, not believing it could be true. "Such generosity, Mr. du Pont. I am moved by your sense of Christianity. For one of a different faith to so accommodate another."

"Nonsense, Father. It is just that I want my people to be content. That's all your Irish seem to worry about—even more than food on their tables—a church of their own to go to on Sundays."

Francis was tingling with emotion. It was true, then, what the powdermen had said of this sainted man.

"Truly, sir," he intoned with reverent sincerity, "the Lord himself has seen fit to direct your hand and heart!"

The old man dismissed the idea, with pure humility. "An employer should take care of his workers, Father. It is as simple as that."

But on his way home that night, Francis was still enthralled with the magnificence of it all. He stopped at the site of his future church and prayed so long kneeling in the withered grass beside his carriage that Thunder set up an impatient stamping to be off for the barn.

The name of the new parish flashed upon him as he drew close to the humble mission he had served so long. "I will name it for the patron saint of workers," he thought. "It will be St. Joseph's— St. Joseph's-on-the-Brandywine!"

Irénée du Pont was content, too, that night as he made ready for bed. He would draft a letter first thing in the morning to commence recruitment of more Irish labor for the mills. They would be eager to come—and to stay. He would even advance the cost of passage and take it out of their pay in small portions as they worked.

As he was dozing off he made another mental note to arrange to have his sons act as trustees in the new parish. They were not Catholics, but he could not imagine Father Reardon or his bishop objecting to that. After all, there would be no church without du Pont generosity. And he had to protect his investment with proper supervision. It was a business affair after all.

Maybe now the fear of explosions would lessen. These people seemed to work more comfortably around danger knowing that their priest was within running distance to give them last rites, just in case.

CHAPTER 39

Slack times at the yards were a boon to the building of the church. Nearly half the powdermen were pressed into service for the project, and all of the heavy tools used for the construction of the massive stone powder mills were made available for the erection of church and rectory.

The walls went up with marvelous speed, lifting the spirits of every soul from Squirrel Run to Chicken Alley. It really did seem too good to be true. It would have been grand enough to have just the land to build on, but here they all were working for their own church and getting paid for it by the Mister. Why even the stone and bricks and mortar and timber—and it was the rumor the roof would be slate—all of it paid for out of the man's pocket. The extent of his generosity strained the mind.

Francis delighted in the childlike happiness of his Irish, and for the first time in his ministry submerged himself in his role as father to his flock.

They had started coming to him for solace and guidance after that first great catastrophe, and on the occasion of every serious accident at the mills since. But it was a long trip from the Brandy-wine to Coffee Run. With the new church barely a half-mile from the yards, and virtually surrounded by employee housing, he was already beginning to get a steady stream of troubled parishioners.

One of them was Blanche Feeney.

Francis was uncomfortable in the woman's company. It had nothing to do with her personally, but she was Noreen Gallagher's sister, and that fact made him uneasy. After all this time he was still beset by his attraction to Noreen....Ah, he might as well be honest with himself: he was in love with her. It was his cross to bear, sweet cross that it was, and somehow he had been given the strength to endure the torment of the unrequited love. As far as he knew, no one, not even Noreen ever suspected his feelings.

He knew that there was an alienation between Blanche and her sister. Blanche rarely even visited her own family. Perhaps it was this very alienation that gave Francis Reardon concern. He was ever afraid that Blanche's detached position might give her a perceptive edge, enough to catch some flicker of emotion in his voice or eye whenever Noreen's name came up.

The day she called on him in the half-finished rectory, however, he had nothing to worry about. The woman was so distraught that she barely greeted him before tumbling out her concerns.

"I'm sorry for the mess, Blanche," he said brushing off a chair, "but I insisted on moving in as soon as the lower floor was finished. I'm afraid that the carpenters are having a difficult time working around these temporary quarters."

"Well, Father Reardon, we are all happy to have you within walking distance at last. And in the nick of time."

"The nick of time...?"

"You'll have to do something about it and quick, Father. Or somebody will. It's a scandal in the making, and my people seem to be ignorant of it."

Francis raised an eyebrow. "Scandal?"

"That's what it will be soon, if it's not already. My niece—"

"Kathleen," he said. "Your sister's daughter?"

"Kate Gallagher is keeping company with one of the new lads at the yards."

Francis was relieved. He began to marshal his pat assurances.

"His name is James Gallagher," Blanche whispered and sat back to wait for her pastor's comment.

Francis did not even make the connection of last names at first. "Oh, yes. He would be the boy living with Patrick and Margaret Gallagher. Is that right?"

Blanche leaned forward and whispered again. "He's Patrick Gallagher's *nephew*, Father."

"His nephew..."

"Kate is his *cousin*."

"Her cousin?"

"Yes, Father. The two of them are first cousins, or close enough to that. And from what I hear they are thick as fleas. Well, you know what I mean, Father. It's a sin, isn't it? I mean, the church says it's a mortal sin for cousins to marry?"

"An impediment, yes," Francis recited automatically as he tried to sort out what Blanche had been saying. "Do you mean that Noreen's daughter is being courted by her own cousin?"

"That's what it looks like to me."

"Perhaps it only seems so, Blanche. Have you seen them? I mean, have you seen them yourself?"

"No, I have not. But the news has come from ones I trust."

He decided it would be better not to pry into her sources of information. It was a problem if it was true.

"What does your sister say about this? I imagine she is quite upset."

"I have not spoken to her of it. Nor to Brendan either."

"I see."

"I thought it best, Father Reardon, that I come to you right away... to see if it was truly wrong.... I mean, before I went to them about it."

"Well, Blanche, if it is true as you say, then it is most seriously wrong indeed. However, I think it would be wise not to stir up things until you speak to Noreen."

Blanche shifted on the chair, and he knew she had taken the comment as a rebuff. "The girl is heading for a marriage with her father's cousin."

"First cousin, once removed," Francis observed. He sounded as if he were reading it directly from the book of canon law. "Within the third degree of kindred. An impediment which, if ignored, is cause for excommunication."

Blanche gasped, "Excommunication!"

"Now I'm sure we are not faced with anything of the kind, Blanche. Certainly Mr. Gallagher would not tolerate such a thing going on

[299]

with someone under his own roof. And as for Kate's mother, well..."
A thought suddenly struck him in midsentence and he floundered.
Noreen Feeney was of independent mind. The old memory rankled
in him again.

Francis rose. The discussion was too tenuous. It might be idle
gossip. He took Blanche's arm as she followed his cue and led her
to the door.

"Speak to your sister and brother-in-law before anything else is
done. The whole thing may be imaginary after all."

Blanche looked doubtful. "If it's imagination, then half of Chicken
Alley is dreaming," she retorted, still smarting at his put-down. "I'll
let you know what she says."

Blanche Feeney rarely came off the hill to spend any time in Chicken
Alley. Her visits home were measured in minutes rather than hours,
and it had been years since she had stayed even long enough to
join her family for dinner.

Noreen was surprised, therefore, to see her sister standing in the
doorway.

"Hello, Noreen. I thought it would be nice if we had a visit,"
she said as if it were the ordinary thing. "Why don't you put the
tea on."

"Come in, Blanche.... It's so cold out. You must be freezing."

She closed the door behind her sister and led her into the kitchen.
"There... Daddy's chair," she said pointing to a wooden armchair
at the head of the plank table. "Let me push it closer to the hearth
so's you can warm a bit."

"Is he home?" She whispered the question.

"No...no. He's...out."

"I see." Prim disapproval mixed with relief. Blanche held out a
parcel wrapped in paper and tied with twine, and when Noreen
made no move to take it, she placed it on the table.

"Those are some things from the house I thought you could use.
Some things might fit you and Kathleen, and there's a jacket of the
Mister's that will fit Daddy. The things are hardly worn, really, and
I would have liked to keep the dress for myself. Of course, that
would not do with my being seen in them at the house."

Noreen looked closely at Blanche, her clothing, the elegant bonnet, her beautiful hair, gray in places, but lovely. And her face... still smooth with few wrinkles around the eyes and none around the mouth. Not a careworn face, that. She wondered how they would compare now. It would not be a draw, surely, and not because of the four-year difference in their ages either. Blanche had done well tucked away from troubles. None of the wrenching sorrows of marriage... well, none of the joys either. She looked like a nun in fancy clothes, preserved and neat.

Blanche pulled off her woolen gloves. "I do think you might take the time to look in a glass, Noreen. You're a young woman still and shouldn't let yourself go. I know it must be hard to keep up with the demands of a cottage full of men, but a woman must keep up appearances."

Noreen could feel the anger begin to rise. "Katie and I manage to..."

"Kathleen. Yes. Now that's who I want to speak to you about."

"I'll get the tea," Noreen said. She filled the kettle from the freshwater bucket. As she swung it over the low coals of the hearth, she heard Blanche sigh deeply.

"Now you must understand that I'm telling you this for the girl's own good, Noreen. Ordinarily, as you well know, I do not like to butt in, but if what I hear is true, something must be done... and quick."

"If you are going to bring up the business of Katie working in the woolen mill again, I won't be listening, thank you."

"It's not about her working there, although that is a sore subject, too. To have her rubbing elbows with the likes of those... every day at that place when she could have a position with one of the family as fast as a wink... well, it's beyond me."

"She does not want to be a servant to the du Ponts."

The color rose in Blanche's cheeks. "All right, then. We'll drop that, but there's the other thing that won't lie still."

The kettle whistled abruptly, and Noreen wrapped her hand with the apron and lifted it from the fire. "What is it, then, Blanche, that brings ye all the way down off the hill to Chicken Alley?"

"James Gallagher."

"Jamie?"

"Himself. Or more to the point, our Kathleen and James Gallagher. They've been seen holding hands, and the Flynn boy tells me that Meg Halloran saw them in each other's arms, kissing to beat the band last Saturday behind the spring by her house."

Noreen laughed suddenly, a happy little chirp that bubbled out of her.

"What in heaven's name are you laughing at, woman?" Blanche demanded.

"Oh, I was thinking it's been so cold lately, and I could just picture Meg scootin' through the bushes behind her house to get a good look. Y'can't see the spring from her house, y'know. She must have been spyin' on them. I don't wonder she got that awful cold she has. Was she crouched there for very long?"

"Noreen, I do not think it's amusing at all. You miss the point."

"I'm sorry, Blanche. What point was that?"

"Saints preserve us, Noreen, she's falling in love with the lout!"

Noreen bridled at the epithet. "He's a good lad, fine and sensitive, if you ask me, and no 'lout' at all. He's a hard worker who'll not be a powderman all his life."

"He's her *cousin!*" Blanche shouted the word so loudly that she nearly screeched. Noreen blinked.

"Well, yes. Of course. In a way. He is really Brendan's cousin, isn't he?"

Blanche sighed with exasperation. "Listen Noreen. The man is halfway to being her first cousin. It's a terrible thing and a scandal in the making. It's against all the laws of the church. Father Reardon says so. . . ."

"What does Father Reardon have to do with all this?"

"Well, I spoke with him about it the moment I heard."

"Why did you go to the priest?"

"*Somebody* had to take the bull by the horns."

"You should not have done that, Blanche. To spoil an innocent little thing."

"Innocent be damned is what they'll be if they're not stopped in their tracks. Mind you, Noreen, he'll be asking for her hand in blasphemous marriage before long or . . . or worse."

"You're makin' a mountain out of a molehill, Blanche. Here, have some tea before it steeps to bitters."

Blanche rose and swished behind the chair, gripping the back and staring down at her. "Huh! How can I get it through your head?

[302]

Listen, the time to stop this thing is right now...before it gets any more serious than it is."

"I think the thing to do now, Blanche, is to sit back down and have a quiet cuppa with me. Let me handle the matter...if it needs handling at all. And I'll thank you not to be gossiping any more about those two."

"Gossip, is it? Well, remember that it didn't start with me."

"The important thing, I'm thinking, is that it stops with you, Blanche."

"I'll not say another word, if that will please you, but I'll have to stop my ears not to hear of it more." She took a sip from the cup and made a face. "And you'll be hearing from others. . . . The father wants to speak to both of you. He said it was his duty to put a stop to public scandal."

"I'll speak to him myself. There's no need to upset Brendan."

Blanche put her cup down. "The whole thing could be set right in a minute, you know. If James were to leave the mills, they wouldn't be thrown together, and it would be over in a month. All it would take would be a word from me to the Mister, and he would—"

Noreen leaped to her feet, and her cup crashed to the floor, shattering with a wet splash. She glared at her sister. "Breathe a word of this to that man, and as God is my witness, Blanche, I'll kill you."

Long after Blanche had left, Noreen sat in the kitchen gazing at the barren treetops just visible through the window over the sink. They were black etchings laced through the pale blue of the winter sky. Months yet before they would bud again and fill her vista with soft greens. If she stood she would see the broad surface of the Brandywine, black-green now with new ice. She did not like to look at the new ice, flat as a sheet of glass, mysterious, like life caught in a dream. After a few days, weeks, if would whiten with cracks, rumpled at the shoreline, perhaps dusted with snow flurries. Water was restless by nature, riffled, tumbling, moving, ever moving. She did not like to see it caught suddenly fast in still green wetness. Even as a child she had not liked to see it so, her face pressed close to the flawless pane that was inches thick, peering into the inky black, straight down, as if she were looking into a night sky without stars. Once while she knelt so on hands and knees, a rumpled leaf had wandered past, tattered from miles of scraping soundless under the ice, a dead thing, and she had scuttled after it, bumping her nose in the eerie chase, wondering if it would get where it was supposed to be before the next layer of cold would lock it up in a green tomb.

Noreen turned her face from the window and trembled. So her secret would come unlocked again. Eighteen years. She had nearly forgotten.

CHAPTER 40

Francis studied the troubled face of Noreen Gallagher as they sat with a pot of tea between them in the rectory kitchen. A shaft of winter sun angled through the east window, catching her graying auburn hair and turning it into a soft halo. She grew more beautiful with the years.

He toyed with a teaspoon and shook his head slowly. "Impossible. The rules of the church are clear in these matters, Noreen. Kate cannot marry her father's first cousin."

He watched her eyes brighten with sparks of anger. "I see no earthly reason why—"

"No *earthly* reason, indeed, Noreen, but we are guarded against offenses of the flesh by God's law."

"And where does this law come from? Did the Lord write it somewhere that Kate and James should not marry because their kin are close? I'd like to know that!"

"Leviticus, eighteen."

Noreen was suddenly out of her depth. She looked away for a moment; then a thought crossed her mind and she spun back.

"What about the du Ponts? One of the girls married her first cousin!"

Francis sighed and dropped his head. "They are not of our faith."

Noreen quickly followed up. "Not Catholic maybe, but don't

they follow the Bible, too? Does the Almighty have a different set of rules for the Mister and his lot?"

"They do not have the gift of faith, as we do, Noreen. We must be the example to show others the way."

"A gift, is it? More like a burden, I'd say, Father Reardon." Noreen was thoughtful, then spoke resignedly, "I've had me fill of burdens, thank you, but if there's no other way out of this thing, I'm about to pick up another." She looked into his eyes steadily. "Or maybe I'm about to drop one on you, Father."

"And that is . . . ?"

Her eyes were still fixed on him so close as she leaned forward that he could see his own image inverted on the lens.

"You remember my confession to you nineteen years ago next summer?"

Ah! After all this time! He was tempted to pretend that he had forgotten, that like a good confessor he had been able to let the seal of confession blot his human memory as well as his tongue, but those eyes would not allow it.

"Yes, my child. Yes, I do remember. Is it your wish to make a good confession now?"

"No. . . ." Noreen appeared confused, but then something clicked, and she added, "Ah, no, Father. I set that all rights within the week . . . with the old priest. You remember. . . ."

He flushed with his own presumption and waved her off. "That's all right, Noreen, I thought . . . Well, I'm sorry to have . . . Never mind." Dear God but he was handling this badly!

There was compassion in the look she gave him now, as if she was suddenly aware of *why* it was that he remembered. He felt his heart begin to pound with fear that she might probe the secret out with those eyes.

Her expression gradually changed, a subtle difference that hardened the lines about her mouth, and her eyes went cold.

"I've never told this to a soul, Father Reardon, but if it means her happiness and my misery, I'll be out with it now."

He waited, and she seemed to brace herself again before she spoke. "Kathleen is not Brendan's child."

"What?"

"Like I said before, she and James are not really cousins at all."

[306]

He was stunned, her words only half registering. A name flashed on his mind, and he uttered it before thinking: "Louis Jardinere!"

Noreen recoiled as though he had struck her. "How did you know it was him?"

Francis's mind reeled with the enormity of his action. In two words he had broken his confessor's vow. He hurried to cover the awful indescretion.

"He...he seemed the logical..."

Noreen paled. "It was Mister du Pont who told you."

"No, no, he would never be so unfeeling, Noreen."

She looked at him steadily until he dropped his eyes and fumbled with the teaspoon. "Then it was Louis himself who said it. Did he pour the whole unlovely tale into your ears, Father?"

Francis stared at his cup and said nothing.

Suddenly she knew, sickened by it all. "He confessed to you, too!" she whispered. "And he told you my *name*?"

The charade was pointless now, Francis thought miserably. How easily he had become duped by Louis's sacrilegious game.

"It was improper for him to do so, but he did."

"And you let him?"

"...before I could stop him."

She dropped back against the chair, slumped with the degradation of it all. She covered her mouth and avoided looking at him.

"And all these years you knew..."

"Not I, Noreen. It was between you and God. I was just the instrument."

She laughed, a miserable little barking sound.

"'Instrument,' is it? I might say that's all me sinful partner was, an instrument. I shudder to think whose instrument he was, though for a time I thought to be in paradise."

He thought miserably of his own affliction. "Love can blind the stoutest heart...."

"Love?" She looked up at him. "Y'would not know of such things, Father, protected by the cloth as you are, but it was lust, not love, that got me in this fix. Lust," she added miserably, "and other things."

They both sat silently for what seemed like minutes. At last she spoke again. "So they can marry after all."

"How... can you be sure of that? Does Brendan know?"

"I know," she said flatly. "The child came early by a few weeks, and she has... his features. And no, Brendan thinks she is his own."

"Everybody does?"

"Everybody."

"Then nothing is changed," he said gently. "The impediment stands."

The color drained from Noreen's face, and she struggled to her feet. Her voice trembled. "In God's name, why? Isn't it enough for me to tell my awful secrets to you so that the innocent ones can be happy? Must I shout it from the bell tower on the church this Sunday?"

He tried to sooth her with as soft a tone as he could manage. It was hard work; the face of Louis Jardinere kept pushing into his mind with an evil, leering smile.

"We must protect the faithful from being scandalized, Noreen. Your Kate is Brendan's child as far as anyone knows. Let it go. Can't you see the harm that will come of publicizing her paternity?"

"Then you won't marry them?"

"I can't."

"You'll drive them from the church."

"No," he said sharply. "They must be made to break it off. Counsel them. Surely when they realize the incestous blasphemy that such a—"

"*Incest*, is it now!" Noreen retorted, her face gone bloodless even to the lips. "You call it incest because of what it seems... not for what it truly is. You would have me tear them apart and use my tired old lie as the reason? And you make this church a tyrant to bend them under the lie?"

"Noreen, Noreen, listen to reason," he begged. "You'll destroy both your families if you don't bury the past. Which is worse, the end of a budding, childish affair or the destruction of lifelong relationships and your own good marriage?"

Noreen turned her back to the priest and walked to the window. When she faced him again she was icy calm and her words flowed without emotion.

"Lifelong relationships and a good marriage, eh? Well, Father, we'll soon see how strong those family ties are... and how good the marriage really is. I'm going to give that pair my blessing, soiled as it is, and..." her speech trembled slightly, "and tell them *why* they're not related, after all."

He could see that further argument was useless. He rose from the table and walked to her side. "Just think it through before you act. That's all I ask, Noreen. The laws and rules seem harsh, I know, but they sometimes help us avoid the pits our hearts can lead us into."

"Like marriage banns?" she asked, thinking of long ago. He was not quite sure of what she meant. Catching the perplexed look on his face, she let it go. "Never mind, Father, you keep your laws and rules, and I'll be following my heart, for a change. I don't suppose you have need for aught else but laws. It must be easier on the mind."

After she left, he wept for the first time since the great mill disaster, not because she had caused him pain, but because, again, he had failed her in her great need.

He was still uncomposed an hour later when a messenger came galloping up to the rectory with a letter from his superiors in Baltimore. The blood pounded in his ears as he tore open the seal and unfolded the single page. The contents were brief and cruelly to the point: "The community of your brethern in Christ wish to inform you of the imminent death of your mother who was stricken yesterday. May God speed you to her side in time for you to give her your priestly blessing before she is taken to her heavenly reward."

Francis was in Wilmington boarding the overnight stagecoach to Baltimore before the sun set on that most unhappy day.

CHAPTER 41

Jardinere grimaced as he saw La Roche apply the whip. The man was a fool to give in so recklessly to wrath and risk mutilation of his own property. It was pointless anyway. After that first welt rose in mute echo of her solitary shriek, the girl was insensible to the rest of the lashing. She hung limp from her wrists at the end of the rope tied to a massive limb of the magnolia, her toes dragging furrows in the dust.

"An example to the rest," La Roche said. He grunted with effort as he swung his arm again, and the rawhide hissed toward her. The tip cracked like a shot against her naked belly, flicking a white crater in the tawny skin under the navel. Louis stared at the wound as it welled red and ran a narrow rivulet into her groin.

"Enough!" he snapped at his partner.

But La Roche had already begun coiling up his lash. He clucked his disapproval with a smirk. "You have a weak stomach, Louis?"

"Why go to the trouble to bring them back if you scar the wretches so badly they can neither work nor be sold?" Louis demanded angrily.

"Nor used to pleasure a man?" La Roche insinuated.

Louis glared at him. "If you will remember, I own a share in this plantation, and I will not stand by while you indulge your rage by destroying our property."

La Roche laughed. "'Indulge,' you say? I suppose that you were not indulging, my dear Louis, when I saw you and this wench together in the tobacco sheds."

Still chuckling, La Roche approached the dangling figure, pulled her head back roughly by the hair, and dumped a pail of water into her face. The shock of the cold water brought an immediate reaction from the girl, and she began to flop like a gaffed fish, her eyes rolling in seizure. With a single tug he slipped the knot, and the girl collapsed backward into the bloodied puddle under her. An occasional moan, barely audible, passed through her open mouth.

Louis turned his back to the sight and strode away from the quarters, away from the tobacco sheds, trying to think only of his rooms and a bath to rid himself of the filth of his journey—and this latest business.

"Larkie, come out and tend to this. Do you hear me, Larkie? Quickly now! And the rest of you... back to work."

La Roche's calling out to his hidden audience further grated on Louis's nerves. He still could not, after months in this dismal place, make out the Negro family connections. Larkie was the oldest female they owned, he knew that, but whether she was related to the unfortunate creature on the ground under the tree, Louis was not certain. But La Roche knew. He knew them all by name and kinship, something these simple people seemed to respect almost as much as his exquisite wrath. Louis had at first marveled at the man's ability to carry on homely conversations with the "folk" as he goaded them to greater production. He could mimic their pidgin phraseology and even slip into the accent, almost as if he were one of them instead of their owner.

"C'mon Marcie. C'mon, now. Whack on them weeds lak Aunt Josie show you, or ah'll tell her on you 'n' she whack on you whens you gits t' quahtuhs 'night," he would say, and the field hands would giggle and hum agreement.

The first time he had heard La Roche speak to them in this way, Louis had thought one of the slaves was speaking until he turned and saw his new partner's lips working. He had been startled at the man's familiarity, wondering if somehow the slaves had taken over their master. A few days later that impression had changed abruptly when he was treated to an example of the La Roche whipping technique. The guillotine seemed humane by comparison.

Louis grimaced with impatience as the decking of the porch creaked under his feet. The place was beginning to depress him.

He was grateful to be spared meeting La Roche's wife in the wide central corridor and walked directly to a staircase whose cantilevered mass swept up in a graceful fanning arc to the balconied rooms above. Louis felt so soiled that he refrained from touching the spotless handrail with his fingertips as he ascended. Despite the fatigue he felt from the morning's events, he rushed up the last few steps with a crawling need to get out of his clothes and bathe.

And then a nap. He deserved that, and it would put him in better spirits for a trip into Richmond tonight. The thought of the ten-mile ride was certainly not something he was looking forward to with pleasure—not after the night-long journey with the captured runaway, but there would be a good bed awaiting him at the end of the road and an eager young thing to share it with.

He was still napping that afternoon when the shipment of iron plows was delivered by the wagon from Philadelphia. The driver was eager to take on a full load of tobacco for his return trip, and spent several hours supervising the loading of his pungent new crop. La Roche was impressed with the man's skill and the care he took with the bundled leaf. This was the best of their crop, and La Roche wanted it to arrive fresh and dry in the lucrative northern market. If he could build a reputation in Philadelphia as a quality grower, the fortunes of Skibbereen would quickly rise.

LaRoche handed the teamster an envelope bearing the address of a tobacco dealer written in the elaborate script of Madame La Roche and a copy of the lading bill.

"You will be paid on delivery," he explained. "Take care of the unloading, and I can guarantee my regular trade."

The driver accepted the documents with a silent nod and went back to work. La Roche watched him a moment longer, idly curious about the purplish scar tissue on his neck, visible under the open collar of his blouse. La Roche wondered if his arms and chest were marked as well, and what had caused the disfiguration. He wanted to ask, but the man's taciturnity was a wall to his curiosity. He shrugged off the thought and took his leave.

The driver took great pains with the loading, so that the tobacco rode high and light in the Conestoga bed with many roomy pockets laid like a maze within the load.

It was dark when he finished and clucked to the team to start north again, so dark, in fact, that Louis did not notice the wagon standing by the sheds when he drove off for his rendezvous in Richmond.

Just after sunrise the following day, La Roche was wild with rage again when the hounds ended their snuffing trail of the four runaway slaves three miles south of the plantation on the banks of the James River. At the spot where the dogs stood bawling their frustration, he could see where a raft had been dragged into the water; a length of rope was still fastened to a freshly driven stake. And there, there in the confusion of footprints in the wet mud, clear as a signed declaration of rebellion, was Larkie's impression, the right foot without a middle toe.

He should have chained that little nigger up after he whipped her. Damn! Now the whole family was gone—Larkie, her son and his wife, and that young one again. They could have drifted all the way to Richmond, or gotten off the raft at a hundred places between. He wondered if the hounds would be able to pick up their scent.

The dogs were pulling and yelping so much as he retraced his steps back to the plantation that he had to use the whip to quiet them. Stupid brutes! They could not tell the difference between the trail going or coming. When he got back to the starting point they set up a greater din than they had at the river.

La Roche gave up in disgust and went up to the house to figure his losses and wait for Louis Jardinere.

North of Fredericksburg, at about the same time La Roche was commiserating with his wife, his shipment of tobacco came to a halt at the Rappahannock ferry crossing. The wagon had made excellent time over the night roads. The driver set his brake and climbed stiffly from the seat. He made a slow circuit of the team, giving close attention to their hooves and checking the harness for chafing. The animals were tired, he knew that, but the pace had not been so hurried that there was any sign of lathering. He was pleased at that. Anyone looking at the rig would presume they had just begun the day's haul.

He looked about the deserted landing for any signs of life, but as far as he could tell there was no one else about. Stepping to the side of the wagon, he opened his pants and urinated with his back to the road. He was huddled so close to the wagon that when he was finished, his knuckles grazed the sideboards. They rapped smartly three times on the wood planks. As he bent over to fasten his pants, his ear was cocked inches from the wagon bed. Just before he straightened up and turned to look across at the approaching ferry, he heard three distinct raps from inside the load.

The message from La Roche reached Louis late in the afternoon. The news infuriated him. How could La Roche let more people slip away the very day he had brought one back? The bungler should be made to get back what he had lost on his own—assume some responsibility for his own lack of security.

"Damn him!" Louis seethed, his mind filled with social delights he would now have to cancel because of the note in his hand. "It would serve him well if I refused."

It was only a moment's dalliance, however, and by the time he reached the plantation much of his anger was spent. His mood was sour but resigned.

La Roche was returning to the stable after another futile search with the hounds when Louis approached.

La Roche glowered, but his voice was subdued. "You are back quickly, eh? It was good of you to come so quickly."

"Which one ran away this time?"

"Larkie's family. All four of them!"

"You mean . . . including the one you whipped yesterday? The girl I just brought back?"

"Yes, yes! That damned little wench. You see, I should have given her more. The lesson . . . the lesson, it must be complete." He grinned wryly. "You were so upset that I spared her. Not to scar your plaything, eh? Now she is gone from you again."

One of the hounds was struggling against the line La Roche had bound to his saddle. With a roaring curse, La Roche leaped from his horse and jerked the bawling dog over on its back. In full stride he kicked the beast so violently that the old bitch rolled over several times howling with pain. She struggled to her feet, still whining, and limped awkwardly away from La Roche. Louis wondered if her ribs were cracked, and when she lowered her muzzle to the ground and began snuffling, he was sure the animal was about to go into convulsions and die on the spot.

But the old hound labored in a straight line to the corner of the drying sheds where she stopped and began to bay mournfully.

La Roche was beside himself. "Look at that! Again she tracks back to the starting point." He began to fumble with the flap of his saddlebag. "The scent a day old, and still the dog calls me off!"

"Calls you off...?"

"Yes! This morning also. She led us first to the river where I saw the footprints... where they boarded the raft... and then in a crazy run back here to the quarters. Ah, the dog's brain is gone. She's worthless." He rummaged about in the saddlebag. "Ah! Here we are, eh?" He pulled out a pistol.

Louis followed his wild-eyed partner to the baying hound. She was sitting on a wheel-rut near the door of the drying shed and gave no sign of seeing La Roche approach with the gun pointed at her head.

Louis was not prepared for the noise of the shot, a crack that stung his ears and left them ringing. And he was appalled at the work of the ball, which carried half the dog's head away.

Louis suddenly felt sick.

La Roche bent over the sprawled carcass, watching it curiously as it twitched. "*Oui*, Louis, it is a businesslike gun, no? One shot only; we must make it count, eh? Not like the toy you carry in your pocket."

Louis turned from the man in disgust, but La Roche seemed not to notice.

"Ah, Louis," he spoke lightly, "there are some things to show you before we go into the unpleasant task of getting back our runaways. While you were resting yesterday our new plows came. I tried one out on the new field we cleared for the golden leaf tobacco."

He tugged Louis by the arm, forcing him to follow him into the storage room. "There they are," he rattled on enthusiastically, pointing to a row of deep-bladed iron plows gleaming with the sheen of fresh black paint.

Louis suddenly came alive. Snatching the lantern from La Roche he crouched by the nearest plowshare, holding the light next to the cast-iron colter beam. The embossed trade name leaped out, and he read it aloud.

"Garrett Iron Works."

La Roche was pleased by Louis's apparent enthusiasm. "Ah, you recognize the name, eh?"

Louis straightened slowly, but he seemed mesmerized by the plow. Then he shook his head and repeated the name in a hoarse whisper, "Thomas Garrett!"

La Roche was confused. "But they are of high quality. The best that money can buy. Yesterday we tried one, and it cut deeply.

"Yesterday? The plows were delivered here...yesterday?"

La Roche nodded.

"In a high covered wagon? Very heavy, with a bed much larger than most?"

"Ah, you saw it then when you left last night for Richmond?"

"Last night? You mean it was here until after dark?" Louis demanded. "Why was it here so long if the plows came early enough for you to try one out?"

"It took him longer to load the tobacco than to take off the plows, eh? The man was very careful in the loading of our first shipment. I saw to that."

"Very careful, yes...I can imagine. Tell me, La Roche, did he have bad scars on his neck and arms?"

"Scars...? Oh, yes, I could see them on his neck, at least." He smiled. "Then you have met this quiet one."

"No, I have never met him. I have never even seen him...his arms only, and at night. But I have indeed heard of the man."

"Well, then...?"

This time it was Louis who took La Roche by the arm, leading him out the door and over to where the dead hound lay on the rutted ground. Louis set the lantern beside the torn head of the animal.

"You see, La Roche, the beast was the only one who knew. She tried to show you what should have been your first suspicion."

La Roche shook his head. "I do not understand."

"The scent led her to the river and back again."

"The old bitch was confused...."

"Have you ever read the classics, La Roche? The fall of Troy?"

"A waste of my time."

"Or the newspapers? You should know your enemies...."

"What are you telling me, Jardinere? I do not understand these riddles!"

"There is much you do not understand, La Roche. But you should understand at least not to buy from an abolitionist like Thomas Garrett, even if he makes fine plows. Nor should you trust his driver with an empty wagon next to your nigger quarters half the night."

La Roche's jaw dropped as the truth dawned. He looked down at the wide tracks from the heavy wagon still sharply pressed in the soft earth, and swore.

"A conductor?"

"Precisely." Louis could not disguise the scorn in his voice.

"We must set out at once. He has a day's lead."

"Not you, La Roche. Leave this to me. I will start out in the morning."

"But you will never catch him if you let him have a two-day start. In three days he will be into Pennsylvania."

"I will catch him, La Roche."

"But it is two hundred miles; no horse—"

"You forget the steam railway from Baltimore."

La Roche snorted. "How can you track a wagon from a rail coach?"

Louis smiled. "I know exactly where your Monsieur Fenn is taking his passengers."

"Will you need help, Louis? What can I do?"

Without looking back, Louis snapped, "You might get a spade and bury your mistake."

CHAPTER 42

A raw northeast wind billowed Francis's cloak as he lugged his heavy black valise from the stable to his new rectory. Turning his face sideways against the buffeting gusts, he looked up at the fresh brick chimney squatting astride the roof. Another disappointment. Not a wisp of smoke. The house would be freezing—and damp, too, probably.

Once inside, he closed all doors leading from the kitchen, heaved his valise on the small table, and set about building a fire in the iron cookstove.

Thank the Lord someone, the Flynn boy probably—or Patrick Gallagher—had stocked the wood box. Sliding off one of the stove lids, he shivered with pleasure to see that the fire box was already laid with a large clump of shavings poking out from under the stacked pile of split starter wood. A handful of lucifers stood ready in a tin on the stovetop.

He selected one of the sulfur-coated sticks, rubbed its phosphorus tip vigorously against a small piece of ground-glass-coated paper, and held it to the wood. With a rewarding crackle the shavings caught and were soon roaring flames in the draft up the flue.

It would be several minutes before the cast-iron plates of the stove began to radiate heat into the room, but he took off his cape and began unstrapping the bulging valise.

He was looking for the documents... and his mother's letter, the one she had not had time to post before she died. Suddenly the thought that it was truly the last letter he would ever get from her was overwhelming, and he began to tremble with more than the chill of this lonely room.

He pulled the packet out and dropped it on the table. The envelope with his mother's letter lay on top. He gazed at it a moment, then turned away and began to busy himself with the teakettle.

He was on the point of pouring his cup of tea when he caught the muffled sound of a horse and trap. Taking a step toward the kitchen window he watched as the rig drew up near the stable and a bundled little figure climbed stiffly from the buggy seat. Even before he could make out the black face swathed in a huge muffler he recognized her.

"Maddie!"

He rushed for the door without pausing for his cloak, and flung himself across the porch like an eager child. When he reached her, a tottering hummock of layered coats and shawls, he squeezed her in a hug that nearly knocked her down.

"Oh!"

Madeleine Toussaint was so weary and cold from the trip—such a short drive really, the five miles from Coffee Run—she could not manage to say anything more. I must be very old, she thought with detachment.

"Inside, Maddie, before you freeze! Here, let me stable the mare." Francis pushed her toward the rectory and went to the animal's head, taking the reins and patting its muzzle like a long-lost pet. "Ah, there, Daphne! Would you like some grain? Do you miss Thunder?"

"Leave the mare in harness, Father; I cannot stay long."

"All right," he said, waving her toward the rectory. "Just a nosebag then, but you get inside the house, madame!"

After he had tended her horse and hurried back inside, he found her sitting placidly at his table pouring tea for them both. A mountain of outerwear was piled on a chair, which she had drawn close to the stove.

She looked up and gave him a smile. Why was she always so struck with his apparently eternal youth? Even now as he came bursting through the door, eyes flashing, hair tousled by the wind, cheeks pink under the stubble of beard, he seemed more like a stripling than a man more than fifty years old.

"How good to see you, Maddie!" he chattered, backing to the stove and rubbing his spare buttocks with his slender hands. "How is Coffee Run? And your mysterious, moneymaking enterprise? Don't tell me, Maddie. Everyone in Delaware knows you are wealthier than du Pont!"

"Come, sit," she ordered, tapping the table with her fingertip. "You are warmed enough, Father Francis, and we have important things to discuss."

He sat obediently. "So, you have finally called upon your pastor, Madame Toussaint." His tone was a self-mocking condescension.

She cut through his patronizing comment. "I was saddened to hear of your mother's death, Father Francis. May she rest in peace."

"Amen," he whispered, the flippancy gone. She watched him sag. His eyes were moist, the edges of his lids suddenly red.

"But she had the full life, eh? And a son in the church to pray her through Purgatory." She knew she was abrupt, but she had to get on to other matters.

"This was her last letter to me," he said mournfully and picked up the envelope. "She wrote it two days before she died."

Maddie drew her shoulders together and leaned forward. She might as well get started. "Tell me, Father Francis, did she mention anything about letters of manumission?"

"Manumission?" He was suddenly on guard.

"The black people on your plantation. Did she mention their freedom in her will? Were they to be freed upon her death?"

"Her will? Why Skibbereen was sold... years ago, Maddie."

"Yes, yes. But you told me that the slaves were given their freedom when the place was sold, a condition of the sale, eh?"

He swallowed hard. "Well, Maddie, that was a long time—"

"Damn you, priest!" She spat angrily. "The truth is what I need! Not some excuse for a conveniently weak memory."

He was so startled by her outburst that he said nothing.

"Speak up, man!" she demanded. "People's lives are at stake."

"They were never freed." His answer was so low that she had to ask him to repeat it. When he did she stiffened with exasperation.

"Agh! I *know* they have not been freed. But were there letters of manumission? The documents, Father Francis. Did you or Madame Reardon—"

"There are no documents." His voice was pleading.

"No agreement? Nothing to use as evidence?"

"None."

"Misplaced, perhaps? Among her papers somewhere?"

"No." Francis sighed and rose, walking heavily to the window. "There never was an agreement."

"You lied!"

"Yes." He stared at the frost as it formed on the windowpane. The shame was a cold weight within him and he fought to justify himself, to shift a portion of the guilt. "My mother had to consider her own financial security, you see. . . ."

"Grow up, Father Francis," Maddie said tiredly. "Do you wish to heap her grave with sins for you to pray away?"

He spun from the window. "That's not fair, madame! You do not know of my anguish when I found out the sacrifice she made for me—for my vocation."

"Not fair, eh? *Something* is not fair." Maddie snorted with scorn, "And your 'anguish?' I know nothing of your 'anguish,' but I do see your neglect."

"It was never my place to dictate to her. . . ."

"Dictate? I imagine not, Francis. But are you still a boy to hide behind her skirt? She is gone. Now you must accept the fact of all the things you have inherited from her." She pointed to the letter lying mute upon the table. "The good and the not so pleasant."

"Believe me, Maddie," he said, entreating her to understand, "I will do all that I can. But there is so little money left. Not enough to buy their. . ."

She shook her head and waved him to silence. "What you must do now is not for money to buy, priest of the church."

"Anything!"

"Anything?" She would see. "Your slaves have been set free, Francis, all of them. Four are on the road as I speak, and the other ten are at this moment on their way to a ship in Chesapeake Bay."

"God be praised."

"The ship's captain is a friend, the ten will come to no harm. But Larkie's family—"

"Larkie!"

"Yes, Larkie and her son's family are coming here."

"Here?"

"Yes. You must hide them in your house until it is safe to move them again." She watched his face pale, and began to doubt the wisdom of her choice.

"*Hide* them? Dear God in heaven, Maddie, don't tell me that they are *fugitives*."

Maddie found it hard to believe the man's naiveté. Did he truly believe that he would be delivered of this responsibility, too? She was angry, but she spoke slowly, patiently, as if explaining a complex problem to a child.

"Yes, Francis. We of the underground have arranged it. But something has gone wrong, and the plantation owner's partner has found me out. My station is no longer safe for them."

He was incredulous. "Found you out? Are *you* involved in these illegal activities?"

Maddie's anger began to soften into fear. He would not be up to the burden after all. She should have picked another place. But there had been so little time, and she thought that he at last would be equal to the task. She covered her own doubts by pressing on. "For years I have been... involved, yes."

"At Coffee Run when I was living there?" He was aghast.

"While you were there, and long before, Father Francis. We have delivered hundreds to safety."

He slipped into a chair, dumbstruck.

"They will be here soon," she went on quietly. "Do you have a room where they will not be seen for a few days?"

"So this is what you called your 'rum and molasses trade,' with all the strange callers at the rectory... that sailing man..."

She cut in. "It is better for us... and you, my priest... to forget as much of that as you can. Now, the room."

A look of confusion crossed his face as though he had heard her for the first time. "A room? No, Maddie, I'm afraid that is out of the question. You know that I cannot in conscience support such a thing. What a sad turn of events, to find that you are party to these misguided, unlawful acts. And sadder still that you should wish to involve the church." He shook his head to emphasize his concern. "The most tragic element of all, of course, is that you

[322]

have made those poor souls accomplices in crime! Poor old Larkie and her family! And the others, terrified in the hold of some freezing vessel, hungry probably, ripped from the only home they've known all their lives." He went on thoughtfully, trying to straighten out the problem as best he could. "Perhaps it is not too late; as their former owner perhaps I could intercede in their behalf. Certainly their master could be made to understand the circumstances, taken as they were against their will by misguided zealots. . . . I will protect your anonymity, of course."

"Fool . . . fool!" Her eyes were smoky black, and her mouth contorted as she leaned over him, not much taller than he was sitting in the chair. "You think their master will understand, eh? Which one? The beast who flayed Larkie's granddaughter bloody with the lash until she was almost dead, or the other one, the sniffing hound who is on their trail, the 'gentleman' who rapes her at his pleasure?"

Francis leaned back to escape her wrath. He had never seen her in such a rage. "Now, Maddie," he soothed, "you must not make too much of what these Quaker abolitionists rant. No family of quality would—"

"Enough!" she roared, inches from his face. "There is not time for Maddie to play your game of manners and philosophy. They will be at your door before nightfall. I have done what I can. Now it is for you, priest, to wrestle with your mind . . . and heart, if it is not all smothered with your cold love of God."

"Maddie, Maddie, be reasonable."

She began putting on the layers of outer clothing. "Reason, reason; that's all that you have now, Francis. A small measure, eh, for a man more than two score into life. No heart . . . no soul maybe . . . only the mind." She shook her head sadly. "Very well, Father Francis, then I tell you to do as Thomas did in your holy book. Ask to see the wounds . . . the ones you *can* see. And then look Larkie in the eye when you tell her your plan."

She was suddenly out the door before he could rise, and by the time he had thrown on his cloak and followed her, she was whipping her horse out of the carriage shed into the cutting wind.

The whole time Madeleine Toussaint had been in the rectory with Father Reardon, Patrick Gallagher was not more than a hundred feet away laying bricks for the church chimney. Except for Patrick and his apprentice grandson, Kevin, the work site was deserted. Construction had stopped until the roof slate arrived because the next phase of the operation called for plastering the interior, and that could not be done until the roof was weathertight.

The chimney had nearly reached the eaves, and Patrick had just troweled on a fresh layer of mortar when he heard a wagon pulling in on the other side of the church. It was a heavy one by the sound of it, and he had to see if the slate shingles had finally started to arrive. He quickly laid a course of brick on the fresh mud, dropped his tools in the ice-skimmed water bucket, and began the long climb down to the ground.

There were five ladders in all, zigzagging down through as many scaffold levels, and by the time he had reached the third, he had to stop for a breathing spell. He stood on the mortar-splattered boards and steadied himself with one hand on the new chimney. He had that dull ache in his chest again.

Yes, well, he would put himself to pasture just as soon as the church was done. It would be a fitting way to tie things up, it would. A month or two more and he could step down with a good feeling. He swung onto the next ladder and continued down.

Now where was that Kevin? He chuckled happily and began walking around to the back of the church. No doubt he was off to nose into that wagon himself. Wanted to be the first to know, and any minute now that strapping broth of a grandson would come thumping back to tell his grandpa the wonderful news.

Patrick smiled. It was wonderful. His only grandson a mason like himself, and a fine one at that. The boy had good hands and a sharp eye; something he himself could not boast of lately. The lad was now twenty-seven, the third generation. No wonder Patrick Gallagher was feeling old. He was becoming a bloody patriarch!

As he rounded the sacristy, he heard Kevin call, "Grandpa! Grandpa!" Kevin came following his own voice so closely that they nearly collided. Patrick staggered back against the wall.

"Mind yer course, lummox! Do ye want to trample me into the sod before me time?"

"Sorry." Kevin reached out a hand to steady his grandfather. His face was blanched with excitement. "But, Grandpa, it's wonderful news!"

"Well, calm yerself, lad. Have ye never seen a wagonload of slate shingles before?"

Kevin shook his head, a great smile spreading across his face. "No, not the shingles!"

"What, then?" Patrick never did like getting news secondhand. "Out with it, y'grinnin' banshee! Or I'll go round and find out fer meself."

Kevin croaked the words through his taut grin: "Uncle Tim is *alive!*"

CHAPTER 43

It was the same old nightmare. He was in the dream, knowing it to be a dream, and clawing helplessly to lift himself free of it. The smooth black handle jutted from its slot in the stone wall, and he saw his hands reach up to clutch it. His brain shouted for them to stop, but the hands pulled down against the pressure, and he heard the crushing rumble of the wheels on the other side. Then the door beside him fell off its hinges, and the falling body dropped from the darkness above. He saw it jerk to a stop, heard the soft snap of bone, and watched horrified as it swung lazily in the doorway. The trousers blackened at the crotch, a spreading stain of hot urine seeping through the cloth along both thighs and down to the knees.

And now the approaching footsteps. They rushed past him into the mill, pointing with horror at the . . . thing hanging there. Dozens of them, all trying to get at the rope inside, trying to cut it down. He fought with the handle. Get it up! Get it up! Stop the thunderous rolling of the wheels. The black cake was too dry, gone to powdering. Stop the grinding, wet the cake, get them out of the place. . . .

As before, the flash brought him full awake, trembling with the guttural moan that had been a splitting scream in his nightmare. He lay there shuddering in a cold sweat, smelling the sourness of his fear. Denis Feeney kept his eyes tightly shut, willing away the light of another day.

His hand fell from the bed and groped for his jug. When his knuckles struck the glazed earthenware, he heard it roll out of reach. Even with his eyes closed he knew it was empty.

He moaned again and dragged himself from the bed. Only when he was standing, supported with one hand against the wall, did he open his eyes.

The daylight, muted by winter and filtered through thin curtains hung at his single window, seared his eyes and sent a stabbing throb to the back of his skull. With one hand over his brow and the other feeling along the wall he made his way to the door.

His only thought was to get at a jug.

"Daddy..."

Noreen's voice out of the kitchen. Not now; no lecture now. What he needed was a drink.

"Come out and sit a minute, Denis."

He felt Brendan take his arm firmly and lead him to the table. His tongue was glued in his mouth and he could not protest. The shakes caught hold of him suddenly, forcing him to grip the seat of his chair with both hands. Noreen put a cup before him on the table.

"Drink up, Denis," Brendan said. "Drink up a drop to celebrate a miracle."

The cup was miracle enough. He snatched it with both hands and drained it off with a shudder of relief.

"And now," Brendan said sliding into the chair beside him, "Norrie has fixed you a good breakfast...."

Denis waved a protesting hand.

"Aye," Brendan insisted, "and after that a shave and clean clothes, eh?"

"Yer not takin' me to mass. Is it Sunday?"

"No, Daddy," Noreen cut in a bit impatiently as she thrust a steaming plate of mush and eggs under his nose. "'Tis more like Wednesday." She slid a mug of strong tea next to the plate.

Denis eyed the food uncertainly. "Well, what's the celebratin' for?"

He noticed Noreen and Brendan exchange a look of mixed apprehension and excitement.

"A visitor come callin'," Brendan said vaguely. "You'll want to look yer best."

"What vis—?"

"Quiet now, and eat, or I'll spoon it in for you!" Noreen said shaking her finger in his face. "I'll go fill his tub, Brendan. You make sure he fills his belly... and not with another drop of the other."

After she had left the room, Denis turned to Brendan with a casual air and lowered voice. "Is there more, then? Ha' ye kept some back I might have?"

Brendan chuckled. "You better eat and make do with the tea, Denis. I think your daughter is in no mood to be crossed."

It was not easy, but he managed to get most of the food inside him and then submitted to a bath. An hour after he had pushed back from the table, Denis Feeney was limping about the house looking more presentable than he had in years.

They wouldn't be wheedled into telling him who the great visitor might be. Probably one of the owner's sons on some fool errand, or the priest—aye, that was it—the good father come to peck away at his sins. He laughed grimly to himself. If only he could be absolved of... Agh! Stow that!

"They're here!" Noreen was at the front window. "Now, Daddy, sit here in the chair."

He could hear voices on the road outside. Kate, Kevin, and another, a man's voice he could not place. But familiar... familiar.

Then Noreen was out the door like some fluttery chicken and Brendan after her. He heard a soft cry, then weeping. The man's voice again, soft, strong, and... familiar. He wanted to get up from the chair and look out the window, but some awful dread rooted him to the seat.

"Yes, he's inside." That was Brendan. The voice was low; Denis had to strain to make out the words. "We'd better go in to him, but go slow. We didn't tell him anything, and the shock..."

He couldn't make out the rest, but it didn't matter. Something told him then. Just as the man's foot stepped through the open door, something told him, and he knew. And there was no shock, not surprise even. But for a moment, Denis Feeney was not quite certain whether his son had returned to life or he himself had slipped into death to meet him.

"I'm sorry, Dad," he heard Tim say with a breaking voice, and

Denis opened his arms to take in his resurrected son. The younger man was on his knees, face pressed against the old man's neck, arms around a body that was now so terribly frail.

Denis soaked up the moment in a confused ecstasy of calm. He never felt a tear rise, but in the great emotion of their embrace he knew the very essence of his expiation.

During the commotion that followed he hobbled about his son, marveling at his size—so much brawnier than when he left—and powerful in his build. How much like the other Tim he seemed, tall and strong and gentle-natured. He tried to listen to what the boy was saying, the exciting tales of his adventures, but it was no use. He could only drink in the music of his voice and the vision of his living. Even the awful burn scars were unimportant, a minor blemish on the miracle.

Later, when Tim had been rushed off by Kevin and Kate to see the Gallaghers, Noreen asked him if he would like a little drink.

"Something, a little," she said, "to calm you down after all the excitement."

He delighted in her new joy, too, and noticed the reborn sparkle in her look. And it seemed as right as rain to ask for tea.

The drummer apparently had been on the road for some time. His clothes bunched in wrinkles as though he had slept in them for several nights. He needed a shave, too, and while that was not uncommon among the usual patrons at Dorgan's Inn, this fellow had the look of someone who should not appear careless.

He ordered a brandy, and poor old Dorgan had to sort among the dusty bottles under the bar for some time before he could locate his single bottle of that rare drink. He dusted it off, squeaked out the stopper, and set it next to a thick mug on the corner table where the drummer sat. Everybody watched as the stranger poured a measure and sipped at the drink.

Louis Jardinere settled back into the corner shadows and nursed his brandy. He nearly gagged on the awful liquor, brackish and raw as it was, but he made no sign of disapproval. It was important to ease into the atmosphere of this grubby place as quickly as he could. He was not here for refreshment or entertainment... not even for rest, although he certainly needed that after three sleepless nights.

The conversation gradually rose in volume as the regular patrons slipped back into their normal patterns. They were like a nest of insects, he thought; all the buzzing stopped dead at the intrusion of an alien movement, but after a time, their dim minds forgot alarm, and the buzzing resumed.

"When I see 'im, I blessed meself twice."

Mild laughter.

"Y'thought 'twas a ghost surely!"

"Aye, a ghost with them purple powder marks along his neck."

"Poor soul. Like a Jonah, I'll bet. Dontcha wonder all that's been goin' through his mind these many years since the blast?"

"What brought him back, I wonder?"

"Teamster, I hear. Lives in Coatesville, up the Crick. Busted a wheel on the Lancaster Pike. Me ma saw his outfit in the church barn this mornin' when she dropped off some bread fer the priest."

They all fell silent for a moment, relishing the gossip and sipping at their pails. Louis leaned forward in his chair, sharply attentive.

"Tim Feeney, right under our noses. It's a wonder none of us ever seen him."

"Ah, small wonder, if y'ask me. When does any of us get to town anyway? I know it's the company store or Dorgan's here fer the lot of us."

After most of the powdermen had gone, Louis Jardinere asked for a room where he might clean himself before moving on. The valise of women's finery worked marvelously in loosening the old proprietor's tongue. Long after he had left the inn, the drummer would be remembered by Dorgan as a smooth talker and slick merchant of such underthings to take a man's breath away. But old Dorgan would have no memory of how many important questions he had answered about other things, which warmed Louis Jardinere more deeply than the brandy ever could.

CHAPTER 44

When supper was done at the Feeney house, Noreen started cleaning up while the others huddled in the front room pumping Tim for news about his travels. They were all so excited by his stories that he had trouble keeping up with their questions. Noreen noticed that she seldom heard her father's voice, but when she looked up from her work, she could see him leaning intently forward, his eyes on Tim constantly.

"And where is your factory, Uncle Tim?" asked Kate.

"Well, Kate, it's not so grand as I'd call it a factory. More like a small shop . . . and it's in Coatesville."

"Coatesville," Brendan said, remembering some of his western trips into Pennsylvania. "So you never left the Crick?"

Tim laughed softly. "Not for long, I guess. The old Brandywine goes right through town up there."

"Dad said you were a cooper, Uncle Tim," Kevin observed thoughtfully.

"Yes. It was easy gettin' work on the farms. They always needed kegs for storage."

"How long after you left did you wander before finding . . ." Brendan stumbled.

"Not more than a week or so. A Quaker farmer took me in. I worked there for a year or so then moved on."

Brendan winced, looking at the burn scars running down Tim's neck and disappearing into his open collar. He wondered how he had survived.

Tim caught the look and smiled grimly. "The Feeney blood. More good luck than good sense. They were good to me."

"Did they ever...?"

"Never once. I think they knew. It was only ten miles north of here. I'm sure they heard the thump, even there. They knew. But they never asked me why."

"How did you get from kegs to wagons?" asked Kate.

"All those barrels and kegs get carted away sometime, I guess, and the wagons break down. So I got to turnin' out a spoke or two in amongst all the staves. Then I found that shrinking an iron tire onto a wood wheel was not much different than fitting hoops on a barrel. Pretty soon I was makin' the whole thing."

Brendan spoke again. "To think y'were just up the Crick at Coatesville all the time. Not thirty miles as the crow flies."

"Just think!" Kate said. "You could have sent us all a letter in a bottle."

Tim looked at her sadly in the sudden awkward silence that followed. They did not quite feel at ease with this man who had abandoned them so long ago.

Noreen walked into the room and over to where he was sitting. "All right now. It's my turn. I want some time with my brother alone if y'don't mind."

They groaned to cover their reprieve, and Kevin made a show of pulling out his watch. "Five o'clock comes pretty early. I'm for the haypile."

Denis spoke only after Brendan and Kevin had left. It was a single question, almost a plea.

"Ye'll not be leaving tomorra?"

"Not tomorrow."

Denis nodded, struggled out of the chair, and limped to his room.

"Why, Tim?" Noreen whispered as soon as they were alone. "Why did you leave us to grieve so?"

"I blamed myself for it all," he said simply.

"But you must know that's daft!"

"I know it now, yes." His look swept past her into some blackness of his own memory. "All I knew then was that I had to go. I hoped at first I would die."

"You must have been in frightful pain." She reached out and ran her fingers over the scarred wrists.

"I saw them in the woods with baskets, you know," he said in a reverie. "I washed up above the dam on the other side and hid in the bushes until after dark. I watched them. I heard Lizzie Dorgan call for Joe...." He raised his hands to cover his ears. His sleeves fell almost to his elbows, and Noreen saw the ugly purple welts. She tugged at his sleeves, pulling them over his arms again and smoothing the cloth down over his wrists.

"You should have let us know you were alive. It wasn't fair," she whispered, her voice breaking. "It wasn't fair."

He leveled hard eyes at her. "It was necessary."

"What in the name of God for?"

"I let the bearings get hot, and the powder cake must have been too dry.... Didn't they find the burned shaft?"

"Of course," she muttered dully.

"Then it was as plain as day, Noreen! I was the one—"

"Tim, you were a cooper, not a powerman. Nobody in his right mind could ever point the finger of blame at you."

She was silent for a moment, thinking how much Denis Feeney had suffered for not being at his post. But it was time to ease off the hurt.

"Can you stay a time with us, Tim? Will you lose your job, I mean?"

"A week or two," he said absently. Then, when she looked up in surprise, he added, "You see, Norrie, I'm owner of me shop. I don't work for wages anymore. I've sixteen men on the payroll with an honest foreman to depend upon."

"Tim!" she almost squealed with delight.

"Aye, I've broken out for good." There was a trace of pride in his saying it, and she was glad for the shift in their mood.

She suddenly thought of something else.

"Are you married, Timmy? Is there a lucky Dutch or Quaker girl that loves ye out there in the wilderness?"

He laughed. "No. Not my luck, Noreen. I don't think very many girls would take to bed with an Irisher cooked to a cinder."

[333]

She looked at him archly. "You might have heard Meg Halloran's a widow five years now. I don't think she'd mind; not if I remember right."

"I've heard. The first thing I heard at Dorgan's." Then, he added, "I've been givin' it some thought."

Noreen let that rest, too, for another time. She thought for a minute and then asked quietly, "Did you have any news of us all that time?"

"I knew about mother... three years after she died. And bits of other news that I could piece together without letting on to strangers."

He saw how deeply it saddened her to hear that he had known of them while they were in darkness about him. He had to set it right with her. "Noreen, there was another reason I could not come back."

She looked up expectantly.

"For many years now I have been working in a thing that nobody must find out about. Before I tell you, y'must swear not to breathe it to another soul—not Daddy, nor Brendan—nobody."

"Mother of God, Tim, you're not in some kind of terrible foolishness?"

"Not foolishness, Norrie," he muttered. "It's just that I help to carry runaway slaves from time to time."

"Runaway slaves..."

"Aye, poor buggers."

"Abolitionist?"

Tim chuckled, "I never thought meself to be an abolitionist; it seems too fancy and political a name for me. No, the others are, I guess; some right here in town are pretty much out with it, even in public."

"Thomas Garrett, the Quaker!"

"You're quick, Norrie. Tom Garrett is the farmer's son who took me in after the blowup. And after me wagon business got goin' good, he talked me into cartin' freight for him. It was always a two-way haul with no deadheads. Brendan would understand that. I always had a load on the return trip, something for delivery to Pennsylvania. There was a proper lading bill, with real stuff in the wagon. O'course, what was stowed underneath was 'unofficial' cargo."

"Haven't you been stopped? There are awful people loose on the roads."

"Many times. But I've had no trouble yet. . . ."

"Oh, Tim, if they catch you at this business here in Delaware, you'll be off to prison surely!"

"*If* they catch me. And there's not much chance of that."

She tilted her head doubtfully.

Tim squeezed her hand and went on. "Look, Norrie, only three people know I'm a conductor for Garrett—besides himself, I mean. Not one of them would ever give a hint. Only Garrett knows my real name, and hardly anyone can connect my face with the conductor called Tim Fenn. Up till today I always moved in the dark of night near Wilmington. Of course, now Father Reardon knows. . . ."

"Why did you tell him? I thought you stopped at the church because of a broken wheel."

"I broke it myself after getting there, to make it seem a natural reason for stopping. No, I was in a hurry to get to the church because my regular station was being watched by a spy from Richmond. I got the word beforehand, while I was still in Maryland."

"Do you mean that Father Reardon is. . . ?"

"Aye. Those poor black wretches are hidden away in his rectory as the two of us are speaking. In a few days another wagon will pick them up, and off they'll go to Kennett Square or someplace north in free territory. By that time I'll have 'fixed' me broken wheel and I'll deliver the tobacco to Philadelphia."

"Father Reardon does not seem like one who—"

"He had no choice, I guess. My people just dumped it on him sudden like. There was such a rush to get them out of the hiding place in me wagon, and then all that confusion of him seein' me back from the dead, as it must have seemed to him, and then your Kevin and Patrick Gallagher all worked up when *they* saw me. I had to work fast to get them all tucked out of sight and into the rectory before Kevin came runnin' back with Mr. Gallagher."

"Why did you agree to work with the abolitionists, Tim?"

"I did it to make up for the ones who died here."

Her voice was warm then, and tender. "Does it help, Little Tim?"

"Three hundred, twenty and seven, counting this last. There's pleasure in knowin' that, Noreen. Y'hafta see the poor things to know my feeling. It's like runnin' a railway from hell to heaven. But no, it doesn't make up for the others. That hurt will go with me to my grave, I'm thinking. But this other helps distract me mind a bit."

Noreen smoothed a wild cowlick in his hair. "A long time ago I used to brush that down. There has been so much we missed, Tim."

He nodded, remembering.

Long after his sister had gone to bed, Tim turned down the lamp and stepped outside to relieve himself before climbing up to the loft. The air had calmed, and a few stars gleamed through openings in the cloud reflected on the ice-skimmed Crick. He stood for a moment to soak up the night, breathe the familiar air of Chicken Alley.

Almost immediately he heard a sound from the front of the house, something moving through the bare branches of a clump of dormant lilac. At first he thought it was a rabbit or skunk out foraging, but the outline of a man took shape moving swiftly up Crick Road. The figure stumbled once, recovered, and faded into the darkness.

Gone to Dorgan's, he thought. It seemed like a pointless trip. The place would soon be closed, and besides, the fellow must have had enough already to go falling into the Feeney lilac bushes and tripping over his own feet. He hoped old Dorgan would not serve the fellow more.

Louis Jardinere had gone to spy at the Feeneys' window for two reasons. First, he wanted to have a private look at Thomas Garrett's faceless conductor. By now he was certain that the man would be on guard at the intrusion of any stranger in the neighborhood, and Louis needed the advantage of instant identification when he made his move. It would not be easy to spot a man whose identity depended on some scars that might be covered up with heavy winter clothing. No, he needed time to observe the agent so as to absorb the nuances of expression and movement that would make him easy to mark in any situation.

He had wanted to see Noreen as well.

Try as he might to put it down, as he had approached the cottage, the old memory returned, and with it the newer fantasies. He found himself becoming almost reckless in his rush to the place, slipping out of the stealthy habits of his new profession.

When he had finally hidden himself in the darkness outside their window, Noreen had been busy in the kitchen end of the house beyond his range of vision. It was some time before he was able to sort out the others in the room by a process of elimination. But when he saw the lovely young girl so raptly listening to Timothy Feeney, the man known as Fenn, he was stunned by the similarity. The girl was the image of Noreen.

But, there was something else familiar about the girl. . . . What had the innkeeper said her name was? Kate. Yes, this Kate reminded him of someone else. It was something in the way she moved about the room . . . and her features had a certain quality.

He shifted his position carefully, and moved closer. The window panes distorted his view as the girl moved past imperfections in the glass, but at last he could make her out clearly, the radiant smile that flashed with sudden impudence, the casual gesture of her hand. Yes, she was Noreen's child. But that fullness of her mouth . . . and the peculiar arch of those eyebrows. Suddenly the image of his own sister fixed itself in Louis's mind, a memory of twenty years earlier. And then Louis knew, with a certainty beyond doubt, that this young version of Noreen, this Kate, was his own flesh and blood as well.

The realization sent a prickling sensation up his neck and he nearly stumbled against the wall of the house. *"Mon Dieu!"* he whispered. As he looked at the girl, a surge of possessive passion seized him . . . not for the child, but for her mother. All of the fantasies he had woven through the years came alive again, a well-spring of renewed desire heightened by this ravishing issue of his paternity.

He did not speculate on the reasons why he was so moved, but when Noreen Gallagher finally took her place with the others in the Feeney sitting room, she stirred Louis Jardinere like no other woman had since last he saw her in the woods so many years before.

She stood in the half-light at the far side of the room, softly radiant in the rosy gloom of the single lamp. He caught his breath, felt his pulse quicken, and the old fiery urge was on him again. Even the bitter cold of his watchful pose went unnoticed in his heat.

How long after that he stared, rooted in the same position, he did not know. Gradually there was a stirring among the family as they made their good nights, their muted voices leaking through the rickety sash, but he had eyes for only one in that room. He drank in the vision of Noreen, her reality making all of his memories pale in the comparison.

When she disappeared at last and the lamp was out, he heard the door close and came stumbling out of hiding.

And on the way to the inn, as he moved on stiff legs, he marveled at the aching in his groin and swore aloud in a whispered promise to himself, "I'll have her again before another day is spent, or may the devil take me!"

Then he remembered her iron obstinacy. Ah, but there were other ways, newer avenues that she could not resist.

How convenient!

He started formulating a plan that included Timothy Feeney and the daughter called Kate.

CHAPTER 45

The next morning Louis Jardinere was up and dressed before first light. As he moved about his chill room at the inn, quickly packing his valise, his mind was buzzing with the day's heavy schedule. The shabby costume of the traveling salesman had been replaced by his usual gentlemanly ensemble, and the thought of quitting this squalid, ill-smelling place was a stimulation of itself.

One of the things he had skillfully elicited from the old proprietor of the place was a method of getting a message to Noreen Gallagher. Like everything else in this tightly knit community, the postal service was tied in with the company network. Each household had a box at the powdermen's store, and nearly all mail, social notes, and company messages were exchanged there.

The last item that Louis picked up before leaving his room was a folded note written on ordinary foolscap, a rather coarse paper that would not attract notice as quality stationery might. The letter was written in pencil and carried the name Noreen G. printed in block letters on the outside.

Louis harnessed his horse between the shafts of his rented trap, removed the garish signs of his tradesman's role from its sides, placed them in the separate trunk with the other drummer trappings, and snapped the lock. The trunk concealed all the elements of his disguise, secure and ready for the next mission.

His first stop would be the du Pont company store, where he would browse as though inspecting a competitor's facility. When it could be done easily without notice, he would drop the letter in the Gallagher box and be off to his other appointments.

Next he would call on the priest to ensure the safekeeping of the runaways...and to renew his old acquaintance. He rather relished the idea of seeing Francis again, a surprise visitor out of the past!

Then to the du Pont residence. He did have some apprehension about that. The memory of his treatment by Irénée du Pont nearly twenty years before still stung raw. But times had changed. Du Pont was an old widower now, and Louis was again a landed gentleman. Equal status. He wondered if the old man had been privy to any gossip from France regarding his most recent social escapade. That would be unfortunate. Still, he did not care much. The possibility of using the mansion as a base for completing his business with Reardon, Feeney, and Noreen appealed to him greatly.

The third appointment! Ah, the *pièce de résistance* of this stimulating day! Their rendezvous, at last. It was a heady thought! He snapped the buggy whip on the horse's rump, driving the sluggish animal into a trot.

He must not become overeager in the matter of Noreen, as delicious as that prospect might be. He promised himself to exercise restraint this time. He would wait until the trap was carefully set.

Shortly after breakfast, when Brendan and the two young Gallaghers, Kevin and Kate, had gone off to their respective jobs, there was a knock on the Feeney door. Noreen was pouring a second coffee for Tim and her father, and she carried the pot with her to the front of the house to see who was calling at the crack of dawn.

She did not recognize the swarthy, thick-set man who waited on the stoop and asked for Tim. He politely refused her offer to come in out of the cold.

"Thankee, ma'am, no. It's an imposition on you as it is, to come sailin' in so early. I just have something to tell Mr. Fenn...Feeney about his tobacco shipment. And I need to be shoving off presently."

Noreen was about to insist when Tim suddenly appeared at her side, smiling easily. He pulled on his coat and slipped past her.

"Thanks, Noreen. I won't keep the man from his trade with us idle coffee drinkers." Tim took the visitor's arm to direct him out to his steaming horse. "You have the papers for me to sign, I'm thinkin'. Well, let's get at them, boyo. I won't be keeping you waitin' in this cold."

Something stabbed at Noreen as she remembered Tim's revelations of the night before, and she stood at the window peering out at the two men. They spoke very earnestly, with Tim nodding much of the time. Then the horseman mounted awkwardly and trotted out of sight up Crick Road toward Dorgan's. She noticed he had produced no papers for Tim to sign.

When her brother came back inside, she was already at the kitchen table filling her cup. Denis Feeney looked up curiously when his son was again seated.

"Anything amiss, Tim?"

"Ah, no, Daddy," he said carelessly between slurps of hot coffee, "Just a bill of lading I had to sign is all. The shipment is redirected to a new shop in Philadelphia."

Noreen felt the fear again. Something was amiss surely. There were no papers. The stranger had not even opened his coat or gone near the saddle bag.

"There is one small... inconvenience," Tim went on. "I'll have to be heading out today with that tobacco... as soon as me wheel is fixed, that is."

Denis looked closely at his son. "Y'*will* be comin' back?"

Tim laughed and patted his father's hand. "Before supper time tomorra night, Dad. An easy haul. One day up; one day back. I'll see you that quick."

He looked sharply at Noreen, though, his eyes demanding her cooperation. "Sorry to leave so quick, Norrie. I guess the Quakers are in desperate need of a good smoke."

She was up and bustling through the pantry without a word. Before Tim had reached the bottom of his mug, she had assembled a meal sack of provisions and plumped it on the table beside him.

"There. Now off to the priest's with ye. Ye'll need all the daytime you can get if that wagon is to be fixed," she said brightly. But her fingers were shaking as she tied a string around the neck of the sack.

A few minutes later Tim was on his way. He had an important stop to make before heading to his wagon and team in the rectory stable, however. It had to do with Brendan Gallagher, and he hated to get the man involved. He cursed when he realized there was no

[341]

alternative, considering the pressures of time and circumstances that David Craith had just laid on him. He would have to talk fast and hard to get Brendan to agree. It might cost him his job with the mills... or worse. Well, it was their only chance.

As he entered the lower yard and headed for the shipping office, a chill ran through him just to be here again. The memory of that other time flooded back like the icy waters of the sullen millrace, and he wanted desperately to go back and explain to Noreen just why he had to put her husband's life on the line. Again.

The pastor of the new powdermen's church sat glumly over his second cup of morning tea. A two-day stubble of beard made his face seem doubly haggard, and his hand shook as he raised the cup to his lips. He had not had much sleep during the night, and this morning for the first time since his ordination he had not offered the sacrifice of holy mass. He could not bring himself to do it this horrible morning. He did not feel worthy of the act.

Larkie.... He shook his head to weather the searing memory of her words. Larkie had spoken to him just once the afternoon before, a tirade about what the poor old woman had endured, what they had all endured because of his dereliction through the years. And then the pitiful wreckage of the girl lying on his bed. Larkie had made him look at her nakedness, her own granddaughter, pulling down the bedcovers, and tenderly stripping the girl of her blood-matted rags. Demanding warm water and cloth to clean the lash-ripped flesh, insisting that he stay until the ghastly task was done. But the worst she kept till last, when finally the shivering fifteen-year-old was cleansed and bandaged, old Larkie had pointed to her rounded belly with a shaking finger and nearly whimpered through the tears that at last began to run from her old eyes.

"An' the other devil-massah has filled her with his child."

She had not said a word to him since, nor had the others. All of his entreaties, his tears of remorse, his promises to make amends had drawn their silence, and he was an outcast in his own home. They had accepted his food without comment, shutting the door of the room after taking the trays. He was a pariah.

At last he could not stand being with himself in the empty kitchen. He threw on a wrap and stepped out into the cold morning. He wandered along the frozen path leading from his back door to the new church building. No sounds came from the place. All work had stopped until the slate arrived for the roof. Even the brickwork for the chimney was stopped because the mortar would freeze before it had a chance to set. His feet followed the lumpy pathway until he was brought up short directly before the yawning doorless opening of the vestibule. Two rough boards were nailed crisscross to the frame barring his entry.

"Huh!" he grunted, laying a hand on the splintery barrier; he would have to crawl under the crossed wood to get in. There was something symbolic in that, he thought ruefully, and got on his knees to squirm through.

The rough-sawn timbers caught on his cassock and held fast. He tugged at the cloth, and heard the fine serge rip as he crashed headlong onto his face to the gritty surface of the floor. He lay there a second, fearful that he might trip on the torn cassock as he tried to rise.

He got to his feet and examined the damage. The fine soutane was ruined. A gaping tear had been ripped down one side, and the seam in front was torn open halfway to the waist.

For some reason the loss of his best cassock did not even register. Neither did the fact that both hands were scraped and bleeding. He was still. He watched each detail of the rough interior take shape as his eyes adjusted to the gloomy light. The chill of the place suddenly overcame him, and he shuddered. Unconsecrated. No church as yet. A pile of stone that could offer no consolation.

As he struggled on hands and knees back under the crossed planks to reach the light outside, Francis found the passage easier to negotiate. But he was filthy with the groveling in the dirt, and his hands stung as he pressed them against the frozen earth.

There was such an emptiness within him as he got to his feet that he even began to wonder if he had lost the gift of faith itself. Strangely, the thought had no great effect on him. He felt only a cold determination to do something for Larkie's poor family.

While Father Francis Reardon was ruining his best cassock crawling into the church, Louis Jardinere was making his own inspection of the parish barn and stables. The elusive conductor had not taken pains to conceal his rig beyond simply closing the barn door. Apparently the people in Garrett's organization did not know about the long-standing connection between the priest and himself. In their haste to arrange a safe station, they had picked a place most accessible to Louis.

Undoubtedly the four slaves were squirreled away in the rectory. It was the only place with heat in this chilling weather. How convenient for him! Unless the priest had changed markedly over the years, his temperament and social background would make him extremely pliable to demands—particularly when they had the force of law.

Louis grinned as he left the outbuildings and headed for the rectory. Another moral dilemma for the theologian! What a marvelous homecoming this was turning out to be.

He was so delighted with his success in sleuthing out the runaways that on entering the empty lower floor of the priest's house, he fixed himself a cup of tea before rising to the second floor and finding the terrified foursome in Francis Reardon's bedroom.

The piercing shriek of the mutilated girl brought Francis crashing into the kitchen, and as he raced through the door leading to the central hallway, he saw a man moving casually down the staircase. The figure turned and faced him with a triumphant smile on his lips and a pistol in his hand. The twin barrels of the small handgun were aimed directly at his chest.

Francis felt his flesh crawl, but it was not because of the dull steel gleam of the pistol barrels. He felt suddenly as if he had stepped on a snake. The years were swept away in a wink, and he was again in the company of the only man he truly believed to be demonic.

"Ah, Francis," Louis purred, "*mon père*, I was afraid I had called while you were not at home." He looked down at the pistol in his hand with mock surprise. "Eh! I forget myself! Forgive me." He slipped the flat little caplock into his pocket and added, "Self-protection, you see; one can never be secure with these poor creatures once they have flown the plantation."

Francis stared dully at him. Larkie's words were running through his mind: "That other devil-massah..." He knew that Louis was the rapacious animal that had ravaged the child upstairs. Had he harmed them further under this very roof?

"Did you...? Are they...?"

Louis arched an eyebrow disdainfully, "*Mon père!* You do Louis a disservice. I am here to protect my property, not to do it further damage. They are merely startled at my sudden appearance. Like errant children who fear the rebuke of their provider." He winked and chuckled. "*Noblesse oblige*, eh? Ah, our burden!"

Louis dismissed the subject and began exploring the lower rooms, drifting in and out of the dining room, the parlor, the reception room, the small office.

"All splendid! Somewhat modest for a man of your upbringing, of course, but then we must recall the austerity of the priestly calling. Ah, Francis, I do forget myself. You did not know that I had purchased a modest share of your lovely Skibbereen, eh?" He paused directly before Francis, watching that bit of news sink in. "You will recall mentioning the estate to me years ago.... To think, if we had not had that little talk, your Jardinere might never have had an interest in the place. God's will, Francis; you were his good instrument in that, eh? To restore poor Louis to his rightful place and best calling." He sighed.

"Ah, enough of this, Francis. Come, into your kitchen. I have taken the liberty to pour myself a cup of tea. Please join me. We have matters to discuss."

Francis followed him to the kitchen and stood while he took a seat at the table and raised his cup. Louis's eyes widened in mock horror as he looked at Francis in the sun-flooded kitchen.

"*Mon dieu*, Francis! Your soutane! And your hands... Have you been working on the church with your own hands?"

Francis jerked his head down to look at himself. He was stunned at the damage to his cassock, torn and smudged with clay stains. "You spoke of other matters, sir! I am interested only in your proposals covering those unfortunate people in my bedroom."

Louis's eyes glittered. "As you wish. My proposal, as you put it, is rather a demand—for the safe return of my property."

"That will not be as easy as you think. You are in Delaware."

Louis laughed. "Ah, and so we are! Your adopted state permits slavery, eh? And are there not penalties for assisting runaways? Is it not the law of fair Delaware to return nigger chattels to their owner?"

"Yes."

"Well then, *mon père*, you must do your priestly duty to uphold the law in Caesar's provinces. God wills it that you constrain your pastoral urges to the duly enacted law of the land, eh?"

"I find it strange, sir, to hear you invoke God's holy name in support of your own wretched perversions!"

"Ah, does Francis sit in judgment of poor Jardinere? My appetites are much the same as yours, is it not so? Hot blood runs to your loins, does it not, good Father Reardon? And is it not true that all the exquisite delights of which I have partaken, you have also ravished in your celibate mind?"

Please, God, Francis thought, do not let him mention her name!

Louis chuckled. "Ah, Francis, has Louis struck a nerve? But we drift away from your point, dear Father. What is this profound enunciation you were about to make vis-à-vis your Delaware?"

Francis was now so agitated that he had nearly forgotten himself. His teeth were on edge as he forced out the words with as much assurance as he could muster. "In Delaware the law requires proof that the Negro is a slave, not the other way around as in Virginia. You will need proof before a magistrate of your ownership of these people before they can be seized."

The instant he had spoken, Francis knew that his last resort had failed. Louis nearly snickered as he made a grand production out of reaching inside his coat, pulling out a sheaf of documents, and casting them carelessly on the kitchen table.

"Voilà!"

When Francis did not respond, Louis reached for the folded bundle of parchment and began to open each sheet, smoothing out the creases with the palm of his hand.

"You see, Francis? Authentic. The official bills of sale graced with the bold strokes of your mother's own hand. The endorsement covering my own interest is written elsewhere into my agreement with La Roche, of course. All very uncomplicated, the identity of each slave clearly stipulated by breeding plan and bloodlines for four generations.

"Well, Francis, my friend, I will leave these proofs, as you call them, in your safekeeping. Please have the slaves ready, eh? I have no wish to encumber your reputation with the local magistrates."

He sauntered toward the door and stopped with his hand on the latch. "Oh, should your errant sheep, Timothy Feeney, decide to attempt anything rash, would you advise him that his sister Noreen's honor may be at stake."

Francis strangled with his anger and spluttered out the words, "You...you are a depraved and lecherous scoundrel!"

Louis gave a deep bow. "At the very least, yes. I accept your accolade, Francis. Until tomorrow, *adieu.*"

"Empty kegs?" The foreman looked at Brendan as if he had not heard right.

"You heard me, Dougherty. Two stacks of empty kegs in the smallest Conestoga. And load them fore and aft to the top of the bows, lash them tight, and put a foot or so of straw on the wagon bed between the stacks."

Dougherty scratched his head. He'd never heard anything so foolish in his life. "Do ye want a tarpaulin over the kegs at the front and back?"

"No tarp. Leave the kegs in plain sight at both ends."

"Look Gallagher, 'tis none of me business to butt in..."

Brendan drew him closer and whispered in his ear.

"Ah! Well, why dintcha say so in the first place?" he said softly. "Haulin' some breakables for the good father, is it? Well, me lips are sealed, Brendan. And no loss to the company either; the team could use a good long run." He winked and bustled off importantly. Brendan noted that it was the first time his second-in-command had ever called him by his first name.

He left the office and strolled to the end of the loading platform where his brother-in-law stood waiting.

"Give me a half-hour, Tim, no more."

Tim nodded and left without comment. In less than a minute he was out of the yards and angling through the woods on a shortcut up the hill to the rectory at St. Joe's. It was a half-mile walk, but he made it in five minutes. He was blowing hard when he rapped sharply on Father Reardon's door.

Exactly twenty-seven minutes later there was a mild commotion in the woods below the church on the Barley Mill Road. Two wagons nearly collided as they passed in opposite directions on the narrow roadbed. One was a high-sided freighter with double teams; the other was a smallish Conestoga canvas-top from the powder yards. It appeared to be loaded with gunpowder, for the wooden kegs were piled high behind the one-armed driver.

Both rigs were halted for a few minutes as the drivers got down between the closely juxtaposed wagons. Apparently they had locked hubs. After a time the driver of the Conestoga climbed aboard and gently coaxed the team forward. They cleared the freighter by inches and continued on up the hill. The driver of the freighter kicked a few handfuls of fresh straw from beside his wagon, climbed up to the high seat, and proceeded down toward the Brandywine. At the foot of the hill the freighter turned downstream, past Chicken Alley and the yards, past Dorgan's, and on eastward. It was a bit out of the way, but a fellow who knew the turns could find his way ultimately to the Philadelphia Turnpike.

A few miles west on the higher ridge of the Brandywine Gorge, the white canvas bonnet of the Conestoga swung along at a slower pace. Black powder teamsters always picked their way carefully. No need to invite trouble. This driver eased along with the slightest jolt to his fragile cargo. The du Pont logo on the canvas was rationale enough for anyone who cared to speculate.

The wagon turned west-northwest at the first junction. This road led to Kennett Square and the Pennsylvania line. It was half a day's journey at his pace, maybe longer, to Quaker and Amish territory... and freedom.

After taking his leave of Francis Reardon, Louis Jardinere drove directly to the du Pont mansion. It was close by, no farther by much than were the powdermen's houses, the mill yards, or the Brandywine itself. Louis took his time. It was still quite early for the household to be up. Of course, he imagined the old man was probably already busy at his office on the grounds, even though his sons had undertaken much of the operation of the industry. He had learned from the innkeeper that only the widowed powdermaker and one of his unattached daughters still lived at the old place. He was suddenly aware of being hungry and looked forward to being invited to breakfast.

That he would be accorded hospitality as houseguest was beyond question. Among his peers such a thing was automatic. One simply did not turn a traveling aristocrat away from one's door. Cordiality was also presumed. Whether that atmosphere was real or feigned was of no concern to Louis. All he needed was a proper location from which to pursue his business over the next few days. Conversation with du Pont did not interest him.

When he reached the house and gave the buggy over to a stableboy who came running up from the barn, Louis took a moment to gaze down over the sloping lawn toward a pathway in the woods. Stripped of leaves, the trees were not nearly so impenetrable as they had been that marvelous, heady summer. He could nearly make out the location of the very rock.

"Before this day is ended," he whispered as he twisted the bell crank. He felt himself quicken with the promise.

CHAPTER 46

The note lay crushed into a ball in the pocket of her apron as Noreen paced her kitchen floor, fighting to control an overwhelming need to give herself up to the release of tears. But she would not allow herself that luxury.

Damn him. Damn the cursed day she first saw him in that awful house whose owner controlled their lives. And damn the awful need that had tripped her up! And then she thought of Kate and almost gave in to the weakness of tears again.

She would not! If that devil was on his way to snare her loved ones and herself again, she would have to be ready to fight, and fight with a clear head. He knew all the tricks.

Suddenly she was aware of the smell of the Crick, and she felt near to drowning. Only this time there was no Brendan to snatch her up.

A dozen times she had started for the door to go for him, to tell him everything, to rid herself of the great lie once and for all. But what a foul slop jar to throw in his face after all these years, he who loved their Kate to the point of pain. She could not do it!

She forced herself to sit at the table and pull out the rumpled note. Even as she read it again she trembled with raging despair: *Ma chérie*, this time do not disappoint me. We have much to discuss regarding your brother's possible arrest and imprisonment for crimes I can swear he has committed. I must insist also on arranging a meeting with our lovely daughter, Kate. Meet me at noon. The usual place. Louis."

She let it lie on the table. It had a curious, mind-clearing effect lying there open to her scrutiny. She forced herself to confront it, as though it were Louis himself. It was, after all, a mere scrap of paper with words. Was he anything more than a man?

Her mind went back to those days with him, remembered the control *she* had over his powers, remembered *his* helplessness under her spell. It was like picking through her own garbage, but gradually she was able to attain a certain degree of detachment, and her anger at last held sway over her desperation.

After a time she calmly folded the paper and put it back into her pocket. She would meet him at noon and learn the worst. Then she would plan.

What had she said to Blanche? Noreen smiled ruefully. Ah, now, that had been wild anger and fright speaking, threatening to do her own sister harm, that silly little thing. Crazy talk. She could never raise her hand against Blanche.

Louis was another matter altogether.

Louis was at the du Pont house for less than a half-hour before he left in a towering rage. Du Pont had not even given him the courtesy of greeting him in person. After keeping him waiting in the music room, the doltish, fat little Irisher who had let him in returned with a scrawled note from du Pont, handed him his hat and cape, and disappeared into the back of the house without a word. He had to let himself out.

The note was brief and to the point: "Your fame precedes you, *débaucheur*. Leave my house." Du Pont had not even signed his name.

His mind stung with the rebuff. He would not let the man get away with it. Somehow, somewhere he would have his satisfaction. He was so tense with anger that he crouched like a race driver in the rig whipping the straining horse, and the gray was in a lather by the time he turned off on the public road.

But above all other things, Louis was a pragmatic schemer. One setback was not going to ruin his day. He let the blowing stallion cool down at a walk as he retraced the route to the rectory.

The priest's house would do just as well as a base for his plans,

[351]

and how could Francis refuse him? He had quite enough leverage to bend the man to his wishes. Unless he was quite off the mark, protecting Noreen would be uppermost in the cleric's mind.

Louis had a sudden fantasy of taking Noreen to bed in the priest's own room! He allowed his thoughts to improvise on the possibilities, including one wildly tantalizing picture of the helpless priest witnessing the act.

His second setback of the day came at precisely eleven-twenty in the morning, when he saw the gaping stable doors at the rectory and the house itself empty of slaves and priest.

As soon as he had helped Tim Feeney get Larkie and her family into the freighter, Francis hurried back into the house, picked up the slave documents and went directly to his study. He rummaged through a heavy leather file box, extracting several faded letters, carefully unfolding each, and smoothing the delicate tissue stationery with his hands.

He studied the script for several minutes and then took a clean sheet, dipped his quill, and began practicing the neat, small characters of his mother's hand. He had covered three sheets before he seemed satisfied with the results.

Then he sighed heavily, raised his eyes with a mumbled prayer, and began a laborious alteration of the parchments Louis had left. The work took nearly an hour. When he had finished, he replaced the letters carefully, folded the parchments, put away his writing gear, and closed up the desk.

He checked the time on the kitchen clock and whistled. Nearly eleven! He wanted to get to Noreen before the noon break spilled dozens of powdermen into Chicken Alley. The news he would be breaking to her had to be private; the fewer witnesses to his visit the better.

Placing the neatly tied bundle of documents on the table where Louis had left them, he threw on his coat, dashed out the door and walked briskly down Barley Mill Road.

"I intend to meet him."

Francis held the wrinkled note Noreen had shown him and looked up incredulously. "You can't be serious. God in heaven, Noreen, after what I've just told you?" He dropped the note on the table as if it were befouled. "This... this challenge means nothing when you consider what Tim and I have done. Let the beast try to have his way with me."

Noreen had to laugh, a bitter little explosive noise that she regretted when she saw how his face dropped.

"I'm sorry, Father, that I have come to mistrust my betters so, but I do not think Louis is interested in you at all." She shook her head. "Nor do I know why he has come back to pester me. Mother of God, I'm nearly a crone, and that's a fact. The man's mind is adrift surely."

"Demonic..."

"Aye, maybe that." She looked at the clock nervously. "He's not really interested in you or me, Father. It's Kate I'm worried over... Kate and Tim."

"Noreen, I've told you about the papers. He'll have a hard time convincing—"

"Ah, Father Reardon! Papers, laws, rules! Do you think those papers will amount to a hill of beans when he finds out? No, while you and Louis are shovin' your paperwork about, it's the likes of us that get hard treatment. It's always been like that. From the waiting for the banns that made us lose our chance to move away to the rules that are trippin' up Kate and James." She ran on hotly.

"You people up there are always settin' down regulations for the likes of us: when to marry, who to marry, when to pray, how to pray, and the lot of you haven't the speck of an idea what it's all about. And now you talk of papers that will make some poor buggers free or slave, as if that means a thing to the God that created them. Even this place is filled to the bursting with poor devils who signed indenture for the right to risk their lives in these bloody mills."

He could not think of a response, but it did not matter anyway. She nearly raged.

"Now you tell me it's too much of a risk to me to go out and meet this devil of a man who's bought *your* slaves, and wants to make my dear ones suffer for it."

She sank into the chair opposite the priest, her anger spent. She did not notice, but her eyes were welling with tears as she whispered hoarsely, "I won't sit by and wait for him to fill Kate's ear, or

Brendan's. And I can't stand the thought of Timmy in some dungeon."

Francis got to his feet. He began putting on his coat. "It's almost time. We had better go."

Noreen was dumbfounded. The idea of his going with her had never crossed her mind. The thought was idiotic, she knew. but it seemed coarse and cheap to think of the priest as her protector. She burned with the shame of it, to drag him along to the scene of her adultery.

"Oh, no."

Francis was busy wrapping a muffler around his neck. "And why not?"

The confessional scene swam up before her again. "Y'don't understand, Father Reardon. We're meeting in the place...I mean, the same place..."

He was pulling on his gloves, regarding her with a firm but kindly eye. "I'm a wiser man than the one who condemned you for meeting him years ago, Noreen, the time I denied you absolution. This time I'll try to make amends. Besides, there's no one else, is there?"

She was weeping, and she shook her head.

"Not even your father can help, and thank the Lord he's not here. I think Denis would put a bullet into Louis as quick as not."

After she left the noontime dinner on the table for her father, they left. It was a good feeling to have the support of Francis Reardon this day, she thought.

Louis Jardinere had no intention of being frustrated in his meeting with Noreen. Neither did he intend to let her brother get away with his chattels. As soon as he found out that the blacks had been taken away in broad daylight, he snatched up the ownership papers from Francis Reardon's table and made a quick run along Crick Road to pick up the wagon's route. The tracks were easy to follow from the church all the way down to the Brandywine. He whipped his horse more than a mile along that route until he had verified the freighter's direction from four different people.

Satisfied that he could overtake the runaways before they made it to the Philadelphia Pike, he raced back for his noon meeting at the rock. He had to laugh despite the setback. Dealing with these people was child's play. He had really come to expect better performance from Thomas Garrett's conductor, but what he had considered clever strategy on Feeney's part was really the result of the gross stupidity of people like his partner, La Roche.

Feeney's dash this morning would bring a dividend. He would be easy to bring down in the town of Wilmington. With the help of a sheriff, the slaves could be penned up near the railway, and he would be free to pursue his other game with Noreen. He mulled over the effect that putting her brother in irons might have in bringing her to heel. That would be a decided advantage! When he reined up on Crick Road where the wood path entered Chicken Alley, he was more delighted than he had been in the early morning.

He did not take pains to cover his moves. There was no need any longer as far as he was concerned. But if he had looked back a few hundred yards along the route he had just retraced, he might have seen a thick-set horseman rein in abruptly as he came into view, and then back his horse quickly behind some trees. The man had a swarthy complexion and did not sit his animal comfortably. He looked very much out of place astride a horse; he was too big for the animal.

But he was patient enough. He sat there gazing over the flat backwater as the Brandywine tried to make up its mind to follow one of its twisting loops. He did keep a sharp eye up the road on the idle carriage, but David Craith was probably thinking how much he would like to be taking the current himself. The *Quaker City* had already missed a week of sailing tides while he piloted this fouled-up business of Madeleine Toussaint's. He spat with disgust.

When Louis was still some distance from their rendezvous he could see the rock plainly. Without the summer foliage, their glade in the cleft of the hill was a disappointment; he might have arranged a more suitable meeting place, he thought, but their meeting would be brief. The next should be in more comfortable surroundings.

He saw her waiting, her eyes full on him as he climbed past the rock, and the very sight of her took his breath away. He paused in midstep, his hand on the smooth granite, and drank her in.

And then he saw the priest.

Francis Reardon had taken a step to Noreen's side, his face clouded with anger, and a trifle pale.

Louis was so upset that he had to resist the urge to pull out his pistol and do away with this sanctimonious curate. But he was outwardly calm, and when he stepped toward them, the hot jealousy came out in sarcasm. "I am surprised, madame, at your indelicacy. I hardly think it in good taste to invite a holy man to our tryst."

Francis shot back, "Keep a civil tongue, Louis. You've caused enough havoc in this good woman's life. Did you expect her to come alone to confront your foul threats?"

Louis kept his eyes on Noreen. "Ah, Noreen, you have made Francis privy to my correspondence, eh?"

She finally spoke, trembling, "Louis, what do you plan to do about Tim...and Kate?"

"Your brother? Well, my dear, that is for the law to decide." He paused. "Rather, I think it is for your good pastor and Tim to decide, eh, Francis? Since it is their joint effort that could bring imprisonment upon them both. As for the lovely young Kate, I believe that is a matter for us to discuss in more private discourse." He glanced at Francis again. "After all, the child should not be made the object of wagging tongues."

Noreen suddenly stepped forward and struck him in the face. Louis reeled backwards.

"You bastard!" she growled hoarsely. "How dare you persecute the innocent!"

Louis rubbed his face and regained his composure. "I should tell you now, so that we can all be spared this little drama, my dear Noreen, that I am aware of your brother's continued crimes against me...this morning's rash escapade, for example. And of the good *père*...his complicity in the affair."

Louis made an elaborate business of pulling out his watch, opening its cover and holding it to the light. "I will tarry no longer, dear friends," he said snapping the watch closed and slipping it under the waistband of his trousers. "Pressing business, as you well know, eh? I will return by the dinner hour with more information pertinent to this...negotiation. We shall meet at the rectory. The three of us."

He gave them a curt little bow and hurried quickly down the path to his trap. They could hear the crack of his whip and the galloping horse as he raced down the Crick on his way to Wilmington.

Noreen had not been near this hateful place in nearly twenty years. It was a nightmare recreated in harsh, dead reality of brown leaves and ground as hard as the blue-gray rock that overshadowed it. Even the run that had fed the summer ferns and grasses was nearly frozen still. Just a few places were bare to the struggling water underneath.

She was terribly close to tears. Francis reached out a comforting hand, his arm encircling her shoulder, his voice low and reassuring. "Surely he took the papers, Noreen. The papers will save Tim . . . and the others."

She tore away from the priest. "Ah, be off with you and yer damnable papers. What good will papers be to croppies and niggers against the word of 'quality'? They're as good as in the jail."

She stormed down the hill toward Chicken Alley. When she was out of sight behind the rock he heard her call, "I'll be to the rectory at six. If I can find a gun, I'll kill him meself!"

CHAPTER 47

A little after noon of the same day, Patrick Gallagher opened his door to find Denis Feeney standing bright-eyed and spruced up like maybe he was on his way to church. Patrick was so stunned by his friend's appearance that he kept him standing in the cold just gawking like a dolt. Finally the little man gave him a push and let himself in.

"Denis Feeney's the name," he cracked. "I believe we met." He limped to the center of the room.

Patrick closed the door slowly without taking his eyes off his visitor. It was hard to believe this was the same man he had seen not a week ago sleeping off a drunk in the gutter beside Dorgan's.

"Well, it's hard to believe that this is the same man I... Well, 'tis hard to believe, Denis, and that's the truth."

Denis grinned wryly. "Don't count on anything yet, boyo. I might look reformed, but I tell you there's a creature clawin' at me belly this minute I'm speakin'."

"You're the fool if ye give in to the craving again, Denis."

Patrick cleared his throat and led the way to the kitchen. He pulled out a chair from the table for Denis and took another for himself.

"Can I get ye anything, Denis?"

Denis remained standing, but he leaned on the back of the chair gratefully. "No. Thanks anyway." He glanced about the quiet house. "I came to see how Maggie..."

"Oh, y'heard about that? I told Kevin not to say anything. She's all right, that girl. A little shock was all it was. Your Tim, y'know, all growed up like he is. Well, the resemblance..."

"I know."

"She's fine. Just restin' a bit."

"Is she asleep?"

"No, no. Why don't you go in the room there and jaw with her a bit, Denis? I have to fetch water from Halloran's anyway. G'wan right in."

Patrick did not give Denis a chance to decide. He scooped up the bucket and was out the door without another word.

Left alone in the house, he had second thoughts about calling on Maggie in her bedroom. It would have been awkward enough if Patrick were there. She didn't think much of Denis Feeney; he knew that all right. Well, the woman had cause enough.

Ah, what the devil... He shrugged and, taking a tiny bite of the lip for courage, limped over to her door and rapped so lightly that he barely heard it himself.

"Come in, Denis," she answered so quickly he was startled.

The latch rattled in his trembling hand, unnerving him further, but he put on a bold front to cover it up.

"So, Mrs. Gallagher, were ye waitin' on me to call?"

She was sitting in a rocker under the window with a heap of knitting in her lap. The bone needles were a flying clatter in her fingers. She looked up briefly between stitches.

"I'd have to be deaf, now wouldn't I, not to hear you two indoors. You're looking well, Denis Feeney."

"I hope you're well, Maggie," he said quietly. He was shocked at how old she had become. "You certainly do look fit, and that's a fact."

"That," she retorted with another birdlike glance, "Is pure blarney."

"I'm terrible sorry you had the fright ye did yesterday noon. I know how you must have felt. They didn't tell me neither."

"Oh, I knew all right. I was in on it from the first. That made it worse, somehow."

[359]

"Still a shock, eh?"

"I was all prepared to meet your little Timmy back from the grave. I didn't think of all the years, him not bein' a boy no more and all. When he came in he was Timothy, all right, but it was *my* Tim, not yours that stopped my heart." Her voice broke on this, and she dropped her head into her palms. The knitting curled out of her lap, slipping silently to the floor.

Denis eased across the space between them and bent painfully to pick up the heap of soft wool. He placed it awkwardly on her knees.

"Is it still so bad, Maggie? I mean after all this time—a whole lifetime—and your life with Patrick and the boys... with Brendan and all."

She spoke as if to herself only, and he had to strain to hear. "I thought so for a long time. But it was another life I led since losing him. I was just... replaced, I guess... replaced with a different Maggie Doran. And all that time, all that lovely, sad, and wonderful time with Patrick and my boys, the other part was still in love with Tim." She looked out the window as the evening sun suddenly dropped behind a wooded hill, leaving them in soft twilight. "I just didn't know it for certain until your Tim marched in here yesterday so tall and strong... so like the uncle he never saw, or even heard of."

Maggie turned to look at him, her face obscured in the sudden shadow of the dim room. "You never did tell any of them about him, did you? Well, one of them knows, Denis. Years ago, before that awful blast, I told Noreen because she was begging me so. And I thought she had the right."

Denis felt his face tighten into a mask.

"Maybe I should not have done it. But, Denis, you ought have told them all yourself. They would have loved you the more for it."

His mask cracked enough to ask, "And you, Maggie? Have you loved me the more for it?" The words came between his teeth, squeezed by his own hurt.

She studied him a long moment before answering, and in the shadow he saw that her eyes were as empty of reproach as was her voice.

"As God will judge us both, Denis Feeney, I never gave you blame or loved you less."

There was a great stillness in the room then. The afterlight dimming to purple as the evening sank heavily along the soft gorge of the Brandywine. Slowly he bent over her and kissed her. Then without a word he limped from her room and out of the house.

He was halfway to Dorgan's, nearly consumed with an ague of trembling, when he remembered. Remembered that Tim would be back at home tomorrow. Remembered all of them at table, waiting supper, Noreen and Brendan, Kevin and Kate . . . all of them waiting for Denis Feeney.

He couldn't bring himself to stop, but he did manage to turn himself around. A long, looping turn across the road to fool himself into thinking it was just a delay. Just a change in direction. A temporary thing.

He would see them at supper first, see Tim. After? Well, he'd worry about that when it became too much to bear. But in the meantime, in the meantime, every step he took was toward home—and away from Dorgan's Inn.

CHAPTER 48

Noreen managed somehow to get through the long afternoon. She filled in the time by scrubbing the house, cleaning places she had not touched for years, and by suppertime she had carried a great mountain of junk out back to be hauled off to the common dump in the woods.

And she had made a huge supper: stew and biscuits, fresh bread, and a pie that would be mushy and sweet, made as it was out of apples that the frost had touched.

It kept her occupied, gave her an excuse for burning off the fright that would have put her in a frenzy otherwise, but her mind was in Wilmington and on the clock.

It also gave her a reason to go to the priest's house at suppertime. She would use the excuse of taking a bite to the pastor, who everybody on the Crick knew did not have a housekeeper yet.

When the hour finally dragged close, and the family started tumbling in, she had a glow that everybody misread as high spirits. She let them delude themselves, but it was terribly hard not to fold up entirely when she saw the beaming face of Denis Feeney.

"Mebbe the boy'll be back tonight instead of tomorra."

"Kevin suddenly looked up at his mother and said, "Oh, I almost forgot. . . . Dad has taken an overnight run. He won't be back until morning."

Noreen did not realize she was clutching her son with both hands until he laughed and pulled her off.

"Ma...Ma, it's all right. He's not haulin' powder. Gosh, I didn't mean to put a scare into you like that."

She was trembling, aware of all their eyes on her.

Kevin tried to be light. "It was supposed to be a secret anyway, but you know how word gets around. Actually he's usin' a company wagon to haul some things for Father Reardon. On the sly, you know."

"For Father Reardon..."

"Yeah. Dad told Dougherty to let me know he wouldn't be back tonight and to let you know. That was all, but you know Dougherty with a secret. He has as tight a mouth as Halloran's pump. Let the cat outta the bag in the same breath. I hope Dad don't get in bad with the Mister."

"Oh, Brendan..."

Kate touched her mother's arm reassuringly. "It's nothing, Mother. The company is always doing things for the church anyway. I don't see..."

Noreen snatched up her shawl and went for the basket sitting near the hearth. "I'm leaving for the priest's now," she said abruptly. "And I may sit with him an hour to let him eat."

Kate looked strangely at her. "Do you want me to walk along? I can have supper after."

"No," Noreen said quickly, hefting the basket. "It's no burden, and it's my own cooking. I'll deliver it myself. You eat now while it's hot and you have the chance."

When she went out the door, Kevin got up from the table and reached for his coat, but Kate stopped him.

"Let her go, Kevin. She'll be all right. Can't you see she needs to do it in her own way?"

But Kate was thoughtful herself as they ate. Her mother had been through enough to break her down. She prayed the old strangeness would not cloud her once again.

"Why didn't you tell me!"

"Tell you what, Noreen?" Francis looked blankly at her as he took the basket and her shawl.

"About Brendan!"

"I know nothing about Brendan. What do you mean?"

"The wagon trip he made for you today."

"Brendan has no wagon business with the church. What do you mean?"

She told him what Kevin had said, struggling to remember his exact words, and then, "He's mixed up somehow with Tim; I know it."

They had no more time to speculate. The clatter of a trap pulling into the yard brought both of them to the window in time to see Louis Jardinere stalking to the sacristy door. He did not pause to knock, but burst in violently and slammed the door behind him.

He glared at them in silence, holding his dark cape tightly over his folded arms. His hat was gone, and the silvered mane of carefully groomed hair had gone into windblown clumps. He trembled with agitation.

"So, my friends, you took Jardinere for the fool. I should have known better than to trust these innocent charades, this pretense at weakness."

Noreen looked to Francis for some explanation. But he was grimly silent.

"I must bow to your ingenuity, *mon père*, the forged alteration of my papers into documents of manumission. Very clever. And your brother's wagon, madame; no sign of the niggers when I had it searched."

He whirled on them. "And so you think that all is well because the black wretches have been spirited off by someone else, and Garrett's conductor—your brother, madame—is safely on his way again to Philadelphia to deliver my tobacco...."

Very slowly Louis let the cape fall away from his arms. He held the pistol to his hand and deliberately pointed it at Noreen.

"Louis!" Francis's voice was like a pistol shot itself.

Louis's laughter rasped. He lowered the weapon. "Do not be alarmed, Francis. I am not a complete fool, but I wanted to get your manly reaction. It would be unthinkable to mar such a delightful bedmate, no? That exquisitely soft flesh! Have you wondered, *mon père*?" Have you *tried* it, I wonder?"

Noreen turned away ashen.

Francis was in a rage. "Speak another word like that, you mis-

[364]

erable toad, and as Christ is my witness, I'll smash you here and now!"

Louis looked at his pistol and shrugged. "I will not tempt you further, dear Francis. But hear me now, please. Your little scheme is but a delay. I will have new documents drawn from the records in Richmond. There will be an accounting under the law, and you, my dear," he turned to Noreen, "you will learn from your daughter's lips the truths that I will fill her ears with."

He strode to the door and turned as he let himself out into the night. "My rooms will be at the Wilmington lodging house. Should you come to your senses, you may find me there."

They did not move to close the door he had left swinging, but listened as his carriage moved out of the drive. Then Francis stepped outside and stood attentive as the rig moved away into the dark until there were no more sounds. He came back into the kitchen, closing the door softly, and went to Noreen.

"He's gone. I could hear him take the road to town."

"It doesn't matter much, does it?" she muttered. "He'll be back in a day, or a week. But he'll be back."

"Let me handle him," he said grimly. "There will be a way, I promise you."

She looked at the priest wearily. "Don't you think you've done quite enough already?"

She picked up her shawl and wrapped it carelessly about her head and shoulders. Her voice was flat. "I'll be goin'."

"Let me walk you, Noreen."

"No. I need the time to think."

She would not be persuaded, so he let her go. Besides, it was such a short walk, she probably *could* use the time to compose herself. No need for her to show up at home looking upset.

"God knows," Francis thought, "I could certainly use a measure of composure." He had not the slightest idea where to turn for help.

Noreen was halfway down Barley Mill Road where the hill flattened somewhat and entered the belt of woodland above the mills and Chicken Alley. She could hear the rumble of the rolling mills even at this distance. The sound seemed doubly ominous at night. Never before this year had they processed gunpowder after dark, but demand for the black stuff was high, and someone had invented a lamp that could be used with little risk of explosion. Or so they said. Now a few dozen men ran a second shift until midnight, grinding out a third six-hour batch of "cake" every working day. The powdermen didn't like it much; they were afraid of the lanterns. "Flame inside a rolling mill?" they would ask. But they went on schedule anyway.

It wasn't too bad. Once the batch was in the tub and wet down, a body could tuck away somewhere and take a snooze. Let the grinding wheels do their work, and wet it down once or twice between. There wasn't much a man could do but watch and listen anyway. Twin mills to watch and listen to for six hours in the night. It was boring. You couldn't blame a man for takin' a snooze.

Just out of sight in the woods somebody else was working a second shift also. He sat alert and attentive to every sound he heard from Barley Mill Road. His weary horse drooped between the shafts of the carriage and slept soundly, unaware even of the foundering stiffness of his overworked legs.

Louis Jardinere would not be cheated of the promise he had made to himself the night before, and when the sound of her footsteps drifted to him over the rumbling groan of the mills, he slipped from the seat and moved swiftly over the hard ground toward Noreen Gallagher.

She did not hear him at all when he stepped out of the woods onto the road behind her. Still she sensed him somehow, a sharp tingle at the back of her neck, and she turned around.

Noreen did not even have a chance to see him clearly before she was in his arms, fighting off his hungry mouth that was all over hers, searching her lips with his hot tongue, pressing her body to his with an iron strength. She twisted, trying to free her arms, but he held fast, smothering her with his panting mouth, flattening her with a viselike grip as he squeezed her against himself.

She tried to scream, but there was no air in her lungs. She bit at the awful darting tongue, but it was now slavering at her throat. She was aware of being lifted bodily off her feet, of kicking empty air, of a terrifying ugly hardness against her thighs.

She was on the point of passing out when he released one arm, and she took a great sobbing breath. And then she felt his searching fingers in her groin.

Arching her back in a great convulsive spasm of disgust, she freed her left arm from the tangle of his cloak. With a whining snarl, she smashed her fist against the side of his head with all her strength, and fell backwards from him as he lost his grip.

She did not stop fighting even as she struck the hard roadway, but rolled away from him, driving with her feet, and clawing on all fours until she was at last in a crouch, lunging down the hill wildly off-balance, and then fully erect, running desperately for the safety of the mills.

She did not even look back until she gained the millrace bridge and darted across. She saw him moving slowly toward her down the hill, still some distance behind, and for a wild moment she thought she might outrun him all the way home.

She decided not to risk it and plunged down the embankment between the rumbling walls of the first two mills. She knew there would be only one millhand and saw light spilling from the open doorway of the one on her right. She dashed for its sanctuary.

Noreen had never been inside an operating mill before, and the massive thunder of the huge grinding wheels was overpowering. The whole building shook with their vibration as they rolled inexorably in an endless track, crushing the wet powdercake in the low-sided tubs. In the dim light of the single shielded lantern high on one wall, the slowly moving wheels and pinion gears threw grotesque shadows everywhere.

She moved tentatively around the grinding machinery in the middle of the crowded room, her back to the wall as she looked for the powderman. He must be on the far side, she thought, the door was open. She wanted to cry out for help, but the drubbing noise would have soaked up her call even before it reached her own ears. She inched along to the corner, gathering her skirts to keep them clear of the lumbering wheels. The operator was not in sight. Then another twenty feet to the next corner. Nothing. The man was keeping just ahead of her. She hurried another twenty feet, and at the corner she heaved a sigh of relief, for she could see his foot in the doorway.

It was then that Noreen screamed, a silent scream smothered by the din of the wheels. It was not the foot of the powderman at all. The man was Louis Jardinere, and he was closing the door.

She huddled in her corner too terrified to move as he approached. When he was standing over her, he began fumbling with the buttons of his pants, and she stared transfixed, cringing against the cold stone that trapped her. His lips were working, forming words she could not hear, would not understand. She pleaded with him, watched his expression change, saw his mouth shape itself into a laugh. Then he reached out and tore open the bodice of her dress.

She pushed him off as he advanced, feeling herself weakening in terror. Drawing from a last reserve she slapped hard at his leering face. He recoiled briefly, mouth and eyes hardening into rage, threw back his cape to free his arm, and swung his fist at her. Noreen jerked her head away, but the blow caught her at the temple, driving her head against the stone wall. As she sagged into unconsciousness, she had a vision of Louis retreating, and knew at least the satisfaction that she had fought him off.

Louis was backing away. The surprise registering on his face gradually transformed into a look of horror as he realized his cape was caught in the mill wheels. His hands flew to the clasp of the cape. He struggled with it, fingers clawing at his neck as he backed away, slowly arching toward the wheels. He let out a piercing scream. Then the wheels drew him in.

Noreen was still unconscious when David Craith came bursting in. She did not see him drag the body of Louis from the mill. She was not even aware of being carried herself. When she came to her senses, she was fighting the awful taste of something being forced between her lips. Her eyes opened, and she found herself propped up against a tree with the man who had spoken to Tim that morning giving her a sip of brandy from a flask.

She pushed away the drink and looked wildly around. "Where is he?" The movement made her dizzy, and the smell of brandy made her sick.

"You have to hurry, missus, before we're seen."

The terror was building again. "But where is he?" she whispered. "He's like a crazy beast. He'll be after me again!"

Craith looked at her closely. It was good that she didn't know. It would simplify things. "No need to worry about him; I've got him safely stowed. He'll not get to you again."

She was not assured. "But it's not just me I'm worried about, you see, there's Tim and—"

"It's all taken care of. Just forget what happened. The Frenchman is gonna take a nice long voyage back to France, and he'll not be back. There are things he has to answer for where he's going, you

[368]

can be sure of it." Craith thought grimly that there was some truth in that, at least. The man was so broken up he would sooner meet his Maker than any court in France.

Noreen leaned against the tree and searched Craith's face. She wanted to believe him, but her mind was all in a daze still, and it seemed too easy somehow. He reached down and pulled her to her feet.

"Look, Mrs. Gallagher, I hate to be rough on you, and I'm sorry I didn't get here before that snake tried what he did. But that's done. For the sake of yer brother and the priest, you must put it all out of yer mind."

Her head throbbed terribly; she must be a sight! What would she tell the ones at home? That she bumped her head on a tree in the woods? She would have to invent something. Dear God, would it never end?

Craith was pushing her along the road. "Just ferget this. You went to the priest and came back; that's all. Understand? Not a word of this ever to anybody—not even Tim Feeney."

She nodded and started toward Chicken Alley. She saw that the man waited until she was safely along, and then he disappeared. When she got home, it was after nine o'clock, and everybody including Kate had gone to bed.

David Craith wasted little time ministering to the unconscious figure in the back of Louis Jardinere's rented buggy. He barely checked to see if he was still alive before whipping the spent horse toward the priest's house. He had little time to spare, and he was not altogether sure that he should tell the cleric much about the affair. Still, it was important that the Gallagher woman not drop a word in the wrong ear. The priest could be insurance.

"Dear God, you say he raped her!"

"Tried to, that's what I said, Reverend." Craith swore to himself, fearing that he had made a mistake in coming to the rectory. The priest's face was livid. "He roughed her up a bit and tore her clothes, but she was holding her own until I got there."

"Where is the beast? We must—"

"I've got him out there in the rig."

Francis made a move for the door, but Craith stopped him with a firm hand. "Leave him be. Before morning he'll sail with me for Le Havre. He's a fugitive from French law, you know."

[369]

"I can imagine!"

"Listen, Reverend, I'm in a rush to make the tide, and the reason I stopped was to tell you about the woman. Make sure she keeps mum about things. With that one in irons," he jerked his head toward the buggy, "the whole thing with the blacks will calm quick. I've got connections to keep his partner quiet, too."

"La Roche."

"Aye, that one will trade off his loss for our Frenchman's share of the plantation."

Craith waited for Francis's understanding nod, then made for the door. As he left, he shot back a warning, "Just a reminder, Reverend, except for the Gallagher woman, you need to keep yer own lips buttoned."

Then he leaped for the seat and whipped his horse again toward the Wilmington docks. He heard Louis moan once as he careened along, and wondered if he had come to. The ship's surgeon would give the poor wretch drugs enough to kill any pain he might still be conscious of, but nobody could ever undo what those iron wheels had done. Craith doubted that the man would survive the next day.

Louis was still breathing an hour later when he pulled up to the *Quaker City* and had the watch crew carry him to his own cabin. If only he would last until they cleared port. What happened at sea was a captain's responsibility. Until then he could simply claim that he was returning a French citizen to face charges in his own country.

Craith's gamble paid off. Louis Jardinere died without ever regaining consciousness as the ship bearing him toward France entered Delaware Bay. He was buried at sea the following morning.

After the ceremony Craith made a proper entry in his log and wrote a brief letter to Madeleine Toussaint. He would hail the first westbound vessel he met to have it posted. The news would set her mind at ease. Before he sealed the message he had a notion that she should notify the priest and that Gallagher woman about Jardinere's death. There was something in that business that went beyond the slave thing. He wasn't sure what exactly, but it prompted him to add the request to the letter.

That afternoon he exchanged mail parcels with a ship bound for Philadelphia. Madeleine Toussaint would have his letter within a week.

The same morning Father Reardon came calling at the Feeneys' to return Noreen's basket. Denis said that his calling was a good thing, and timely, because Noreen was still abed from bumping her head on a branch in the woods and taking a nasty fall. He and the priest chattered about little things until she was dressed, and then the old fellow limped out to "take a walk by the Crick and give them some privacy."

Francis did not mince words. "The man Craith called on me last night and told me what happened at the mill."

Noreen looked at the priest dully. She started to speak, her throat working in little spasms, but gave up with a dismal wave of her hand.

"I know that I am of no help to you now, Noreen, but there are some things I want you to know for the safety of others, for peace in your own life later on, and for my own peace of mind."

He shifted awkwardly on the sitting room bench and cleared his throat as though arranging each bit of a carefully prepared speech. His discomfort was that of a very young man, certainly not the stern priest she had known.

"First of all, the less said about last night, the better it will be for all concerned. As far as Craith knows, we are the only people who can make the connection between Louis and the owner of the runaways. When the man fails to return, his share of the plantation will no doubt be snapped up by his partner. Craith says the man is quite greedy, and the matter can be handled discreetly.

"Secondly, I have arranged through Craith and another person I know to see to the well-being of those slaves who were my parents' and mine, by signing over my inheritance to them. It is not much, but it will give them some security."

Noreen found her tongue and interrupted. "Father Reardon, you have no need to confess to me."

Francis shook his head. "I have more need than you will ever imagine. Please let me finish, and then I will be gone to let you rest."

He paused again to collect himself. "The money left to me by my mother was to have provided me with travel and a chance to move up within the church." He shot Noreen a quick look. "I think she had visions of my being the pope."

There was hope for humor in that, but Noreen was not up to it, not today. "So all of her money went to you?"

Francis laughed. "No, not nearly, Noreen. Most of it she donated to the church... to be spent on the needy and the education of the priests."

Noreen got up and began poking at the coals in the hearth. She hefted the teakettle to estimate how much water remained and placed it directly on the embers.

"Excuse me, Father, I'm in such a dither today I forgot to fix you a cuppa."

"Don't bother, Noreen. I must be off soon anyway."

She ignored his refusal and began setting out the pot and cups automatically, her mind preoccupied with something else. "It seems like a shame and a waste to me...."

"A waste?"

"The sale of your place, I mean."

"I don't understand..."

"Well, now it's all of it gone...the lot of it. Your piece to the black people, the most of it sent somewhere in the church bank."

Francis drew himself up proudly. "Yes, all of it. I don't regret the loss of a penny, Noreen. It is a fitting last sacrifice to the memory of my mother. A living memorial."

"But I was thinkin', Father Francis," she said thoughtfully as she measured out the tea into the pot. "It would have been better, wouldn't it, to have given the whole place to the people in the first place."

He was incredulous. "To the *nigras?*"

"Aye, the poor niggers, Father. Then there wouldn't be this awful mess to worry over, with people gettin' hurt and killed. Your mother could have stayed on until she died, the black people would have been able to keep their home, and you would have had a place to visit now and then."

Francis had a fleeting vision of the field hands taking up residence in Skibbereen, and the picture was so outlandish that he looked hard at Noreen to see if she was not making some kind of joke. When he was satisfied that she was not, he decided to change the subject—and leave. He was suddenly very weary.

"Ah, well, Noreen, it's water over the dam, at any rate." He went to the clothes tree by the front door and began pulling on his cloak. "I'm sorry that I cannot stay for the tea. There are still so many things to attend to. But please remember this. Forget about the past. All that business is over and done with.

"Let those ghosts die with last night. Nobody," he repeated with emphasis, "*nobody* else needs to know about Louis Jardinere."

Less than a week later Francis was back again, however, and this time he had news of a real ghost. He could not mask his relief at the news of Louis's death and burial at sea.

"God moves in strange ways, Noreen. We must accept it as a mixed blessing of his divine will."

She felt a little sick at the news. She hoped he had felt some contrition in the end, but his death was only a stay of her punishment, not a reprieve.

Francis sensed her thoughts. "Put him from your mind, Noreen. If you can find it in your heart to pray for the saving of his soul, do that, of course; but for the other business, well, forget it. Put it away forever."

CHAPTER 49

The next two weeks were such a whirl that Noreen thought of her argument with Blanche only once—when her sister came to call after Tim's sudden reappearance.

Blanche was holding court in a sitting room, chattering away as though it was a rare holiday with her dropping in like the distant relative she had become. Noreen noticed how shy her father behaved, keeping to himself in the background. She caught Blanche stealing a curious look at her father as if she couldn't quite measure the change in him.

But soon they were laughing at a story her sister was telling about the Mister's children, and the whole room seemed merry. Even Denis Feeney was chuckling.

Then James Gallagher came calling.

Kate shot to her feet to answer the door and usher him in. There was no mistaking the look on their faces as Kate led him to a chair and seated herself on the floor next to him. They were in love, surely; this was no tender family friendship.

Noreen's own realization came as a kind of pleasant shock, as though she had been truly unaware of it before. She let her eyes play across the faces in the room to see if the others were aware. Brendan gave no sign, nor did Kevin or Tim. Her father did not appear to notice. Then she looked at her sister.

The accusation in those eyes made her cringe. If Blanche only knew the real truth! The horror of the whole sordid nightmare of Louis now haunted her. She shrank from Blanche's stare, but it was the memory of that awful accounting that bore her down. The conversation in the room faded to a dismal buzzing in her ears. Her hands felt terribly cold as she glanced furtively from one face to the next. "Are y'well, Norrie?" Brendan's face expressed concern. The others had stopped talking. She could feel them looking.

"Do y'want to lie down? Can I get you something? Y'look so pale, darlin'."

"No... no, I'm fine. Just chilled a bit..."

"Then let me warm yer tea."

She nodded eagerly, grasping for diversion, and touched his cheek briefly with her cold hand.

"Well, I must be off," said Blanche. "I think Noreen should rest. These last few days have been a strain, to be sure, and she must have much on her mind."

The comment was inflected as a direction to James as well as an excuse for herself. Noreen bridled at her presumption. She looked up to see Jamie starting to rise.

"Stay, James," she snapped with more energy than she intended. "I'll see Blanche to the door."

"Well, Noreen, I really think..."

"It's all right, Blanche," she said evenly, cutting her off. "Are you sure you won't stay for supper?"

Blanche pulled on her coat. "It'll be dark then. I don't like cuttin' through the woods after dark on a cold night like this."

"I'd be happy t'walk ye home, Miss Blanche."

It was James who had left his chair to come over to the two women. The offer flustered Blanche, and she fumbled with her gloves.

"'Twould be no trouble at all," he insisted.

"Thank you, no, James," she answered finally and gave him a quick, frozen little smile. "We're shorthanded on the hill anyway, and I'll be needed."

The others rose as she reached for the latch, and Blanche caught Tim's eye. "You'll be back from time to time, Brother Tim?"

"From time to time."

She nodded. "Then I'll see you again."

As she went through the doorway, she gave Noreen a little tug on the sleeve to follow. Noreen stepped out after her and pulled the door closed. The air was bitter cold, and Noreen shivered. Blanche gave Noreen a sharp look.

"It's as plain as day, now, isn't it?"

"That they're fond of each other? Yes, I think so."

"Think so! Agh, Noreen, it's as clear as the ice on the Crick. I know you told me to mind me tongue, but I can't let tragedy happen to my niece."

"There'll be no tragedy, Blanche. Just mind your tongue," Noreen said easily.

"Just look to your Christian duty as a mother, then," Blanche said shaking her finger. Then she sighed and shook her head. "It's true that the lout is a fine-looking man; no wonder he was able to turn the poor girl's head!"

"Good-bye, Blanche," Noreen said as she stepped back into the warmth of the house and closed the door after her, leaving her sister standing on the stoop.

The renewed prodding from Blanche sent Noreen up to St. Joe's the following morning. It was pleasant on the way up the hill, and when she had cleared the woods the warm sun was just warm enough to lift her spirits a little.

Francis Reardon was in high spirits, too, running about the new church in shabby workpants and a black sweater as he watched a swarm of workmen finishing the roof and laying on the stucco. He was like a youth at a festival, trying to be everywhere at once.

When he saw Noreen, he ran over to her. "Just think, Noreen, tonight they start heating the place! Tomorrow if it's warm enough inside, the plastering will begin.

He braced both hands behind his hips and looked up at the steeple. It gleamed with the new coat of yellow stucco, and the copper flashings looked like hammered gold against the slate roof.

"Tower of Ivory, House of God." The words drifted from her mouth without her even thinking them.

He turned his eyes from the steeple and looked down at her with surprise. "That's amazing, Noreen. I was just thinking of Christmas and Our Lady . . . and you caught the exact phrase! From the litany."

She laughed a little. "I always remember that one, from me childhood, y'know. It just popped out."

"A beautiful image," he said, "full of majesty, purity and richness."

"To tell the truth, Father, it always puts me in mind of fairies— fairies and castles and treasures. Mostly treasure."

She laughed at her irreverence. "I shouldn't be lookin' at prayer for an answer to my greed."

"G'wan with yeh," he teased, affecting a brogue. "The Irish have a right to dream of wealth, having been without it for so long a time."

They both laughed. "You've been listening to Denis Feeney too much, Father Francis. Those are his words exactly."

The lightness subsided, and they watched as the workmen began drifting down the ladders to clean up for their dinner break.

"Oh, I hope it is ready for Christmas," he said. "So many of the people can hardly wait."

It seemed like a good place to start, Noreen thought, and so she did. "I can think of two who would like it to be finished right quick."

He gave her a questioning glance.

"I mean, there are two who will want to march up to the altar together."

"You were not able to convince them to break it off?"

"Coax a fly from honey? No. I wouldn't even try. 'Tis a lovely thing they have for each other. I know it in me bones."

"Well, Noreen, I can't see that anything is changed. The people would be scandalized. You haven't told Brendan, have you?"

"I plan to. . . . I will if it will change things."

He reached out and gripped her arm. "You must not do that to him. Oh, Noreen, Noreen, it would crush him so!"

"You don't give my man much credit for strength, do you, Father?"

"Do *you*, Noreen?" he asked quietly. "You've kept it from him since the day she was born."

CHAPTER 50

It was a grand speech she had made to the priest, but that's all it was, a speech. As Noreen hurried toward home, she had no idea what to do once she got there.

Each time she tried to plan what she should do next, the consequences of the act would fill her with an awful dread, and the picture would shatter into painful little scenes, horrible, angry, hurtful things. She would have to start with Brendan. Oh, God, why hadn't she made a clean breast of it all before! And then Kate, dear sweet, bright Kate who had propped her up through the long years of her... confusion, after the twins had died. What would it do to her to find out her daddy wasn't Brendan after all? And Kevin... would he ever be able to look his mother in the eye again? And Tim, and her father, and Maggie... and Patrick.

She felt the knot in her throat again and fought it down. Was she hell-bent on her own destruction and that of her loved ones, too, as the priest had said? God help me, she thought. It's like carrying a torch to light my way out of a powder mill.

At least I'll have the house to myself today, she remembered, grateful for the chance to compose herself in privacy. Her own three would still be at work, and Denis Feeney had planned to call on Patrick. Tim would be at Meg Halloran's again. At least *that* business was off to a good start.

Smoke was rising from their chimney as she turned onto the path to the Feeney cottage, and she was grateful that someone had remembered to bank the fire. She shuddered involuntarily just thinking of getting into her warm kitchen and ran the last few steps to the door.

It opened before she touched the latch, and Brendan stood there waiting for her. A tiny alarm went off in her head as he ushered her in, and across the sitting room she saw Kate and James sitting together. Kate was weeping.

"What on earth...?" She pulled off her shawl and looked at Brendan, who stood grimly with his good arm across his chest gripping the stump of the other.

"Blanche was here," he said.

She bit her lip to stifle a curse, and turned back toward Kate. She was huddled against Jamie, face crushed against his chest. As she took a step toward them, Brendan stopped her with a firm grip on her arm.

"We have to talk, Norrie," he said, "just you and me."

When Brendan closed their bedroom door, she could hardly get the words out. "What did she say to them?"

"She's been at Kate with tales of deformed babies and other rotten trash. Wild nightmare stuff to stop the girl from keeping company with James there."

"I warned her to—"

"Says she *knows* what happens when cousins marry, that God sends them all sorts of pestilence and grief.... Oh, she gave the poor thing an earful."

"Mother of God!"

"Told her that she'd be excommunicated from the church and go straight to hell in a basket." The anger began to ebb in him as he spoke, but he was more furious than ever she remembered, even more than the day he stormed in with the news of their vanished freight line. "My God, Noreen, what kind of a wasp is that woman?"

"She'll hear from me," Noreen muttered, but that would be pointless now, and she knew it.

"That's not all," he went on. "James was fired yesterday. Just told to clear out. I guess you know who arranged that."

"Oh, Blanche..."

Brendan shook his head miserably. "No, not Blanche, though she must have put a bug in his ear. No, Norrie, it was me own father who went to the Mister."

Noreen was suddenly dizzy. She felt Brendan's arm around her as she sank to the edge of the bed. Visions of meeting du Pont by the rock in the woods spun past, the smell of bruised moss was in her nose, and she stared at her trembling hands afraid she might find on them again the purple stain of pokeweed.

"I had it out with him this morning when I got the news. Ah, Noreen, it's hard to be upset with the old man. He was nearly in tears himself after doin' it. Said he was tryin' to save Kate from getting hurt, the meddling old fool."

"Is there aught to be done for James?"

"His work? No. That's done. He's always been a good worker, no disputin' that; but some think him a troublemaker—you know, callin' the Mister 'His Lordship' and all. No, I think he was out soon or late anyway." Brendan smiled faintly. "I don't think Jamie is much upset at that. It's the other thing, his plan to marry our Kathleen."

"What do *you* think about the two of them . . . ?"

"Me? Well, I think he is a fine lad, Norrie. Kate could do far worse, if y'ask me."

"No, Brendan. I mean about their being cousins—this whole business of marrying kin."

"Oh, *that.*"

"Well, yes. That is what the whole wild turmoil is about, isn't it? Or am I gone soft in the head again?"

Brendan held her hand tenderly for a while before he seemed able to answer. He squeezed her fingers gently as he spoke. "Well, they're not truly cousins anyway, are they, Norrie? You and I know that, now don't we?"

She was stunned. At first she was certain she had not heard him right, but as they sat together on the bed, a great warmth enveloped them. She could feel it in him as well as in herself. He knew! He had always known! And the great joy of it was in the final knowing of this greatest love he had for her, unquestioned, deep and unquenchable, steady through all those years.

She was unable to say anything, but there was no need, really. His being with her said it all.

[380]

At last it was he who broke the tender silence. "I think, Norrie, it's time the two of us broke the news to Jamie and Kate."

She kissed him, then, suddenly aflame with love herself, and felt the doubling of their strength as they went in to break their secret together.

Later that evening it was Brendan Gallagher who knocked on Francis Reardon's door. When the priest swung it open, Brendan took off his cap, tucked it under his stump of an arm, and stepped in.

"Good evenin' to you, Father. I hope I'm not bargin' in on yer suppertime."

"No, no, Brendan. It's good to see you. This is your first time in the rectory, isn't it? You've been working on the church of course, but... Would you like to see the place? Or would you like a cuppa?" It was obvious that Father Reardon was delighted for the company, but Brendan was ill at ease.

"Another time, Father, if y'don't mind. I've got something on me mind I need to clear up."

Francis pointed to a chair and took one himself.

"I'll speak plainly, Father, if ye don't mind. It will go easier that way."

He cleared his throat and began.

"The way I see it, Father, y'owe me a favor. What with me cartin' yer black folks to Kennett Square, tuckin' them in safe with that Quaker bunch."

Francis nodded. "As I said before, Brendan, only God will understand how much I am in your debt."

"Ah, well, it was nothin' much to me. To tell the God's truth, I enjoyed the excitement of bein' on the road again." He grinned sheepishly and went on. "But it was a big thing to you, Father, to see how much it meant fer them niggers to be set off on their own, free as birds."

Brendan cleared his throat again. "Well, the favor I want, y'see, is sorta like that. I got a couple of kids down there by the Crick that want to be off on their own, and the only thing keepin' them apart is some rule that says they ain't free to go like others are."

"Kate and James."

"The same."

"Well, Brendan, the rule against cousins—"

"Ah, Father, that rule was not made fer them. You know it, I know it, Noreen knows it, and now the kids know it, too."

Francis examined Brendan's expression for a long time before he responded. "Did Noreen tell you?"

"About the Frenchman? Ah, Father, a hundred times. It's not a thing husband or wife can keep from one another. I've known fer years—or thought so anyway. It's the same thing."

Francis was stunned. "My God, man, why didn't you ever discuss it with her?"

Brendan looked away. "It's hard to put me finger on, except I was afraid at first of losing her. Y'know how headstrong she can be. And then when she got so . . . sick after the twins died—I was afraid it might be too much for her to take. Oh, she was as touchy as glass in them days. I wouldn't risk it."

"And afterward?"

"It didn't seem to matter much. I mean, it was like we both knew about it, but it didn't matter anymore."

Francis said nothing.

"I tell ye, Father," Brendan went on, "that darlin' Kate is the light of me life. God strike me but I love her more than Kevin, and that's a fact."

Francis got up and paced around the room. "It's a marvelous thing you're telling me, Brendan Gallagher. It has opened my mind on many things; I can tell you that." He stopped and pointed a finger at Brendan. "But you can't have me make an announcement to all of Chicken Alley that because your daughter is not truly a Gallagher, she can go off and marry James. The tongues would wag, and your life here would be wrecked . . . yours and Noreen's."

"That's what I come to ask about, Father. You don't have to mention a word. Just give them a . . . a dispensation."

"Dispensation."

Francis collapsed like a sack. Dear God in Heaven, did the man think he was a bishop?

"Aye, a dispensation. Just scratch out a few words that say they're fit to marry, and it's done."

"You don't understand, Brendan. These things can't be done by a priest. We'd have to go to Baltimore, even to the Vatican Curia. It would not be legal if I—"

"No, Father. Dontcha see? It would be *legal* to the folks at Chicken Alley; it would satisfy them. O' course we would know the paper for what it was."

"A forgery."

"Aye, Father Francis! Now y'get it. Just like the slave papers you fixed. They was bogus, too, but all the time God knew he had created them niggers free as air from the start."

"Negroes."

"Aye. Father, your black folks."

Francis sank into the chair again and regarded Brendan for a long time. His chin was cupped in the heel of his hand, and his fingers covered his mouth. Brendan could not tell if he was smiling or frowning. Then he got up and went into the next room.

Brendan squirmed in his chair, spinning his cap nervously in his good hand. After a while he could hear a quill pen scratching away behind the door.

CHAPTER 51

Maggie Gallagher picked irritably at small flecks of lint on the patchwork quilt. There were a few out of reach down by her knees that she would have liked to get at, but she was too exhausted to sit up. It was a mortal embarrassment to have to lie in bed through the long days, the first time she had been down since giving birth to the twins. It was hard even to carry on a decent conversation flat on her back, not allowed to fuss about the kitchen or even sit in the rocker with her sewing.

"So Father Francis finally gave in, eh?"

"Finally." Noreen's face lit up, and she added, "He told me that he had taken to breaking so many rules lately that he might have to become an Episcopalian."

Maggie chuckled at that, a wheezing, ropy kind of noise that almost made her cough again.

No chance o'that," she whispered. "He's not rich enough."

Noreen smiled.

"So it will be two weddings then?"

"Two, Maggie. Tim and Meg together after all these years, and my Kate with your James."

"*My* Kate, too. Ye'll not be cheatin' me out of my only granddaughter."

"God bless you for sayin' that, Maggie Gallagher," Noreen said unsteadily. "And for loving her so since the day you helped me bring her into the world."

Maggie blinked a few times and plucked at the quilt. "So the four of them will move to Pennsylvania. Up the Crick, I hear."

"Yes, Coatesville."

"I never heard of it, Noreen. But then, I've not been off the Crick since the day the boat dropped us here."

"It's not far. About thirty miles, Brendan says. James will work with Tim, y'know."

"T'other side o' the moon. It might as well be County Kildare; I'll never see it." Maggie paused to get a breath. It was a strange sickness that left her as weak as a new chick. "It's nice the two of them can work together."

"And Meg will be a help to Kate."

Maggie grinned. "More like the other way around."

Noreen laughed aloud. She would have to leave soon and let the woman rest. The doctor had warned her.

"Maggie, Brendan told me you knew about Kate all along."

"Almost from the first. But that's forgot, child."

"That time when Brendan was gone so long, and we fought."

Maggie waved it off. "Two and two makes four! Later, when I saw those hands, that chin. I knew."

"You never let on."

"She was a new life, Noreen. God knows we all needed her in those black days. She's been nothing but a joy to me."

"Brendan says he talked to you about it long ago. . . ."

"When your babies died. Aye, we spoke of it."

"Was he very upset . . . with me? I thought that God had taken the twins because—"

"Ah, no, girl. Brendan wanted only to ease your mind, to let you know he felt the fault himself. I said to leave it in the past, God forgive me. I might have let him spare your grief."

She closed her eyes then, and Noreen let her rest, hoping she might sleep until Patrick returned with the doctor. But after only a few minutes, Maggie spoke again.

"Noreen?"

"Yes, Maggie."

"Out in the cupboard, my house money jar. Would y'bring it?"

Noreen gave her a questioning look, but went for the earthen jar, as familiar to her as Maggie's kitchen itself. When she returned, Maggie motioned for her to dump it on the bed. It was quite full of coins, and when she poured them on the quilt, a small flannel bag flopped heavily on the pile. Maggie picked it up and handed it to Noreen.

"Give this to her...on the wedding day."

"What is it, Maggie?"

"Something to start her life with. Just a bag o' dreams."

"Well, Maggie, they plan to visit you on the day of the wedding. Kate wouldn't miss that, now, would she? Why don't you give it to her then?"

Maggie looked at Noreen hard before she smiled and closed her eyes again. Then she spoke so softly that the words were almost lost.

"Because I may be out of town."

She had hoped to see another Christmas, or to last long enough at least to see Kate in her mother's wedding gown, but Margaret Gallagher missed both events and was buried in the old Powderman's Cemetery below the new church.

They postponed the wedding out of respect.

When the two couples were married in a double ceremony three weeks later, they held a subdued reception at the Gallagher home, because the Feeney place was too small. Only the immediate families were invited, and Father Reardon, of course. Meg Halloran's children by her first husband, who was killed, were there, all three grownups now. And a few others.

Of course, Blanche Feeney came down from the big house, because she could not miss a wedding in the family. She did spend considerable time in a discussion with Father Francis about the dispensation, saying what a wonder it was the way the Holy Ghost could inspire Holy Mother Church.

Father Francis just smiled and agreed with everything she said. And when she got on about the scandalous du Pont marriages between first cousins, she was quick to point out how different it was with James and Kate. It was plain enough that they were hardly related at all, as the church had so wisely pointed out.

Kate even let her see the dispensation with her own eyes. An official document of the Catholic church! That was enough, as far as she was concerned. She was satisfied. And so would be anyone else who might dare to ask Blanche Feeney any day thereafter.

The newlyweds were going to leave for Coatesville in the morning, all four of them, so the party lasted well into the night. Father Francis stayed until the last horn. Maggie would have loved that.

CHAPTER 52

The barn swallow glided over the Crick in a shallow arc, a blue steel blur of speed, and scissored his sharp wings at the last second to brake his dive inches above the glistening mud flat. A dauber wasp buzzed up from his work at the disturbance, and then settled back to the tiny lump of muck he had dragged together, gathered it up with his spindly legs, and droned off sluggishly into the trees.

The bird tracked the insect with one eye, cocking his head toward the easy meal. Something kept him from the pursuit, and he stood fast, stiff legs half submerged in the syrupy ooze of the muddy shore. Soon he was scratching up a ball of sticky soil himself, and when it was about the size of a fat lima bean, he plucked it up and flew straight downstream in the direction of some low stone buildings.

As he passed the third mill, his wings snipped again, turning him into an opening under the flimsy eaves. In the sudden darkness of the interior, he had to grope for the massive ceiling beam. He fluttered so clumsily that he nearly dropped the soggy ball from his beak. As his pupils dilated in the reduced light, he was able to make out the new place, a fresh corner under the sloping roof where a crossbeam met its rafter almost precisely in the center of the single room.

He flew to it, to the drying cone of nest that was nearly complete.

For a moment he rested there, cocking his head this way and that, inspecting the rim. Finally he picked a spot and pressed the mudball into place.

As he was poking the soft mass into its pocket, his beak struck something hard, rasping an unfamiliar grating vibration into his brain. He pushed at the offensive center of the mud, worrying it until it was jutting through the wall of the nest. He fluffed about on the inside, brushing the wet stuff until it was even with the rest. Then he gave it a last inspection, flew down toward the shaft of light in the eaves, and disappeared into the sunny afternoon.

A drop of moisture beaded on the small outcropping, grew as it was fed moisture from the mass around it, and eventually dripped away. It splattered onto one of the rolling wheels of the mill and was gone instantly, absorbed into the damp cake of gunpowder underneath.

The vibrations of the twin cast-iron grinding wheels traveled through the stone floor, up the thick walls, and into the rafters. The swallow's nest trembled with the rhythm but stuck fast. And mortared firmly in the drying mud, the shard of flinty stone glinted feebly at its washed point.

Patrick stooped at the edge of the mounded earth of her grave and plucked a stone chip from the raked smoothness of the red clay. One end of the piece was rounded, and it fit comfortably in the soft fleshiness of his palm. It was an egg-sized pebble, newly fractured across the middle. He could see the tiny pockmark where the gravedigger's mattock had struck. The raw stone gleamed harsh and blue, the old roundness aged into a mellow rust. "Gabbro," he thought, and remembered the millions of hammer blows to wrestle the granite from bedrock into mills and dams and miles of races and yes, the walls of that very church. He was going to toss it by, rubble defacing her grave, but he put it into his pocket instead. It lay there, making a bulge in his coat, adding to the weight hanging in his chest.

"I think I was a Judas goat sometimes, Denis," he muttered sweeping his eyes over the mounds and the older, sinking plots.

"What d'ye mean, Patrick?"

"Well, look around here. How many have we put under the sod?

Fifty? A hundred, do y'think?" He shook his head. "And how many of them graves is nothin' but an empty box because they couldn't find enough left to bury?"

"Ah, man, don't be thinking of that now."

"But it's true. I was the Mister's fisher, y'know what I mean. I called them in from the old country by the droves, didn't I? Come on over, lads; make a new start for yourselves. A good job, a roof over your head, food to get fat on in the New World."

Denis hobbled closer to his friend and gripped his arm. "Come on now, Pat. It's only that y'feel so low with losin' dear Maggie there. Don't go heapin' the weight of a millstone around your neck."

"No, it's true, Denis." He pointed to the grave. "She told me so herself, one time. . . . The night y'nearly stretched your neck. . . . Said that we was as much to blame as any to have got in such a fix. But it was me she meant, to get the blame off you, I guess. And it's true all right. I was always the one to keep you all on at the mills, and send for more when the supply of men ran short."

Denis tugged at his arm. "Me leg's killin' me. Let's go now."

They leaned into each other and walked stiffly to the buggy and let Tim help them aboard. The three said nothing as the rig rolled slowly down Barley Mill toward the Crick. When they slipped into the cool shade of the woods above Crick Road, Denis spoke up. "You're wrong about all that back there, Patrick. Maybe I put it backwards. . . . I mean, you were right all along, but I just had trouble seein' it clear."

Patrick chuckled. "Ah, Feeney, you'll argue fer the sheer love of contention to yer dyin' day . . . even if it means takin' sides against yourself."

Denis did not smile and went on as if he had not heard. "Y'see, Patrick, it was pride we were after, wasn't it, now? It wasn't the job, so much—the security, I mean. It wasn't that what kept us here. It was the pride of bein' powdermen, of bein' the Irish up the Crick. It was the danger and bein' different than the rest."

"I dunno," Patrick mumbled, but the words were seeping into him like a salve. "I sometimes think we been played fer fools by the higher-ups . . . the Mister, I mean, and the priest, too, mebbe."

"It doesn't matter, my friend," Denis said quietly. "Look at us now, both fit to tumble into the ground in a minute. And there's du Pont in his fine house just waitin' fer the same appointment.

Does he feel any finer in his old age for havin' all those mills and such? Not likely, I'm thinkin'. What's he got to look backwards at that can outshine what we done?"

Patrick heard himself protest weakly. "Well, his grub is a bit tastier, and the view ain't bad."

"Agh, Patrick, the man has not had teeth worth a damn since forty years ago, and like as not his eyes can't see beyond the tips of his propped-up toes where he sits on that fancy veranda."

"But he owns it all."

Denis nodded solemnly. "Aye, but that's all. We built and ran the goddam thing. We're the ones that made it *go*, Patrick."

"And he gets to leave it all to his kids."

Denis smiled, and gripped Patrick's knee; his pale blue eyes almost twinkled.

"Let 'em have it. It's their trap now, too big fer them to let it go. Our kids," he looked lovingly at Tim's back hunched over the reins, "our kids are free to play with the works...or let them go, as they damned well please."

"Still and all, Denis, I'd like to be havin' just a piece of it to pass on to me own."

"Tell me one good reason why."

"I'll give ye two," Patrick said sharply. "With a inheritance from me they wouldn't be facing a life of backbreakin' work from dawn to dark. The second is I want t'leave them something to remember me by."

Denis chuckled. "Ah, Patrick, ye never learn, do ye? You're as bad as du Pont. Do you realize that? Let it go, man. Don't be tryin' to control the kids from yer grave. Let them work out their own problems."

"You were right about the house, Denis. I shouldn't a give it to the Mister. Now all I got is that six-foot lot fer me and Maggie."

Denis shook his head. "No. You was right and I was wrong about that. But we was right and wrong for the wrong reasons. If you had held out, you woulda been an island surrounded by the company. It was just a matter of time anyway."

Patrick was exasperated. "Jesus Christ, Feeney, I think the creature has burned out yer brain...or mebee the old age dried it up. Y'make no sense at all, and that's a fact!"

"The fact, if you really want to know it, is that we can none of

[391]

us take aught with us in the end. Even that grave up there by the church will be sold out·from under ye someday to buy some fancy fixture fer the altar or such. You can be holdin' on to the clay with both arms, boyo, huggin' it fer all yer worth, but it won't make any difference. We all end up part of the landscape."

"I'm cuttin a headstone for Maggie and me out of Brandywine granite," Patrick mused. "Have y'seen it? The Flynn boy will carve the message."

Denis looked at him for a minute, the heat of argument softened by compassion. Still, he could not resist the opening. "Even stone gets moved in time. My God, Patrick, you of all people should know that."

They were rolling smoothly along the Crick Road now, the old familiar smells of the yard drifting toward them, getting stronger as they approached the gate. It was pleasant; hardly a sound of their moving in the sprung buggy. Even the sounds of horse's hooves were muted by the soft, damp earth of the roadway. Soon they could hear the somber groaning of the first pair of rolling mills, and glimpses of their heavy walls through the emerald green of the new foliage were like snatches of some enchanted vision. Squatting windowless castles out of the mossy past, the deep millrace a moat cutting them off from the road. It would be easy to give in to the spell and think they were on the moors of Ireland again, breathless with the view of some old battlement inhabited only by fairies.

"I have to see the Halloran boy for a minute. His ma wants me to check up on him. Misses her youngest, I guess." It was the first time Tim had spoken since they left the cemetery. He was taking his new role as stepfather very seriously. Denis winked at Patrick.

Tim guided the rig onto a grassy spot beside a young dogwood lush with pink blossoms. Green leaves were beginning to sprout from the black branches, and as Tim got down from his seat, he brushed the tree, sending a sprinkle of petals spinning to the black water. Patrick watched as two of the flower fragments were caught in the sucking current to the mill and shot through the turbine grate. He and Denis sat like stone men, listening to the mills.

Abruptly the rumbling stopped, and their heads turned together toward the twin buildings across the bridge on the other side of the race.

"He must've shut them down fer dinner," Denis said. "This was my pair of mills, Patrick. Four years I run this set . . . and you built 'em."

They fell silent again, remembering. Then Patrick heaved himself out of the seat and began climbing down from the buggy.

"Come on, Denis. Let's give the old thing a once-over. See if these young fellers know what they're doin'."

It was a struggle for the two of them to get down from the rig and make it down the slope below the race to the lower level of the mills. Dennis's knee had stiffened terribly during the ride, and Patrick's support was shaky as they inched their way down to the level clearing outside the first mill's narrow door.

"Hey, old-timers, now you can't come in here!" They looked up at the voice piping out of the mouth of a youngster dressed in a knee-length leather apron. His face was charcoal black with the grime of the trade.

"Humph!" Patrick snorted. What was this lad blatherin' about to think they wouldn't know that, what with almost forty years' experience apiece. "Back off, lad; we won't be hurtin' yer mill."

"Beggin' yer pardon, but it's not the mill I care about, but me own tender neck. Visitors make me . . . Oh, it's yourself, Mr. Gallagher. I didn't—"

Tim cut in. "Halloran here is about to have his dinner while he gives this batch a final roll. Three hundred pounds of blasting powder is in the tub."

Denis looked at the Halloran boy. "It's been a few years, lad. Wouldja let an old powderman start it up one more time?"

The boy grinned, his teeth a white swath in the blackened face. "Why not, Mr. Feeney, go right ahead, but mind you pull it slow." He pointed to the lever just outside the door of the mill. And no goin' inside the place."

Denis hobbled to the wooden handle and eased it down. They could hear the gears engage inside the mill, and the ground trembled lightly as the massive cast-iron wheels began to roll again.

"Is the blowout wall still up?" Patrick asked.

"No," the boy answered as he rummaged through the dinner pail Tim had brought. I took it all down last week when it looked like spring was here for sure. Why? Do you want to take a look?"

"Aye, one last look. Come on, Denis."

They ambled toward the corner of the mill together, about to turn the corner and step out on the inspection walk that lay between the open wall of the mill and the racing waters of the Crick.

Halloran turned to Tim and chuckled. "That's yer dad, ain't it?"

Tim nodded with a slight smile as he watched the pair disappear around the corner of the mill. "They're both getting pretty old. I hope they don't slip and fall in."

When they had reached the center of the stone platform, the two powdermen stopped to watch the twin iron wheels rumble through their turns, grinding the tubful of powder into a finer mix.

"Have y'seen enough, Patrick? Me leg..."

Patrick put an arm over Denis's shoulder and felt his friend's hand grip him on the back of the neck.

"You're right, Denis. It ain't so much what ye end up with—or where—as long as ye have the grand time gettin' there."

"Aye, boyo, that says it all. Now let's be going."

They both saw the swallow's nest break loose from the great trembling crossbrace and drop into the tub in front of the grinding wheel. Neither saw the fragment of flinty stone jutting from the rubble of dried mud.

It didn't matter. There was not time for them to make it around the corner of the mill to safety. They were still arm in arm when the blast caught them.

At Dorgan's everybody said Patrick would have been proud of the way the walls stood up to the explosion. Not one stone was pushed aside. Tim and Mickey Halloran weren't even scratched.

And it was a lovely way to go, wasn't it, now? For two old powdermen like Denis and Patrick.

"Gone across the Crick."

Together.